He was her
only sin...

NOW SUZANNE FORSTER PRESENTS HER MOST
TANTALIZING TALE OF INTRIGUE AND SEDUCTION...

INNOCENCE

Sub: Today's Assignment

Your destination is 6723 Melrose. Three P.M. sharp. This customer must not be kept waiting.

He's expecting a dewy brunette with a red satchel and the requisite cluster of cherries. You know what to do in that regard. Do it.

He has only one hang-up. Innocence. Break out your Catholic schoolgirl's uniform. And pray...

Berkley Books by Suzanne Forster

SHAMELESS

COME MIDNIGHT

BLUSH

INNOCENCE

INNOCENCE

SUZANNE FORSTER

BERKLEY BOOKS, NEW YORK

INNOCENCE

A Berkley Book / published by arrangement with
the author

PRINTING HISTORY
Berkley edition / February 1997

All rights reserved.
Copyright © 1997 by Suzanne Forster.
Book design by Casey Hampton.
This book may not be reproduced in whole or in part,
by mimeograph or any other means, without permission.
For information address: The Berkley Publishing Group,
200 Madison Avenue, New York, New York 10016.

The Putnam Berkley World Wide Web site address is
http://www.berkley.com/berkley

ISBN: 0-425-15663-X

BERKLEY®
Berkley Books are published by The Berkley Publishing Group,
200 Madison Avenue, New York, New York 10016.
BERKLEY and the "B" design
are trademarks belonging to Berkley Publishing Corporation.

PRINTED IN THE UNITED STATES OF AMERICA

10 9 8 7 6 5 4 3 2

For Natasha, my feline writing buddy and constant companion for thirteen years.

This is your book, sweet girl, even though you weren't here to see it finished. Your struggle to survive opened my heart in so many ways, it surely must have made me a better writer too.

Rest in peace and in the knowledge that you were dearly loved.

INNOCENCE

PROLOGUE

INTERNET GATEWAY   97/04/11   09:14

FROM: 75024.527@CYBERSERVE.COM@INET01#1
TO: 206724.291@GENESIS.GEIS.COM
RETURN-PATH: 75024.527@CYBERSERVE.COM

SUB: TODAY'S ASSIGNMENT

YOUR DESTINATION IS 6723 MELROSE. THREE P.M. SHARP.
THIS CUSTOMER MUST NOT BE KEPT WAITING.

HE'S EXPECTING A DEWY BRUNETTE WITH A RED SATCHEL AND
THE REQUISITE CLUSTER OF CHERRIES. YOU KNOW WHAT TO DO
IN THAT REGARD. DO IT.

HE HAS ONLY ONE HANG-UP. INNOCENCE. BREAK OUT YOUR
CATHOLIC SCHOOLGIRL'S UNIFORM. AND PRAY.

WINK ;)

Blue Brandenburg read the E-mail message on her computer screen with a delicious quiver of excitement. She'd done it. She'd snagged the crucial assignment, but there was a problem—the anonymous voice on her phone machine last night. Apparently she'd taken one too many risks recently, and someone knew what she was up to.

If she kept this date, it could be her last.

The screen flickered wildly as she brought up her personal address book and scrolled through the names, searching for one in particular. She had to find someone to take her place. Someone who was innocent in the extreme. Someone who *couldn't* refuse her.

Thank God she knew exactly who that woman was.

1

"*Mary Frances Murphy's as pure as Ivory fucking soap.*"

No one in the dusty little desert town of Sweetwater, California, could remember who first uttered that disgraceful, eyebrow-raising declaration about their precious Mary Frances, but if they were being honest, they had to admit it was the God's truth. There were nice girls, there were nice Irish-Catholic girls, and then there was Mary Frances, who gave new meaning to the word *saintly,* which was why not a one of them could believe it when the rumors of her shocking improprieties began to surface.

Improper young women didn't wear plain white cotton panties to bed under their nighties, floss their teeth after meals, or pay off their credit-card balances every month. They certainly didn't enter St. Gertrude's Holy Order on their twenty-first birthday with the full intention of taking the Lord as their perfect bridegroom.

To know Mary Frances was to approve of her. "A diligent worker," the high-school principal had pronounced

when he handed her the shiny roll of vellum a decade earlier on her graduation day. "And if I may be so bold, the
perfect little lady."

The scarlet cords on Mary Frances's diploma had
swung like a stripper's tassels, but everyone in atten-
dance that misty June morning had agreed, some with a
nod and a smile. The town's few eligible bachelors understood that she was far too good for them. The married
men were known to hold her up as a standard to their
wayward daughters, and their wives spoke fondly of her
hand-crocheted sweater sets and matching ankle socks,
so adorably old-fashioned when most girls her age were
having their noses made smaller and their breasts made
larger. And sex. They were having that, too.

But not Mary Frances. She didn't even insert tampons.

Perhaps that's why it came as such a shock when she
was booted out of St. Gertrude's for sins of impurity in
thought, word, and deed. Mortal sins, the rumors went,
committed with the full consent of the will.

The town of Sweetwater hardly knew what to think. If
Mary Frances wasn't the perfect candidate for a life of
chastity, poverty, and obedience, who was? The scandal
forced her parents into seclusion and left the locals to
grapple with the enormity of the disgrace on their own.
St. Gertrude's would not reveal her most grievous tran-
gressions, but it was widely circulated that, as a prelude
to some unspeakable act in the infirmary, she had been
caught praying for sex, and she hadn't been particular
who with.

"I know this is my life's calling," she'd been heard to
whisper at matins the morning that was to be her last.
"It's the nunnery or burn in hell eternal. I've accepted
that, but please don't let me die without knowing the bliss
of male penetration. Maybe the gardener could lose his

head and defile my person in his toolshed. Actually, now that I think about it, the UPS man's a little younger, and he has better calves. I've seen them both in walking shorts—"

She was said to have twisted her rosary beads into a knot as she must have realized that she was on the brink of bargaining her immortal soul for preferred male body parts. "Oh, I don't care," she'd pleaded. "Really, send anybody you want, even Brother Timothy, though there's been no evidence he has the necessary organ. Just don't let me die unmolested."

Unfortunately Brother Timothy had heard her supplication that morning and taken exception. Mary Frances was said to have argued that her shame could not be that much greater than St. Augustine's, who'd prayed to God to send him the gift of chastity, but not yet. Nevertheless, she was history by vespers, the first of her family line to be so banished. But if the town was reeling, Mary Frances was not. Oh, there'd been tears and contrition and a biblical flood of guilt, but in her heart of hearts, in the sanctity of her true mind, there was only relief. There might even have been joy if it hadn't been for the Murphy family curse.

For two hundred years, dating back to the family's modest linen-shop beginnings in County Kerry, the youngest female of each generation had been expected to join a holy order, and those who hadn't were said to have met tragic ends. Most had been taken in their prime in various, hideous ways—two by lightning, one by a shower of firebricks, another by way of a large furniture delivery truck. All of them were youngest daughters, and according to legend, all might have prevented their untimely deaths with one simple act: take up the veil and become a nun.

Mary Frances Murphy had been living with the evidence of her mortality for as long as she could remember. It wasn't just that she was going to die. Everybody bought the farm eventually, but not everyone knew exactly how, when, and why. She did.

Four daughters in as many generations.

Mary Frances was next.

Some churches were known for their architectural splendor, others for their funereal gloom. Our Lady Queen of Martyrs, situated in the darkest, dankest heart of a Santa Ana barrio, was known for its weeping statue of St. Catherine of the Strict Observance, patron saint of the sick and infirm—and for its feverish parishioners. Whether out of fear or respect, neighborhood gangs had long ago declared the short block a demilitarized zone, leaving the faithful free to congregate at St. Catherine's feet and compare miracles.

This particular Saturday morning the statue had drawn its usual fervent crowd, which was probably why no one seemed to notice when a yellow cab careened around the corner and pulled to the curb in front of the church. The slender, harried blonde inside rummaged through her purse and dug out some money for the driver, unaware as she scrambled from the idling car that the bills were fluttering to the front seat, and the driver was squinting after her in disbelief.

Confused cabbies were the last thing on Blue Brandenburg's mind. She was running for her life. There was only one person who could help her now, and even that depended on whether or not she'd come to the right place. She was certain of nothing these last few days, including where to find the woman she sought.

The heavy soles of her Bass sandals slapped against

concrete as she climbed tier after tier of steps and rushed past the murmurous crowds. She felt like a plain, frightened little bird in flight in her cutoff jeans, cropped sweater, and naked face. Her profession required more exotic plumage—alluring evening wear, silks, sequins, and the most expensive perfumes. And high heels, of course. Men liked high heels.

She burst into the adobe church and hesitated, disoriented by its numinous darkness. Wafting incense and the rows of flickering votive candles were her beacon. Calla lilies ringed the altar like a graceful white necklace, apparently left over from Easter mass the weekend before.

Someone was whispering in hushed, passionate tones, and the sound drew Blue to the communion rail, where a young woman draped in black knelt in prayer. Blue gasped softly as she realized who it was. "Mary Frances, you did it," she said. "You took the vows!"

The woman looked up, her expressive green eyes wide and startled. But wariness followed swiftly on the heels of recognition.

The two women knew each other from convent school, but they were never friends. If anything, their aspirations had pitted them against one another. Mary Frances had seemed to be vying for sainthood, while poor little rich girl, Amanda Brandenburg, tagged "Blue" because of her blueblood background, had sought every possible way to exasperate the nuns and get herself expelled.

Blue had been best friends with Mary Frances's older sister, Brianna, and both had been boy crazy, while Mary Frances had never seemed interested in boys or pretty enough to interest them. Some years later, when Mary Frances entered St. Gertrude's Holy Order as a postulant, everyone had thought she was fulfilling her destiny, that she would be the perfect woman of the cloth.

Gazing at her now, Blue wondered if they were right. She hadn't seen Mary Frances since eighth grade, but there was something intriguingly restless stirring in the woman's veiled glances, and undoubtedly in her soul as well. Not only that, she was quite pretty, albeit in an unconventional way. Freckles fanned her cheekbones like lace and her unadorned eyes seemed too large for the boyish angles of her face, but her raven hair had an occasional hint of fire that brought out the richness of its russet tones. It was a nice, sensual touch, even severely restrained as it was with plaits and coils and combs.

Well, bless my soul, Blue thought ironically. Maybe I have come to the right person. Mary Frances Murphy looks like a damsel who desperately wants to be in distress, if only someone would show her how. Sin was a teapot on simmer in those dark green eyes.

The church doors banged open, and Blue glanced over her shoulder, searching the brightness until she'd convinced herself it was another parishioner and not someone following her. Not someone who wanted her dead. *He hadn't found her yet.*

Her shoulders dropped with relief. Fortunately, Mary Frances didn't seem to have noticed her apprehension, and as the other woman rose and shook the wrinkles from her skirt, Blue realized the dark linen dress she'd mistaken for a nun's habit was actually streetwear.

"Have you left the convent?" Blue asked. "Or is this lay clothing?"

Mary Frances touched the delicate gold saint's medal she wore around her neck, sliding it between her thumb and forefinger, and Blue was left to peer at her expectantly. The other woman had drawn inward in the swift, dramatic way that Blue remembered from their childhood. She'd always seemed to be escaping to some private, secret world, the garden of her own mind. It was a habit that used to exasperate Blue terribly. She hated it when people were able to tune her out, no matter how industriously she tried to keep their attention. Mary Frances had been able to do that. She'd been able to tune everyone out, the whole damn rest of the world.

"At St. Gertrude's we were trained to confine the body in order to free the spirit," Mary Frances said by way of explanation, adding mysteriously that she had apparently never gotten the knack of it. "I was expelled from the Holy Order several months ago, *before* I took my vows."

Blue was startled. She couldn't imagine what someone as dutiful and disciplined as the Mary Frances she'd known could have done to get herself expelled. But she refrained from probing as Mary Frances explained that she'd been working in the church rectory at Our Lady ever since, as a favor to a friend.

"I'm also planning to pursue the nurse's training I started while I was in the convent," she confided. "How could I not? It's such a useful occupation."

But not one she loved, Blue suspected. She didn't quite know what to make of her former schoolmate's strange revelation, but this wasn't the time to puzzle it out. Her own situation was too urgent. There wasn't a doubt in her mind that the news she brought would horrify Mary Frances, which was all the more reason she had to be told.

"I need your help," she said. "I'm in trouble. Serious trouble." Aware that she now had the other woman's full attention, Blue cautiously explained that she'd infiltrated the West Coast operation of a society escort service to investigate the death of a friend.

"My friend Celeste—" Blue glanced around, feeling a little foolish as she drew Mary Frances aside and lowered her voice. "That wasn't her real name, but the service preferred their escorts be anonymous, and Celeste was the alias I knew her by. Anyway, she was killed in a hit-and-run accident six months ago. Only I don't believe it was an accident. I think one of the service's clients was responsible—Calderon, Webb Calderon."

Mary Frances visibly started. She gaped at Blue, her face draining of blood.

"Do you know him?" Blue asked.

"No," she said abruptly, "not at all." But she touched the saint's medal as if to compose herself. "It's nothing, I—I saw him once on a tabloid television show, and I'll never forget the way he looked into the camera. Those strange silver eyes. Frightening, I still dream—"

Their whispery tones were attracting attention, Blue realized. An elderly woman in a black scarf had looked up from her prayers.

"He was involved in an art scandal," Mary Frances added.

"Right." Blue urged her toward the doorway of the sacristy, the small room where the sacred vestments were kept. "He owns galleries all over the world, very prestigious. You probably heard about the Featherstone scandal—the twins who inherited the family retailing empire—Lake and Lily? They had a multimillion-dollar collection, but they were stealing art like thieves. Guess who their private and personal dealer was? Then last month there was that record-breaking sale of a Rodin statue to the son of a notorious South American dictator. Calderon, again."

Mary Frances's dark gaze was lit with curiosity. "I saw the Featherstone story, too," she admitted, her voice taking on a hush reminiscent of confessional booths. "It was on *Hard Copy*, wasn't it? Or *Inside Story*? I can't remember which. *Geraldo*?"

Blue briefly contemplated the prospect of a convent dropout hooked on trash TV and decided not to pursue it. "I broke into the service's computerized files and checked out Calderon's dossier," she explained. "There were some coded references that had to do with art smuggling, I'm reasonably certain of that. But the guy's cagey. He's never been caught at anything or even implicated."

Mary Frances was caressing the saint's medal again, her fingers twined in the feathery gold chain, and there was an unconscious sensuality to the act that made Blue stop and stare. Blue's sexual preferences were strictly heterosexual, but her stomach was aflutter watching this. There was no missing the latent eroticism in the languid lacing of fingers—and almost everything else Mary Frances did, yet she clearly wasn't aware of it. She was a siren in sackcloth and ashes.

Blue remembered the saint's medal from their Catholic-school days as an heirloom passed down through the Murphy family line. She'd once teased Mary Frances about the curse it was supposed to protect her from—and had her foot uncharitably stomped on. The adult woman was probably too polite to tromp on toes, but that didn't stop her from playing with the piece of jewelry like it was a sex toy.

"Calderon used this . . . escort service you mentioned?" Mary Frances asked.

Blue shook off the errant thoughts. "Celeste had a date with him the night she died. I got a strange phone call from her, and she told me she had to get away from the service, that someone was trying to hurt her, but she wouldn't say anything more. She seemed reluctant to keep the date, and she was frightened of Calderon, I'm sure of that."

"And you think he actually had her *killed*? Why would he do that?"

Blue glanced around at the door. "I found her diary. She kept a journal on the purse computer the escorts use to communicate with the service. It went into detail about the sexual stuff she was into, incredibly kinky stuff with one particular client. She didn't mention his name, but I'm sure it was Calderon."

Blue was reluctant to say more, but there was more, lots of it. "I don't know why she died, but I must be getting close to the truth, because now someone's threatening to kill me."

"There's been an attempt on your life?"

"Not an actual attempt, just phone threats. But my apartment was broken into, and someone's been following me ever since." She glanced back at the church doors. "I took several detours coming here. I even changed taxis just to be sure no one was tailing me."

"Have you notified the police?"

"I went to them first, but apparently they had better things to do than investigate the death of yet another 'hooker'—I think that's the way they put it—especially one that was so cleverly made to look like an accident."

Anger and fear tightened Blue's voice as she tried to clarify what had happened. She'd taken many risks to get information on Calderon, first breaking into the escort service's files and then visiting his gallery in Beverly Hills. She'd pretended to be ill in order to slip into his gallery office and help herself to his Filofax, only to have someone break into her apartment that same night and

steal the appointment book back. Since then she'd been
getting anonymous phone threats to back off or be
killed.

"I think the service is a cover." Blue's mouth went
bone-dry as she admitted her suspicions aloud. The impli-
cations terrified her. "It caters exclusively to heads of state
and business barons and is well-known in those elite inner
circles, but I think it's more than that. I think it's a network
for industrial espionage and black-market operations of all
kinds. If I'm right, they're smuggling everything from
fine art and antiquities to classified information and prototype microchips."

Mary Frances brought the medal to her lips. It seemed
an involuntary response, as if she were in the process of
crossing herself. "I still don't understand how I can help
you," she said.

"You're the only one who *can* help me now," Blue explained, realizing she could no longer hold back the most
important part of her story. "Celeste? The escort who was
murdered? She was your sister, Brianna."

Rich, buttery sunlight dappled Our Lady's modest rectory, pouring through the door that opened onto the San
Joaquin hills in the distance. A stand of weeping willows
bordered the missionlike group of buildings that flanked
the church, their feathery branches transforming the flood
of light into waves and the tiny office into a golden
aquarium.

Mary Frances stood frozen in a pool of undulating
warmth, her back to the woman who had brought her the
news of her sister.

"Brianna?" she murmured. "Dead?" Her first reaction
had been utter denial, followed quickly by confusion and
guilt. She was still confounded. She'd left the nave to

catch her breath and try to make sense of the utter chaos that was threatening to engulf her. She needed to be alone. She'd told Blue that, but the other woman had followed her.

"I'm sorry," Blue kept repeating. She'd begun to babble. She was trying to explain why she'd had to break the news so bluntly, but Mary Frances wasn't listening anymore. She was struggling to understand the impossible. The Murphy family had never been notified of her older sister's death, and Mary Frances could only assume it was because Brianna had broken all ties years ago. She and her sister had been sworn enemies for most of their childhood, at odds in almost every way. For many reasons, Mary Frances knew it was impossible for her to grieve the way a sister should, but she also couldn't accept that Brianna was dead. She was the boldest of them all in convent school, virtually indestructible.

The day Mary Frances announced to her family that she would take up the second oldest profession and enter the convent, her sister had announced her intention to take up the first oldest and become a call girl. She hadn't stolen Mary Frances's thunder. She'd blasted it from the heavens.

"I need your help," Blue was saying, her tone urgent. "I need you to help me catch her murderer."

But Blue's desperation fell on deaf ears. Though Mary Frances had fought all her life to suppress the feelings, she'd resented her older sister terribly. Brianna, the beauty. Brianna, the brazen. No one else had existed when Brianna was around. Her sister had lived to shock and offend the public morals, even to horrify; while Mary Frances had fought to subdue her worldly passions and desires, Brianna had openly indulged hers.

Brianna was bold and Mary Frances was a coward.
Brianna was dead. *Good.*

Mary Frances shuddered violently, her horror complete. It was so much more than resentment. She had deeply envied her sister for being at the center of everything. There were times when she had lashed out at Brianna in her fantasies and times when she had wished her dead. Dear Lord, she had.

"I can't help you," she whispered.

Blue touched her arm. "Mary Frances, you don't mean that. There's no one else I can turn to. At least listen to me. Let me tell you how I planned to expose him—"

"No, I *can't.*"

Bells rang hauntingly in the distance. Had they come from the steeple? Mary Frances couldn't tell. The traffic outside was noisy, smelly. Cars backfired and belched. Drivers cursed each other in heavily accented English.

Blue caught her by the arm and turned her around. "Listen to me, dammit! Your sister's been *killed.*"

Another shudder silenced Mary Frances. Blue's fingers dug into her flesh. The woman's clear blue-gray eyes, never warm, were as cold and hard as gemstones.

"Calderon uses the service regularly," Blue was saying, "but it's not for female companionship, I'd bet my life on that. I think the escorts are unwitting couriers for whatever he's smuggling. He has a small, intimate party planned for one of his clients—Alejandro Cordes, that South American dictator's son I mentioned. Cordes is here on another art-buying trip, and I volunteered myself as one of the hostesses through the service."

She drew a breath. It was audible, painful. "It's not safe for me to go . . . that's where you came in. I needed you to take my place, to be me. There'd be an interview first. Calderon always personally interviews new escorts, but I could coach you through that."

"Be you? How is that possible?"

"No one knows who the escorts are. We get our instructions through the Internet. You'd have to use my password and ID number to communicate with them. That way they wouldn't know they're weren't dealing with me, but you could use any identity you wanted with Calderon."

Mary Frances pulled away and walked to the door. The street traffic was still congested, but she couldn't hear the noise anymore. It was strangely muted and distant, like the bells. Perhaps she shouldn't have been surprised that Brianna would continue to dominate her life, even in death. It seemed she would never be able to escape her sister's reach.

"You risked your life to find Brianna's murderer," she said. "Why are you doing this?"

"Lots of reasons. Let's just say your sister was a friend, and I owed her, okay? Now I don't have any choice. Whoever did this to her is after me, too. I want to get to him before he gets to me."

Mary Frances shook her head and a feeling of profound sadness overtook her. "I can't help you."

"Jesus, Mary Frances." Blue's whisper was incredulous. "I know you didn't like her, but—"

Tears filled Mary Frances's eyes. They blurred the ugliness of the traffic and the dark beauty of the hills. The graceful willows bled emerald ribbons into the cobalt horizon, but she could do nothing to stop the rivulets that washed her face.

"No, I didn't like her—" Her voice was raw as she

turned to Blue. "I hated her. I hated her because I wanted to be her!"

Blue's stunned silence turned into a shaky sigh of relief. "Well then . . . this is your chance."

2

"What? No fishnet stockings, no black leather mini? I'm disappointed! I expected hooker chic."

Mary Frances's sudden smile was as piquant and ironic as her remark. Captured like a Victorian cameo in the medicine-cabinet mirror, her inquisitive features were poised on the cusp of disbelief and amused self-mockery.

"I'm not finished," Blue assured her, laboring to free the woman's plentiful cherry Coke tresses from the coils and combs that imprisoned them. "If Julia Roberts can be led out of Valley of the Shadow of Slutdom, you can be led into it. Have a little faith, Sister. This is *Pretty Woman* in reverse, and I'm your call-girl guide."

Mary Frances's nose twitched as if she'd just sniffed something peppery and were about to sneeze. "This is going to take more than faith," she informed Blue. "The heavens are going to have to open, the seas part, and—"

"Bushes burn." Blue deadpanned the double entendre. "Don't forget the burning bushes."

Blue checked for a response, but Mary Frances seemed

to have missed the punch line entirely. Something Blue suspected was often the case. The boat neck of Mary Frances's black linen blouse had slipped off her shoulder, revealing a sedate black slip strap. Quick to put everything right, she settled her hands in her lap and released a little sigh of accomplishment, as if pleased to have done her bit for world order, no matter how small.

For the life of her, Blue did not understand how a woman could be dreamy and distracted and intense *and* sensual at the same time, something Mary Frances managed with the aplomb of a Disney cartoon heroine. It was clearly as natural to her as breathing. Those deep forest eyes were gone one minute and back the next, piercing you like a light ray.

A moment later that very same gaze flicked back to Blue's reflection in the mirror as if Mary Frances had just remembered she wasn't meditating in the garden at St. Gertrude's. "How does that line go?" she asked. "You can take the woman out of the convent, but you can't take the convent out of the woman?"

Blue had the sinking feeling her odd new friend had never been more right, but Blue wouldn't have admitted it if Brad Pitt had appeared in the flesh and offered himself as a reward for her honesty. Well . . . maybe if he'd been wearing leather chaps and grown his hair long again. Never mind!

"Country," Blue said emphatically. "You can't take the *country* out of a woman—and it's not true. You can. Women can be sluts if they want to. Camille Paglia said so."

Blue moved around the other woman, whom she'd positioned on an old wooden stool in front of the mirror. It wouldn't have surprised her if Mary Frances had read Paglia's cracked manifestos about love, sex, and feminism in the nineties. Blue didn't put much stock in contemporary pop philosophy, but she liked irreverence and iconoclasm and even bombast on occasion, and Paglia delivered on all counts.

She liked gutsy women as well. Fortunately, Mary Frances was showing some promise in that area. She'd surprised Blue by agreeing so readily to go to the interview with Calderon that afternoon in Blue's place. Blue had a sneaking hunch Mary Frances harbored considerable unresolved guilt where Brianna was concerned, but it was more than that. Her reaction to Webb Calderon had been nothing short of riveting. If she wasn't obsessed with the man already, she soon would be, whether she wanted to admit it or not.

Once they'd agreed to temporarily trade lives, the two of them had walked the few blocks to Mary France's tiny squirrel cage of an apartment, where Blue had immediately hauled Mary Frances into the bathroom, stood her in front of the mirror, and then sent up a prayer to Max Factor.

It seemed Max was listening.

Blue had already done a light application of facial makeup with dramatic results. The woman had skin like fine china. Plus she had killer bones and, of course, the eyes. They made you stop and wonder, those eyes. Was this oddly exotic creature really as prim as she looked? Even Blue was curious. There was only her hair to go, and if that could be whipped into some kind of shape, they'd be nearly there. The color defied description. Its hot burgundy highlights put Blue in mind of vintage wines from the Côte d'Or. But when she tried to tell Mary Frances so, the other woman merely shook her head.

"It's not blond," she said dismissively. "Men prefer that, don't they? I thought it was genetic."

"Not Calderon," Blue assured her. "He requested long dark tresses and innocence. That's you, babe. If I were going, I'd have to wear a wig and duct-tape my mouth shut."

Long dark tresses and innocence. Mary Frances's hand flew to her throat, a reflex that brought a sharp glance from Blue. Embarrassed at the intensity of her response, she quickly forced all thought of Webb Calderon from her mind. She had her own considered opinions about her hair color anyway. She found it frighteningly close to the wet cranberry glow of Sister Mary Margaret's Christmas gelatin compote, and she couldn't imagine how anyone— man, woman, or beast—could find that attractive, especially settled on someone's head. Now, Brianna's hair, there was an incredibly lush strawberry-blond ice-cream sundae of sensuality. Touch that and a man must have wondered if he'd fallen into a honey pot and drowned.

Her sister would have been the perfect consort, she imagined. The Murphy girls had been trained in the ways of a man's world from the cradle, perhaps unwittingly, by their father, who had raised both of them alone, and who clearly believed that women were either Madonnas or whores, and there was nothing much of significance in between.

Their sainted mother, Abigail, had undoubtedly fulfilled her womanly function in his eyes by having given birth to his daughters in rapid succession and then contracting pneumonia and dying shortly thereafter. "A good wife," he'd lamented throughout the house for years after her death, tears in his eyes and genuinely grieved. "Abigail was a righteous woman."

As the youngest, Mary Frances's birthright had destined her to be the Madonna, which only left one way for Brianna to go, if she didn't want to be outdone by her younger sibling. It was all quite simple, really, except that now Brianna was gone, and Mary Frances was about to become the family harlot.

Perhaps it was fortunate that Michael Benjamin Murphy had died quickly and freakishly when his fishing dinghy sprang a leak. He'd been sound asleep and gone down like a weight and tackle, or so the game warden had said. At least he would never have to deal with the way *both* his daughters had defiled his vision of a good woman. Mary Frances consoled herself with that. His need to see things in absolute terms—right or wrong, good or bad—would undoubtedly have kept him from recognizing how their need to please him and win his love had played into their life decisions. He would have blamed all of it on the workings of the devil.

"Tell me about this service Brianna worked for." Mary Frances watched intently as Blue removed the last few pins from her hair and let the kinky, thickish mane fall in waves around her shoulders.

"Well, it's called Cherries—"

"Cherries?"

Blue forged on, seemingly oblivious to Mary Frances's incredulity as she whisked a brush from the Formica countertop that served as a vanity. "Some of the escorts actually have a little cluster of cherries tattooed on the inside of their ankle," she explained. "I have no idea how the service decides who gets one or what they mean. Brianna had one. I didn't, but I did get the works at the spa, and that's one out*rage*ous flesh fest."

"Flesh fest?" This time she nearly came off the stool.

"Oh, no"—Blue laughed—"the only flesh involved is your own, but what they do to it! You'll come out of there looking incredible, more radiant than you ever believed possible."

"Sounds like a makeover."

"The mother of all makeovers, trust me. The place is like a Grecian temple, and the staff—well, you gotta be there to believe it. Everything's far-flung and fabulous."

Far-flung and fabulous? Mary Frances stole a look around her and smiled. Everything about her one-bedroom garden apartment was quaintly old-fashioned and on the brink of obsolescence, especially this closet-size bathroom with its ornate brass faucets that leaked steadily into the cracked porcelain sink. Mary Frances hadn't rented the place for its charm, however. She couldn't afford anything else. Ex-postulant church secretaries didn't live high on the hog.

"I'll bet the service has the convent beat for codes of conduct," Blue opined, working diligently to brush some spring and shine into Mary Frances's hair. "They're fanatics about taste and etiquette. They don't want any of their titled, tony clients publically embarrassed, so the escorts aren't allowed to accept gifts, drink liquor, take drugs, or wear provocative clothing while working."

Mary Frances winced as the bristles dug into her scalp. Blue was either stronger or more anxious than her lithe, angular frame suggested. "We are talking about an escort service, aren't we?"

"Not like any service you've ever heard of." Blue laughed. "They discourage spike heels and bustiers, even rhinestones. Ankle bracelets are a capital offense."

A suggestion of cinnamon rose from a row of unlit candles in tins, hand-painted with autumn leaves. They were gift items made by the nuns to help support St. Gertrude's, and the zesty scents had been Mary Frances's idea. She was wild for apple-pie spices and even carried a cinnamon sachet in her bag.

"We did have our moments at St. Gertrude's." Mary Frances's sigh was wistful. "Once we got blitzed on dandelion wine at the Feast of All Saints, and the reverend mother showed us her collection of phallic fertility statues from missionary work she'd done around the world. Somehow I can't imagine her making much of a fuss over an ankle bracelet."

Not like the fuss she'd made when Mary Frances and some of the other postulants had "borrowed" one of those phalluses, the ebony-black member of a male bison—huge, petrified, and hard as stone.

As Blue continued describing the service's policies Mary Frances came to a realization. Blue had no idea she was still sexually inexperienced, and Mary Frances had no intention of telling her. She actually wanted to do this crazy thing Blue was suggesting, even if she wasn't quite ready to examine all the reasons. The tight little flutters in her chest wouldn't let her deny the anticipation that was building there, no matter how strange and disturbing it felt. Besides, sex in all its infinite variety was not a given on a "date," according to Blue, but a mutual choice made by the escort and the client. If escorts chose to participate, the fees increased dramatically. But Mary Frances wasn't doing this for the money, and she was reasonably certain she could find ways to avoid the very things she'd been praying for at St. Gertrude's.

The leaky faucet had become the muted heartbeat of the bathroom, Mary Frances realized. Each drip was a marker, a countdown toward something waiting to make itself known to her. Life itself, perhaps. She would have leaned over and cranked the faucet handle if it would have done any good.

"Maybe you'd better tell me about Brianna's diary,"

she suggested. "Where did you find it, and what did it say?"

"You mean specifics?" Blue seemed startled.

"Well, yes, specifics. I doubt Calderon is hiring escorts to do his laundry, so it would probably help if I knew what was expected." Her matter-of-fact tone belied a burning curiosity. She had to be curious if she was about to place herself in harm's way, but this went beyond that. If her reaction to Webb Calderon in person was anything close to her reaction on the screen, then she was in for an experience beyond her wildest imaginings. And Mary Frances's imaginings had already landed her in a great deal of trouble.

Some emotion had darkened Blue's expression. She set down the brush, picked up the jumbo curling iron she'd brought in her makeup tote, and as she expertly rolled up one fat section of Mary Frances's hair after another, she described a cornucopia of forbidden erotic delights.

"Calderon is a wicked man." She glanced up from her task and mouthed the words conspiratorially to Mary Frances's reflection. "You saw his eyes. They can peel clothes off a woman like he was paring an apple, one strip at a time. They're gray, but they should be yellow. He's a demon, trust me."

Yes, she'd seen his eyes. When Calderon had walked into the courtroom, the entire mood of the place had changed. He'd brought the rains with him like a displeased demigod, and Mary Frances's first impression had been of the golden immortals from the Roman pantheon. A bit extreme, she realized now, but there had been that quality of arrogance and command about him. And coldness. It nipped at her skin even now, that sensation. Polar ice.

The camera's close-up *had* immortalized him in her

mind. There was no way to avoid his eyes as he looked into the lens. They were chilling and marbled gray, not unlike the qualities Blue described. They didn't stare, they perforated. Mary Frances had felt them piercing her like icicles before he looked away. Cold, cruel beauty. She'd heard the term countless times, but it had never been more apt. His face had no softness. None. The lean, jutting bones that dominated its contours looked sharp enough to cut yourself on, and though his mouth was wide and sensually shaped, it was not soft. His hair was ice white where the sun had touched it and dark, dark gold everywhere else.

The dead-on shot had actually stunned her for a second. She'd had to blink to be sure her eyes weren't playing tricks. He most assuredly was not a man who inspired confidence. You couldn't feel safe with Webb Calderon. Never, not for a second . . . but then Mary Frances had been safe for so long.

"And Brianna was with *him*?" she asked.

"Many times, according to her diary. Apparently he nearly drove her mad with pleasure. She must have been seeing him right up until the night she was killed, but the last entry in her electronic diary was made months before she died. I think she—or someone—erased the rest of them."

The steadily dripping water sounded almost musical. "Drove her mad?" Mary Frances was aware of the softness that had crept into her voice, the hushed shock.

Blue shrugged, clearly nonchalant about these things. "She mentioned things like aphrodisiacs and love potions and erogenous zones she hadn't known existed. One of them involved the ball of her foot, as I remember. There was kink, too—bondage and blindfolds and spankings that made her 'scream' with ecstasy."

"No? Spankings?"

Blue grinned and winked. "Lucky you, wish I was coming along."

But Mary Frances couldn't fathom it. "Do you mean he actually . . . with his hand, he—"

"*Mmmm-hmmm*, he used an Oriental paddle, too, one woven with wicker and silk, and apparently he knew exactly how to wield it. She described the experience as pleasure that broke every boundary, said it brought tears of joy to her eyes."

"Oh . . . my." It shouldn't have surprised her that Brianna was into that sort of thing. She just didn't know what else to say or how to respond. Some emotion had turned her throat into a cinch. Her head was spinning dizzily, and it wasn't entirely from shock. Worse, Blue hadn't told her everything. Mary Frances sensed strongly that the other woman was holding something back. "There's more, isn't there?" she insisted. "Tell me the rest of it, Blue."

"Well, the escorts who've been with him swear he's not made of flesh and blood," Blue admitted. "They say he's incapable of feeling physical sensation. Pleasure and pain are one and the same to him."

Mary Frances stayed Blue's hand. "What do you mean?"

"One of the escorts claims she saw him do things that would have been excruciating for a normal man. She said he had a keepsake from his childhood, a ruby-studded cross that belonged to his mother. It was a jagged, spiky thing, and yet once, in a cold fury over something, he crushed it in his hand. That was how she described him, in a 'cold, silent fury.' When he opened his fist, she noticed a scar on his palm. It was an exact replica of the cross. She said his hand should have been cut to ribbons, but there was no pain and not a trace of blood. She swears it's true."

The dripping water sounded like waves crashing against rocks. Mary Frances's hands were clasped in her lap, a gesture that had been associated with reverence in the convent. Now it was to stop them from moving. "Did you believe her?" she asked.

"She had no reason to lie." Blue exchanged the curling iron for the brush and began to comb through the abundant dark curls. "She claims he feels no pleasure, either— not even from the sex act. He rarely requests an escort's services in that way anymore . . . although there is this persistent myth about his superhuman endurance."

"Pleasure and pain." Mary Frances echoed the phrase as Blue did magical things with her hair. Her eyes were dark with wonder as she watched herself being transformed, but she wasn't thinking about the woman who was emerging. She was thinking about the deeper significance of Webb Calderon's acts, though he may have intended none. She'd made a study of the lives of the saints and their inhuman ability to endure pain and hardship. They'd drawn their strength from spiritual sources. She didn't know where Calderon drew his from, but the cross on his palm was frighteningly symbolic.

"I went through his dossier. . . ." Blue was saying.

Mary Frances forced herself to listen as Blue described a life of extreme contrasts, of wealth and indulgence, followed by brutal hardships. Calderon's mother and natural father were divorced even before he was born, and his stepfather was in the diplomatic service. Webb had been just nine when his entire family got caught in a brutal military coup in Central America. His stepfather, mother, and sister had been tortured and executed, one by one, while Webb, the youngest, was forced to watch and wait his turn. He'd been spared only because the president's mistress had admired his blond hair and long, slender limbs and decided to make him her personal errand boy.

When the president discovered his mistress's true interest in Webb, he'd had the boy imprisoned and tortured with barbaric methods that included water and electrical current. Three years later a guerrilla's bomb had blown up the crumbling stone gulag, and the zombielike teenager had escaped. Calderon had his freedom, but he was as good as dead in every other way.

Mary Frances couldn't help herself. She was touched by the story. Her compassionate nature had been stirred, but Blue warned her against sentimentality.

"He's ruthless," Blue reminded her. "He felt no compassion for Brianna."

Despite Blue's warning, Mary Frances could feel the hot breath of destiny breathing down her neck. She'd been born with a sense of ultimate purpose, but she'd always thought she would make her mark through good works, not detective work. She wasn't suited for a cloistered life, that much was abundantly clear, and yet what had she done but trade the convent for the church office, one cloister for another? She'd gone back into hiding when her heart had craved danger. Her heart had wanted to be jolted to life.

She fingered the lacy gold chain that roped her neck. Engraved on the filigreed pendant was a single rose, surrounded by drifts of snow, thriving in the bitterest kind of cold. These were the symbols of Rita of Cascia, patron of impossible causes, the rose who bloomed in winter.

The medal had been handed down through generations of Murphies and was believed to protect the youngest daughter and keep her safe until she could enter the convent. Mary Frances didn't know whether she believed that or not, but it had been given her on her confirmation day, and she'd worn it ever since.

"That has to go," Blue said.

Mary Frances closed her hand over the medal. "No! Why?"

"Sweetie, escorts don't as a rule have patron saints."

Mary Frances removed the necklace with unsteady fingers and spread it on the countertop. Over the years the medal had come to feel as much like a charm as a safeguard, though Sister Fulgentia, mistress of postulants, would have disapproved of the idea of magical charms. Still, Mary Frances wondered if her luck would change now. It hadn't been that good to begin with, she thought ironically.

"Here, let me," she said finally. She took the brush from Blue's hand, aware that the curved wooden handle felt good in her grip, solid. Bending over, she shook out her long hair, then flipped her head back up and began to wield the brush vigorously, taking pleasure in the firm strokes, in the cascading waves and flying curls. She still couldn't decide if this was a move in the direction of freedom or utter recklessness. But it felt like freedom, and it seemed to be working.

She was becoming consumed with the desire to solve the mystery of her sister's death. She wanted to know everything about Webb Calderon. Who he was. What he'd done. But before she could enter his world, she had to successfully pass his interview. Somehow she had to transform herself into the kind of woman he couldn't resist.

Blue had a very specific look in mind. She knew exactly what she wanted for Mary Frances's transformation, and clothing flew every which way as she searched through her meager wardrobe for something suitable. Littered with needlepoint pillows and hand-crocheted touches, Mary Frances's bedroom had a certain Quakerish charm to it. Unfortunately, her clothing did, too. The colors ranged from brown to black with the obligatory gray cardigan sweater thrown in.

Blue was almost ready to despair when she discovered a long, flowing ivory-and-lace dress, straight out of the sixties.

As Mary Frances gingerly undressed, leaving on far more than she took off, she explained how she'd come to have the dress. One of the parishioners at Our Lady had been jilted on the day of her wedding. In a perfect fury she'd ripped the dress off as she was storming out of the church and left it in a heap in the aisle. No one had claimed it, and Mary Frances had thought it so lovely, she'd had it cleaned and brought it home. But there'd never been an occasion to wear it.

"I'm undressed," she announced at last, having carefully arranged her skirt and blouse over the back of a chair. Her black slip could have been tarpaulin material from an army-surplus store. Many women wore less clothing to work every day.

"Let us pray," Blue murmured under her breath.

Moments later, sans slip, Mary Frances tried the dress on, and Blue knew immediately that it was perfect. She quickly and expertly altered the neckline so that it dipped invitingly over Mary Frances's breasts, then accessorized it with a floppy straw hat and a huge red rose that made her look like a dewy, impossibly sexy ingenue.

Blue loved working with fabric and design. Her family connections had opened professional doors, including her most recent legit job as an assistant curator at a museum, but that had been her mother's choice. Blue might have pursued design in college if there'd been any support. Instead she'd been faced with "We don't really know the sort of people who do that for a living, dear," and other equally vague discouragements.

"Well?" Mary Frances asked, angling to get a look at herself in the full-length mirror.

If Mary Frances had a special appeal, Blue realized with some relief, it wasn't the earthy sexiness, high-fashion glamour, or cool sophistication of the other women who worked for Cherries. It was exactly what she needed for this assignment, the allure of innocence. She might not consciously practice feminine wiles, but she had an abundance of natural sensuality in her darkly lashed gaze, inquisitive glances, and slow, hot blushes of awareness. If only she would unleash some of that simmering energy, Blue thought. She'd be a force to reckon with.

As Blue stepped back to have another look at her handiwork, she heard a low wolf whistle come from behind. She turned to find herself confronting one of the sexiest-looking roughnecks she'd ever seen. He was wearing ripped blue jeans and a paint-smudged white T-shirt with the sleeves rolled up. He looked as if he'd been doing physical labor, and Blue was immediately intrigued. The men in her life had always been sophisticated and moneyed, whether old wealth or new, including her dates from Cherries. This man was none of those things. He was a rogue at heart—a rebel, like her.

"Who's your friend, Murf?" Blue whispered.

"His name's Rick Caruso. He's not your type," Mary Frances warned.

That's all it took to hook Blue. Was she being warned off because he *was* Mary Frances's type? Was he the reason she had been expelled from the holy order? But something in the nature of her friend's greeting as she invited the man in told Blue they were only friends.

"Not my type," Blue murmured, smiling. She'd been on the run since her apartment was broken into. Her intention was to hide out in Mary Frances's place for a while. But if Rick Caruso here was to be her neighbor, perhaps lying low won't be as boring as she imagined.

3

Sixty-seven twenty-three Melrose turned out to be a dusty little antique shop, tucked in between a clothing boutique and a boulangerie at the less fashionable end of the famous avenue. The leaded-glass panel in the carved oak door was inscribed with the words ANTI-QUARIAN ATTIC, and according to the sign hanging from the inside doorknob, the shop was closed, even though it was not yet three in the afternoon.

Mary Frances pulled her car to the curb and ducked down to peer out the passenger-side window, wondering if she had the right place. Calderon was an art dealer, so it was possible he owned the shop and kept an office there, but the glare of the late-afternoon sun as it sheened every exposed surface with fire made it difficult to see if a proprietor's name was listed on the door.

Her ailing VW bug expired with a wheezing shudder before she could turn off the ignition. She'd bought the car from a young Latina seeking refuge from gang reprisals at Our Lady. Everyone had told Mary Frances she was making a mistake buying a "kid's" car, but the price had been right and she'd loved the color. Dandelion yellow.

Cradled in the worn bucket seat next to her was the red leather Cherries' satchel, its handcrafted curves as velvety soft as chamois could possibly be. Expensive and seductive, it looked as out of place in her car as she was going to feel carrying it. She was not a red leather kind of woman, even in her fantasies. She had, however, fantasized about many other things, including wearing a man's trench coat, a gold ankle bracelet from Tiffany's . . . and nothing else.

It was Brianna's satchel, and it was loaded with Cherries' gear—a beeper, a tiny cell phone, and a purse computer for communicating with the service. Blue had briefed her on the other contents, which she'd said were *de rigueur* in a society call girl's bag of tricks. Rattling around with the obligatory sex toys was a first-aid kit stocked with nitrogylcerin for heart patients, Prozac for the suddenly depressed, and a vial of exotic knockout drops that could be lethal if dosed incorrectly. Unfortunately Mary Frances's nurse's training hadn't dealt with Chinese herbs.

The rearview mirror gave out a groan as she twisted it to see how her huge hat had fared. It was amazing what soft golden straw, a red velvet rose, and long, shiny, freshly washed black hair could do for green eyes. Hers looked as big and bright as a startled child's. She hadn't wanted to admit it to Blue, but she loved the look Blue had created. She felt as if she'd stepped out of a portrait by Sargent.

Mary Frances had always preferred solemn colors. The drab grays and browns of the convent had never depressed her as they had other novices, perhaps because up to the point of entering the holy order, she'd rarely questioned the belief that it was her calling. Oh, there'd been moments, especially when Brianna had vehemently tried to talk her out of "sacrificing her entire life." And their mother's sister, Aunt Celeste, whose name Brianna had apparently borrowed, had drawn her aside once, too, deeply concerned about her decision.

But most everyone else had sincerely believed that she was suited, and they'd offered her own quiet nature as proof. It hadn't occurred to any of them—or to her—that she might be depressed or in denial. Her father had made it clear that she wasn't just living out his wishes. This was the sovereign test of Murphy mettle, the most holy of family traditions, and no other path was possible.

No one but Brianna had spoken of sacrifice. As far as the rest of them were concerned, Mary Frances could simply pack up any romantic notions she might have had in a hope chest, take them to the storeroom, and lock and bolt the door, which was exactly what she'd done. She'd relegated all errant physical urges to the equivalent of a storm cellar, where they'd eventually whipped up a tornado that had blown off the roof.

Now she touched the flower on her hat and pursed her lips. This outfit, this vibrance, was like giving herself permission to be alive, to want, to *need.* She was greedy for those feelings, but more than a little frightened of them. It felt dangerous, being alive.

With another searching glance at the shop, she let herself out of the car and went to investigate, leaving the satchel where it sat. The shop's address was inscribed on a bronze plaque above the door's leaded glass inset, so she couldn't have made a mistake. But there didn't seem to be anyone inside. She might have called Blue on the cell phone if she hadn't still been suspicious of anything that didn't plug into the wall in some fashion. Life in a cloister hadn't prepared her for the fast lane of the information superhighway, and Blue's crash course in high-tech communications had been designed to show her only how to E-mail the service so that she could report in and get her instructions.

She tapped on the glass and peered in, inspecting the musty environs, then jumped back as the door swung open. "Sorry," she rushed to explain. "I thought the store was closed."

"It is." A wiry-limbed young man gazed back at her through the thick, smudged lenses of his horn-rim glasses. He looked more like a math nerd than an antiquer. "You were expected," he assured her.

After inviting her in and locking the door behind her, he led her through a shop lit only by antique lamps—brilliantly bejeweled Tiffanies, Venetian chandeliers, and rococo wall sconces. Elegant old pieces of furniture and art graced every inch of space, making it difficult for Mary Frances to navigate as she followed his swift, catlike progress toward the back of the room.

The ambience was turn-of-the-century, a Victorian drawing room. An antique secretary held an array of liqueurs in crystal decanters, perhaps for customers to sip as they browsed, and the air was perfumed with the richness of brandied peaches and spice. Clocks ticked everywhere in soft bewildering profusion. The one that caught Mary Frances's eye was a green teak ship's clock sitting on a Carrera marble mantel.

"It's so beautiful here," she said, imagining herself arranged on a brocade sofa, sipping tea and nibbling cucumber sandwiches.

"Come this way." He acknowledged her with little more than a nod as he indicated an enormous armoire that stood against the back wall, its walnut face carved with winged angels and cherubs.

It was nothing more than a shell, Mary Frances realized as he drew open the doors. The interior had no shelves or drawers, no racks for hanging clothes, and it was large enough to step inside. When he did step inside, as Mary Frances had somehow known he would, the back walls slid open. It had been made with doors on both ends and a stairway that descended into darkness.

Mary Frances watched the young man disappear, wondering what to do as he called up for her to follow him. The armoire creaked under her weight as she stepped inside and peered down. Tiny lights lit the stair treads on each side like a movie-theater aisle.

Apprehension stirred inside her. She hesitated with the awareness that she was crossing some kind of portal, descending into the realm of the unknown. It made her think of St. Patrick's purgatory, that dwelling place where the devil himself carried you off if you fell asleep. To take the steps was to commit herself to whatever Calderon had in mind. But perhaps it wasn't as macabre as it seemed, she told herself. If his office was on the lower floor, this might be nothing more than a clever way to enhance the shop's old-world ambience.

The young man waited at the bottom, gazing up at her, unsmiling. She wanted to call down and ask where he was taking her. It was the rational thing to do. Any reasonably assertive contemporary woman would have asked, but either Mary Frances's nature, or her training, didn't allow for that. She'd been schooled in the healing virtues—humility, meekness, chastity, and temperance among them—and she had learned her lessons well. Besides, she was supposed to be an escort, a woman who knew her way around.

She started down the stairs, wondering if he knew about her, if he could tell from simply looking at her that she wasn't what she pretended to be, a woman schooled in the vices rather than the virtues.

The young man smiled.

The hallway at the bottom was low-lit with modern, recessed lighting and lined with booths that looked like the narrow dressing rooms in a department store. He stopped at the last one and surprised her by asking if he could take a picture of her. "He'll want to see you this way," he said.

Mary Frances didn't know what on earth that meant, and before she could ask, a flashcube had popped in her face, blinding her. She ducked her head and bumped up against the wall, the strangest thought crossing her mind. She was wondering if she'd dislodged her hat. When she could see again, the young man was framed in a greenish aura and holding open the door of one of the booths, apparently for her.

"I'll wait here," he said, reassuring her with a boyishly polite smile that was faintly chilling. "You'll need to take everything off and put on the body suit and kimono you'll find inside."

This was as far as even Mary Frances's compliance would stretch. "I don't understand," she said. "Why are you taking pictures? And why am I changing my clothes?"

"Oh, I'm sorry, didn't the service tell you?" He didn't seem surprised in the slightest at having to explain. "Mr. Calderon is in Paris. He'll be interviewing you via the Internet in a 'virtual' private lounge."

The apprehension lifted, leaving her weightless and filled with disbelief. She'd always thought of virtual reality as some kind of game you played while wearing a Darth Vader space helmet and shooting starfighters out of the galaxy. Even if she'd been aware that it was possible for people to conduct transatlantic interviews in private lounges, she wouldn't have thought of it as something that could touch her life. Her brief stint working in Our Lady's rectory hadn't prepared her for this, though perhaps it should have. The church had a computer one of the parishioners had donated, and she'd learned to use it for bookkeeping purposes.

"Why am I doing this?" That question sprang to her lips repeatedly as she removed her hat and gingerly began to undress. She reached to unclasp her medal and remembered it was gone. She was naked, truly naked. If she had any protection at all, it would have to be her sense of purpose. She was doing this because no one else would or could. Brianna's death had been ruled an accident, and Blue had already been to the police. Now Blue's life was in danger, and that left only Mary Frances.

But those were just the mechanics. This was deeply personal to Mary Frances. She needed to resolve her own troubled relationship with Brianna, as well as the mysteries of her sister's life and death. But more than any of that, and perhaps for the first time, she was doing something for herself. Her life was calling and she had to answer. She had to take some chances before she dried up and blew away. The circumstances of her birth had destined her to be a sacrificial lamb. If she couldn't escape that fate, at least she could choose her own altar.

Moments later, clothed in nothing but the metallic glow of a spandexlike silver body glove and draped by a short black silk kimono, she was taken to a circular room, painted with electric-blue skies and white clouds. A far cry from the antique shop, she thought. This was turn-of-the-twenty-first century.

He led her to something in the center that might have

been a computer terminal, but she wasn't at all sure. The wraparound console was equipped with spidery-armed sensors, tiny video cameras, and a headset.

Feeling slightly ridiculous, and wondering why Blue hadn't told her about any of this, Mary Frances arranged herself in a lead-white ergonomic chair and listened carefully to the young man's instructions while he calibrated the equipment and prepared her as if for a shuttle launch. He even restrained her arms and legs with leather straps, telling her that any movement would disrupt the sensors and cut off the feedback they were designed to pick up and transmit.

His brief, but explicit directions took all her concentration. "I'll be attaching several electrodelike devices that will monitor your physical and emotional responses," he said. "The helmet you'll wear has sensors that will track your eye movements, so there's no need for you to do anything but relax and watch what happens. It won't be necessary to talk or type or touch any controls. Everything will be done for you, all right?"

Mary Frances nodded, and he began quickly and expertly to attach electrodes to her palms, her forehead, and the base of her throat. She wouldn't have realized she was nervous except for the flutters in her stomach. He didn't leave her time to think about it.

Anticipation built as she stared into the opaque black landscape of her headset. Other than the grid at the top that apparently recorded her eye movements, it seemed an endless void. She'd begun to feel lulled by it, sleepy, until a crack of light opened the screen like a sunrise, and the next thing she knew, she was surrounded by a radiant blue sky. The young man, who'd described himself as a technician, had told her she would see a three-dimensional graphic landscape, but this was so real she could have reached out and touched the clouds floating by.

Scenic vistas began to soar at her as if she were hang-gliding the heavens . . . misty mountain lakes and lush green islands. A glassy mirror of water, bright enough to reflect her image, appeared below her, and a moment later the swirling momentum stopped, and she was earth-bound again. But this wasn't anything like the earth she was familiar with. She was sitting on a snowy-white chaise atop a dramatic cliff, and nearby a cobalt-blue swimming pool overlooked a sea that could easily have been the Aegean.

It was a breathtaking scene, but it wasn't actually her sitting there on the chaise, she realized. It was a virtual replica of her. She was still seated in the ergonomic chair and very much aware of watching herself on the screen. It was a bizarre experience, since the replica looked as real as if it had been an actual videotape of her. Even the freckles across her nose were the same.

She was still trying to orient herself when the silhou-ette of a man appeared on the other side of the pool. The sun shone directly on him, but the details of his face couldn't be seen. He had no features, she realized as he walked toward her. He was a negative image, a virtual shadow, even in the bright light.

Her clothing shivered on her body, the fabric cold and damp. The black kimono seemed to be trembling in the wind, and she could feel it against her skin as if she had nothing else on. She'd always had strong intuitive re-sponses to people and a gift for judging character that had grown so keen over the years it approached telepathy. But her finest gift was an uncanny ability to sense when she was in the presence of evil. Her skin would draw tight, pulling until even her scalp grew sensitive and painful to the touch. Her heart would hush. As it had now.

She was surprised when he spoke. She hadn't heard any other sounds until that moment, but now she could hear the water crashing against the cliffs below, and the cries of seabirds in the distance.

"Apparently you haven't done this before," he said, with just the faintest hint of irony. "The robe . . . you're supposed to stand and remove it."

The ergonomic chair creaked in protest, though Mary Frances hadn't moved. She couldn't have. Even if she hadn't been restrained, she was rocked by disbelief. What was more incredible, her counterpart on the screen had risen without hesitation and she was calmly undoing the kimono ties.

Watching her, Mary Frances felt a sense of personal violation that set off a war within her own body. From what little she knew of virtual reality, the user controlled the virtual image through remote devices or with simple physical movements, but that didn't seem to be the case here. She tried to counteract her double's exhibitionism, but the more she struggled against the restraints, the tighter they got. They cinched her like a car seat belt that had locked in place on impact.

"An initiate . . . is that what they've sent me?"

She could barely hear him, and yet his voice was everywhere. It seemed to have taken on the reverberations of an echo chamber. It shimmered in her head. Something was controlling the image on the screen. Was it that, his voice?

"Show me who you are, initiate . . . show me your secrets."

She couldn't lift an arm, and yet she felt as if she were doing everything her counterpart was. All of the musculoskeletal sensations of standing were flooding her body. Her muscles pulled and her bones strained against them. The backs of her knees gripped the seat of the chair. She could even feel the sea breezes on her skin and was shocked to see the silk kimono slide from the other woman's body and catch in the crooks of her outstretched arms.

She was naked under the robe.

Nothing could have confounded Mary Frances more than witnessing herself that way. And it *was* her. Her body was pale, luminous. Moonglow. Freckles dappled her breasts like golden sequins. She couldn't explain any of it, except that the body glove and headset she wore were feeding physiological information to the computer. But it wasn't the mechanics of the situation that concerned her. It was the fact that *she'd never even been seen by a man in her underwear before.*

"Your darkest secrets, initiate . . . the ones you can't admit to anyone, not even to yourself."

Her skin rippled with gooseflesh and the most sensitive parts of her anatomy leaped to attention, tingling and tightening. And if that weren't enough, something reciprocal was happening. Apparently her own bodily sensations were being transmitted to the screen, and she and her virtual counterpart were picking up each other's responses. The other woman's belly clenched and her nipples peaked, drawing tightly on pink, wind-flushed breasts. A delicate shudder rippled through her flesh.

"You can't decide whether you like this or not, can you?" Calderon laughed softly. "Be glad the choice isn't yours to make. All that matters is whether or not I like it."

Shock had a taste, Mary Frances realized. So did anger. It was bitingly hot and sour, unfamiliar in her mouth. It didn't surprise her that he was the kind of man who took

pleasure in others' discomfort. She had seen that quality
in his eyes when he'd stared into the camera. The women
in her former profession were expected to be forgiving of
sin, to seek grace and goodness in others. Her instincts
told her that this was a predator who fed on his victims'
shock, on their fear and outrage. She imagined that it
would bother him very little to have a woman shrink from
his touch. He might even enjoy it.

There was no doubt in her mind that this faceless evil
was Webb Calderon. Though she couldn't see him, she
could feel his cold scrutiny and knew that her intuition
was right. He didn't operate within the same moral
boundaries as the rest of the world. He played god when
it suited him, creating and destroying without remorse.
He also believed it his right to wield the whip hand and
mete out punishment, twisted as that logic might be. She
sensed his contempt for humanity, which undoubtedly
stemmed from his tragic childhood experiences. He'd
been tortured. He had witnessed the execution of his entire family, the ultimate degradation of his mother and
sister.

Still, only a saint could have felt compassion for Webb
Calderon in this situation, and yet Mary Frances knew it
would be her saving grace. She understood the power of
forgiveness. It was one of the seven works of mercy, and
paradoxical as it seemed, if she could summon empathy
for him, it would protect her.

She'd come across a teaching in her religious studies
that said the only way to conquer evil was to let it be
smothered within a willing, living human being. *When it
was absorbed there, like a spear thrown into one's heart,*
the author had counseled, *it lost its power and could go
no further.*

She believed that implicitly. If she could open herself

to love and compassion, she could stop the arrow. But there was no forgiveness to be found in her searching heart, only anger. The emotion fired her spirit and steamed her blood like the milk Sister Fulgentia used to scald for rice pudding. It felt good, anger did, and that made it dangerous.

"You don't really see a woman until she moves," Calderon said. "Let me see you move . . . walk to the edge of the cliff."

The woman on the screen wasn't calm anymore. Her jerky steps gave her away, but she didn't question what she'd been told to do. Haltingly, she ventured toward the precipice, and Mary Frances felt herself moving, too, cool breezes flowing over naked skin. Preoccupied as she was, she was aware of the air. The onshore currents held traces of wild orchids, and they seemed to be bathing her, arousing her as gently as fragrant bathwater.

The woman reached the edge and slowly turned around, her head bowed. Her cheeks were stained pink with embarrassment and her breathing was shallow, but her dark hair rippled with the sensuality of a water nymph who'd risen from the sea. Something seemed to be happening to her as she stood there; a strange, perhaps even sweet transfiguration was taking place that made her tremble from within.

The sight of her riveted Mary Frances, although she found it almost impossible to watch as the woman began to lift her arms, seemingly in supplication. The kimono trailed behind her, a dark veil caressed by scented breezes. Her fingers were splayed as if some kind of ecstasy might be within her grasp. Her eyes were closed, her flesh quaking.

Not supplication, Mary Frances realized. This was release, some kind of joyous release. She was offering herself.

The conflict that rose within Mary Frances was almost unbearable. The humiliation of being reduced to such a display of abandon appalled her. It disgusted her, and yet in some undeniable way, it enthralled her, too. She'd only seen this kind of passion, this kind of surrender, in a religious context, and then the purity had made it powerful. Something else made this powerful . . . something carnal.

The singing inside her head rose to a crescendo, like choirs of angels and demons vying to outshout each other. Anger, she told herself. Anger was dangerous, volatile. She had given in to it, and it had stirred the beast. She was hot with anger, tasting it, hot with something that could undo her if she let it.

"Naked." The winds sighed softly as he approached her. "I want you completely naked, unable to hide anything."

Mary Frances felt her arms drop to her sides and the robe slide to the ground in a heap around her feet. She jerked to cover herself, but the restraints locked brutally. *Pick it up!* she wanted to shout at the other woman. *Cover yourself! Don't give in!*

Mary Frances grew still then. In her mind she grew still, aware that some change had taken place within her, too. She was shaking from head to toe and yet totally at one with the naked body on the screen. She felt the woman's emotions as if they were her own. They *were* her own. There was no other woman any longer. Calderon was scrutinizing *her,* moving around *her.* She had become her counterpart.

Postulants were tutored rigorously in the secrets of mortifying the flesh and routing its desires, but all of that discipline seemed to have failed her now. The hours upon hours of deep contemplation and prayer, the Great Silences, the slavish adherence to ritual. She'd forsaken the rites and opened herself to dangerous emotions. Anger had ignited the fires of excitement. Fear had given way to a fever of anticipation.

She'd fought the tyranny of feelings all her life, but she could feel the power in surrendering to them now. The release alone could save her from this awful quaking. It would transport her. That must have been why her counterpart had given in. She'd known.

He'd moved closer. She still couldn't see any detail of his features, but she could feel his presence as surely as if the sensors were feeding her information about him. The wind had enveloped her in its embrace, and it felt disturbingly sweet, as hynoptic as the orchids, only this breeze had weight and pressure and heat. It was as sensual and unhurried as a seductive touch. Was he touching her? *Was this what it felt like to have a man's hands on your body?*

"What are you doing?" she wanted to know. "Wait! Stop! You don't have the right—"

"Don't have the right to touch you? I'm about to buy you, intitiate. And if I do, your body will be mine to do whatever I choose with. Mine to touch and fondle and fu—"

She shrank back in horror.

The shadow flared and receded. He was moving away from her with a force that told her he was angry, walking toward the cliffs on the other side of the pool.

"Besides," he said, "I didn't do what you were demanding I stop. I never touched you. Whatever you felt you created in your own imagination. You generated a feedback loop that made you feel touched because you wanted to be touched . . . and most likely by me."

Unquestionably by him, though that made no sense to her now.

She closed her eyes, willing herself to withdraw, to retreat to the haven of her own mind, but the low resonance of his voice stole through every barrier she put up.

"Each escort has her own specialty," he said. "Even the initiates. I'm trying to imagine what yours might be."

Mary Frances felt the restraints tighten on her wrists. Until now she hadn't realized how symbolic the gesture of clasped hands was. Deceptively humble, it created its own feedback loop, warding off evil and providing invisible protection. Calderon had deprived her of every possible defense against him, but he may have just given her a way out. Blue had told her he might ask about her specialty and they'd picked one Mary Frances was well suited for.

"The Golden Needles of Ecstasy—" She hesitated for a reaction. "I can give you the most intense pleasure imaginable. I can take away pain, too."

"But can you *give* pain?" he asked. "*That* would be a gift."

Pain, a gift? She didn't understand what he meant, but there was a quality in his laughter that made her throat tighten. It was raw, exposed. It was also the first glimpse of vulnerability he'd given her, the first glimpse of anything human, and she seized on it, glad that she had some medical training.

"I was trained as a nurse," she said. "The Golden Needles are really just an exotic form of acupuncture, but they do stimulate nerve pathways and open the body up to more feeling. They can make you experience things much more intensely."

"Things? Like orgasms?"

"Well, yes . . . and arousal."

It struck her as borderline crazy that she was discussing an exotic sexual technique she'd never done while poised stark naked on a cliff, being interviewed by a phantom, who was actually in Paris. She wanted to laugh. Could she ever have done anything resembling this in real life?

Still, it was a relief to talk about something she knew and to regain some control of the situation. Since he'd done nothing yet to discourage her, she went on about the efficacity of acupuncture, hesitating only when she saw a picture flash onto the corner of the screen. It was her likeness, the snapshot the technician had taken before she'd changed.

The big droopy hat nearly hid her raven hair, but there was no concealing the startled green eyes and liberal sprinkling of freckles. That should please him, Mary Frances thought. It was hard to beat Snow White for innocence. Her pale skin was as translucent as the ivory lace dress, and both were perfectly complemented by the deep red of the rose.

But the phantom's demeanor had changed. His mood had darkened with frightening swiftness. Interest had become anger, more than anger. She sensed rage. He'd been overtaken by some primal and ancient fury. It had crystallized inside him—frozen shards of agony that could rip her to ribbons if freed.

"Why were you dressed like her?" he demanded.

"Like who?" She had to think that he meant Brianna, but that wasn't an outfit her sister would have worn, not on a bet. Brianna was a red leather kind of girl, which was all the more reason why Mary Frances didn't understand Calderon's attraction to her, or hers to him. If Calderon really did prefer innocence, then Brianna would not have been his choice of companion.

"Who are you?" he asked. Shadows flew across the

screen, concealing his presence, but the volume of his voice had increased thunderously, and it seemed to be coming at her from everywhere. She felt as if she were about to be annihilated.

"A nun," she heard herself whispering, yet couldn't imagine that she was actually saying it. Or that he would believe it. "I was going to be a nun until I committed a sin of impurity."

Suddenly all the color on the screen was being sucked up into a vortex. Everything, including her image, was disappearing into a tiny black pinhole. With a loud pop, the screen went dark, creating a void that accentuated the ringing chaos in her head. What had happened?

He'd aborted the interview.

Mary Frances sagged in the chair. Relief overwhelmed every other consideration, even the awareness that she might have failed her interview with him. The straps came loose, allowing her to slip her hands from them and remove the headset. She quickly undid the restraints that held her feet, and by the time she was free, she realized the technician was gone. She was alone in the room. Now all she had to do was find a way to escape this place.

4

It was midnight, Paris time.

His office was as cold and dark as a tomb. The only light in the enormous, octagonal room was the glowing computer monitor on his glass-and-iron desk. The only heat was his breath. He preferred it that way. Cold. Dark. He had every material thing a man could want, virtually at his fingertips, but life's comforts meant nothing. The knife's edge was where he lived, where he had to live in order to feel anything at all. What others found uncomfortable, even painful, he found merely stimulating.

Tonight he was stimulated.

She was fucking with him. Or someone was. He'd known it the moment her picture appeared on the screen. Naked, she'd been just another expensive Cherries' whore. But clothed in lace and with the gigantic red rose weighing down the brim of her floppy straw hat, she could have been a turn-of-the-century waif, her dewy-eyed innocence captured on canvas by Cassatt or Goddard.

She could have been Blush, he admitted.

He swung around, chair wheels caterwauling beneath him on the red marble floor. He'd had the tiles imported from Africa to accent the Italian postmodern look of the office suite. The place was a showpiece in black and gold, according to the international art press, every bit as spectacular as his five-floor gallery, but the decadent furnishings had lost their appeal for Webb long ago. He found them garish now, especially when contrasted with the dreamy portrait that hung on the wall adjacent to his desk.

They called her Blush, and Webb had understood why the moment he'd seen her. She was kissing her own reflection in a mirror, misting the glass with lips that were softened and swollen with longing. Her fingers caressed the ornate frame as if it were a man's shoulders, and the lovesick droop of her lashes had told Webb what she longed for . . . initiation into the mysteries of life—the secrets of the heart, the body. This was kissing practice for some phantom lover, a man who had yet to touch her, perhaps even to notice her.

Sadly, Webb knew she would lose her innocence the moment she *was* touched. *The imagined was pure and perfect. Her lover wouldn't be. He might ease her physical longings, but he could never meet the needs of a dreamer's heart. They were pristine, like dewdrops clinging to a leaf. The sun's glory made them radiant, but only for a moment before it destroyed them.*

Webb remembered his thoughts word for word and with the same clarity he had the day he'd first seen the painting. He remembered them because he knew all about that kind of destruction. He specialized in it.

An antique ruby-studded cross lay in a small silver box

on the credenza behind his desk. It had belonged to his
mother, a family heirloom she'd slipped to him moments
before her death. Webb scooped it up now, studying its
spiked edges and cruel beauty. What twisted urge made
men hurt what they loved? Why did they need to defile
innocence instead of protecting it? Christ if he knew. Yet
the urge lived within him. It clawed to get out. The innocent weren't safe around Webb Calderon, and yet that
very quality drew him in all its forms, drew him irresistibly, perhaps because he'd lost his own innocence in
such an early, violent way.

The silk of his short-sleeved shirt was liquid ice
against his skin as he returned the cross to its container.
Assaulted by the chill, his flesh rose in protest, but any
sensation of pain was absent. That was a memory, too,
his most vivid recollection being the morning the Goddard portrait arrived in his Beverly Hills gallery. He'd
wondered who had inspired such a fever of longing in
her, what sort of man. A tiny, whiplike nerve had stung
deep in his jaw as he'd surrendered control of his ob-
jectivity for a moment and allowed himself to imagine
the touch of her trembling lips, the sweet taste of her
innocence. It was the closest thing he'd felt to an emotion in years.

The original portrait was now encased in bulletproof
glass in that showroom, but he'd had prints made for
the two other offices where he spent the most time, this
one and the one in Milan, and there'd been the inevitable gossip that the painting was a "thing" with
him. They were right. But cold was a thing with him,
too. So was darkness. There was very little in this
world that pricked his senses and allowed him to feel.

When he found something that did, he kept it close at hand.

The soft whir and glide of precision machinery drew his attention. He turned back to the desk, found the remote device that controlled his computer software, and with a few perfunctory clicks brought the office lights up. He could manipulate the utilities and the security of his entire gallery from this computer if he chose to. High technology had taken much of the guesswork out of running his business, and for that very reason, it bored him. He liked guesswork. He liked the risk, but he preferred guessing right. Fortunately, he almost always did.

A color copy of the snapshot slowly emerged from his laser printer. He rose from the chair and watched it drop into the tray. Her eyes were dark green. It was the first thing he noticed. Their color wasn't particularly striking, except in contrast to her translucent skin. Surrounded by the smoky lace of her lashes, they gave her an ethereal quality that struck out at your senses and defied you to look away.

He had no desire to try. He rather liked the feeling that tugged at his gut as he studied her. It was like being massaged from the inside. The price of being surgically cut off from one's own feelings was that he couldn't feel the good things either. He couldn't feel the things a girl like this could do to him.

She wasn't beautiful, he decided. Not beautiful at all. Timeless, perhaps. Like a Raphael Madonna. Hers wasn't the face of a prostitute, but then neither was Mary Magdalene's, and that had been her profession before she was chosen.

He took the copy from the tray, wishing he had some

natural light. His gallery, viewing room, and storage space took up the top three floors of the five-story Empire Building and his office suite was in the medieval tower that abutted the penthouse showroom. Hazy streetlight slanted through the window overlooking Rue de George V, which was quiet and uncongested at this hour. It sprinkled the moonlike chamber with a silvery incandescence, but it wasn't strong enough to see by.

Backlit by office light, he could see himself reflected in the window as if he were looking in a mirror. The heavy waves of his dark gold hair were combed back from his forehead, but silvery, sunwhitened tendrils curled uncontrollably at his temples and nape. It was a look that might have softened another man, but Webb's steely bones and bleak gray eyes militated against any such thing. He looked dangerous, and he knew it was because of her. She'd brought something out in him, a hunger he hadn't felt this strongly in years. If it was the twisted urge that dwelled within him, it was also something more, something surprisingly close to pain. It went without saying that he wanted information about her. Answers. He wanted to know who she was, why she'd dressed that way, and what she was up to. But he wanted more than that. More.

Searching green eyes gazed up at him as he studied her likeness. She couldn't possibly be a prostitute, he reasoned, not even one whose game was innocence. She didn't have that wary, weary look about the mouth. Her features were open, unclouded by suspicion. He knew that look of veiled hostility toward everything male, and this one didn't have it. She hadn't been tested or tried. She hadn't been damaged like the others . . . or like him.

Which was exactly why he couldn't take his eyes off her.

"Jesus Christ," he murmured. A knowing smile crept into his thoughts, though it didn't touch his mouth. If someone was using her to get to him, they couldn't have picked better bait.

5

Perhaps Blue Brandenburg wasn't even aware that she'd lost that vital voice within her, the one peculiar to women that warned them when they were about to venture into dangerous territory involving men and sex. When it was working that voice cautioned, "This doesn't feel right. Think twice, then don't do it."

When it was working.

It was possible Blue had never had a voice like that. She'd certainly had her share of trouble with men, starting with the day her mother had accused her of trying to seduce her own father and then shipped her off to convent school as punishment. Blue'd had no way of knowing that her mother was sick and pathologically jealous of the close relationship between her husband and her ten-year-old daughter. Blue also hadn't understood why her father, the man she adored above all other humans, the man she worshiped as God, hadn't intervened. He'd let his wife scream and stomp and hurl accusations at Blue as if she'd been some tramp he was having an affair with. He'd refused even to look at his only child.

No, Blue didn't have one of those vital voices. She only had Kaye Brandenburg's voice, calling her a filthy little whore who wanted to sleep with her own father. Her mother had said those words over and over, as if she were clutching rosary beads and reciting Hail Marys. Spewing Hail Marys like bullets.

Maybe it was fortunate that this afternoon Blue didn't even have that voice, her mother's. All she could hear as she ran the exercise wheel in Mary Frances's squirrel cage of an apartment was the desperate scream of her nervous system for something heavily spiked with white sugar and dark chocolate and at least three pulls of unadulterated Italian espresso. She had a craving for a triple iced mocha supremo that was as powerful as a cry for heroin or some other fatally addictive drug.

"*Mufuh.*" The vulgarity, a favorite from Blue's convent-school days, dropped out of her mouth as she caught sight of her pallid self in the warped mirror of Mary Frances's dresser. She looked like a derelict street person. Her friend's saint's medal lay on the dark wood surface like an offering, but Blue was preoccupied with her own deficiencies. She needed makeup. Without it, she looked like warmed-over au gratin potatoes—a pale, lumpy, and unappealing face under a glob of stringy orange hair.

No one would ever believe that men had paid thousands of dollars to be with her since she'd been at Cherries. Sometimes she couldn't believe it herself, though she'd been told her whole life that she was the sinfully seductive kind of beauty who shipwrecked men on the rocks of sexual ruin. She'd had that drummed into her head, first by her mother and then by the nuns.

Hands planted on her hips, she peered into the ocean

waves of Mary Frances's mirror. The damn thing made her dizzy, but she had to know if they were telling the truth, and this mirror belonged to an ex-nun. It wouldn't lie.

She couldn't deny the woman glowering back at her possessed cheekbones that with a bit of color, artfully applied, had the arch of a bullfighter's spine. Good eyes, too. Merciless. Flashing with lights that couldn't completely hide the deep wells of blue-gray water. Men were struck dumb by her eyes when she "did" them, the sweepy black lashes thickly coated with waterproof mascara. And okay, she thought, sighing, her caramel-blond hair with its long shag cut, when fluffed and fringed around her face, was killer, too.

"Get your act together, Brandenburg," she ordered. "Go out for coffee. Maybe you'll shipwreck a man on the way."

Twenty minutes later, looking fashionably funky in her cutoff Calvins and the snug white tank top she found in one of Mary Frances's drawers, and which was undoubtedly intended to be underwear, Blue was ready to boogie and wondering whether or not she should leave a note. Mary Frances had left for the interview with Calderon over an hour ago, but the drive from Santa Ana to Los Angeles alone would take that long.

To be safe, she scribbled down a message on the marker board hanging next to the kitchen phone. She'd sat Mary Frances down before she'd left and taught her how to contact Cherries on the computer and pick up her E-mail. She'd also had her send a message saying she was on her way to the interview. Now she wanted to remind her to check back in as soon as she returned. Otherwise the service might become suspicions.

As she locked up the second-floor apartment with the

key Mary Frances left and headed down the rickety stairway to the street entrance, she felt an unfamiliar sensation, perhaps triggered by the stained walls and general
shabbiness of the building, as well as the spartan quality
of Mary Frances's lifestyle. The kid was living in a dump,
Blue admitted, and Blue herself was feeling guilt. Pangs
of it.

She trailed her fingers lightly down the banister, aware
of the squishy give of the moldering wooden steps. She
hadn't told Mary Frances the whole truth. She would
have if she hadn't been afraid of scaring her off, which,
now that she thought about it, didn't seem likely. It would
have been more difficult to talk Mary Frances out of the
interview than it was to talk to her into it, Blue suspected.
But it wasn't the interview Blue was worried about. It was
the party. If Mary Frances was spotted as a fake, she became a threat to Calderon and an obstacle to others. Her
life would be in danger, too, only Mary Frances would
have nowhere to hide.

"It will still be the truth when she gets back." Blue
pushed through the door and heard the hiss and click of
security locks as it closed behind her. "I'll tell her then.
Everything."

Her sandals clip-clopped thunderously as she took another short flight of steps to the street, aware that she
would have nothing to do for the next couple days except
live Mary Frances's life. Oddly, that felt more freeing
than confining, but she couldn't afford to take needless
risks. Mary Frances had become the decoy, but someone
had broken into Blue's apartment, apparently for the express purpose of stealing Calderon's appointment book.
Whoever it was knew Blue's identity and might be looking for her now.

She glanced around and decided Mary Frances lived in

a ghost town. The dust of the ages coated the few parked cars that lined the deserted street, and windows were broken out in a nearly vacant strip mall across the way. One doughnut shop appeared to be operational and the X-rated video shop was doing a thriving business, which said something about the law of supply and demand on a Friday night. A main thoroughfare ran a few blocks to the north. She and Mary Frances had come that way from the church, so she struck out to retrace their steps, her thoughts cluttered with the details of her plan.

Calderon's party was scheduled for Saturday night, but the escorts would be expected to stay the weekend. If everything went well, Mary Frances would be back to work in the rectory office by Monday morning, hopefully with some tangible evidence that would implicate Calderon in her sister's death.

Blue had coached her on what to look for, the artifact that had vanished from Brianna's apartment after Brianna stole it from the briefcase she was to give to Calderon that night—a pre-Colombian blue jade pendant—plus anything else that might indicate Calderon had a motive for murder.

Blue hadn't decided what her own next move would be at that point, except that she wasn't going back to either escorting or assistant curating. That museum gig was a joke anyway. Her mother's connections had made it possible. Blue had been unemployed and grateful at the time, but after twenty-seven years, she'd finally figured out that if she continued to let her mother pull strings for her, she would always feel obligated to live up to the woman's expectations.

Blue's dad had died tragically a few years back in circumstances Blue tried not to think about anymore, though she knew she might never be free of her guilt and confusion. He probably wouldn't have approved of what she was trying to do either, but it was the realization that she hadn't been put on earth so Kaye Brandenburg would have someone to disapprove of and feel superior to that had freed Blue to quit the museum and start investigating Brianna's death. And though she deeply regretted the circumstances, she'd never felt more alive or involved.

Someone whistled and catcalled obscenely as Blue strolled down the sidewalk, basking in the dusky pink rays of the setting sun and loving the feel of its warmth in her hair. She picked up her pace, but didn't look around. The neighborhood she'd ventured into was a rough one. She'd already passed a couple of cars that looked as if they'd been stolen and stripped, and the kids loitering around the video arcades weren't smoking Camels.

Blue had noticed the unsavory elements when she'd walked Mary Frances back from the church earlier that day, but she hadn't actually considered the possibility that there wouldn't be a safe haven somewhere nearby. A coffeehouse. Every neighborhood had one of those, didn't it?

Now she realized how naive she'd been. This neighborhood specialized in substances much stronger than coffee. A small group of men were ambling along about a half block behind her, grinning, jostling each other, and making suggestive remarks. She couldn't decide whether they were following her or not, but she wasn't taking any chances. She abandoned her quest for caffeine and set out in search of Our Lady, Queen of Martyrs, knowing she couldn't be very far away. She only hoped she could remember where the church was.

Turning in a circle, she searched the skyline and saw a spire in the near distance. It rose above the dingy iridescence of an all-night diner whose neon signs were already aglow. Limestone white, the spire stood out against the black hills behind it like a guidepost for lost souls.

As she turned the corner a moment later and saw the crumbling, yet dignified adobe structure a few blocks down, she let out a shaky sigh. Her mad dash across the busy street triggered yells and blasting horns from the last of the evening commuter traffic on this, that most important day of the week, Friday. There were no parishioners gathered around the statue when she got there, but a scatter of rose blossoms and a wreath that appeared to be made of laurel leaves had been left at the saint's feet.

Blue was oddly touched as she passed the offerings, but by the time she reached the church doors, she'd squelched the sentiment as corny. She really did wonder at the gullibility of some people. When would they learn that you made your own luck? It didn't come because you littered a churchyard with posies.

A big, skinny marmalade tom lurked in the bushes next to the entrance, grooming himself and looking as if he could use a good meal. Blue had nothing to give him, but she stooped to scratch his ruff. He purred noisily and rubbed himself against her knee.

"Back in a flash with some grub," she promised.

The interior of Our Lady was quiet and serene, untouched by the Friday-night chaos outside. Lancet windows on each side of the nave shimmered with the rosy hues of twilight, but darkness and candlefire prevailed. Healing darkness. Blue could feel its balm and wondered why she'd always found the worship services so fearsome and oppressive as a child. Nothing had changed except her. The bogeymen in her life were real now, not imagined. Obviously that had given her a different perspective.

There were a few worshipers sitting quietly, their gazes

fixed on the golden crucifix behind the altar. Others were kneeling to pray. Not wanting to disturb them, she made her way quietly down the outer aisle of the nave, with one thought only, to find that place where the church held its social gatherings and bingo nights. They always served coffee in those rooms.

A doorway led to the small, missionlike building that housed the rectory, where the priests lived and the church office was located, as well as what appeared to be a small community room. Blue checked out the tiny church office as she passed and found it unoccupied. Noises were coming from the community room at the end of the hall, which was where she was headed.

She peeked in the door and saw Rick Caruso in ripped-out jeans and a paint-spattered chambray work shirt, talking to a tearful teenage girl. All she knew about him was that he was a friend of Mary Frances's, but that alone told her he must have some involvement with the church. The room looked like it was being remodeled, and she imagined he was donating his time, which impressed her favorably. He was probably in his mid-thirties and most guys that age had other things on their mind than volunteering to counsel teenagers.

Blue couldn't hear their conversation, but they seemed to be finishing up their talk. The girl had risen from the chair next to Rick's and she was tugging down the hot-pink cardigan sweater that covered her flowered leggings.

"Thank you, Father," she said, her tone almost trembling with reverence.

Rick smiled at her as he rose, a certain tenderness in his expression. "You're welcome, Gina. I want you to call me if there's any more trouble. I'll talk to your mother, okay?"

She nodded and skipped from the room, a delighted smile lighting her face until she spotted Blue. Her tennis shoes could have laid skid marks, she came to a stop so abruptly "Who's she?" Her startled gaze needled Blue with suspicion, and then she spun back to Rick as if certain he would need her help in dealing with this blond interloper.

"It's okay, Gina. I know the lady."

His reassurances appeared to have little effect. The teenager slunk past Blue, silently, unhappily, and left.

Rick seemed to be assessing the situation as he took his sweet time getting across the room to Blue. A faint grin wreathed his blunt, boyish features, and his cobalt eyes shimmered with curiosity. Blue's heart took an odd skip and a hop. The sensation reminded her of young girls playing jump rope. Her eyes hadn't deceived her. He was just as impossibly masculine and sexy as she remembered from their brief meeting earlier that morning in Mary Frances's apartment.

Hoping to shipwreck him, she flashed him her best this-is-your-lucky-day smile. "Do all the nubile young girls call you Father?" she asked. "How quaint. And how kinky."

Something in his expression caught her off guard. There were traces of gravity, perhaps even of sadness, beneath the good-natured grin. He tucked his hands in his jeans pocket and slouched his shoulders a bit as he gazed at her, taking in her tight T-shirt and her shiny blond hair.

"Here's a real thrill for you, Amanda," he said quietly. "Some of them even call me Holy Father. I'm a priest."

"A priest?" Blue had an urge to look around for the lifeboat. Now she was virtually certain there was going to be a shipwreck. The only thing in question was whose boat was headed for the rocks.

• • •

Mary Frances spotted the note from Blue the moment she walked in the front door. Her apartment complex, the Casa Rialto, was straight out of the fifties, when two-story, runway-roofed adobes with sliding-glass patio doors and combination kitchen–living rooms were as prevalent as outdoor movies and bowling alleys.

Her place was situated on the second floor above the utility room—an undesirable location that had saved her fifty dollars a month in rent—and true to architectural tradition, the two main rooms were separated by a white Formica breakfast bar, all of which gave Mary Frances a clear shot of the marker board next to the wall phone. And Blue's note.

She didn't stop to read it, however. As irresistibly as the note called to her, it would have to wait until she'd retrieved her medal. The sky was going to fall in otherwise. She hated being so superstitious, but it really did feel as if she'd pushed her luck as far as she could. Perhaps too far. Family curse or not, the medal had always made her feel protected and she wasn't taking it off again, for any reason or any one. She couldn't help but wonder how the interview with Calderon would have gone if she'd worn it. Certainly she wouldn't have felt as vulnerable.

The red satchel landed in her cushioned rocker with a soft plop and her straw hat sailed toward the breakfast bar as she strode through Casa Murphy on her way to the bedroom.

Antique eighteen-carat gold glinted brightly from the dressertop. Mary Frances scooped up the delicate chain, laced it around her neck, and secured the clasp with a sureness that came from years of familiarity. Once she had it lined up with the vertebrae at the nape of her neck and the medal resting on her breastbone—a ritual begun in Catholic school—the world felt a good deal safer.

She changed her clothes in front of the refrigerator while reading Blue's note. Her Levi's were zipped and buttoned before she pulled the lace dress over her head, and the soft white cardigan sweater she'd grabbed from the drawer was already looped around her waist, ready for her to slip her arms inside. She had never been nude at St. Gertrude's. The nuns generally had more clothes on when they were undressing than at any other time, a paradox that still made Mary Frances want to smile.

The situation with Blue did not. It didn't surprise her that Blue had gone out for a walk, only that she'd braved this neighborhood. Her restless streak had been legendary, even in school. She'd always had the curiosity of a cat, and she'd always landed on her feet. It was the last reference in her note that had Mary Frances uneasy, the part about checking in with the service as soon as she got back. Did Blue really mean for Mary Frances to do that on her own? She'd only had the one crash course in using that strange little computer, and though she'd memorized every step of the process, she would have preferred some moral support.

Mary Frances left the dress in an ivory heap on the kitchen linoleum and turned to the bay window in the living room, hoping to see Blue on her way back from wherever she'd wandered off to. Clearly Webb Calderon hadn't been enchanted with the way the interview had gone, and Mary Frances was concerned that he might report back to the service with specifics that would blow Blue's cover. It was the "nun" comment that worried her most. Blue had been a prostitute, but she'd never been a postulant.

"Where did she go?" Mary Frances's stomach growled

noisily as she searched the street. She'd had a decadently moist bran muffin and a steaming cup of hot tea for breakfast, but nothing since. She was growing too nervous to eat now, too nervous to do anything but check her ten-year-old Timex and search the street.

Where *was* Blue?

In truth, she was burning to contact the service and see what might have come of her interview with Calderon, but wasn't sure how she would explain herself if the anonymous Cherries' contact started asking questions for which she had no answers. The one she'd dealt with earlier had used the nickname "Wink," and had signed off with a semicolon followed by a parenthesis. The "emoticon" had confused Mary Frances until Blue had told her to tilt her head to the left and look at it again. Then she'd seen it, a smiling wink lying on its side.

Within moments Mary Frances's sense of urgency won out.

How much longer could she wait? The note had said to contact them as soon as she got back. Fortunately she already had some hands-on experience with the computer at the church. Father Rick had taught her the basics, but she'd drawn the line at learning Shock Wave Assault, a computer game he particularly loved.

Resolving to see what she could do, she fetched the purse computer and cell phone from the satchel and sat down with it at the kitchen table. It took some trial and error, but she finally succeeded in getting through and accessing Blue's E-mail. There were already several messages demanding to know Blue's whereabouts and requesting that she check in, each one more emphatic than the last. But it was the most recent message that rocked Mary Frances back in the kitchen chair. She could hardly believe what she was reading.

INTERNET GATEWAY
97/04/11
FROM: 75024.527@CYBERSERVE.COM@INET01#1
TO: 206724.2910@GENESIS.GEIS.COM
RETURN-PATH: 75024.527@CYBERSERVE.COM

SUB: YOUR FUTURE

APPARENTLY YOU MADE A VERY FAVORABLE IMPRESSION ON
THE CLIENT. WEBB CALDERON HAS ISSUED A PRIORITY RE-
QUEST FOR YOU.

APPARENTLY YOU ALSO NEED A REFRESHER COURSE IN CHER-
RIES' PROTOCOL. YOU ARE TO REPORT IMMEDIATELY TO THE
SPA TO BE "DONE." A LIMO WILL PICK YOU UP THERE AND
TAKE YOU TO CALDERON'S HACIENDA IN SANTA BARBARA.
THE PARTY STARTS TOMORROW, BUT CALDERON WANTS YOU
THERE TONIGHT.

A WORD OF ADVICE? IF YOU FUCK THIS UP, YOU'RE HISTORY.
WINK. ;)

6

"If this cat goes for my balls, they'll hear the screams in Outer Mongolia."

Blue nearly choked on the sip of coffee she'd just taken. As it was, a stream of the hot brew slopped over, baptizing her fingers. "Shit," she gurgled, setting the heavy china cup down with a clunk and popping one of the burned fingers into her mouth as she grabbed for a napkin.

Father Rick Caruso did look highly, highly uncomfortable sitting across the dinette booth from her. She might have taken it personally if she hadn't known he had the marmalade tom hidden inside his yellow rain slicker. She'd coaxed the reluctant priest into joining her for a cup of coffee, and the cat had been waiting for them at the door of the church, looking gaunt and hopeful as they'd left. A hasty search of the rectory kitchen had turned up nothing edible for felines, so Rick had agreed to stow the cat away in his coat. And now that they were at Rio

Grande, the diner Blue had seen around the corner from the church, a double order of fish tacos was on its way.

Rick watched Blue nurse the scalded knuckle with mordant interest. A smile fought for its life and lost the battle as he added conversationally, "Contrary to popular opinion, we don't check 'em at the seminary door."

Blue exerted amazing control this time. She finished the mop-up, then removed the impediment from her mouth. "Oh, I'm sure not," she said, assuming they were still on the subject of balls. His balls. "Forgive me if I'm not used to discussing male genitalia with priests."

"If you consider that a deficiency, we could talk about my manroot."

Blue was pink! She wouldn't have bet a longshoreman could entertain her this well, much less a priest. Not that she didn't like it. She did. She loved nothing more than to be kept off balance, and this guy had an interesting curve-ball. Maybe two. A smile puckered her nose and she colored again. Heaven only knew what else Father Caruso had in store. Blue had every intention of finding out.

"I'd love to know all there is to know about your manroot," she assured him, "but could we talk about why you became a priest first? Somehow I think that's the real story."

In fact, she was sure of it. The slight bend in the bridge of his nose told her it had probably been broken, and there was a spidery scar on one cheekbone that looked as if it might have been a nasty cut. He'd earned his stripes the hard way, she suspected, but the battle scars barely put a crimp in his Irresistibility Quotient.

Coppery flourishes in his black coffee hair brought out the warm tones in his skin, and a lean, wide-angle jaw lent his rugged features a charming boyishness. He also had eyes the color of her name, but his were the truest shade she'd ever seen—the blue that could sometimes be discerned in a flame when it burned very hot. Searing, his eyes, and faintly sad. They could blaze right through a girl's heart, she imagined.

"It's a long story," he said. "I don't think the cat's interested."

But Blue was. Fixated wouldn't have been too strong a word. She couldn't imagine that Rick Caruso's decision to enter the priesthood wasn't a compelling one. For the life of her, she couldn't figure out why a man that sexy would give it all up. He didn't appear to be the quiet, contemplative type, and he didn't seem to have any desire to be a shining example to the heathen.

He didn't seem too happy about rescuing stray cats either. At the moment his entire concentration was on the bedlam taking place inside his clothing. The slicker bunched and bulged with frantic activity and a throttled-down mewling issued forth.

Rick's grimace of despair brought a sympathetic smile to Blue's lips. "Either Cardinal Fang's in love," she pointed out. "Or he needs some air. Can he breathe in there?"

Blue had wanted to name the tom Baby Hughie, but Rick had insisted on Cardinal Fang, which did have a certain logic to it, considering where the cat did his panhandling. The slicker's gaping placket answered Blue's question. Cardinal Fang did not need air. He wanted his freedom. Or maybe Rick's balls.

"Here, give him to me." She indicated that Rick should pass the cat to her under the table. "I'll bribe him with some coffee cream until the fish tacos get here. The waitress'll never see him on the seat."

Emancipating an annoyed cat must be a lot like saving a panicked sinner, Blue decided, watching Rick struggle.

The priest had met his match. It looked like he was trying
to give birth to Rosemary's baby! She glanced around the
restaurant to see if anyone else had noticed the commotion in the front booth. Luckily, the place was nearly
empty. Two men sat at the counter, conversing passionately in Spanish and nibbling on coffee-soaked dough-
nuts, and a couple in a booth at the other end of the
restaurant were conversing passionately in body language and nibbling on each other's faces. No one seemed
to have heard Cardinal Fang's howls of rage.

"Come on," she urged. "There must be a cat in there
somewhere."

He flashed her a dark look. "Want to see my scars?"

A quick intercessory prayer seemed to do the trick.
Rick closed his eyes, mumbled a fervent plea and miraculously the big orange tom settled down and allowed
himself to be extricated and discreetly transferred.

Once Blue had him lapping up a splash of milk off her
coffee-cup saucer and purring contentedly, she decided to
indulge herself as well. Hot and sweet, just like me, she
thought as she ripped open another packet of sugar and
poured the entire thing into her coffee. Tonight she'd
gone for the steaming, black, no-frills variety, just like
the restaurant. And the man, she admitted. No iced-
mocha frippery for this guy. He'd eat coffee grounds first.

"So," she said, friendly-like, "I guess you work with
kids?"

It was his second dark glance. That should have been
enough to warn her off. Unfortunately it did anything but.
Moody, she thought, realizing she might just have sealed
her fate. He was moody. She *loved* men who were remote
and forbidding and in all ways difficult bastards. The
kind women were told to fight off with cans of pepper
spray. It was a failing of hers. One of many.

"You don't work with kids?" she persisted. "Or you don't *like* working with kids?"

He picked up his nearly full coffee cup with both hands and held it to his lips, but didn't drink. Instead, he raised his gaze as slowly as an antiaircraft gun sighting its target. "Yeah, I *love* working with kids," he said, riddling her with bullets. "Is that what you wanted to hear? Working with kids is my life."

He stared out the window at a cluster of teen greasers on the street and the low-riders slinking by like land subs. "Who the hell would want to work with kids like that?" he asked, his voice barbed with sarcasm. "*Vatos locos* who'd just as soon pump holes through you as look at you? The kids in this neighborhood don't need me, they need a good emergency room. They've got two career paths open to them. They can either be drug-dealing murderers or drug-dealing corpses. Some of them get to be both."

Something in his profile told her not to say a word. He was angry. But it was anger smoldering in a sea of a desolation. She had just witnessed a silent shout, a declaration of his helplessness, and it moved her in ways she didn't understand. He wanted to be there for these kids. He just didn't know how.

She reached for the cat and pulled him onto her lap, stroking him absently. "I'm sorry," she said. "I didn't realize it was that bad. There must be some way to—"

"Help?" He was still preoccupied with the street scene, though it clearly pained him to watch the furtive goings-on. "These kids groove to guns, drugs, and Phantasmagoria. How'm I supposed to compete with that? And even if I could come up with the money to fund a program for them, do you think they'd care? They'd laugh their asses off."

"Phantasmagoria?"

"A video game of death and destruction." He managed a gallows smile. "I'm pretty good at it."

His preoccupation had given her a chance to observe him, and she took full advantage of it until he suddenly turned the tables on her. He glanced around and gave her a look as unflinchingly probing as that of any man she'd ever dealt with. He searched her up and down, considering every aspect of her, the burned sugar-hair, the pearl-blue eyes, the breasts that jiggled beneath the tantalizingly tight T-shirt when she moved. He saw everything that she was on the surface. But perhaps he probed her soul as well as her body.

A shaky sensation formed in the pit of her stomach. She could feel herself holding the cat tighter, wanting to rock it in her arms like a baby. She could feel her heart working.

"How well do you know Mary Frances?" he asked.

"What?"

"Mary Frances is not a woman of the world," he said, summing things up quite nicely. "Just how good a friend are you?"

Not a friend at all, Blue thought, especially now. She couldn't admit that, however. Rick Caruso was clearly protective of Mary Frances, and she couldn't allow him to interfere with her plans. Envy welled, sharp little pangs of it. Would that some white knight like Rick Caruso galloped up on his charger to protect her. Men were never that way toward her. The only one who ever had been was her father. He'd doted on her when she was a kid, and then disappointed her unforgivably. She'd never allowed anyone that close since, but idiot that she was, she apparently still longed for sheltering arms, a sheltering heart.

"We've known each other since convent school." She

busied herself with the cat, who was nearly drunk with pleasure at all the attention he was getting.

"Funny she's never mentioned you."

"I was better friends with her sister, actually." She imagined he'd buy that, since it was the truth anyway. When Rick had stopped by Mary Frances's apartment that morning, Mary Frances had introduced him as an old friend of the Murphy family, someone she'd known since she was a kid, when he'd worked weekends as an auto detailer in her father's busy body shop.

The urgency of the situation hadn't permitted much more conversation than that. As it was, Blue had just barely stopped Mary Frances from telling Rick the news of Brianna's death. Blue had hurried to explain that Mary Frances's aunt Celeste was ill, and Mary Frances was needed at home. She'd known revealing Brianna's death would prompt all kinds of dangerous questions. She'd also had the presence of mind to tell him she would be staying in the apartment while Mary Frances was gone, and then, hoping to create a distraction, she'd brandished Mary Frances's pincushion and offered to repair his clothing. Now she understood why he'd made tracks.

"Of course, I was the slutty one," she added impishly, waiting for the inevitable questions. How ill was Celeste, how long would Mary Frances be gone? Had Brianna been notified? Any friend of the family would have ventured to ask the first two, and she was hoping he might even pick up on her last remark. *Slutty? A lovely young thing like you? Impossible.*

But he didn't. He just gazed at her with much deeper questions in his eyes until she felt as if she wanted to confess everything to him, as if she could find her way out of hell through this man. Could Rick Caruso save her? And what did she need to be saved from, anyway?

"Did you grow up in Sweetwater?" she asked. Anything to break his concentration. She was about to offer condolences in case he had when he shook his head.

"Sweetwater was the first town I hit on my way east, and the rest is history. I was just like those kids out there on the street. At seventeen I was already a punk, I'd already done jail time. I had to get out of town, only I didn't get very far. I needed money, and luckily, Ben Murphy needed a detailer. He was the one who counseled me to consider the seminary."

It was an opening, but the waitress plugged the hole. A friendly, bony, gum-chewing grandmotherly type, she plunked the plate of fish tacos down on the table and hoisted a coffeepot with a bright green collar. "More java?" she asked.

"Hit me." Blue pushed her cup forward, sighing as she watched the coffee level rise. "Hard." Any minute her nervous system would stop screaming. A little more caffeine, a little more sugar, and she'd be fine.

Rick didn't want any more java. He shook his head when the waitress attempted to fill his cup, but she grinned and topped it off anyway. *You couldn't possibly know what's good for you,* she seemed to be saying. *You're just a guy and a priest at that.*

"Hope your cat enjoys the tacos," she said with a sly nod.

Blue glanced at Father Rick Caruso. They both smiled, only Rick's smile was the saddest, most adorable thing Blue had ever seen. Blue's heart wrenched hard, and she knew something unequivocally. Cardinal Fang wasn't the only one in danger of falling in love.

•   •   •

You couldn't get to the twentieth floor of the ultra-swanky Pratt-Anderson Building on the regular elevator.

You had to be escorted up in a private lift by a special security escort who knew the numbered code to open the doors. The spa on that floor was said to cater to a very exclusive clientele that ranged from movie divas like Demi Moore and Sharon Stone to famous lady lawyers, business baronesses, and wives of foreign royalty, but the most fascinating rumors about the spa had to do with its unique services.

If the myth was true, exotic European and Oriental beauty rituals combined the secrets of the ages with the biochemistry of the next millennium. They offered herbal brews that melted off pounds and electro-acupuncture that made traditional cosmetic surgery obsolete. Even the usual spa fare, massages and wraps, were rumored to be vastly superior. Most startling were claims that a woman's youth and fertility could be sustained indefinitely with certain powerful potions the FDA had undoubtedly never heard of. And that her sexual appetites and stamina could be homeopathically enhanced.

There was even talk of controversial medical procedures—implants and electrodes capable of augmenting pleasure in various ways that included stimulating nerve pathways. But if the legalities of such procedures were somewhat cloudy, the power and political clout of the consumers who wanted them were not. Within the elite circle who knew of the spa's existence, it was widely believed that regulatory agencies looked the other way, that the powers who ran local law enforcement were prominent among the spa's paying customers, or had spouses who were, and that the security was airtight.

Mary Frances was not one of those elite few. She'd never heard of the spa before today. To her the Pratt-Anderson Building was a gleaming superstructure in the toniest area of Century City, where the most beautiful and powerful people in Los Angeles spent their days doing whatever beautiful, powerful people did. She knew nothing of the secrets of the wealthy and privileged.

All that was about to change.

Her security escort was a tall, lithe Asian man in a khaki jumpsuit, who never once looked at her as they wooshed upward in a great golden-mirrored box toward the spa. His gaze was cast down in a manner that made her think of a convent practice called custody of the eyes. Except with him the deference seemed sinister rather than humble, and she sensed intuitively that he missed nothing, including her nervousness.

She slipped her hands into the pockets of her jeans and her shoulders dropped with a taut inner sigh. If someone had asked her to describe a CIA operative, it would have been this guy. Dark, silent, lethal. One wrong move, and she would be immobilized. He wouldn't stop to ask questions. A hand would flash out, crush her windpipe as if it were made of toothpicks, and her neck would be broken.

Easy, Murphy, she thought. Too much reality TV. She'd often wondered if a steady diet of those "live" cop shows could induce paranoid fantasies. Somehow she'd gotten herself hooked on them after leaving the convent, but even so, she knew her premonition had nothing to do with television. Her intuition was so keenly honed from meditation and contemplation that she had learned to trust it implicitly. She would have to now. This felt dangerous. It felt as if she had never encountered anything this dangerous, possibly even in her imagination.

The elevator slowed and settled with a smoothness that made her look around to see if they'd actually stopped. Curiosity overrode her fear as he tapped out the combination of numbers that would open the doors. After getting the message from the service, she'd found the spa's address in a computerized black book that must have been either Blue's or Brianna's, and then she'd been faced with a difficult decision—whether or not to follow the orders she'd been given.

You are to report immediately to the spa to be "done," the E-mail had directed. *If you fuck this up, you're history.*

While she'd waited for Blue to return, she'd tried to remember what the other woman had said about the spa. It had only been mentioned in passing, but even that had been enough to suggest activities that had little to do with manicures and pedicures. The place catered to a society escort service, after all. There might even be organized-crime connections.

The elevator doors shuddered and swept open like the curtain of a great Broadway theater, revealing a panoramic landscape of jade-green marble, white Corinthian columns, and cool blue pools. Immediately in front of her was a cresent-shaped ante area, cordoned off by balustrades of alabaster and graceful Kentia palms. Beyond it, the place looked like a movie set, something out of *The Greek Tycoon,* that film based on the life of Onassis.

A disembodied male voice greeted her, deep and resonant. "Welcome to Fantasy Island," it rumbled. Low laughter rippled through the anteroom like a roll of thundering timpani.

Mary Frances wasn't ready to disembark. She tilted forward, glancing around until she saw the man who'd spoken. And what a man he was! Tall and muscular, black as ebony, he wore flowing robes as white as cirrus clouds. Long, gleaming, snakelike dreadlocks had been gathered into a ponytail that fell down his back, and a gold chain roped one of his ankles. It glittered wildly against the dark skin of his bare foot.

"Come in," he insisted. "I've been waiting for you."

Mary Frances had very little choice. The security escort had moved in behind her and there was nowhere else to go. Elevator doors whooshed shut behind her as soon as she stepped out onto the sea of green marble.

"I'm Africa," the black man crooned, his voice as deep and musical as a cello. "Your faithful cosmetician." He introduced himself with a slow, courteous nod, but his dark rich eyes flickered over her with all the intimacy of a lover's, taking in her hair and features, the freckles, the hints of cleavage. Everything.

"Let's see what we have," he said, approaching her. "Ah, yes, very nice, quite promising . . ."

Mary Frances couldn't imagine what she was supposed to do as he came to her and looked her over with a certain detached professionalism. He seemed to be enjoying himself immensely as he reached out a dark, elegant hand and toyed with her hair, lifting it from her face, tucking it behind her ears, and then stroking her skin with his fingertips. She felt like expensive goods being examined by a customs officer—gingerly, but always with the suspicion of soon-to-be-discovered fraud.

"The skin is good," he said softly, reverberantly. "Just the right quality of translucence. And now for the breasts? So important, you realize . . ."

She looked down in disbelief and realized the bodice of her sweater was already unbuttoned and he was helping himself to a searching look at her bare bosom.

"Mmm, yes, these will do nicely," he said, reaching to cup her. His touch was so light, so fleeting, Mary Frances wasn't sure if she'd imagined the whole thing. Surely he hadn't fondled her breasts in a hallway in front of the elevator? A wild shivering shock bloomed in the pit of her stomach, and her body seemed to be promising her that this was only the beginning. She was about to be immersed in the secret indulgences of the decadent rich, a woman with no more life experience than an adolescent girl. Possibly less! She wanted to speak but that didn't seem to be possible.

"We'll make you even more beautiful," he was saying. "Men will be aroused to physical pain at the mere sight of you, you know. They will harden uncontrollably and the weakest of them will even moisten their clothing, poor fools!"

He laughed again, uproariously, and the gauzy robe billowed behind him as he beckoned her to enter the spa. "Come in, come in! Come and discover your power, my fair Irish rose. You *are* Irish, aren't you? Be the woman you were meant to be. Born to the temptations of pleasure, just like the biblical Eve."

Mary Frances did as he asked, her limbs strangely fluid. She didn't seem to have any choice but to follow the irresistible music of her Pied Piper just as the children of Hamlin had followed theirs. The chords of his mellifluous invitation reverberated inside her and her heartbeat clashed softly, reminiscent of a distant cymbal. Her body was already beginning to deliver on its promise.

7

Africa was as good as his promises, too. Mary Frances was subjected to nearly every exotic ritual and cosmetic ablution known to womankind, with the notable exception of a pelvic exam. She wasn't sure how the spa personnel had missed that nook and cranny. They hadn't missed any others. Even the insides of her nostrils had been cleansed and stimulated.

The spa itself was the modern version of a Grecian palace, classically simple yet grand in scale, with open and airy colonnandes, all beautifully spare of decor other than sleek marble benches and Hellenistic friezes. Africa took her first to the Korean baths, and left her in a huge tiled room of hissing pools with a group of women who spoke no English except to issue the simplest requests. "Arm, leg, sit, stand."

Mary Frances hid her surprise when the women surrounded and began to undress her. She had prepared herself for the prospect of nudity, but not to be gang-stripped. At least it was women, she told herself—as myriad hands and fingers probed and poked and unbuttoned—and not Africa himself, which would have been a true test of her spiritual mettle.

Once she was totally naked, except for her St. Rita's medal, which she now refused to remove, she was immersed in a warm pool to soak and given an amber concoction to drink that tasted like a honeyed infusion of oranges, rose-hips tea, and ambrosia. She thought the woman had called it Angel Water.

A short time later she was bodily lifted from the bath, stretched out on a marble slab, and sloshed with a bucket of warm water before being scrubbed down with loofahs and scented liquid soap. What followed was a Yoni massage, an herbal shampoo, and a facial mask of pulpy cucumbers before she was finally robed in plush white terry and fetched by Africa.

"Take these," he said, handing her a small packet of pills as he arranged her in a reclining apparatus that reminded her of a futuristic dental chair. It had a surprising number of moving parts, including adjustable rests for the arms and legs. The private lounge he'd brought her to had walls that were softly illuminated with recessed panels and a ceiling that was lined with black mirrored tiles. The sounds of splashing water and tinkling wind chimes made her wonder if there was a fountain nearby.

She took the crystal goblet of Angel Water he offered, but continued to scrutinize the pills. "What are they?"

"Nature's finest," he assured her. "Supplements for the skin and the hair, the internal organs, even the senses. You will glow like a firefly when I'm done with you. Everyone will want you. Even women, even children."

"Children?" Mary Frances hoped he didn't mean—

He smiled and touched her hand. "Take the pills."

The constriction in her throat made it difficult to swal-

low at first. It also told her she hadn't wholly surrendered
herself to this bizarre and fantastical situation. Some protective mechanism must have distanced her from the apprehension she would normally have felt at being so
vulnerable. She'd assumed she was calmly going along
with everything because she had no other choice, simply
a matter of faith and acceptance, not unlike her religious
training. But underlying the calm, her muscles still
wanted to cling to something, despite the hot soaks and
massages.

Once she had all the pills down, she lay back and tried
to settle herself as he moved over her. The leather chair
was heavenly soft, and fully reclined, it was like being
held in the palm of a huge, warm hand. But still she found
it difficult to relax, especially as he began to slowly and
gently lay open her robe, starting at her ankles and working from the bottom up.

"Now we free the sensual creature within you," he
crooned. "The nymph trapped in this warm, erotic co-
coon. . . ."

His voice stroked her caressingly as he moved gently
up her legs and stopped discreetly at her thighs, not
touching the sash that was tied at her waist and leaving
the rest of her body covered. His enormous hands and
long fingers were as dark and lush as panne velvet against
the milk-white terry cloth and the pink of her skin, and
the scent that emanated from him was pungently laced
with ginger, one of the spices she loved.

Maybe he wasn't attracted to women? she thought,
wondering if that was supposed to relieve or disappoint
her. From the painstaking care he took, she had a sinking
feeling he loved everything about women and prided
himself on making their senses swirl. The entire situation
had stimulated her imagination to the point that she

couldn't suppress a rising curiosity about whether any of
what he did was arousing to him.

It was impossible to tell with the flowing robes he
wore, which might be the reason he wore them. She
hadn't had any personal experience with aroused men,
but she wasn't totally naive, despite her convent background. She'd seen them naked in the hospital where
she'd trained.

She knew what an adult male penis looked like and, in
theory, what it did.

He parted her legs next, with the help of the chair.

What was he doing? Mary Frances fought the urge to
jackknife up as she felt the leg rests opening and her
lower body being even more intimately exposed. What in
the world? She glanced down to see him position himself
on a stool at her feet and realized with some horror that
he must be able to see parts of her that no man had ever
seen before.

The wind chimes soared and tinkled. Water thundered
and crashed, and through the bewildering cacophony,
Africa gazed back at her from between the narrow V of
her legs, his smile revealing a glimpse of brilliant white
teeth, the glow of onyx eyes, and perhaps the reassurance
that he did this every day, to women who were as nonchalant about the procedure as he was.

"Relax," he said, his voice erupting in a low musical
rumble. "Haven't you ever had anyone make love to your
feet?"

She fought for breath as he took one of her feet into the
lush velvet cradle of his large, masterful hands. She
strongly sensed that about him now, that he was a gentle
man, but supremely domineering, and that his total control of the situation and his knowledge of secrets ancient
and arcane would be frighteningly seductive. As power-

ful as her resistance was to these things, she could feel the edges of her will melting away already. And what good would resistance have done her anyway? The kind she had in mind would give her away as a novice—at life, at everything.

"Are you comfortable?" he asked.

She took a moment. "I am."

"Good," he said, massaging the sole of her foot with his thumbs. The strokes were slow and easy, yet with deepening pressure. They were wonderful, like the long, rhythmic pull of oars dipping deep in the water, propelling a boat.

Tension trickled away. . . .

She could feel herself sighing. Her body was sighing. Her will was sighing. *Let go . . . give in . . . stop struggling.*

"You will feel this everywhere," he told her, lulling her senses with the sensual tug of his voice. "There are seven thousand nerve endings in the soles of your feet alone, and by manipulating them gently, I can touch you everywhere, intimately, inside and out. Each zone is rich in nerves and longing to be stimulated. . . ."

His chuckle sounded soft and wicked, as if he were thoroughly delighted with the power at his fingertips. "By the time we're done, you'll be quite incoherent with pleasure, I suspect. Mmm, yes. For the most part, there will be only the sensation of profound relaxation and release. Any trace of pain or pressure indicates blockage and tells us where we need to concentrate. But even that will feel sublime . . . trust me."

Lowering his voice to a murmur, he began to work in earnest. His thumb walked the lower arch of her sole, flooding her belly with sensations too delicious to describe. It purled the delicate curve of her upper arch and made sensual spirals across her metatarsal. Like a silken inchworm, it tickled and tantalized, creeping over every crease and crevice.

Glorious. It was glorious. She was going to faint, it was so glorious. The urge to protest, to fight this incredibly pleasurable subjugation, rose and fell within Mary Frances. At St. Gertrude's they hadn't been allowed to show even the backs of their knees or their underarms. Her whole life had been an apprenticeship in the denial of the physical. But it had also been a primer in acceptance. In the convent she had rigorously disciplined herself to submit in ways she would not have thought possible, even to things that went against the grain. Incomprehensible as it seemed now, she knew if she could call on the years of mental and spiritual training, it would allow her to get through this . . . ordeal.

"The adrenal reflex," he said, applying light pressure at the base of her toes before his fingertips slid into the tender spaces between them. "Do you feel it?"

"Yes—" A little groan filled her throat.

"Was that pleasure or pain?"

"I don't know."

"Ah . . . good, both." He laughed softly and brushed his lips over her arch, then rose and came to her side. "You're very responsive, much more so than most of the escorts. They tend to tune out after a while. They come to think of it as a business, which of course, it is not. It's an art form. Giving pleasure is an art form. Don't ever forget that."

She stared up at him, quite sure she never would, even if she wanted to.

"You can turn over now," he told her.

The knowing smile on his face confused her.

"Did you think we were done?" he asked. "Just because you're humming in certain places? We must tend to those places that are still silent. Before we're through, you'll be one sweet, soaring chorus, a choir of angels."

Mary Frances wondered at his choice of metaphors, but there wasn't time to question it. He untied her sash and opened her robe, lifting her out of it. With a flick of his strong arms and hands, he rolled her onto her stomach, handling her so effortlessly that she didn't immediately realize what else he'd done. Her robe had not made the trip with her. He had swept it off and she was totally naked.

Her sense of shock was real, but it felt more like a quiver of excitement than fear. She was so limp with sensation, her body seemed totally attuned to his ministrations now. Was it the baths, the Angel Water they'd been plying her with, the pills, the massage, or some combination of all of it? She'd been touched all too rarely in the last several years, and never intimately. Apparently she was going to make up for all that in one evening.

"Now we are going for the chorus," he said softly. "A massage the Japanese call Rainstorm. I'm going to apply a whisk of thin bamboo reeds to your back. Very invigorating, I promise. And though it might nip a little at first, your nerves will habituate almost instantly, and the pleasure will be intense. Close your eyes now."

She did, aware of how exposed she was. It surprised her how little concern she had for the fact that he'd hinted there would be pain. She'd developed a certain tolerance for physical hardship in the convent, but she'd never been vulnerable in this way. The wooziness she felt made her wonder if one of the pills she'd been given might have been a sedative. Perhaps that was why she couldn't seem to work up any concern for what was about to happen. She couldn't even seem to hold a thought.

"Inhale," he said. "And then exhale slowly . . . empty your lungs."

When the last drop of air left her lungs, he began to switch her lightly with the reeds. The crackle they made registered before the needling impact did, but when the feathery, paper-thin sticks struck her bare skin, she squealed in surprise.

"Ayyy!" she gasped. It felt like a hundred tiny little switches coming down on her shoulders all at once. It wasn't painful, exactly, but it was close enough to get her attention.

He worked his way down her back, stimulating every inch of her skin, gently whipping the sensitive flesh of her buttocks, the back of her thighs, and the crook of her knees. The sharpness of it passed almost immediately, leaving only the sense of being wonderfully pricked and tickled by a hail of tiny, feathery switches. It was sublimely sensual. Every nerve ending sang out in response, and as he reached the soles of her feet, the pleasure became almost intolerable. It was like being held down and having your feet tickled, and nothing made her more wild than that.

By the time he was done with the reeds, she was vibrating from head to toe and unable to do anything but breathe out a moan. His low laughter soothed her, blending with the water and the wind chimes to create the choir he spoke of. But the intensity of her reaction made her remember how it felt to give herself over to something entirely, how she'd immersed herself in the spiritual and believed that was all she could and should want, until something passionate and not at all religious ignited inside her, a fire she could in no way control. Now she was being immersed in the physical. Entirely immersed. Her body loved the sensations, the stronger the better. It craved them in a way she couldn't explain.

"You aren't done?" she asked as the whipping ceased. She was aware of the plea in her voice. Maybe he would think she wanted him to stop, but just the opposite was true.

"Don't open your eyes yet," he cautioned. "I'm going to bring you back around and finish the treatment."

She felt herself being lifted and rolled to her back, but she couldn't muster the energy to participate. She was far too limp and sated. Once she was settled, she felt a cool compress being applied to her eyes, and then one of her arms was lifted into his grasp. Using both hands, he began to massage something that felt like cream into her skin. She felt the heat of it immediately.

"Mmm," she breathed.

"Feel good?"

Staring into the darkness of her closed lids, she realized she was smiling, that she couldn't stop smiling. The warmth of whatever he was using felt as if it could penetrate clear to her bones, but there was another sensation as well. It was getting hot. It was beginning to burn.

"Too hot," she mumbled, barely finding the energy to speak. "It stings . . . why does it sting?"

His voice seemed to come from far away, the thunder of a river that ran through a distant canyon. "Oh, that's just the poison, darling," he said. "Your skin is absorbing it. Once it's in your system, you'll won't feel a thing."

"Poison?"

"Yes, didn't I tell you? It's going to make your skin very pale and beautiful. There won't be any more freckles or flaws. You'll be perfect."

"No, I like—" She wanted to tell him she liked her freckles, although that wasn't true. She'd always wanted to be rid of them, especially the ones on her breasts and the bridge of her nose. But he was still talking, and she didn't seem to know how to form the words she needed— or any words, for that matter.

He spoke again, but his voice sounded as if it were coming from another plane. "You remember how women used to ingest arsenic to give them a pale, fragile look?" he asked. "That's what I'm doing to you. Only my poison is topical. That way there's less damage to the liver."

She tried to protest. She felt herself rising up, yet nothing happened.

He relinquished her arm and began to work on her shoulders, where the freckles were massed like daisies. With every deepening circular stroke, the heels of his hands dropped lower until they were pressing intimately into the swells of each breast.

She shook her head, trying to tell him to stop. The burning was severe now. It was making her queasy. Though her eyes were closed, an image flashed through her head of a woman lying naked on the chair, her body reflected by the black mirrors in the ceiling, and a large, grinning man hovering over her. The woman was trying to get up, but something was restraining her. The arm and leg rests had closed around her limbs.

No! No, please! She could hear herself shrieking the words, but the sound wasn't tearing from her throat. It was ricocheting around inside her head. She couldn't make her mouth work. She couldn't speak or open her eyes or even blink or swallow her own spit. She was slowly becoming paralyzed, losing consciousness. Poison. He'd poisoned her. She was going to die . . . and she had never lived.

8

His fellow clerics would have armed themselves with faith. Rick Caruso carried a gun. He'd had the Smith & Wesson .38 Special since the bloodstained days of his youthful excesses in an inner-city gang. The weapon had saved his life more than once, a mixed blessing that had made him feel invincible, godlike. It had made him reckless, too, and others had paid the price for his fancied omnipotence. He'd taken lives, innocent lives. Far more than protection now, the gun was a reminder, a symbol of tragedy. It was the reason Rick Caruso was a priest. The reason he couldn't be anything *but* a priest.

Nevertheless, he was glad to have the revolver tonight. The streetlights had been shot out from Laredo to Carson, probably in preparation for a gang war. The neighborhood appeared deserted, another bad sign, and the silence was charged with negative ions. There was a storm coming. The heavens were about to crack open and disgorge their fury, and Rick Caruso was walking into the vomit.

He glanced upward, curious about the possibility of divine intervention, and realized he'd pressed his hand to his chest at the same time, assuring himself that the gun was there, where he always carried it in a holsterlike pocket in the lining of his slicker. Another crisis of faith, he thought. How many did this make in the ten years since he'd left the seminary?

Too many. And now there was her.

He'd walked Blue Brandenburg and her adopted stray safely home from the restaurant, prince of a guy that he was. But when he'd left her at the door of Mary Frances's apartment, she'd invited him in. "I can offer you cocoa," she'd said ruefully. "I haven't figured out where Mary Frances hides the booze."

He'd never wanted a cup of cocoa so badly in his life, and he hated the stuff. He'd taken a rain check, congratulating himself on the smartest move of his life. His only goal from that point on should have been to get himself back to Our Lady in one piece, but his thoughts kept veering back to her.

She was trouble. A blindfolded tightrope walker in the center ring of the circus could have spotted that. She was holding something back about the situation with Mary Frances. Maybe about herself as well. She looked over her shoulder too often for him not to think that she was running from something. Everything considered, there was nothing about her sudden appearance in their lives that should have reassured him, including this, the fact that he couldn't get her out of his head—

"Hey, gringo!"

The shout did what Rick couldn't. It got rid of Blue Brandenburg. A small pack of homeboys were ambling toward him from the opposite direction. He could just make out their smirking grins in the falling light. A half dozen of them, undoubtedly armed to the teeth and looking to play some real-life Phantasmagoria . . . the same way he had been nearly twenty years ago.

"Wachew want?" one of them demanded. "This is El Diablos' turf. You got a beef with the Diablos?"

The kid who spoke couldn't have been much more than fourteen, although some of the others looked older. He wore baggy khakis, a huge denim shirt jacket, and his head was shaved to the scalp, except for a wide strip that ran from his forehead to a skinny ponytail in the back. His crazy, glittery smile was almost as disturbing as the way his hand had snaked inside his jacket at the belt line. He was packing deadly force. It was only a question of how deadly.

"No beef," Rick assured him in level tones, "not with the Diablos."

"Smack, then?" Laughter erupted, veritable howls of it as the ringleader yanked a cellophane bag of what looked like bath powder out of the myriad folds of his voluminous costume. "You want to get *smacked*?"

Heroin. They thought he was out to score drugs. Rick returned their sneers with an unflinching stare. His gaze locked with the ringleader's, and he did something that made their smiles vanish. He slowly slid his hand inside the front opening of his coat, knowing full well what would happen as he reached into the inner pocket. Before his fingers could find what they sought, he had six gun barrels flashing in his face. His question of how much deadly force had been answered. A half-dozen hammers cocked with a thunderous roar. As many bullets were chambered.

"Wachew lookin' for, gringo?" someone snarled. "Your *cojones*?"

"Blow 'em off!" another shrieked. "Kill the fucker!"

A furor ensued. Angry howls and hisses. Rick was an interloper, an *intruso*, and the Diablos were enraged by his lack of fear, not to mention his lack of respect for their power.

Rick could feel the heavy slam of his heart beneath his hand. He should have been dead, six times over. Six feet under. Dead. And maybe he would be. Maybe this was how it was supposed to end. Or maybe this was a test. Was God still up there in His heaven? Father Caruso hadn't felt His presence in some time now.

"Drop it, gringo! *Drop the fucking gun!*"

The snarled threat exploded in his head. Imminent death by a hail of gunfire should have been more than enough incentive to back off, but Rick wasn't subject to the forces that had shaped other men. He didn't always understand what motivated him, but in this case, he knew that his thundering heart had gone silent, that his spine had locked in a frozen arc, and that his hand, as he reached into his coat, never faltered.

He had a mission, but it wasn't the Diablos' rage that spurred him on. It was their shock as he found what he was looking for and drew it out of his coat, that brought him the truest satisfaction. They couldn't believe their eyes.

A black clerical collar. He produced it with the quiet flair of a magician and popped it around his neck, tucking it into his work shirt.

They gaped at him, their surprise as silent as his heart.

"Fuck, he's a priest?" someone whispered.

If I weren't, you'd be dead by now. The thought flared into Rick's head, but he said nothing. Instead, he indicated the bag of heroin with a tip of his head. "No thanks." With a polite nod, he stepped back and turned to cross the street.

"Esta pinche guey, esta loco!" he heard someone mutter as he walked away. "Dude's fucking crazy!"

Rick contemplated that possibility as he walked the remaining blocks to his church. Yeah, he was crazy. Maybe even fucking crazy, but not for the reasons the kid thought. He was crazy because he kept beating his head against the wall of impossible odds, trying to help kids who didn't want it and to crack the very system that had relegated him to this no-man's-land.

The local diocese had spotted him as a maverick in seminary school, and the power playing had been going on ever since. Even some men of God weren't above jerking each other's chains. He'd originally shared duties with another parish priest, a gentle older man, but Father Patrick had fallen ill over a year ago, and no one had been assigned to replace him, leaving Rick to carry the entire load himself. Beyond that, his efforts to set up an outreach program and secure support for the barrio kids' special educational needs had been discouraged as impractical, despite the fact that his parishioners were desperately poor.

The kids he dealt with played video games with a passion, and Rick was sure he could transfer that passion to computers and the sprawling vastness of cyberspace with its riches of information, if he could only get the funding for classrooms and equipment. The gangbangers were virtually unemployable because of their problems with school and the law, which was why they resorted to more crime, a vicious cycle. Internet expertise was the hot ticket in marketable job skills, and he could give them that. He could give them futures. All he needed was money.

What he got were exhortations to be patient and pray.

Shit, he *was* praying, and with every Amen he uttered,

there was another dead body on the street. He'd even considered appealing to less-than-holy sources in order to get what he needed. He had access to that kind of money, large amounts of it, but for now had decided against it. He'd done enough bargaining with his own conscience to last him a lifetime.

The taste of salt on his lips made him realize he was perspiring. The spring night was too warm for an overcoat. As he pulled his off and draped it over his arm, he caught the wafting odors of frying meat and onions. It was coming from the diner the next block over, the tiny place where he and Blue had had their coffee.

The pungently rich and greasy smells made his mouth water. At least this was an appetite he could indulge, he told himself. Better a hamburger and fries than her.

Blue Brandenburg was some kind of harbinger, he decided as he walked into the diner a moment later and glanced at the booth where they'd been sitting. The place was crowded with dinner customers now, and a young couple sat there, studying the menu, while their two toddlers played in the water glasses and spritzed everyone within firing distance with their chubby fingers.

Rick headed for the counter, nodding at those who murmured, "Good evening, Father."

He'd thought of Blue as trouble, but she was more than that. She was that bit of chaos that lingered inside every soul, waiting for expression. It stirred irresistibly, as he well knew, especially when times got tedious. It caught your attention and made you want to drop whatever you were doing and look for the hurricane's eye, bring order out of chaos as the reference went. But if you made the mistake of staring at it too closely in the hopes of finding symmetry there, you could get sucked right into the vortex.

• • •

"Welcome back, Irish."

The rich voice was familiar. She recognized the bass tones and the seductive vibrato, but there were too many other sensations competing for her attention. Chimes and chirruping birds and gurgling fountains. Her head soared with celestial chords, but underneath the music there was a nagging drumbeat, a rhythm whose pulse couldn't be ignored.

Pain. She was in pain. A hot, spiky sensation radiated from inside her leg, down low . . . her ankle. It felt as if pins were pricking her. Stinging her. Bees, a swarm of angry bees. She had to get up, but she couldn't even seem to open her eyes.

A moan filled her throat, burning because she couldn't express it.

"Easy, Irish," the voice soothed.

Her eyes fluttered open to a bewildering sea of nymphs and satyrs floating above her, naked and cavorting. Shock rippled through her as she tried to make sense of what she was seeing. Unless she was hallucinating, the images were fornicating in ways probably not even depicted in the *Kama-sutra.*

"Where am I?" she murmured, struggling to bring her surroundings into focus as a dark form blocked her field of vision.

"It's time to go, Irish."

Who was Irish and why was he calling her that? She couldn't quite make out the details of his face, but his name crept into her consciousness as his towering presence nudged her back toward reality. He was named for a continent, the dark continent. Africa. It all came sifting back then . . . the spa, the baths, the *poison cream.* It hadn't killed her, she realized, still strangely detached from her surroundings. She was alive, minus some freckles perhaps, but alive and breathing.

"My ankle," she said, trying to decide what kind of effort would be involved in sitting up. The pain forking up the inside of her left leg sharpened with her effort to sit. It felt as if she'd stepped in a bed of nettles. "It hurts."

"Of course it does." Africa's calm certainty bubbled with mirth. "You've been stewed, blued, and tattoed, child."

Mary Frances had no idea what he meant until he helped her sit up and pointed out the cluster of cherries that looked as if they'd been painted on the inside of her ankle. They looked as red and plump with juice as fruit that had ripened on a tree.

"What's that for?" Her faint voice was the only thing that acknowledged the dread forming in the pit of her stomach. *Was* that a tattoo? She wasn't sure she wanted to know.

"It's your ticket to ride," he explained. "All Cherries' escorts carry such a mark. Without it you wouldn't be allowed into the Calderon affair or any other Cherries-related function. It's your identification."

Ticket to ride? She ran her fingers over the still-inflamed area, aware of the heat. "A tattoo?"

"The process is similar, but much more sophisticated. We do it with lasers."

Dear Lord above! She was about to ask if it was permanent when she realized there was someone else in the room. A uniformed man stood behind Africa, his head erect, his eyes focused somewhere other than his immediate surroundings. She recognized it as a military stance.

"Your driver," Africa explained, sweeping his hand toward the man, who acknowledged the comment with a barely perceptible nod.

They weren't in the massage room anymore, Mary

Frances realized. This was a grotto, with a waterfall the length of one wall. Ferns branched from craggy, black volcanic rocks and a gentle mist lifted off the shallow pool, where bright red fish swam lazily. She was lying on a bed, she realized, not one of those strange dental-chair contraptions.

A bamboo credenza was set with wines in crystal decanters, crackers and cheeses, pâtés, mousses, and fresh fruits. A midnight snack? she wondered as Africa plucked a piece of fruit from the centerpiece bowl.

"It's show time," the cosmetician went on, his voice musical with laughter. Sparkling white teeth flashed as he crunched into a shiny red apple and munched the mouthful with great gusto. "We've done our best, and now it's up to you. Here," he said, setting down the apple to come over and clasp her hand, "have a look at yourself. Not bad, *n'est-ce pas?*"

Mary Frances grasped his hand as she felt the chair moving beneath her. It rocked gently and tilted forward until her feet touched the pedestal the chair was mounted on. Africa's powerful grip urged her to a standing position, and the next thing she knew, she was gazing into a mirrored surface and the woman gazing back at her was one of the loveliest creatures she'd ever seen.

Hair tumbled around her face like black satin ruffles on a petticoat. The dress she was wearing was a long gossamer concoction of wine-colored voile and visible through the sheer material was a lace body stocking of the same color. The effect was both sexy and demure, and the rich, warm color made her eyes look as verdantly green as the ferns.

She touched her St. Rita's medal, gathering it up, and felt the warmth of her breasts nestling against her knuckles. She might have brought the medal to her lips, except for the irresistible softness of her own flesh. The dress's bodice was discreetly unbuttoned to reveal the plunging neckline of the body stocking and a décolletage that was sprinkled with gold.

"Freckles?" she whispered.

He seemed to enjoy her startlement. "We didn't get rid of your freckles, Irish. We just turned them to stars. Now you have a rainbow of stardust riding the bridge of your nose and the crest of your breasts."

"They look like gold motes," she said.

"Ravishing, yes."

It was a statement, not a question, and she could hardly dispute it as she gazed upon herself once more. It had never dawned on her that she could be so beautiful. Postulants were not encouraged to dwell on their looks, quite the opposite. To do so was to invite the sin of pride. Besides, Brianna had been the beauty in the family, not her. What kind of magic had they worked on her? She couldn't help but wonder if this was what Webb Calderon had requested she look like. Or if she would even be with Webb Calderon. The assignment was a glamorous party. Other escorts would be there too, undoubtedly.

Unsettling thoughts flashed through her mind, visions of slave auctions and being sold for the night to the highest bidder. Save the dramatics, she told herself. Cherries was an escort service. She'd already been bought and sold. Calderon had made that clear.

The driver stepped forward, startling her. He hadn't moved in so long she'd begun to think of him as inanimate.

"Couldn't I drive myself?" she asked Africa in wheedling tones. "Just give me directions. I'm good with directions. I got here—"

The cosmetician shook his head. "Oh my, no, you're still much too woozy to drive. Your car's in the building's garage, and the security here is marvelous, best in the city. It'll be safer than in your carport at home."

Again, she touched the delicate gold chain roping her neck and ran the medal between her fingers. Was that a good guess, or did he know she had a carport?

"You're a very lucky girl."

Whatever Africa meant, the insinuation in his tone alone made her nervous. The driver had resumed his zombie-like state, but Africa now sported a grin that would have made a Cheshire cat look somber. His abundant good humor was beginning to get on her nerves. "Lucky? Why, pray tell?"

He retrieved the apple and took another bite that sounded so crunchy and luscious it made her mouth water. "Would you like one?" he asked, indicating the fruit bowl.

For some reason, she shook her head no, although she would have loved a piece of fruit, anything. Her mouth was dry and cottony, probably from whatever they'd given her to put her to sleep. It was interesting that she so often said no when she meant yes, especially if pleasure was in some way involved. She had so little capacity within her to enjoy pleasure, even the simple pleasures like fruit. Enjoyment of anything beyond the spiritual had always seemed wrong somehow. Was that in the Bible? Her catechism? She didn't think so, perhaps it was just in her head, or something her father had conveyed with his prudish leanings.

"Are you familiar with the legend of Bluebeard?" Africa asked.

Mary Frances had some recollection of it as a rather grisly story as fairy tales went, but she couldn't remember the specifics. "Didn't he have several wives that died mysteriously?"

"Yes, but there was nothing very mysterious about it. He killed them. Not totally out of malice, of course; he had little choice. He was quite a guy, highly sexed as a bull, and aces in the sack, so they say. A virtuoso. He kept his wives locked in their bedrooms, awaiting his amorous visitations, and apparently he was so gifted they were happy to be his captives. He also had only one rule. He gave each of them a ring with a key to every room in the house. But there was one room they were forbidden to enter. The key to that room was solid gold, but they were instructed *never* to use it."

Mary Frances shuddered, remembering. "The room where he kept his dead wives? Weren't they hanging from the ceiling on hooks?"

Africa nodded, oddly jubilant, given the subject matter. "Yes, but each one of his wives in turn disobeyed him and visited the room, and as soon as they saw what he'd done to the others, he had to kill them, too, of course."

"What does that have to do with my being lucky?"

He laughed uproariously. "I assumed you knew. Rumor has it that Webb Calderon is a Bluebeard for the modern age."

"What do you mean? He has several dead wives hanging in a room somewhere?" She was being sarcastic now, which wasn't like her, but she could hardly bear his tone.

"Not wives, per se," he explained with seemingly inexhaustible good nature, "but he does have a room in the cellar of his hacienda that's said to be outfitted with an authentic *camera de tortura*, and whenever a Cherries' escort turns up missing, the rumor is that he's got her locked up there."

"Dead?"

He winked lasciviously. "Well, we don't know that, do we? I maintain that he simply detains them for his own amusement, and that he, like Bluebeard, is so gifted, he drives them mad with pleasure and they kill themselves." He walked over to her and smoothed an errant lock of her hair. "Delicious, isn't it?" he crooned. "You're going to have so much fun."

Fun? "How many escorts are missing?"

"Oh, several, I'd say."

Several escorts had disappeared? Blue hadn't mentioned that. Or was Africa simply tormenting her again? If he wasn't, she couldn't help but wonder if they'd all gone the way of Brianna. Were they all dead?

"Did I mention the riddle?" He blurted the question so suddenly Mary Frances couldn't tell if his concern was sincere.

"What riddle?" she asked.

He whirled away from her and turned back, robes flying. "How could I have forgotten that? The riddle holds the key to the mystery of women's power over men. If any one of Bluebeard's wives had known the answer, well, who knows . . . it might have saved her."

His hesitation seemed strategic, as if he were making sure he had Mary Frances's undivided attention. "Listen carefully now, Irish. And answer carefully. What is the *strongest* of all things?"

"Love, I suppose. No, that's too simple. Faith?" she said swiftly, quite sure of herself.

"Ahhh." His sigh was crestfallen, his expression sad. "You made the same mistake Bluebeard's wives did, child. You overlooked the obvious."

"The answer's not faith? Are you sure? What is it, then? Diamonds? Aren't diamonds supposed to be the hardest surface in nature?"

Africa began to shake uncontrollably. Mary Frances thought it was pain at first, then realized it was laughter rocking him. She wasn't amused. Neither was her driver.

"Well?" she demanded.

"Faith *does* move mountains and diamonds *are* the hardest substance of all, but neither is the right answer." Still laughing, he walked to the door and opened it, signaling her to go through. Apparently he'd said all he was going to.

As the driver glanced at Mary Frances, his cold eyes running over her like an icy bath, she had to fight the urge to cross herself. Who were these people? And what kind of monster was she being delivered to?

"Mr. Calderon would like you to think of his house as your house." The petite blond housekeeper bestowed a practiced smile on Mary Frances, then busied herself unzipping the luxury luggage Mary Frances had brought with her, a garment bag full of clothing and a weekender packed with makeup and other essentials, all provided by Africa.

The woman was undeniably efficient, but she apparently couldn't hear. When she'd arrived at the hacienda, Mary Frances had been relieved to find that a perfectly normal-looking person worked for Calderon as his housekeeper, and then, when that normal-looking person, who'd introduced herself as Traci, had told her that Calderon wouldn't be back until the next morning, she was even more relieved.

She'd been given a brief tour of the breathtakingly beautiful Spanish mansion and brought to her room, at which point it had all gone downhill. Not that the room wasn't beautiful. It was a suite, actually, on the second floor, overlooking an enormous sun-struck edge pool.

The glittering water seemed to empty into the vast blue Pacific below, a sheer, straight drop from the cliffs that looked to be one hundred feet at least.

Africa had not exaggerated. The two-story adobe hacienda was magnificent. Moodily elegant, its mazelike interior surprised the eye with richly appointed salons and secret alcoves, and just when you thought you were lost, the darkness was relieved by a sunny tiled courtyard, abloom with dogwood trees. Even some of the smaller cathedrals Mary Frances had visited in Europe prior to entering the convent hadn't achieved the brooding ambience or soaring dimensions.

But Traci had blithely ignored Mary Frances's polite request for time alone to freshen up, and what concerned Mary Frances most at the moment was the housekeeper's enthusiasm over her luggage. Mary Frances had had no chance to go through it herself, so she had no idea what the woman might find in there. Scanty lingerie? Sex toys?

"The house is yours," Traci repeated, briskly whipping one lovely outfit after another from the garment bag and bustling to hang them in the spacious walk-in closet. "Please do make yourself comfortable, or Mr. Calderon will be offended."

Another practiced smile. "However," she said, "there are a couple areas that your host wishes to be left undisturbed. His office and workroom, for obvious reasons, and a small gallery of antiques on the lowest floor where he takes customers only by special appointment."

The gallery that Africa mentioned, Mary Frances realized, the *camera de tortura*. The housekeeper was gazing at Mary Frances searchingly, seeming to want some confirmation that she understood.

"Of course, I wouldn't dream of disturbing Mr.

Calderon's private gallery or his work space," Mary Frances assured her, secretly resolving that the office would be the first place she searched, the gallery the second, the very moment she had a safe opportunity.

Blue had told her the police had found nothing when they'd gone through Brianna's apartment. But Blue firmly believed that whoever killed Brianna had gotten there first and taken the jade pendant, and Blue's plan had been to search Calderon's house for it, which was why she'd finagled the party assignment.

Blue also believed Alejandro Cordes, the guest of honor, was involved in some way. Brianna had dated him, too, at one time, and apparently she'd told Blue the pendant was reputed to be part of a cache of looted national treasures the Cordes family had claimed as theirs, and that Alejandro had approached Webb about selling them on the international black market.

Now it was up to Mary Frances to find the pendant, and she could hardly believe her good luck at having the entire night to do it, although she would have to be cautious with Traci around. Given the way the woman was going through her things, it was clear she missed nothing.

"Thank you." Mary Frances braced her normally soft voice with a forceful tone and quite liked the sound of it. "I'll finish that."

She whisked a black satin jumpsuit from Traci's clutches and faced the woman squarely. If it was going to take a confrontation to get the housekeeper out of her room, so be it. She couldn't let Traci go through the Cherries satchel, which was what she seemed to be headed for now that she'd unpacked the weekender and garment bag.

It was an interesting way to check out visitors, Mary Frances realized as the housekeeper nodded curtly and excused herself. The moment she was alone, Mary Frances took the satchel from the armoire and slipped it under the bed. She would look for a better hiding place later. Right now she needed to figure out how to let Blue know what had happened. An ornate gold telephone sat on an antique writing desk, but she wasn't sure the phone was safe. She also had the computer and cell phone, but that only gave her the option of communicating with Cherries. Still, she had to check in. Blue's failure to do so had already made the service very unhappy.

"Okay, Wink," she said, referring to the nickname the Cherries' contact used, "you're on."

Moments later, sitting at the writing desk, she accessed the messages for Blue and found one requesting that she report in. She did so with a brief reply that let them know she was now at Calderon's, alone, and that he was expected in the next day.

The response was immediate.

GOOD, YOU'RE THERE. PLEASE REVIEW CHERRIES' SAFETY AND PROTOCOL PROCEDURES. I KNOW IT'S BORING, BUT WE HAVE TWENTY-FIVE YEARS OF STERLING SERVICE AND AN IN-TERNATIONAL REPUTATION TO MAINTAIN. YOU WOULDN'T WANT TO BE THE ONE TO TARNISH A PERFECT RECORD, WOULD YOU?

Mary Frances curbed the rebellious desire to type in *Hell, yes, I'd like nothing better.* Instead she typed *No* and the procedures began scrolling down the screen.

CHERRIES' ESCORTS ARE ALWAYS DEFERENTIAL, GRACIOUS, AND EVER MINDFUL OF CHERRIES' CREDO: PERFECT PLEA-SURE THROUGH PERFECT SERVICE. . . .

They were right, she thought as more instructions scrolled by. They were boring, not to mention utterly chauvinistic. She also realized with some irony that this was her second service-oriented organization, only in the convent she wasn't given an emergency E-mail address to use if things got dangerous.

Brianna would have picked the locks on Calderon's computer files faster than Houdini. But Mary Frances was not Brianna or Houdini. She let out a sigh of exasperation and dropped back in the leather executive chair, heedless of the deep groan of its springs.

It was the dead of night and she'd found Calderon's office easily enough. A quick search of the room had turned up nothing, but she'd noticed the computer as she'd been about to leave and wondered if it was the reason the housekeeper had warned her about this room. She'd decided to have a look, but her attempts to bring up any of Calderon's files had been blocked by her ignorance of the access codes. He had a gallery right here in the house, so there was a good chance they contained nothing more than customer account information, but she wanted to know that for sure.

Frustration burned so high and hot it brought a flashback of Sister Fulgentia's exhortations about patience. The mistress of postulants had believed patience to be the essence of perfection and the mother of all other virtues, and she'd said so at every opportunity. If she was right, Mary Frances was a hopelessly flawed orphan.

The utter futility of her efforts had reminded her of Brianna's skill with computers. Her sister had a love affair going with the school's one rickety microprocessor. It was the only thing she did love besides tormenting the boys with her beauty. Still, she'd been good. The only hacker in parochial school, she'd known all about locked files and access codes.

Mary Frances also recalled that Brianna had used the short form of a very dirty word to access her own private stuff. Brianna and Blue had mumbled the word under their breath during prayers just loudly enough that the other girls could hear and the sisters would think they were actually praying. It always brought down the house—and made Mary Frances nearly ill. Her sister had loved stirring the pot—she'd lived for it—so, of course, she'd picked the most offensive word she could think of, given the situation.

Now, staring at a blinking prompt, Mary Frances could identify with Brianna's urge to shake things up. Thoroughly frustrated, she wanted to type in the profanity just to see what the program's response would be. She'd been scrolling through a subdirectory and come across a file called "Diary" that had intrigued her, but when she'd tried to bring it up, the program had once again blocked her, mocking her ignorance in large caps.

ADMITTANCE DENIED! ACCESS CODE REQUIRED! REENTER CODE!

Oh, what the hell! She began to type, keying in the word on impulse. "Mu . . . fuh," she said under her breath, quelling nervous laughter. She pressed the enter key with a sharp jab and what happened next made her sit back in the seat and stare at the screen in wonder. The dated entries that materialized appeared to be from an actual diary. Whoever had written it had a sex life that put Anais Nin's fantasies to shame.

Mary Frances forgot to breathe as she read through the entries. In the most poetic of terms, the diarist described her dark and thrilling encounters with a client who was a "secret garden of sensual delights," a man who had lured her into an erotic Eden of carnal desires and introduced her to her own latent, yet rampant needs. *He's wholly ensnared me,* she wrote, *body, mind, and soul . . . and Lord, it is the sweetest kind of subjugation imaginable. I've become a wanton, hedonistic creature who can think of nothing but my own flesh and the pleasure he brings to it. I would do anything for him.*

Mary Frances read on avidly, unable to stop herself. She skimmed through weeks of entries until she came to one that made her gasp. Her fingers were unsteady on the keyboard. She read it several times before she could believe what she was seeing.

I asked him to call me by a special name tonight, the diarist wrote. *I must be insane! I am insane when I'm with him. I'm someone I don't even know, but I can't seem to help myself. I crave having the most decadent things done to me in the name of pleasure. God, the wickedness of being called a sacred family name while you're tied to a four-poster and being roughly pleasured with all manner of deliciously evil things . . . slender silken whips that sting like bees, yet drip with honey so sweet it makes your throat tighten with longing. . . .*

The last line read, *I asked him to call me Celeste.*

Mary Frances fell back in the chair. This was Brianna's diary, the one Blue had mentioned. It had to be. Mary Frances was stunned, though perhaps she shouldn't have been. Brianna was an escort, Calderon a client. Still, the inner trembling was violent now. She barely had the control to go on with what she was doing, yet she had to look at the remaining entries. Her breath sounded like low moans as she forced herself to depress the arrow key.

Each entry was more erotic than the next, until the last few, where there were vague references to things the man had done that had frightened Brianna and perhaps caused her pain, and then the entries abruptly ended.

Mary Frances felt weighed down with confusion and exhaustion. She was still grappling with the meaning of what she'd found when the soft creak of footsteps caught her attention. She froze, listening for a split second before she ducked under the desk and then remembered the blinking computer. It was on! She groped the wall, found the plug to something, and praying it was the computer, yanked it.

The creaking was coming from the floor above, she realized. She wasn't aware that Calderon had any household help other than Traci, which meant that it was either the housekeeper or Calderon himself had returned. Hidden in the gloom of his office, huddled beneath his desk, she tried to make sense of what she'd found. If Calderon was the one who'd had Brianna killed, he wouldn't want the police to find a diary on her computer that might implicate him, so he'd erased the incriminating parts and copied the rest, perhaps as a little memento of their time together.

Springing to crouch, Mary Frances realized that she had to get out of this room immediately, before she was discovered, because there was no way to explain her presence here. That was her first objective, and then, at the next opportunity, she had to find Webb Calderon's camera de tortura and search it thoroughly.

9

Mary Frances awoke at dawn with the crystalline awareness that she wasn't alone in the room. She'd slept badly. Her head was spinning with dreams of discovery, but this wasn't the stuff of dreams, unless they were nightmares. He could have been her virtual-reality experience all over again, only this man wasn't a shadow. He was standing on the balcony, his back to the radiant sunrise, watching her through open doors.

Her heart hushed, sensing an enemy. It was too late to pretend she was asleep. In the convent, she'd trained herself to sleep on her back on a wooden bench and to do without a pillow. It was one of her many attempts to "confine the body and free the spirit." She still slept that way, motionless, a deathlike rest, but he must have seen her open her eyes.

She'd already felt his darkness, and her body was responding as if to a threat. Her scalp had drawn painfully tight, and she knew she ought to be afraid, yet she wasn't, not the way another woman might be. Her nurse's training had prepared her to deal with crises, and she'd come to grips with her fears of death and destruction in the convent, partly through reading the horrendous ordeals of the religious martyrs.

What she didn't know, and could have had no way of knowing, was that death and destruction were as natural a state of being to Webb Calderon as breathing. He was raised on the casual brutality of terrorists. Death could be a gift, he had learned long ago. There were many things worse.

Mary Frances gathered the sheets around her and sat up. She wore one of the nightgowns that had been packed in the weekender, an Empire design with a deep neckline and yards of sheer white silk that draped to the floor when she stood. It was modest in comparison to the others, but the volume of material in no way made up for the fact that it was nearly transparent.

Custody of the eyes. She had not looked at him yet, not fully. To look at him was to engage him, and that could endanger her. He could reach her through her eyes, violate her spirit in incalculable ways. Animals knew that. Animals avoided the direct gaze, knowing it was deadly. Still, she would have to take the risk. It was the only gauge she had to confirm what she was sensing.

A darting glance. That's all it was intended to be, but there was no way to avoid *his* eyes as she looked up. They were even more forbidding than she remembered from the televised trial. Wintry and marbled with ice, they didn't look *at* you, they looked through you, and the sensation was one of raw, aching cold.

The phrase she'd used that night to describe him was inadequate, she realized. Cold, cruel beauty didn't begin to do him justice. The sensual width of his mouth was a fascinating contrast to the whiplash contours of his handsome face. He was tall enough to seem towering to a woman lying in bed, and yet at the same time he was as submerged and dangerous a presence as an iceberg. Approaching him would be a perilous thing, but how could you not be drawn to such incandescence? Even Brianna, who lived to torment men, had been helplessly ensnared by this one. Was he the one who seduced her sister with all manner of erotic delights?

She waited for him to speak, but he never did. Instead, he entered the room and walked to a huge carved Spanish cabinet that stood against the far wall. Housed inside the black-ash panels and doors was a large-screen television, a VCR, and a stereo CD player, all gleaming with chrome and electronic wizardry.

A remote control lay on one of the shelves. He picked it up and activated a videocassette in the VCR. A shadow person materialized on the screen, and once again Mary Frances was struck by a sense of virtual reality. She watched silently as the form hovered near the walls of a hallway, slinking more than walking.

There was a loud burst of static and the scene changed abruptly. Now the light was slightly higher and the shadow could be seen. The room was Webb Calderon's office in this very house and the woman going through his file cabinets like a thief in the night was Mary Frances herself. He'd taped her entire search of his office.

The video played on, but she could no longer watch. She'd been caught. There was nothing she could do. Somewhere beyond the open balcony doors, gulls cried and roaring waves crashed against rocks. She'd barely heard those things before. Now they thundered in her head, threatening to explode. The air smelled pungently of ocean brine and fear.

She was aware of him without seeing him. He was still

watching the video. A loud click dropped the room into a pit of silence. The screen went black, and he turned toward her.

He was taking off his belt as Mary Frances glanced up.

There was a moment of shock, of disbelief, but it passed with a shudder of understanding. As he walked toward her she held out her hands, wrists together. Her awareness of his intentions was deep and intuitive. It came from years of contemplation and reflection, years of enforced silence. She was taught that submission was more powerful than persecution, that humility was holy.

"Tell me about this sin of impurity," he said, still some distance from her.

She'd never been able to lie. Like Emerson, she had always believed a piece of the soul died with every untruth. Unfortunately what was a virtue in the convent might be her undoing in Webb Calderon's world, she realized.

"I didn't want to die without knowing what it felt like to be with a man," she admitted. There was more, but she wouldn't reveal it unless asked.

The silence welled again. This time he was the contemplative. After a moment he walked to the foot of her bed and drew the sheet off her, exposing the sheer nightgown and the tattoo on the inside of her ankle.

"So you decided to sell your body," he said.

His mouth curled with a contempt that confused her, considering the things he'd done to and with her sister. But there was something else: ghosts haunted his eyes. Memories, she realized. Tragedies.

"Yes, in a way." She couldn't lie, but she couldn't give him what he was asking for either. Somehow she understood that he wanted her to be pure and innocent, to be everything he wasn't.

"Convince me that I shouldn't kill you," he told her.

"How would I do that?"

His voice dropped to a whisper. He didn't like what he was saying. He didn't like her. "You're a whore. Prove it."

Mary Frances couldn't do it, not even to save her life. She knew it and somehow so did he. She was not Brianna. Nor was she the frightened, sensation-starved young woman who once lost her head and prayed for sex at morning prayers. She had options now, the full range of sexual experience to choose from, and because of that, she wanted something more than mere experience. She wanted love. She wanted to be transported by passion so incandescent it fired her soul the way religion never could. She couldn't have cold, mechanical sex. It would destroy her.

She was touching the medal, running it through her fingers, resisting the impulse to bring it to her lips. She knew he was watching her, but she couldn't help herself. It was an intimate, desperate urge for contact.

Rita, she thought, carry me through, make me strong.

Not caring if he saw her, she brought the sacred thing to her mouth and touched it lightly to her lips. Sweetly anguished, she felt her breath tremble uncontrollably. A soft, bleating sound caught in her throat.

She couldn't look up for a moment, and when she did, she found him scrutinizing her as if he couldn't decide whether she was innocence or evil incarnate, the sweetest, most seductive thing he'd ever seen—or the most sinister. Suddenly things were reversed and she was the one who was suspect, not him. That was odd.

What was evil? she wondered. *Who* was evil?

"We're all whores," she told him. "We're all saints, even you. But I doubt you can prove it."

It wasn't the answer he wanted. "Who are you?" he asked. "Why were you going through my things?"

She didn't respond, and her silence seemed to galvanize him. He strode to the bed, looped his belt around her crossed wrists, threaded it through the buckle, and pulled it tight.

"You can be made to talk," he said. "Anyone can be made to do anything."

"Not anyone," she responded. "Not me." It wasn't a challenge, though she knew he might take it that way. She also knew there was no torture he could invent that would force her to violate a vow of secrecy. She had mental resources even he couldn't understand.

Moments later, her white nightgown billowing behind her, she awkwardly descended a stairway to the cellar. Her hands were still bound, and Webb Calderon was right behind her. He'd given her one last chance to tell him what she was looking for, and when she hadn't done it, his eyes had gone as blue white as lasers. It was the coldest fury she'd ever seen. He'd pulled her to her feet with the lash end of his belt and forced her into the hallway. He hadn't told her where they were going, but she already knew. Bluebeard's lair, where a gallery full of ancient torture equipment awaited her.

Rick Caruso was having a rotten day. He was being stalked by a blond bombshell, and he might be a priest, but he was no saint. He understood now why Blue Brandenburg had suddenly appeared in his life. This had nothing to do with Mary Frances. Blue had been sent by the devil to test him.

That explained everything, including why she'd arrived at the rectory at the crack of dawn this morning, before he'd even finished his first cup of coffee. The rectory was a priest's living quarters as well as the church office, and Rick's room was on the second floor. Fortunately he was up and dressed when she bounced in, but he hadn't beat her by much. It also explained why she was wearing an outfit hell wouldn't have—button-fly blue jeans, cut off to her dimples and riding low enough on her hips to bare her succulent belly button—

The coffee cup he was holding crashed to the desk, and he shook his head. *Succulent* belly button? Was he already reduced to thinking in those terms? He had the ten A.M. mass to prepare, and what was he doing? Staring at a computer screen and fighting off images of the cropped blouse she'd tied at her midriff and the tanned toes of her bare feet. She hadn't even bothered with shoes? Did the woman know what naked toes did to a man?

His housekeeper had let her in. He intended to have a talk with the woman, but that would have to wait. At the moment, for reasons that escaped him, the two of them— Blue and his housekeeper—were engaged in earnest conversation in the small kitchen that adjoined the rectory office. He could see them clearly. He could almost hear them they, were so close.

Mariana Delgado was a young, unhappily married mother of four, whose husband refused to come in for counseling. It wouldn't have surprised him if Blue was advising her on the joys of divorce, a subject about which Rick himself was increasingly ambivalent, considering Mariana's situation. It troubled him how little help he'd been able to offer her. He'd finally told her to follow her conscience, a solution that didn't resolve his questions or her predicament. When a woman's husband seemed incapable of finding a job, drank too much, and generally behaved like an ass, it felt condescending suggesting that she console herself with the rewards that awaited her in the afterlife.

He fell back in the creaky desk chair, cheeks puffed like a blowfish as he let off some steam. With a long stretch of his arm and a few taps of his fingers on the keyboard, he saved the sermon he'd been working on and brought up his E-mail, thinking that might distract him. He'd long been fascinated with the idea of cyberspace and was one of the early users of the Internet, not to mention one of the first priests to use it.

According to the list that came up, he had several messages waiting to be read, one of which had nothing to do with his church work and needed immediate attention, by its return address. It was of a confidential nature, so he shot a quick look over his shoulder to make sure no one was coming up behind him. He should have been happy Blue had found something to occupy herself, although it bugged him that she was essentially rustling one of the sheep from *his* flock. If he had qualms about the practicality of his advice to Mariana, she clearly had no such qualms about hers.

He'd just hit the key to bring up the E-mail when Blue gave up a snort of moral outrage that warned him she was about to grace his presence. He'd been trying to listen in on her hushed conversation all morning. Now, suddenly, she was going to make him a part of it?

"Unbeleeevable!" she muttered.

He barely got the message off the screen before she strode into the office. Mariana could be seen making her escape through the side door of the rectory. She clearly wanted nothing to do with her new friend's pique.

Blue's exquisite features were hot with indignation. "Were you aware that your housekeeper's husband threw a punch at a neighbor and nearly broke his nose? All because the neighbor called him a parasite on society?"

Rick barely squelched an expletive. "I'd have punched him, too. If you're talking about Armando Delgado, the man is under a lot of pressure. He doesn't need people calling him names."

"He's a powder keg with lips! Mariana says he throws tantrums and stomps around like a caged rhino. The kids won't come out of their rooms they're so terrified. I told her to pack up the *niños* and get out of there."

Deep forbearing sigh. "And what purpose would that serve?"

"It would get his attention, for one thing. He needs a wake-up call."

"Or it could push him over the edge. He's a man of great pride who feels like a failure in every way." Rick had stopped by the Delgados' home recently at Mariana's request, but with disastrous results. Armando was humiliated that Mariana had confided their circumstances to anyone, even a priest. To him it was the final betrayal— even his wife thought him incompetent— and a crushing blow to his masculinity. Instead of improving the situation, things had gone from bad to worse.

"Mariana already has four children," Blue argued. "She doesn't need a fifth. What is it with men and their pride? I told her to do what's best for herself and the kids."

She looked Rick up and down, as much indignation as bold interest in her expression. Her layered blond hair swung in a shivery arcs as she cocked her head to one side and propped her fists on her hips, issuing an unspoken challenge. Maybe that was one of the things he liked about her, her boldness. Maybe he actually liked it.

"And . . . what did she say?" he asked.

"She said you told her the same thing."

Rick drew up defensively, hitching his hands into the pockets of his Levi's. He rarely wore the robes anymore, except for Sunday mass, holidays, and special observances. "That's not true. I didn't tell her to leave. I told her to follow her conscience."

"Like I said, padre. Same thing."

She beamed and touched his bare arm, sending ripples of awareness through him. He felt like a pond she'd just thrown a penny into, but oddly, he didn't want to tell her. He didn't want to admit it, although that's how he would normally have handled something like this. He would have told her. He'd told other women when he'd felt those physical pangs. It was a way of clearing the air and creating the emotional distance they would both need to function. But with her it was different.

She wasn't just beautiful. In fact, that was the least of it, although if he was being honest, he had spent most of the morning trying to figure out what she had on under her blouse. Nothing, he'd decided, both glad and sorry to have the burning question answered. Because the moment he'd satisfied his curiosity, other parts of him had become dissatisfied. What really intrigued him about Blue Brandenburg was her flat-out ballsiness. She had no respect for anything, including him and his calling. That made her a challenge. One he couldn't resist, unfortunately.

"I think my work here is done," she said with more than a tinge of irony, "at least for today." And with that, she turned and left."

"That's a handful," Rick observed softly, not at all unmindful of the sway in her stroll and the lean, tan line of her thighs as he watched her close the door. "Two handfuls."

As he returned to his desk he remembered the E-mail. A glance at his watch told him there wasn't going to be time to answer it now. He had less than an hour until mass and still hadn't prepared his sermon. But when he tried to bring the message up to save it, he discovered it wasn't there to answer. He'd lost it somehow while he was trying to clear the screen.

Blue death strikes again, he thought. Should be a video game.

Try as he might, Father Rick Caruso never did get his sermon done on that morning of blond bombshells. He never did find the E-mail either. What he did instead was pace. Pace and soul-search and agonizingly reassess, or whatever they called it when you felt as if the Rug of Life had been pulled out from under you. He'd been attracted to women before, even flirted with the idea of leaving the priesthood for an exotic dancer once, but he'd always come back to the same indisputable truth. He had to be a priest.

Maybe he even knew that at fifteen when he knelt over a thirteen-year-old boy's dead body and realized that he'd taken a life for no other reason than that the kid had dissed him in front of his gangbanger friends. He'd bargained with God that day. "If you can forgive me for this," he'd said, tears soaking his face, "my life is yours. I'll find some way to serve you, some way to save kids like this."

His answer had been the wail of sirens. He'd done his time in the California Youth Authority, and his only visitor had been the dead boy's mother. His own parents had turned him out at fourteen, baffling him with their references to "tough love." They washed their hands of him the following year when he was found guilty of manslaughter and remanded to custody, but this woman wouldn't leave him alone. She'd haunted him in the visitors' room, railing at him from the depths of her crushing pain, and then she'd broken his heart with her forgiveness. He hadn't realized until later—years later—that she had been God's answer.

He stopped his pacing now long enough to look at the various citations and plaques hanging on his wall, all of them recognition for his work with juveniles. His throat began to burn and his eyes threatened to mist as he realized what he'd been allowed to accomplish in his miserable life, the good he'd been blessed to see come into people's lives. Could he give all that up? More to the point, could he give it up for a woman named Blue?

He shook his head, laughing huskily, mostly because it was better than crying. What? Was he crazy? How could he possibly consider such a thing? She didn't even have the vision to see that Cardinal Fang was the perfect name for a cat who hung around a churchyard, raiding Dumpsters and panhandling for fish tacos.

10

He had the black heart and the icy intelligence of a grand inquisitor. He was capable of anything. Even murder.

Mary Frances understood that as surely as she knew confession was not necessarily good for the soul. In her case it would bring about her destruction. "*Kyrie, eleison; Christe eleison,*" she said, murmuring a plea for mercy from the mass under her breath. She could feel the drawing ache of her own skin and the delicate gold chain burning around her neck as she stood where Webb Calderon had placed her, near a torture device with steel spikes called the Great Wheel.

The dimly lit medieval chamber had a malevolence about it that made her want to shield her eyes, only that wasn't possible with her hands bound. She was surrounded by instruments of punishment that looked as lethal as they were primitive. Racks and iron maidens, thumbscrews and beds of gleaming spikes. Lucifer's Cradle, a chairlike device suspended from the ceiling by chains, creaked as if there were an updraft in the room making it swing. Some of the machinery was so macabre, she couldn't imagine its purpose, but the possibility that he had actually tortured some hapless victim down here was beyond her comprehension.

She was finding it increasingly difficult to believe that the brutality of his childhood could have made him this way. If anyone seemed born to evil, it was Webb Calderon. And yet she knew what they'd done to him. They'd taken a child of nine, stripped him of everything vital, and left his remains to the carrion. That should have made her compassionate, but she could find nothing in her heart, nothing to fill the void but horror.

Gallows humor curved his fine, hard mouth as he turned toward her. The wide scoop of his dark, hunter-green sweater revealed powerful neck muscles and strong, burnished features. His linen slacks were baggy around the ankles in the current European fashion, and his feet, surprisingly, were bare.

"You've heard of the Serpent's Eye?" he asked.

He'd just taken a bejeweled serpentine object from a locked display case, and now he held it up for her to see. The sleek and gleaming thing was over a foot long, and with the exception of the emerald embedded in its head, a daggerlike handle and guards of ivory tusk, it looked very much like a fer-de-lance, the large and lethal South American viper, that had been preserved and mounted.

When she didn't respond to his question, he gripped the handle and freed a steel blade that made her shudder in the very depths of her being. The thing he called the Serpent's Eye was actually the dagger's sheath, she realized, but the blade itself was every bit as riveting. The scimitar shape was as sinuous and deadly beautiful as its scrimshaw design.

"Why should I have heard of that?" she asked. "We didn't have a lot of use for daggers at St. Gertrude's."

His bleak smile made her realize how cynical she sounded. Where was that coming from? Fear? She'd never been cynical. That was Brianna.

He didn't give her time to ruminate on sisterly differences. He'd sheathed the knife, but seemed to have decided she was in need of further instruction. "I thought you might have heard of it," he said, his voice edged with irony. "It was a popular item in seventeenth-century Spain for deflowering heretical nuns."

Her wrists jerked against the belt, making the gold buckle scrape and the tongue rasp noisily. "A *dagger*?"

"No, the sheath." He indicated the snake's phallic contours. "The church had a field day. They even accused their own nuns of having sex with Satan. It was a witch-hunt, literally."

She knew a little something about the Spanish Inquisition and the torture involved herself, but the last thing she wanted to do was distract him with the facts. The longer he talked the better. He seemed to be relishing the perverse subject matter anyway, which should *not* have surprised her.

"Proving witchcraft was merely a formality," he said. "Everybody knew an actual witch had a devil's teat stashed away somewhere on her body—" He glanced up at her, his thumb leisurely stroking the sinister sheath. "Stop me if you've heard this, but the teat was supposed to be a hidden nipple where the witch gave suck to her master—Satan himself. All the inquisitioner general and his honchos had to do was find the thing."

Stop him? Mary Frances would have loved to stop the bastard, but for some reason, she was perversely fascinated. She flinched inwardly at her choice of words. He

did have the capacity to bring out the ungodly worst in
her, the *bastard*.

"That's where the Serpent's Eye came in." Now he was
circling the gemstone on the snake's head with his thumb.
"It was reputed to change color when it came into contact
with the nipple, a mood stone for the dark ages, I'd guess
you'd call it."

He considered the sheath and its generous proportions
in a way that made her think he might not be terribly
averse to playing inquisitor himself. It was difficult not to
imagine that prospect, considering the way he was
fondling the object, but even the thought made her weak
with disgust. It was a monstrous thing. Long and dark and
hideously erotic! If he came anywhere near her with it,
she would shriek to the heavens. She, who had spent
months upon years in stoic contemplation. She, who was
the quietest of postulants.

"When they found the teat," he went on, "which they
always did, they also made sure the wicked witch was no
longer a virgin, assuming she'd been one to begin with.
Confessions to sex with doorknobs probably weren't unusual, given the White Hoods' enthusiasm for extracting
the 'truth'."

He strolled over to one of the baffling devices that had
caught her attention earlier, a wooden contraption that for
all the world had made her think of a Thighmaster. Sister
Fulgentia would have said she'd been watching too many
infomercials, and the mistress of postulants would have
been right. TV had been Mary Frances's first vice when
she'd left the convent, her only vice to date. Withering
sarcasm was to be her second apparently.

"This ingenious little thing was a brace made to force
the nun's knees apart so she could be 'searched,' " he ex-

plained, using the snake as a pointer to emphasize the cleverness of the wooden contraption's design.

Helpful, isn't he? she thought acidly. The inside of her own thighs actually ached from straining against the imaginary thing. She was surprised that he didn't transfer his probing gaze to that part of her body as he glanced around at her, a feat that must have taken quite a little restraint.

"How do you like my camera de tortura . . . Irish?"

She must be gaping. She was as surprised by the raw, husky way he mouthed the sobriquet as by the fact that he knew it. And he, of course, seemed pleased to have gotten a reaction out of her. She might actually have seen a spark ignite in his "clinically dead" blue eyes.

"That *was* the name you typed in when the security program on my computer asked you to identify yourself, wasn't it?"

She'd typed in many things in the frustration of trying to access her sister's diary. She supposed that might have been one of them. A sharp, icy sensation shivered her spine as she remembered Brianna's impassioned words. *He's wholly ensnared me, body, mind, and soul . . . and Lord, it is the sweetest kind of subjugation imaginable. I've become a wanton, hedonsitic creature who can think of nothing but my own flesh and the pleasure he brings to it.*

"You've heard of the rack?" His tone said he was about to introduce her to the nasty-looking piece of equipment that resembled an elongated bed with leather thongs and straps and pullies. "They say it can stretch a man—or any part of him—to twice its normal size."

"Really?" He was going to have to do better than that. She'd not only heard of the rack, she knew a great deal

more about its use in torture than most. Her instruction in
Christian martyrdom had been quite thorough.

"And women," she asked, "what does it do to them?"

The quality of his smile changed as he gazed at her. It
flickered with something that might even have thrilled
her in another situation. Hunger? The gleam in his eyes
darkened as he let his attention drift down the body of the
woman he'd taken prisoner. She could feel her breasts
rising and falling under his inspection. Her heartbeat had
gone shallow and sharp, and she had never felt more
naked.

"You could donate your body to medical science and
find out," he suggested blandly.

"And I'll bet you'd love to play doctor." She said it
with such low force, it couldn't have been discernible to
the human ear, proving he wasn't human when his smile
darkened. Had she ever doubted it?

"Every little boy loves that," he assured her, "as long
as he's got an obedient little girl to practice on."

"How utterly sexist. Women are doctors, too, have
been for generations."

"But not you—" His gaze was knowing, evil. "The student nurse? You look like the perfect patient to me."

She thought he might be going to strap her down and
demonstrate. She actually thought he might be going to
do that, and her mouth went bone-dry at the possibility.
Instead he opted to play tour guide for the torture culture
of the seventeenth century, moving around the room, cat
graceful in his hunter-green garb, his white-and-gold hair
glimmering in the low light as he described the instruments. There were scaffolds for suspending sinners by
their hair, massive stone balls to hang from their feet, and
cudgels to inflict beatings.

"Creative, hmm?" was his only comment.

He is a monster, she thought, averting her eyes as he directed her attention to what looked like a smaller version of a gymnastic pommel horse with leather straps at the base of each of its four legs.

"Don't bother," she snapped. "I know what that's for."

He pulled a thick bamboo cane from its leather-strap sheath and swacked the horse smartly. "A public whipping was meant to humiliate the victim rather than extract a confession," he said. "Did you know that?"

Scare tactics, she told herself, all of it. Webb Calderon was a prominent art dealer with galleries all over the world. This very room was a gallery and these devices were authentic antiquities, some of them probably priceless. He wouldn't risk damaging them, even that ridiculous pommel horse. She knew a bit about human nature, and the louder and longer people threatened, the less likely they were to carry out their threats. He'd been going on for far too long. If he were going to torture her, he'd be doing it instead of talking about it. This *was* the twentieth century. People didn't use the Iron Maiden of Nuremberg to get information. They used sodium pentathol.

She relaxed a little, reasonably certain that she was right and pleased with her analysis. She'd always been the family's cool head. It was another of the traits that had made everyone think she was the perfect candidate for holiness. No one knew, however, about the secret, erotic life of her mind. She'd been able to keep that under wraps, and she'd always thought the fantasies would miraculously vanish when she entered the convent, that she would be cleansed. She'd prayed for that. But something had changed as her postulancy progressed and she contemplated the sacrifices to be made. As a novitiate, she would receive the habit, a new name, and be required to go into strict enclosure. It would become imperative that she get control of her thoughts, curb her unruly, sex-soaked imagination—

"Anyone can be made to talk," he said, repeating the threat he'd made earlier.

The zing of sharp metal set her heart on edge. He'd freed the dagger again, and the emerald set in its case gleamed unnaturally in the mustard glow of a wall sconce. Unexpectedly, he brandished the knife, cutting the golden pool into quadrants, as if it were so many pieces of a pie. The blade left a sizzling arc in its wake.

Mary Frances heard a whistling thud before she realized the knife had been thrown. Against the far wall of the gallery was a wooden cross large enough for an adult man, except that it was pivoted in the shape of an X. The dagger was quivering at its center, its blade stuck fast in ancient wood.

She imagined she could hear the screams of the people who had died there. Another moment passed before she realized that Calderon had crossed the room and pulled the weapon free. She was only absently aware of what he was doing because the object of her intense focus had changed. She wasn't staring at the dagger anymore. She was staring at the cross.

"St. Andrew's Cross?" she asked. She remembered its uses from her studies. The victims were mainly women and the abuses were sexual, including the deflowerings he'd mentioned. But what they did to men was every bit as heinous.

"You know it?" Tendrils of gold had fallen across his forehead, giving him a curiously careless look. Boyish even. An utterly depraved child, she decided as he absently flicked the hair back.

"The cross was introduced at the height of the Inquisition," he went on, oblivious to her withering scrutiny, "to make witches and heretics confess their sins and beg for a quick and merciful death. It's said to have inspired some of the most ingenious tortures ever devised."

Which explains its appeal to you, she thought. "Why don't you just burn me at the stake? It would be simpler, wouldn't it? Than all of this?"

"Sure, but think of the fun we'd miss." His gaze brushed over her again, swiftly, but with far more heat than before. She could feel the friction. She could almost see sparks. If he kept looking at her like that, he wasn't going to need a stake, she realized. He would set her afire without one.

Her next realization was even more disturbing. This man made her vital signs flare out of control like nothing else in her life. He made her heart rate soar. It was adrenaline, of course, but this was more complicated than simple fear. If he weren't a suspect in her sister's death, and if she'd met him under entirely different circumstances, she would probably have been half-infatuated with him already.

It was the appalling truth, but she didn't understand why. The nuns had taught her there was nothing more tempting, nothing more irresistible, than evil in all its guises, but it couldn't be that—

Lucifer's Cradle groaned softly, still swinging.

Her bonds rasped as she pulled against them. "No doubt it's inspired *you*," she mumbled, referring to the fun he mentioned.

If he picked up on her embittered tone, he did nothing to acknowledge it. She was waiting for some reaction, a warning glance. Instead, he walked back to where he'd left the sheath, replaced the dagger with a soundless slice, and returned it to the display case.

End of lecture? she wondered.

His back was to her as he shut the glass doors and locked them. He made no effort to hide the fact that he kept the key in a secret drawer in the cabinet's molding. She considered the possibility of trying to make a run for it while he was occupied, but when he turned around, she saw the scimitar glinting in his hand.

He lifted it to the light, admiring the blade like another man might have a glass of wine. "Did I mention that it's so sharp a man could bleed to death before he even knew his balls were gone?"

Effect, she repeated, shuddering. This was all for effect.

He held a tissue in his hand and demonstrated by draping it over the blade. It floated to the floor in two perfect pieces, severed by the blade's razor edge.

"*The Bodyguard,*" she said faintly, referring to a movie she'd seen on television with Kevin Costner and Whitney Houston. The stars had ended up kissing after Costner's sword trick. It had all been a prelude to passion.

Calderon's eyes glared like sun on a patch of ice.

"What are you *doing*?" she gasped softly. The question was unnecessary. He was walking toward her, gripping the dagger like an assailant who intended to open her throat.

"Apparently my demonstration wasn't persuasive."

"It was, believe me!" She backed into the Great Wheel and had trouble freeing herself from its spokes. Her bound hands flew up as she tried to regain her balance. Fortunately she hadn't stepped on the steel spikes that lined the floor beneath it. A quick glance around told her she was being forced into a corner. There was nowhere to go and he was still coming at her.

"Clearly you need to be convinced," he said.

"No, I don't! No—" Her protest broke off in a sharp cry. With as little effort as he'd cut the tissue, he reached her and opened her nightgown from top to bottom. The scapel-edged blade never touched her skin, but the sound of ripping fabric and the flashes of steel left her faint.

"Convinced now?" he asked softly. "It's quite sharp."

"I am," she breathed. "It is."

A raspy vibration had invaded her voice, but she continued to stare at the knife as if it were alive and hungry. She didn't fully grasp what he'd done to her until she looked down and saw her nightgown fall open. The slowness with which it unfurled struck her as unreal. Invisible hands might have been undressing her, lifting the fabric, folding it back. But as she gaped at her own delicate, shivering flesh, reality finally sank in. There was blood on her body. He'd cut her. There was a thin red line on her belly, and she hadn't even felt it.

She slumped against the wall and heard his voice through her reeling confusion.

"It's just a nick . . . this time."

Her neck snapped back, and she stared at him in horror. There was blood on the knife, too. He was wiping the blade clean with the tissue he'd severed. She was wrong. He didn't want a reaction. He wanted a confession, and he wasn't going to stop until he had one. Her hands worked to bring the thin fabric of her nightgown together, but she couldn't seem to manage it. What did he care whether or not she was naked? He had cut her. Just as her hands couldn't grasp the material, her mind couldn't grasp that fact.

She hadn't believed he would hurt her. She really hadn't.

She closed her eyes dizzily and felt a heaviness pulling

at the lids. Lethargy made her sway and then catch herself. No! Oh, please God! She couldn't pass out. Consciousness was the only protection she had with him. Her mind was as strong as his, stronger. Her will to prevail was indomitable. Those qualities were her only weapons. She had to think and fight, to live.

He was right there in front of her when she opened her eyes. The knife was gone. He must have set it aside somewhere, but he didn't need it. His ice-blue gaze impaled her.

"I'm ready to hear your confession," he told her. "Are you ready to bare your soul?"

"I have nothing to confess to you." She felt woozy, but it couldn't be the blood she'd lost. He said he'd only nicked her.

"You committed a sin of impurity."

The creaking and groaning of chains was everywhere. She didn't understand . . . was that what he wanted, to know her sins? She struggled to hold her head up, to stay awake. His eyes were like nails, the only thing holding her up. They pierced her senses, but she couldn't look away or she would be lost in the oblivion that threatened to engulf her.

"Why do you care about my sins?" she asked him. "They have nothing to do with you."

"But the sin of impurity has everything to do with *you,* doesn't it? It's who you are. It's what you need, Irish. I want to know what you need . . . down there where you live . . . in that sweet, soft, naked part of you."

My sex, she thought.

"Your soul," he said.

His expression had changed. There was a strange caress in his features now. He wanted to know why she'd sinned for some reason that was personal to him. It was almost as if she'd transgressed against him.

"I can't tell you that—" She slumped against the wall, her head lolling back. "I can't tell you anything."

"Then you leave me no choice." He took a small bottle from his shirt pocket and held it up, close enough for her to see that there were capsules inside. "There was a drug on the blade of my knife. I introduced it into your bloodstream when I nicked you, and that's *all* it was, a nick. I have the antidote right here if you want it. It's your choice. You can probably feel the effects taking hold already."

"A drug? You drugged—"

"A wonder drug, love. It makes you very talkative and then it makes you sleep."

"Forever?"

"If I wanted you dead, you wouldn't be wasting my time with these questions."

Truth serum? He'd done that? She swayed forward and felt him catch her. His hand buttressed her shoulder and eased her back against the wall. She cared more about the rape of her psyche than the threat to her life. The bastard! The unholy bastard! She would never have given him the information willingly, and he knew that. No torture would have wrung it from her. There was nothing he could have done to break her, so he'd taken the information the only way he could. It was rape, it was!

"No," she gasped, "I would never have told—"

He released her, and she staggered forward uncontrollably, collapsing into his arms again. A shudder raked her as he gathered her up and held her there, his body hot and powerful against her nakedness, his voice reverberating against her temple. And oddly respectful.

"I know," he said, something whispering in the admission, perhaps regret. "You're much tougher than I am, Irish. But you can't win, not against me. I play dirty—"

"*Coward!*" She sobbed the word and felt him react. His chest jerked against her lolling head. She'd struck home. He knew he couldn't beat her in a fair fight, and he didn't like what he'd had to do. But possibly, just possibly, he couldn't bring himself to torture her either. Did even Webb Calderon have a conscience?

Something inside her wanted to scream and fight, but her drugged body had already succumbed. She was as limp as a fainting child, and when he caught her beneath the knees and lifted her into his arms, she sank there like a stone. He cradled her with a strength that magnified her helplessness, but there was an odd quality of tenderness in his power. His voice washed in and out of her consciousness. Or was it his voice? She couldn't be sure anymore. There were so many bewildering thoughts in her head, so many sounds. She had no idea what was real and what wasn't.

What was the strongest of all things?

The question came from out of nowhere, electrifying her groggy mind. Someone had told her Bluebeard's wives could have saved themselves if they'd known. The answer seemed vitally important, but even the question eluded her as she felt herself spiraling into another reality, one that was impossible to distinguish from fantasy.

Was he carrying her at all? Had he picked her up?

She didn't have the strength to open her eyes, and yet somehow she could see everything that was happening. It was there on the screen of her mind. He'd laid her down on the floor and was kneeling over her, searching her face, talking to her, though she couldn't hear his voice. She had just begun to think he was trying to revive her when another screen appeared, another man. . . .

She couldn't see him clearly, this other man, this phantom who was carrying her, but she was limp and faint in his arms, her skin pale against his dark clothing. He'd drawn her gown together and picked her up, and now he was carrying her to the St. Andrew's Cross. She'd always had an ungovernable imagination, but what she was experiencing now could only be a dream. This could *not* be happening. It was a fantasy right out of her readings about religious persecution.

Objects darted in and out of her mind like serpents. She couldn't tell if they were real or simply visions. The huge cross was no longer standing against the wall. It was hanging horizontally a few feet above the floor, each end post of the X supported by some invisible chain from the ceiling. The leather straps could only be meant for her arms and legs.

No, this couldn't be happening. Everything was floating and surreal. She was floating. This had to be the drug. . . .

She could feel her body being arranged on the wooden planks with a carefulness that seemed almost obsessive. The gown had fallen open and the bright red ribbon of blood against the luminosity of her belly made her look like the sacrificial offerings she had read about, a lovely, raven-haired virgin. Atonement to the gods? she wondered. Or bribe to the devil?

Shame washed over her as she fought the images that were taking hold of her. She had dreamed this before—erotic reveries of a phantom carrying her off and sweetly torturing her into submission. But he hadn't wanted information; he'd wanted her. *More than anything in heaven or hell, he'd wanted her.* He'd stolen into her consciousness while she slept and taken her captive with his dark desires. His touch had made her shake.

Was he really touching her now? Or was she only dreaming?

Every stroke of his fingers made her back arch and her body lift off the planks, but it was their tenderness that threatened to destroy her. He was violating the sanctity of her thoughts, forcing her to betray herself, as well as anyone she might implicate. That was coercion. How could tenderness be any part of it?

"How were you impure, Irish?"

The whisper of a caress floated over her belly and down her thighs. Like a charge of static electricity hovering just above her skin, it made her hair rise and shiver. Her flesh prickled, reaching to meet its source. It was not his hands, she told herself. No human touch was that light, that stimulating.

She twisted against the wrist cuffs, her hips rolling.

Her very helplessness seemed wanton. Much as she wanted to, she couldn't stop the sensations that were blooming inside her. Anticipation was unfurling like petals. She could see herself on the screen, and her breasts were as full as the moon. They shimmered with every little movement. Rosebud red, her nipples had puckered and tightened as the rest of her body was opening. Long white legs fanned from a rich black delta that invited the eyes, the fingers, to explore her mysteries.

A sigh slipped out of her. She was swimming in her own senses, in the startling beauty of her own flesh. Perfume rose from her frustration, a heavy floral bouquet. Heat fanned up her legs and she knew his hands were there. They were at her ankles, sliding up her calves, sprinkling her thighs. . . .

"The truth now, Irish. Who are you? Who sent you?"

"I can't give you that," she told him, not sure if she was

actually speaking or only thinking. *Anything but that. I'll give you anything but that.*

Something brushed her face, hot and soft. His fingers?

"Then give me this," he said, touching her mouth, pressing into its fullness. "Give me the lips that trembled against a saint's medal. Let me taste their longing, feel their unsteadiness—"

His voice was suddenly harsh, roughened with need. It touched her in a way his fingers never could. *Give me this,* he said. *It's all I'll ever know of innocence.*

She lifted to him, but he was gone. . . .

Purple night. It enveloped her. She was falling through it like a star, lost. Weightless. The strange beauty of her descent lulled her. She didn't even exist, except in spirit. Gravity tugged gently, coaxing her to give in and let herself fall. She wanted to. She might have if she hadn't known the truth, that it had to end. Even infinity ended somewhere.

She was imagining the impact when the screen of her mind opened like Pandora's box. The noise was earsplitting. She tried to cover her ears, but her hands were tied. Daggers whistled through air and snakes spat obscenely.

"Tell me who sent you!" he thundered, hooded and horrible.

The echoing screams warned her what happened to women like her, women who didn't give the grand inquisitor what he wanted. They were branded as heretics and burned at the stake. Nothing could save her. He had never intended to save her. He was drawn to her innocence because he could never reclaim his. He wanted it so he could destroy it. Throughout the ages people had sought to destroy what they couldn't have. It was easier than living with the proof of your own defectiveness.

Darkness loomed and a glowing iron brand flashed into her consciousness. The noise rose again, piercing her eardrums—howls and grunts, snarls and moans. The white-hot iron flew at her like a spear, hissing as it touched her bare flesh. The last sound she heard was her own keening scream.

11

A bouquet of lavender flowers lay on the concrete as Blue sashayed out of the church, fresh from her semivictorious encounter with Father Rick. Petunias, she realized, surprised and delighted as she crouched to pick up the wilted arrangement. They'd been her favorites when she was a kid. Every time her dad had gone on a trip, he'd come back with some kind of trinket for her personal petunia garden—clothing, stationery, ornamental soap for her bathroom. She'd even had a toilet seat with petunias on it.

She touched the petals, remembering and smiling foolishly. She didn't believe in signs, but it was hard not to think that these flowers were meant for her, that they signified something. Odd that she'd found them in front of his church.

"Ma'am? Those flowers, they're—"

Blue turned to see a young boy waving at her. He was laboring to get to her, a hitch in his gait that made her realize he was wearing a leg brace.

"I dropped them," he said, huffing and puffing, his face red from the exertion. "But you can have them if you want them." He was rail-thin and dusky with dark hair and round black eyes, a cute little guy who couldn't have been more than seven or eight.

"Oh, no." She couldn't take his flowers, but she was aware by her vise grip on the bouquet that she did not want to give them up. "Not if they're yours."

He wobbled, touching her arm as if to keep his balance. "They're pretty, aren't they? You like them? You take them, okay?" He grinned up at her expectantly, obviously waiting for something.

Blue stared at him, wondering what it was, and then she saw his other hand creeping out. His fingers were curled inward as if he were holding something, but she could see nothing there. Suddenly Blue understood. He *was* expecting something. Money. She heaved a sigh. He was one of those street-corner kids who knocked on car windows and hustled flowers. Now they were wearing leg braces to wring sympathy from the public. What next? She cast him a reproachful look.

"How much are they?" she wanted to know. This kid knew a sucker when he saw one.

"The flowers?" He scratched his head.

Another ploy! He was probably going to double the price. She clamped the flowers between her teeth long enough to dig in her bag for a ten-dollar bill. That ought to get rid of him.

"You don't like them?" he asked, crestfallen.

"I love 'em, okay? They're friggin' beautiful. Here, take this and go buy yourself a fake Rolex." She thrust the ten dollars at him, disgusted at what the youth of America had stooped to. It was probably because she'd been silly enough to think the petunias meant something.

But still, a grade-school kid shouldn't be so devious. She shuddered to think what he'd be selling when he was a teenager.

He drew his hand back. "I don't want your money, lady," he said. "The flowers were for St. Catherine of Siena."

"St. Catherine? Do you mean the statue?" The stonework she spoke of was the centerpiece of the crumbling courtyard several feet beyond them, a woman in tattered robes, her head thrown back as if in a state of ecstasy that bordered on pain, or vice versa. Blue could never figure out which it was.

"She's *not* a statue." He regarded Blue warily, indignantly. "She's one of the holiest women who ever lived. My mom told me so. She said St. Catherine once drained the pus from the sores of a dying nun who'd been really mean to her. She drank the pus to show her love and forgiveness."

"Euuuuw! There are easier ways to say I love you."

He chattered on, apparently not put off in the slightest by Blue's distaste. "Sister Dominic told us she slept on a board and had a brick for a pillow. She never ate, y'know. Lived for years on one lettuce leaf."

Now that was impressive, Blue thought. "Quite a little dieter," she said, and meant it sincerely. Blue couldn't seem to give up anything, especially if it was in one of the four essential food groups—sugar, chocolate, caffeine, or booze.

He seemed pleased to have prevailed upon such a woman of the world as Blue Brandenburg. "Anyway," he went on, "if you lay the flowers at her feet and say a novena—and *if* your heart is right, and you don't ask for something for yourself, like hot wheels or Power Rangers —she might send you a blessing."

Blue was bewildered. "You're not selling flowers?"

He shook his head slowly. "I brought 'em for her, the saint. My mom and dad aren't getting along, and I thought this might help."

Blue still couldn't believe this wasn't a ploy. Kids didn't really bring offerings to statues nowadays, did they? She couldn't remember anything like that back in her own Catholic-school days, and kids were far more innocent then. Of course, they hadn't had a famous statue, one who wept real tears.

"You keep the flowers, okay?" he insisted. "My mom says doing stuff for other people brings good luck, and besides, you looked kinda sad before."

"Sad . . . when?"

"When you saw the flowers. I wuz afraid you might cry for a minute there." He wrinkled his nose in distaste. "I hate it when my mom cries."

Blue could have cried. She honestly could have. He was for real, she thought. Holy shit. She was in the presence of a good and honorable man, and it was the second time today. This was almost more than her cynical nature could handle.

He had a St. Christopher's medal clutched in his hand, which apparently he was also going to offer. He must have been trying to give it to her earlier . . . because she had looked sad.

Her heart wrenched. She didn't want anyone to know that about her, that she was sad. She thought she hid it so cleverly, behind anger and bravado, but he'd seen through her easily. Either she was a total wuss or he was a special kid. She hoped to heaven it was the latter.

"I can't take your medal," she told him. "You must keep it and wear it and be protected by it. But I will take the flowers, and I will offer them to St. Catherine."

And I know just how I want to be blessed, she thought. I want a man who can look into my heart the way this child can.

Her arm was missing. Mary Frances could feel nothing beyond her shoulder. Her mind was telling her to lift her hand and clench her fingers, but she couldn't. There was no hand, no fingers to clench. That was her first groggy awareness upon awakening, that and the faint rasp of metal scraping against metal. Next came the fuzzy suspicion that she must have dozed off with her arm above her head and it had fallen asleep . . . as opposed to falling off.

She opened her eyes to the murky darkness of predawn and wondered why her alarm hadn't rung. Had she overslept again?

Late. She was going to be late for work!

"Ah!" Something jerked her backward as she tried to sit up. She let out another confused moan as her head hit the pillow. It was the arm she'd lost. The dull, buzzing pain that ran from wrist to shoulder told her where it was, high above her head, but she couldn't move it because it was attached to something.

Something that rasped and whined like an old saw.

"You're handcuffed to the bed."

"What?" Mary Frances reared up again and was jerked back. "Ouch!" she cried.

"Keep jumping around like that, and you'll pull your arm out of its socket."

It was a male voice, barbed with irony. She turned in its direction, but all she could see was the glowing black form of a man, fringed by the moonlight of patio doors.

"Handcuffed?" Her question echoed ominously. She could feel it now, a metal ring digging into her flesh. She started to ask why, and then it all came flooding back to her, who he was, where she was, *what he'd done*.

He'd branded her with a glowing iron. Her breast! He'd scored her flesh and made her cry out. The stench of burned hair and skin had torn shrieks of pain from her, and then she'd blacked out.

The handcuff hissed obscenely as she craned to see the wound on her breast. The light was too dim, even at close range, but she was still wearing the nightgown he'd sliced up the middle, and her St. Rita's medal hung around her neck. Her right hand was free, and she could touch herself, but she couldn't detect anything resembling a burn wound. Her heart felt as if it were trying to escape through her fingertips as she explored her hot, feverish skin. But there were no raised marks, no oozing sores that she could find.

"What are you doing?"

It was his voice again, and when she didn't answer, the room lit up with a sudden, painful burst. Floorboards creaked, whispering a warning that he was coming toward her.

"So it's true," he said. "You are fresh out of the convent. St. Gertrude's, wasn't it?"

"How do you know that?" She'd ducked her head in order to avoid the glare of the overhead light, but she couldn't avoid his voice. It was low and sonorous, with an afterlife that reminded her of an echo chamber more than a torture chamber. There was coldness, yes, but it was the kind of chill that has an ache in it, not frozen crystals, not dead like his eyes.

"You told me," he was saying. "You also told me your name is Mary Frances Murphy, and that you think I killed your sister."

A fiery sensation shot through her eyes as she looked

up at him. "The drug," she whispered. "Truth serum. I'll never forgive you for that."

He seemed to understand what she meant, that he'd forced her to violate her own ethical code and tell him things she wouldn't have otherwise, even under the agony of torture.

His frigid gaze thawed a little. "Ah, Irish," he said, "would you rather I'd hurt you to get you to talk?"

"You did." She touched her breast as if to present him with the proof and realized there was no wound. Her skin was as fresh and pink as the day she was christened. He hadn't burned her. She must have dreamed it. She checked her free wrist to see if there were any marks from the leather straps, and found nothing.

"It was the drug," he said.

The handcuff rasped helplessly against its restriction. It was locked to a bar in the brass bedstead.

"The drug?" She found the bandage on her belly. It was a gauze strip and she ripped it off, wincing at the pain. There was nothing more than a razor-thin red line about three inches long. Soon it would be gone without a trace, but at least she knew that much was real. He had nicked her with the knife.

"Was everything the drug?" she asked him. "Even the way you—"

"Touched you? Spoke to you?"

The color that had congested beneath her fingertips flared in her cheeks. He'd touched her in places she hadn't touched herself. He'd violated her physical boundaries and made her writhe. But he'd also told her that she was all he would ever know of innocence. And his voice, with its strange echoes, had gone painfully harsh . . . or had she only dreamed that, too?

"Did you like what you thought I did?" he asked.

"No."

"Did it excite you, any of it?"

"Perhaps . . . yes, it did." She couldn't lie. "But I didn't like it. I hated it, I think. And you." That was true, too.

He began to walk the room, and she watched him, his long, elegantly muscled frame and fine golden head a study in brutal beauty. At their Serengeti best, lions weren't as regal. Or as indolent. How could she have responded so strongly to the touch of a man who might have tortured and killed her sister? That wasn't right. It wasn't moral. She prayed this didn't have anything to do with her lifelong rivalry with Brianna, but what else was there to explain the powerful connection she felt?

You can't win, not against me, he'd said. *I play dirty,* he'd said.

"Are you going to kill me?" she asked. "Now that you know who I really am?"

"Yes, unfortunately, I'll have to." He said it without hesitation, and then he sighed. "But not quite yet. That wouldn't be expedient."

Mary Frances couldn't quell a shudder. "Why?"

"Why wait?" he asked.

"Yes, why wait? Why not kill me now and get it over with?" *Maybe I can play dirty, too,* she thought. *Maybe I can.*

He stopped walking, but didn't look at her. Instead he seemed to be studying the haze that had whitewashed the horizon. Its harsh brilliance glared against the panes of the patio doors.

"Because you're not a hustler like the others. You were recruited for this, but for some reason, you're still holding out. There are things you haven't told me yet, such as why you were wearing that dress and hat for the interview. I also believe there are other people involved in this mission of yours, and I want to know who they are."

So she hadn't told him everything? Thank God for that. "This is not a conspiracy," she said. "It's me, investigating my sister's death."

His sidelong glance had the slicing edge of one of his knives. "I'd like to believe you, but I don't think you have a clue what you've stumbled into. My work puts me in personal contact with the most powerful figures in the world—heads of state, heads of industry. There are people who would pay any price to get to me, and yet you strolled into my life dressed like a girl in one of my paintings. Why?"

She had no idea why, but it wouldn't have mattered. He didn't wait for an answer.

"Do you have any proof that I killed your sister?" he wanted to know. "Or had her killed, or had *anything* whatsoever to do with her death? Do you even know if she's actually dead?"

She didn't mention the diary she'd found on his computer, or her sister's references to her sexual enslavement by some unidentified man who could only be Webb Calderon. She only voiced what she knew to be true. "Brianna was hit by a car and pronounced dead on arrival at a hospital."

"Did you see her? Did you identify the body?"

"No, but—"

He cut her off with a patronizing look and started for the door. "I have things to do," he informed her. "You and I have some unfinished business, Irish, and when I return to finish it, I won't be bluffing. In the meantime, don't do anything foolish. You're under surveillance in this house. You're always under surveillance."

Mary Frances heard the door click shut and lock from

the outside. She fell against the brass bars with a taut sigh and closed her eyes. By bluffing he could only mean that he hadn't given her a lethal drug. He'd forced the truth out of her, but he hadn't taken her life . . . that time.

She opened her eyes and saw what she'd already felt in every fiber. She was vibrating with nerves, raw with them. She had to do something, but what? She quickly surveyed her surroundings. She was back in the small suite where the housekeeper had first brought her, and her clothing and other belongings were still there, too. Hopefully the red satchel was under the bed where she'd slipped it.

Her visual check of the room was meant to detect surveillance cameras and any possible escape routes. She found neither, but the flash of gold that caught her eye was an ankle bracelet, she realized. He, or someone, had looped a lacy chain around her left ankle, the one that had the Cherries insignia tattooed on the inside.

She drew her foot up to examine it and felt movement in the bar that her wrist was cuffed to. The brass rod was loose. She tested it again, cautiously, and realized that it screwed into the horizontal railings above and below. Her breath hitched in painfully. How careless of him, she thought, almost afraid to believe her good fortune. She was reasonably sure she could get it free with a little effort and slip the cuff off, but she couldn't risk acting immediately. She would wait for a better moment, like the party tonight.

It had already occurred to her that Calderon might want her to escape so that he could keep her under further surveillance. He made her feel like a lab rat in a maze, as if she were something he could amuse himself with. She wanted to think it was possible that Webb Calderon was not infallible, not Lucifer incarnate, just a calculatingly

evil man who had seriously underestimated her resourcefulness. She wanted to think he'd made his first mistake
this time, one of many. And yet she knew he wasn't careless.

She fingered the medal around her throat, felt its
golden warmth, and calmed fractionally. She would have
to be cautious, extremely cautious, and yes, she might
even have to play dirty. At the very least, he would be in
for a surprise when he returned to "finish" his business.

12

*S*he was the enemy. Webb Calderon didn't need tarot cards to tell him that. Nevertheless he opened the pack with a practiced flick of his thumb, drew a card at random from the deck, and laid it on his worktable, face-down.

He had no intention of turning it over.

He'd been collecting art tarot for a decade at least, and this particular deck by Dali was seductively beautiful. Surrealistic circles pinwheeled into Webb's focus. The effect was hypnotic, the pull tremendous. He was curious, certainly. The card was an icy tickle in his gut. But this was an exercise of the will. He had his own use for the tarot, but it wasn't to predict events. He'd never needed to. The future hadn't held any secrets for him in a long time.

Very few people understood that destiny was an out-moded concept in the electronic age. So was the random play of circumstance, for that matter. The future was already charted and mapped. Not by the stars, but by men who would own the stars. Prediction was the game of the powerless, those without the resources to make things happen. Webb knew in advance the outcome of ninety-nine percent of what affected his world, either directly or indirectly. He'd spent his entire adult life amassing secret power the way other men amassed secret money.

He didn't have to predict Fate. He was Fate. He read the tarot only for his own amusement, to see if the cards could predict him. He never read for himself. Ever.

He'd never wanted to until now. . . .

His hand hovered above the card he'd dealt and a mordant smile crept into the muscles of his jaw. She was that one percent. That *fucking* one percent that couldn't be controlled with any amount of contingency planning. She couldn't be bought or bullied or broken. Her belief system, whatever the hell it was, was too strong. That's why he was going to have to get rid of her, the virginal little imp. Otherwise, he'd be frozen over a pack of tarot cards for the indeterminate future.

The morning's quiet was shattered by the riotous chatter of cliff swallows, nesting in the dogwood trees outside. The noise reminded him of the half-finished tasks that still needed his attention. A Henry Moore sculpture was waiting to be uncrated, and he'd left his office computer blinking in midtransaction. He'd been using an electronic service called ArtNet to check the sales histories on a couple of Peploe oils he had under consideration. But more pressing than any of that were the preparations for tonight's transaction. The triplight laser he'd had installed for the meeting with Alejandro Cordes had to be tested to ensure there were no flaws in the operation.

He reached for the tarot card, intending to return it to the deck. As his fingertips brushed the glossy surface, the contact triggered an urge as potent as anything he'd ever known. It flared upward, burning brightly in all his nerve endings. Megawatts of voltage. Gallows laughter set fire to his throat. He so seldom had the pleasure of pain.

He wanted to look at that card. Fuck. This was why she was the enemy. She made him want to do things he'd never done or had any need to do.

All morning he'd been plagued by visions of long white loveliness, restrained by leather, and naked skin as painfully bright to the eye as a hazy spring morning. Her body had contrasts of tone and texture that would have defied even Rembrandt's gifts. The ruby flowerings at her nipples and the dark, smoldering curls at her pubis were as carnal as the charms of a biblical harlot, and yet somehow, on her, they were emblems of innocence. Everything was. Gold dappled her pale cheeks like stardust. It had taken him a moment to realize they were freckles.

Even the crimson cut on her belly seemed to purify her. She was a martyr to her own sensuality, he realized. Her beauty couldn't be defiled. That kind of innocence was indestructible. It was too powerful, even for him, who specialized in those things—

A flash of color bounced from the mirror of a framed photograph.

It was his housekeeper. "Did you want something, Traci?" Her startled brown eyes and teal blouse were caught in the glass of an Ansel Adams landscape, sitting on an easel. She'd been with him four months, and though she'd come with the highest recommendations from trusted sources—and hadn't done anything overtly suspicious until this moment—it took very little to trigger Webb's instincts. He couldn't afford to be complacent

about his help. It wasn't her capability in question as
much as her loyalty.

"The caterers are here," she explained. "They need to
set up for the party tonight."

Webb continued to observe her as she approached.
She'd always been quiet to the point of stealthiness, and
just now she'd come into his workroom through his office, something he'd told her never to do. He restored and
authenticated art as well as dealing it, and he worked on
priceless pieces in this room, readying them for auction
or private sale. He didn't want *anyone* coming up behind
him. The environment was climate-controlled, and normally he kept the room locked, even when he was working inside, but he'd been distracted today—by visions of
naked martyrs.

"Do you read the cards, Mr. Calderon?" she asked,
spotting the tarot deck on his table. "I thought you only
collected them." She craned to see the design, seeming
fascinated by the abstract images on the package.

"Incredible, aren't they?" He slid the pack toward her
to give her a better look. "It's one of Dali's tarots. I
brought it back with me from Paris."

"Salvador Dali?" She studied it appreciatively, lifting
her gaze to Webb with the same intensity. "I know so little about fine art," she admitted. Laughter swelled in her
throat, breathless and confessional. "I was hoping to learn
more, working here."

She colored slightly, and he realized she'd embarrassed
herself. He also realized she was nervous, but his faint
smile of reassurance only seemed to fluster her more. It
was possible she was acting, although it wasn't unusual
for women to be uneasy with him. It was something
about his eyes. He'd heard it all his life. Their marble-
gray quality had been described as disturbing, and that,

coupled with his Nordic features and the icy streaks in his golden hair, apparently had an unsettling effect at times.

A woman friend had once confided that he put her in mind of a beautiful Nazi S.S. officer. Those had been her exact words, which she'd insisted were meant as a compliment. The irony was Webb didn't have a drop of German blood. His mother was Scandinavian and his biological father, Spanish and English. David Calderon was a doctor his mother had been involved with briefly in Madrid before he'd gone off to be a missionary and vanished in the wilds. They'd never married and Webb had been raised by his stepfather, but it was his real father's name he'd taken when he escaped the prison in San Carlos. He'd had to. His entire family had been executed as enemies of the republic, and Webb had been forced to assume a new identity.

"Oh, you *are* reading," Traci exclaimed softly, pointing at the card he'd dealt. "Which one is that?"

Before Webb could stop her, she'd reached out and flicked it over, stunning both of them. "I'm sorry!" Her color rose sharply as she saw the expression on his face.

Webb swept the card up and returned it to the deck, but not without seeing what it was, the death card. "I don't read," he reminded her tersely. "I collect."

He didn't give her a chance to do or say anything more.

"Tell the caterers to go ahead," he told her as he walked her to the door with instructions for the party that evening, "but make sure they stay on this floor. Is that clear, Traci? Under no circumstances is anyone to go upstairs. I want the security beefed up outside, guards at every entrance. Our diplomatic relations with San Carlos are strained as it is, and I don't want anything unforeseen to happen to the only son of the president while he's here."

With that, he locked the door on her alarmed expression and took a moment to compose himself. The card Traci had turned over didn't concern him nearly as much as her erratic behavior did. His assistant wasn't good enough to make him think she was a professional saboteur, but she was also too efficient for such heedless behavior.

While he'd been gone recently on one of his buying trips, she'd allowed a computer repair person into his office to do maintenance on his equipment that he hadn't ordered. She'd been told it was part of his service contract with the company, but when Webb had called to verify this, the customer service rep hadn't been able to confirm that anyone had been sent. Webb had chalked it up to incompetence on the company's part. He was less sure of that now.

The tarot deck seemed to move eerily as he returned to the worktable, an optical illusion created by the spirals. His only thought was to get them out of his sight. There was a small safe built into the drawers that supported the table. He stashed the cards there for safekeeping, making a mental note to put them in the display case at his Beverly Hills gallery with the rest of his collection.

He'd broken his own cardinal rule, thanks to Traci. He'd read the tarot for himself. The figure on the card she'd turned over had been the skeleton in armor, representing death. It rarely meant the obvious, but in this case Webb knew with certainty that it did. Someone was going to die. The cards had been right about that part, but they'd predicted the wrong victim. The ax would fall, and heads would roll, but Webb's wouldn't be among them.

The birds had stopped their chattering and the room was silent as he slid onto the worktable stool. He depressed a button on the floor with his foot, activating the

infrared sensor. To test the invisible beam that ran beneath the table, he had to interrupt it. A simple swing of
his leg set everything in motion, and before he'd returned
his foot to the rung, he'd witnessed a miracle of modern
technology. A panel in the table flashed open so quickly
his eyes couldn't perceive the movement, even though he
was staring directly at it.

He settled himself on the stool and watched the rest of
the operation with a cold smile that mirrored what was
happening inside him. To say that Webb Calderon's veins
ran with ice water was to reduce a Siberian glacier to a
snowflake. Whatever was human had been blast-frozen
to hell when he was a child. Since then he'd existed in absolute zero. Every shriek of pain, every animal fear, every
prayer for mercy had been sealed off. There was no other
way to live with the atrocities he'd witnessed and not be
annihilated by them.

A song pierced his thoughts, the sweet notes of a Sun-
day-school hymn frozen in time. It was the clear, quavering voice of his eight-year-old sister before the insurgents
opened her throat with a machete to silence her. He was
spared only because the new president's mistress had a
perverse fascination with young, blond boys. She'd intervened when the rebel soldiers turned on Webb, but her
motives had been anything but noble.

She'd made Webb her houseboy, brought him along
when the presidential entourage took a villa in Cap Ferrat that summer, and used him greedily. But it wasn't her
perversions that had destroyed him. She'd given him the
only sick, guilty pleasure he'd known during that time. It
wasn't even what happened when he was shipped back to
San Carlos and imprisoned. The water baths and electrical current had reduced him to a subhuman state. But the
little girl who wouldn't stop singing was his only true tor-

ture. Her soaring faith had been unbearable. He'd had to find a way to destroy it, even if it meant destroying himself. . . .

Only now was the rage that had crystallized inside Webb beginning to quiver and breathe. Only now was the glaciar rumbling. His hand shook as he touched the fake Maya figurine that had miraculously appeared from nowhere. It worked. He was ready. Everything was ready.

YOUR HOST IS PARTIAL TO PASSAGEWAYS. THE IRON VIRGIN IS YOUR WAY OUT, BUT DON'T MAKE YOUR ATTEMPT DURING THE PARTY. WAIT UNTIL CORDES IS GONE, THE HOUSE IS QUIET, AND EVERYONE'S ASLEEP. SECURITY WILL BE RELAXED THEN.

USE THE ZIN QUAI IF NECESSARY. A FEW DROPS CAUSE SLEEP, MORE, PARALYSIS AND DEATH. DON'T BE STINGY. HE WON'T LET YOU LEAVE ALIVE. DON'T LEAVE HIM ALIVE.

WINK ;)

Mary Frances stared at the vibrant blue screen of her purse computer in mute disbelief. By "host," they could only mean Webb Calderon. She had no idea whom she was communicating with at Cherries or why they would want her to take the life of an important client, but something was going on here beyond what Blue had told her. Something terrifying.

She typed an urgent question: HOW DO I HANDLE THE SURVEILLANCE CAMERAS?"

The response was immediate. EXIT BY WAY OF THE GALLERY. THAT CAMERA'S BEEN TAKEN CARE OF. THE ONLY OTHER CAMERAS YOU NEED TO WORRY ABOUT ARE IN HIS OFFICE AND WORKROOM. STAY OUT OF THOSE AREAS AND YOU'LL BE FINE."

She keyed in her sign-off, then turned the computer off

and silently dropped it and the cell phone into the red satchel. She was alone in the pitch-dark bedroom, huddled next to the armoire in an attempt to be out of range of any surveillance cameras. She decided to stay that way for a while. Her head was spinning and so was her heart. How did they know so much about Calderon and this house? They seemed intimately familiar with the surveillance system and secret passageways.

She found the medal around her neck and clasped it tightly. Don't leave him alive? She couldn't even entertain the idea of taking a human life in self-defense. Her first priority was to escape, and she wasn't going to take Wink's advice on that score either. She was getting out now.

A woman's giggle floated out the open doorway of Webb Calderon's workroom. "So, Alejandro!" came a throaty, feminine voice, the Latin accent thick and slurred. "What did one lesbian frog say to the other one after they make love? Eh? Do you know, *enamorado*?"

Stony silence greeted the woman's question.

Mary Frances crept along the hallway, scanning the walls for surveillance cameras, and aware that she was going to have to pass the open door up ahead to get to the cellar stairway. The heavy black oxfords she'd worn as a postulant at St. Gertrude's had forced her to tred lightly or risk leaving unsightly scuff marks on the glowing wooden floors. Many associated the gliding walk of nuns with deep spirituality when it was really just everyday necessity.

The party for Alejandro Cordes was in full swing, and Mary Frances had chosen the back hall, hoping the crowd had gathered out on the veranda by the pool, where food and drinks were being served. She could hear laughter

and the music of the strolling mariachis drift in from outside, but unfortunately someone seemed to be having
their own party in Calderon's workroom.

"The frog licked her lips and said, 'They're right. We
do taste like chicken'!" The woman gurgled with a soft
squeal of delight. "Whas wrong with you, Alex? Don't
you get it? Frog legs? Chicken?"

Uneasy male laughter made Mary Frances hesitate at
the doorway and cautiously peek inside. There were several people in the room, including Webb Calderon, who
was seated at a lighted worktable, seemingly oblivious of
his guests as he examined a small ceramic figurine of
what looked like an Indian woman in ceremonial dress,
holding a musical instrument.

She assumed it was some sort of antiquity, but it was
Webb who drew her eye, not the statue. His features were
alternately bathed in the glow of a halogen lamp and
cloaked in gloom, creating the illusion of some vaguely
sinister activity. It was probably the Banana Republic ca-
sualness of his clothing that kept him from looking like a
medieval sorcerer. Feathery gold hair curled to the collar
of his indigo shirt in back, and the khaki suit jacket
draped over the back of his stool matched linen slacks,
drawn tight over his bent knees. Mary Frances could even
see the crease of a thigh muscle where the light fabric
hugged.

"We dance later? Yes, Alejandro?"

There was one woman among the four and she was sipping champagne and clinging tipsily to the man Mary
Frances assumed was Alejandro Cordes, the guest of
honor. She'd locked her arm in his and was frantically
trying to get his attention.

For his part, Cordes seemed uncomfortable with her
antics, yet he still managed to look cool and immacu-

lately groomed. His wavy dark hair was casually tousled, though obviously cut and styled to perfection by some hairdresser to the stars. Even the wrinkles in his fashionably rumpled black linen jacket and slacks looked intentionally pressed in.

Mary Frances recognized him from newspaper and magazine accounts of his continent-hopping lifestyle. He seemed to spend more time aboard the Concorde than he did on land, and the media loved him almost as much as women did. According to the press, he was heir to his ailing father's wealth and title, ruthlessly driven to have both, and rumored to be every bit as charismatic and corrupt as Ruben Cordes. Mary Frances's addiction to tabloid television and "details at eleven" had paid off again, it seemed. *Hard Copy* had done a segment on Latin lovers that featured him, and she'd been glued to the tube.

A third man stood apart from the others, observing the scene. Thirtyish, his thin face bisected by wire spectacles, he was the one Mary Frances needed to watch out for. He had the darting eyes of a hawk. They missed nothing. Right now, fortunately, he was preoccupied with Cordes and the woman.

"I had my hair done this morning, but Alex doesn't like my new 'do.' *Do* you, Alex?" she crooned. She tried to lean over and plant a kiss on Cordes's cheek, but he clearly had something less affectionate in mind. His attempt to take her drink away sloshed champagne everywhere and splashed both of them as the flute fell to the floor.

Mary Frances thought him unnecessarily rough, and apparently so did the woman, who couldn't have been a Cherries escort by her behavior. The tile floor was swimming with champagne and slippery as a skating rink.

"Shit!" the woman cried, struggling to keep her balance in heels that would have made Mary Frances wobble on dry land.

Cordes tried to catch her as she went down, and they both lost their balance. Her screams evaporated in a thud as she landed in a soggy heap and pulled him down on top of her. It was quite a sight—legs and arms and designer clothing flying every which way. Suddenly Alejandro Cordes was immaculate no more.

Forgetting for an instant to be careful, Mary Frances craned around for a better look. A glimmer of light caught her eye as Calderon rose, too, and she ducked back, even more astonished by what happened next. Webb Calderon didn't spring from the table as any host normally would to help a guest. Instead he stretched out his leg, passing it through a nearly invisible laser of light. Mary Frances might never have noticed it if his trouser leg hadn't cut off its path.

The commotion on the floor had everyone's attention except hers. From her vantage point she could see the worktable clearly, and the ceramic figurine seemed to have moved of its own accord. Her brain told her it was an optical illusion, but it appeared that the panel in the worktable had done a flash revolution—turning in a full circle—and the statue had vanished and then reappeared.

By now Calderon was up and moving to help his guest.

Mary Frances backed away, confused and wondering what she'd seen. None of it made sense until she realized that it wasn't the original statue that had reappeared. Much more likely, it was an identical one, hidden behind the panel. A switch had been made, possibly a fake for the authentic artifact.

Calderon was a thief *and* a killer?

Mary Frances's impulse to escape was stronger than ever, but something made her hesitate. She chanced another look and saw the aide helping Cordes to his feet. The guest of honor seemed shaken but not injured and insisted that he was fine as Calderon offered to call for medical care. The woman was already on her feet, greatly subdued and quietly trying to put herself back together.

"There's a bathroom in my office," Calderon suggested.

"Thank you." She glanced at Cordes first and then at her host. She was clearly embarrassed, but Mary Frances caught a glimpse of something else in the woman's gaze as she left the room. Fear. Quivering instinctive fear.

Cordes shook his jacket free of its crimps and bunches, did the same with his slacks, and then raked his fingers through his dark hair. A quick, engaging smile seemed to complete the restoration process as he again reassured Calderon that he was fine. "One should choose assistants very carefully," he said.

Calderon agreed. "I just hired one myself. The breaking-in process is difficult." He indicated a settee and chairs by the door that led to his office. "Why don't you have a seat while I finish looking at the piece. It won't take me long."

Cordes's refusal was polite, but chilly. His smile had grown cold, too, though he tried to hide it with an expansive shrug. "The breaking-in process," he said, echoing Calderon. "Ah, yes, that can be painful. Isn't it unfortunate that Cherries doesn't provide clerical help as well as the rest of it. Their escorts are exquisitely trained."

The conversation had just taken an unexpected turn, Mary Frances realized. She detected a sudden wariness between the two men, and the tension mounted when Calderon didn't respond to the comment. Instead, he excused himself and returned to the worktable. The aide had already resumed his post near the far wall, flanking the table.

As Calderon continued his examination of the statue Cordes casually looked over various pieces of art, some of which were still in crates, others perched on easels. "Not like Celeste," he said, apparently referring to the training of escorts. "She was beyond compare."

Mary Frances barely registered Calderon's quiet "Yes." The shock of hearing her sister's assumed name had drowned him out. She leaned against the wall for support, trying not to make any noise and to concentrate on what else was being said.

Cordes's tone sounded vaguely accusatory as he approached the table. "Her death was a tragic waste, don't you agree?" he said. "I've decided to conduct my own private investigation. Someone should pay."

"Someone should." Calderon barely looked up. "The question is who."

"Indeed." Cordes's stare was piercing. A nerve twitched in his lip. Apparently he wanted to say a great deal more. Instead he inquired about the artifact. "What is it worth, do you think?"

"Nothing," Webb informed him evenly. "It's a fake."

"*What?* What the fuck are you saying?"

Mary Frances realized something as she watched these two powerful men. She was observing more than a clash of eyes; she was observing a clash of wills. Not only were there deep-rooted suspicions between them, but they'd just accused each other of her sister's death, and Mary Frances was virtually certain one of them was responsible. She even thought she knew which one.

It was no longer a question of escaping. There was something she had to do first. The switch of the artifacts had given her an idea. It was deceptively simple, yet the risk was staggering, almost beyond her comprehension. All she had to do now was beat Webb Calderon at his own game.

13

Torch songs, a parquet dance floor, and a sultry tenor sax, that was what Blue Brandenburg was in the mood for. God, but she wanted to slow-dance with a man and be crazy, out of her mind in love, even if only for one night. Love was a flood that could wash away all the other junk in its path, fears and failings and regrets. She wanted that, a baptism. She wanted to thrum with feeling and forget everything else but the pleasurable ache in her belly.

". . . zzzzttpffssssbbzzzzzztpfffft another hour of vintage Barry Manilow, the man and his musssspffftzzzff-sssppt—"

She flung out an arm, thumped the stuttering clock radio on its head, and put it out of its misery. She'd been lying in the dark for the last hour, trying to fall asleep, mainly because what else was there to do in a failed nun's apartment at ten o'clock at night? What she needed was body and soul, and all she could get out of the tinny contraption was static and mortuary music.

Mary Frances, where is your appreciation of the finer, funkier things in life, the stuff that feeds the fantasies of an entire nation of lovelorn losers? We can't exist on Campbell's soup, Ritz crackers, and clock radios! We don't unwind with Lipton's tea. We need a smoky cabaret, a bottle of Merlot, a tureen of bouillabaisse, and triple hits of Italian espresso, okay? You hearing this, Sister? The soul can't live on hope alone.

Bedsprings squeaked mournfully as she sat up and tugged at the flannel granny gown she'd found in Mary Frances's dresser. Hell, the mattress made better noise than the radio. Mary Frances was the nearest living equivalent to a religious martyr, she reminded herself. The woman had no appreciation of anything except self-sacrifice and disinfectant-based cleaning agents.

She sniffed the air and winced. Lysol. The apartment reeked of it. She was holed up in an emergency room.

Blue could remember things about Mary Frances no one would have believed. While the other kids were playing doctor and checking out each other's personals, she was doing "crafty" shit like crocheting sweaters and matching ankle socks in powder pastels. And that was just during recess. She was even more obnoxious in the classroom. She raised her hand, always placed in the spelling bees, and won awards for her cursive writing!

"That was our mistake," Blue mumbled, groping for the bedside lamp. "We let her live." The sudden burst of light made her wince again, but it also prompted her to sit up, clear her head, and take a sober look at her situation.

Things were not good. Someone was trying to kill her, she'd been forced to hide out in Gangland, U.S.A., which was arguably the most dangerous " 'hood" in the country, her friend and decoy had disappeared, and what was she, Blue Brandenburg, obsessing about? Slow dancing.

With him.

The pleasurable little ache inside her responded help-lessly at the mere thought of him. It rolled over and opened up like a kitten hoping to have its belly scratched. She was suddenly languid, needy, a melting, dripping ice-cream cone of need.

But torch music and a priest? Mufuh.

Get your butt up, Blue. Go watch reruns. Never mind that the TV set is a black-and-white Motorola with rab-bit ears that gets three channels on a clear day and emits a high-pitched whine that blocks the sound. Never mind all that. Reading lips will be a good distraction.

She gathered up the scratchy wool blanket and pillow that felt like it was stuffed with wood shavings, then grabbed the blue chenille spread for good measure, and dragged them all with her as she slid off the bed. She would need provisions for her trip to television land, which in this case was the living room.

"Ritz crackers," she murmured, snatching the box from the night table and adding it to her heap. "A must!"

As she scanned the bare-bones room for any other treasures it might yield, her eye skipped over tiny pil-lows, needlepointed with inspirational sayings, and hand-crocheted doilies. A Whistler's Mother rocker graced the corner and a bouquet of plastic dime-store posies bloomed on the dresser. This was exactly how Blue's own personal hell would be furnished.

"Why am I subjecting myself to this?" she wondered aloud, giving voice to the question that had been on her lips all day. She didn't just mean Mary Frances's apart-ment, although it was certainly included in the lament. She'd been in jeopardy of one kind or another from the moment she took up the investigation of Brianna's hit-and-run. She'd been followed and subjected to threats of violence and death. It was too late to back out now, but the real issue was why she'd ever begun.

A heavy sigh welled up as she struggled to get the chenille spread under control and make her way out of the bedroom. The answer was ringingly clear. *Brianna Murphy would be alive today if it weren't for her.*

Blue had cleverly managed to avoid taking responsibility for most of the unpleasantness in her life, probably as a defense against all the nastiness her mother had dumped on her. But the buck stopped with Blue in this case. She was the one who'd introduced Brianna to Cherries. She'd picked up some hot gossip about the tony escort service during a brief stint at the *L.A. Times* as a stringer for the arts and society pages.

The Brandenburgs had undergone a crippling financial reversal the year before when Blue's bank-chairman father was found guilty of defrauding the government and sent to federal prison. Unable to cope with the public humiliation, Sy Brandenburg had hanged himself in his cell and left his wife and only daughter with staggering bills, as well as the emotional devastation. Blue's liberal-arts education hadn't prepared her for the grim realities of making a living, but she had heard that an escort at this particular service could make several thousand a night.

Driven by equal parts desperation and curiosity, she coaxed Brianna into coming along to a meeting with the elderly man who owned and operated Cherries, a male Heidi Fleiss who happened to be a retired superior court judge. But when it actually came time for the first date, Blue chickened out. Brianna, it seemed, was the true adventuress. Not only did she take to "escorting" the rich

and famous, she called Blue frequently with stories of
her fabulous experiences.

Blue was actually envious, especially when Brianna
turned mysterious. Her friend said she'd fallen in love
with one of the service's clients and was going to be
married, but was secretive about the details. Blue didn't
hear from Brianna for over a month, and with the next
call, everything changed abruptly. Brianna had a date
that night with Webb Calderon, and was afraid for her
safety. She'd even asked Blue to notify the police if she
didn't check back within twenty-four hours.

The next day Blue was notified of Brianna's death,
and it was an unbelievable blow. It had been impossible
to overcome the guilt, and she still couldn't help but
think that Brianna would be alive now if she hadn't
been coaxed to that interview.

The memories made Blue grip tighter the lumpy
cargo she was carrying. That was the reason she was
stranded here in Mary Poppins land, waiting for word
from her decoy and watching the equivalent of test-pat-
tern television . . . all of which went violently against
her nature.

The marmalade tom was sitting on the breakfast bar,
industriously cleaning his private parts, when Blue staggered into the living room, loaded down with bedding.

"Faaaang," she moaned, "do you have to do that? I'm
trying to get my mind *off* men and sex!"

The cat glanced up at her with an expression that said,
*If you had the goods and could get to them, you'd be
doing it, too, babe*. She could have sworn he winked,
and then he immediately resumed his lewd efforts,
which could be heard throughout the room.

Moments later, apparently having completed his mission, the cat hopped on her lap and curled up content-

edly in the oceans of chenille she'd wrapped around her. She'd arranged herself on the couch, surrounded by vital supplies, to watch TV, and was glad for his company, until she began to stroke his head. He kneaded her thigh with his sharp little claws and purred like a drunken castanet player, in rattles and bursts and wheezy little snorts.

The house of horrible noises, she thought.

Some old issues of *Woman's World* magazine lay on the wicker occasional table next to the couch. Desperate for anything diverting, she picked one up and leafed through it, grimacing at the plethora of articles about baking cookies and toilet training toddlers. "Accck." She was about to put the magazine down when a pop-psychology quiz caught her eye. "'How sensitive are you?'" she murmured.

Absently scratching the cat's head, she skimmed the test, reading snatches of it aloud.

"Okay, Fangman, here you go. Let's see how sensitive you are. 'A coworker tells you your blouse isn't flattering. Would you: (a) Never wear it again, or (b) Put her comment in context? After all, she's not a fashion expert.'"

Blue didn't even have to think about it. "Neither, I'd fill out a change-of-address card and have her mail rerouted to Bosnia, but I suppose that's not the right answer."

Fang might have been smiling. Blue couldn't tell. She supposed his lack of interest had to do with the fact that he didn't wear blouses. At least he wasn't snoring.

She tried another one and snorted before she even had the question out. "'Have you ever taken a salesperson's mood personally?'" Blue's helpless gurgle of laughter failed to get Fang's attention, but she was having too much fun remembering the incident to care.

"Does spitting in her coffee when she's not looking count as taking it personally?"

By this time Fang had roused himself, but only enough to lick his paws indolently. The cat was a tough audience.

Undaunted, Blue searched the page, looking for her place and the next question. She found it, but almost wished she hadn't. " 'Have you ever felt sudden tenderness for someone?' " she asked him, hesitating as she read the answers. " '(a) Often, or (b) Seldom'?"

Seldom, she thought . . . until very recently.

Her throat tightened swiftly, oddly.

"Aw, pooh." She sighed with frustration and tossed the magazine. "These tests are rigged anyway." Settling back, she began to gently thumb and knuckle his muzzle. "You get around some, Fangman. What do you think? Is the priest completely immune to women, or is it just me?"

The cat closed his eyes and stuck out his chin, encouraging her to continue scratching. He had her trained already.

"Oh, what's the point?" she said, suddenly disgusted with herself and the whole idea. "He's a man of God, dedicated to saving souls and converting sinners. He's made a profession of being immune to women. He's supposed to be immune to them. If I had any sense, I'd leave him alone . . . but when did I ever, and God, he *is* the sexiest man of God I've ever seen. Is that redundant, Fang? I don't think he's happy at what he's doing, do you?"

Growling sounds of pleasure issued forth from Fang's throat. He probably couldn't hear her over the noise he

was making, but Blue was getting used to being ignored.

"So . . ." she went on, "if it's me he's immune to,
what do you think I'm doing wrong? Do I come on too
strong? Am I too outspoken? Am I threatening his male
ego? Do priests have those? Or did he check that at the
door, too? Along with his penis?"

She sighed and flopped back on the couch, miserable.
"I suppose it's because I'm not sensitive, right?"

The Fangman cocked his ear at that last reference.

Blue took it as a sign.

Taking a shower was a dangerous proposition for Rick
Caruso tonight, all that hot, steamy water sluicing over
him, the slickness of the soap as it floated over his torso,
and the subtle pressure of his own hands, scrubbing and
swirling.

His skin was so responsive he felt guilty touching
himself.

Was this what a woman would feel if she put her
hands on him? he wondered. A sierra of hot, slippery
flesh? Dark hair and hard contours, drenched by soft,
cascading bubbles. His biceps quivered and bunched as
he grazed the solid white bar over them, and before he
could banish the thought, he was imagining other muscles tightening and relaxing, rippling up and down his
body in a living stream. They lifted, strained to the
touch. A woman's touch.

Even the faint, flowery aroma of the soap smelled of
woman. What was it? Heather? Sage? He couldn't tell.
He'd never noticed it before. His senses were jumbled.
Pleasantly confused.

"It-shay!" The pig-latin word erupted softly as he realized that he had to get out of the shower and get out

fast. Things were happening. But even as he turned off
the water and stepped from the narrow stall, something
deep inside him coiled and kicked like a mule. It caught
him in the groin and flared to the pit of his stomach so
quickly he groaned aloud. He'd dealt with physical
arousal before, many times. There was a whole list of
things he could have done to bring his body under control, but this was different. He didn't want to bring it
under control. The pleasure was so quick and sharp, he
wanted to go with it for a moment, let it take him somewhere he hadn't been in a long time.

He was dripping all over the floor of the small alcove
that abutted his room and aware of his environment in
ways he'd never thought much about before. Steam
clung to the walls in patches and fogged the oval mirror
that hung over the basin. The sweaty blue tile floor was
so granite-hard and slippery it felt as if his feet might fly
out from under him at any moment.

Praise God, he was wet. Everything was wet. The
streaming water had already begun to bead on his body,
and now those droplets were hardening to ice. His nipples strained to be even harder than the russet stones
they already were, and he could feel the contours of his
lengthening penis as vibrantly as if this were the first
time he'd ever had a lustful thought.

No, he hadn't checked it at the door. *Too bad.*

He made a fist of his hand, then a radiant fan.

An aching tightness shot up his arm.

"Don't go there," he bit out, and reached for a towel.
"You won't get back alive." The church was very explicit about that particular sin of the flesh. He remembered being taught in the seminary that the term for it
came from *manus* and *turbatio,* Latin roots meaning
"hand" and "agitation," and that it was a mortal sin.

But it wasn't the fear of sin that had stopped him, then or now. He'd never believed true faith came through fear. That was coerced faith, believing because you were afraid not to. But there had been times when he'd felt his body was a battleground between the flesh and the spirit. He'd won the battles—most of them anyway—because he'd wanted to believe there were things stronger than physical urges. He'd prayed about that on more than one occasion, and each time whichever saints heard the earthbound fumblings of priests had granted him the grace to prevail. He would prevail again.

The pangs of celibacy are a little crucifixion.

Remembering the words of St. John Chrysostom, he concentrated on getting himself dry. It didn't take him long. A few brisk swipes of the terry towel, a hacksaw motion across his back, and a couple of whisks and whacks down his legs finished the job off.

He had a bath sheet wrapped around his waist and was toweling his hair moments later when he realized he wasn't alone in the room. Someone was watching him. He saw her reflection through the steam on the mirror. Blue Brandenburg was standing in the doorway he hadn't thought to close, and he wondered how long she'd been there. Had she seen him before? Naked?

Our Lady was an old church, and the rectory, where the priests resided, was housed in a missionlike building that was attached to the church itself. The office, kitchen, and dining area were downstairs and the sleeping quarters upstairs. Spare and simple, the bedrooms were organized like monastery cells.

At the moment his visitor was surveying the alcove that housed his toilet and basin, the severe iron bedstead and large wooden cross that hung on the wall above it, with an air of rapt disbelief. "Is this your room?" she asked, clearly struggling with the idea.

He tossed the wet towel aside, though he hadn't finished with his hair. "It's where I sleep and shower. It's all I need."

"Is it?" Her voice was husky and dry, as if she were coming down with a cold. Her long shaggy cut was all over the place. It looked hastily pinned up, with blond wisps flying this way and that. She was wearing the cut-off jeans he'd begun to think she slept in and a little white cardigan that he vaguely remembered as Mary Frances's. It was an incongruous combination, the sex-kitten jeans and the convent-school sweater, especially the way she had the thing buttoned, or should he say *un-buttoned.* He'd never seen anything more seductive. Despite his resolutions of a few moments before, it made his mouth go papery.

"All you need," she echoed, apparently not convinced that anyone's needs could be met in such humble surroundings. She'd finished her inspection of the room and now she was studying him with a force in her eyes that felt hard and soft all at once, as if she not only knew what he needed, but just happened to have brought some of it along with her. Her gray-flecked gaze was very blue, and she seemed less scattered than usual. He imagined her having gathered all her nervous energy into a ball and focused it on him.

He thought of a line from the Bible about a man having nothing, yet possessing all things, but didn't say it. Too preachy, he decided. Besides, she would have known it was subterfuge.

"What are you doing here?" he asked. "It's after eleven." Mariana must have left the rectory door unlocked. She often did things like that lately, probably because of her other concerns.

He hadn't meant his question to be an invitation to enter, but Blue did anyway. "I wanted to apologize for interfering," she explained as she slipped gracefully into the room and drew the door shut behind her. "With Mariana," she added when he didn't respond. "I hope I didn't cause problems."

She leaned against the closed door, gazing at him in a way that made his chest feel heavy with expectation. Her eyes brushed the dark hair feathering his pectorals and the bulge in his biceps with more than a little interest. He resisted the urge to cross his arms, but it was a powerful thing. Still, her lingering glance wasn't as seductive as it was challenging, he decided, the kind of look a civilian male knew meant action, *if* he played his cards right.

The room floated with a hazy glow, lit only by his bedside reading lamp and her sensual wattage. Steam from the shower had saturated the air with the lingering scent of sage and heather.

"Mariana will be fine," he assured her, uncomfortable with how patronizing he sounded. "I have every reason to believe things will work out between her and her husband. They're good people in a tough situation."

His hair was still wet and tendrils clung to his face. The sticky dampness was driving him nuts. He combed it back with an angry sweep of his fingers and then checked the knot in his towel. Busy hands, he thought. Keep them busy. His favorite carnival ride as a kid had been the Tilt-A-Whirl. It still was, but that didn't mean he wanted to live his life with his stomach in his throat. He had no ready resources for dealing with her. None of the strategies that kept his stomach where it belonged seemed to work. And for that reason alone he wanted her out of his sight. He wanted the door open and her gone.

"You do? Every reason to believe? I'm glad to hear it." Her cocked head said she enjoyed a challenge wherever she found one, and that she had gone out of her way to find this one. It also said she was no respecter of custom or convention, and the fact that he wore robes or a collar on occasion did not give him special dispensation in her book.

To be fair he'd never been big on custom either. He'd always believed you had to earn your right to wear the collar and vestments, which was why he hadn't been wearing his lately, why he'd been questioning everything about his religious calling.

"You didn't come all this way to talk about Mariana, did you?" His tone was firm, almost stern, and she seemed a little taken aback by it, which was exactly what he wanted.

A hangnail had caught her attention. She ran her thumb over it, examining her manicure at some length.

He couldn't tell whether this was part of the act or she was actually flustered. Either way he persisted. "It was concern about my housekeeper that brought you here at this time of night?"

She colored slightly. "Well, no, actually . . . I came for—"

"No need to explain." Suddenly he didn't want to hear what he'd pushed her to say. Maybe she was actually flustered, which meant his performance wouldn't win any medals for sensitivity. But that had never been an option with her anyway. He was far too susceptible himself to give her the benefit of the doubt. He just wanted her gone. Now. While he was still ahead.

He started toward the door, thinking to open it and usher her out, then made the mistake of hesitating. He stared at her just long enough to be hit by a wall of sudden and surprising force. Their eyes locked and that Tilt-A-Whirl he'd loved as a kid picked him up and spun him around. Hard. He was having trouble getting enough air, and the startled gaze on her face told him she'd felt it, too.

"There's something I need to know," she said.

He stopped her with a shake of his head, certain he'd already figured out what was coming. "Let's see if I can make this quick and painless for both of us, okay? No, I'm not a virgin. Yes, I have been with a woman. Yes, I'm attracted to you, and no, I'm not going to do anything about it."

"I'm flattered . . . I think. But that wasn't what I wanted to know."

Now her face was flushed with laughter, but it was his turn to be flustered. "No? Then what?"

Her gaze dropped to the floor, and she looked like a reluctant child all of a sudden, with her shifting feet and her intense preoccupation with a certain cracked tile. Her fingers had discovered a tendril of blond hair and yanked it toward her mouth. He found it all oddly charming and wondered if he was wrong about her. Maybe she *was* looking for a father figure—and maybe he was losing his mind along with his faith.

Finally she lifted her head. "Am I sensitive?"

"I beg your pardon?"

"Me. Sensitive. Do you find me sensitive?"

This was not what he expected, not in his wildest, and yet he could see that it wasn't a frivolous question. He couldn't have lied to her anyway, he realized, even if he hadn't recognized the vulnerability she'd risked to ask.

"Yeah, I do, actually," he admitted.

"Really?" Wariness made her look up. Surprise made her gaze at him as if she wanted to hear more.

This was important to her, important enough that Rick knew he had to find some way to explain what he meant. "You're sensitive," he assured her with total sincerity, "very sensitive. Probably more than most. You don't wear it on your sleeve, but it's there, inside. In fact, maybe it's because I skipped dessert tonight, but sometimes you remind me of a peach."

She made a face. "A peach?"

"Yeah, a peach—fuzzy and thick-skinned and pretty much inedible on the outside, but the inside's another story."

"Another story?"

She really was going to make him say it. "Sure . . . you know, sweet, juicy, tender. Very tender." He had to stop and clear his throat of the huskiness. "Worth every bit of the trouble to peel it."

There was a flash of yearning in her eyes before she ruthlessly cut it off. "No need to be sarcastic," she snapped. "If we're going to resort to fruit analogies, I'm more like a pomegranate than a peach—sour enough to make people wince and full of seeds they have to spit out."

"Hey, I wasn't being sarcastic," he insisted. "Believe me, I wasn't. I'd bet the rent you're tender. One careless touch and you bruise, am I right? Just like a peach, a pink fuzzy-wuzzy peach . . . ?"

He was trying hard to make her laugh, risking foolishness. Instead she went quiet and looked away, a child again. He could see the sadness in her so clearly now, and it struck straight at his heart. Someone had hurt her—some asshole boyfriend, probably—and he found himself wanting to shake the guy's teeth loose.

In a voice he had to concentrate to keep even, he said, "Someone's done a number on you, haven't they? Someone has hurt you badly."

The faintest little moan imaginable came out of her. "Everyone's had a number done on them, probably even you."

His hunch was right. The brashness was an act to get attention. But it wasn't what she wanted. It sprang from pain. All of it sprang from pain. Her sarcasm and defensiveness, her sexy come-ons. She did it to protect the tenderness he'd just described. He'd probably always sensed that about her, but it was obvious now. She wore her heart on her sleeve, and God help him, he didn't know what to do with it. He wanted her to leave. *Needed* her to leave, but it wasn't in him to be that selfish. She needed something, too, a compassion he felt barely capable of giving her under the circumstances. But he had to try.

"Blue—" Saying her name was another struggle, an effort that made his throat ache with the need to be gentle. He could feel something tugging at him, yanking him in two different directions as he walked to her.

"Don't be such a priest," she said. "I hate pity."

"This isn't pity, it's compassion."

"I hate that, too. It's not what I want from you."

He was afraid to ask. He didn't *have* to ask.

"Blue—"

She looked up suddenly, defying him to be kind and fearlessly meeting his stare. Her eyes glittered with some wild, reckless emotion. "You've been touched that way, too, haven't you?" she said. "Carelessly? Like this?"

She stroked his face, feathering the line of his jaw. He had the feeling she was holding her breath. He knew he was. And then, as if expecting him to stop her, she brushed her fingers lightly over his lips. Desire made him convulse. Her touch was light and silky, the way he'd always thought the air in paradise would be. Her expression was bold, but he could feel her trembling as she stroked his mouth.

It slammed into him again, that savage kick to the pit of his stomach. "Don't," he said, grabbing her wrist.

The hurt dancing in her eyes made him ache in ways he'd hoped never to ache again. This wasn't about sex, it was about need. Her need. His own. It was pure, unadulterated male longing to be with a woman, to find the solace his starved flesh needed within her. He'd forgotten how powerful the bodily hungers could be. He'd willed them into oblivion, but they all flared inside him now. Lust, wanting, longing. He saw them mirrored in her gaze, everything he felt, everything he'd denied himself, and he knew what was missing, why he had been so at odds with himself. This was it. This was what he needed.

"Jesus," he uttered, but it was prayer more than profanity. He was asking for help. Disbelief threatened to choke him. Frustration welled that he could feel these things, that she could make him feel these things with such perfect clarity.

"Oh, my God." She breathed the words as if the sharp longing pouring through him had just engulfed her. And then more softly. "Oh, my God."

His grip tightened on her wrist until he knew it must be painful. He told himself he was gathering the strength to push her away, but instead he let out a shaky breath and pulled her closer. "Blue—"

A whimper caught in her throat and the sound of it nearly destroyed him. He was lost now. He knew that. With his fingertips, he touched her face, her lips, the way she had his. The need that welled inside him was uncontrollable, yet somehow he held her off, held himself off and thrust her away.

"Leave," he rasped. "Go now. Get out of here!" There was anger in his voice. Contempt. He could hear it, but it was contempt for himself. Not her.

She stepped back, stricken. Her eyes blinked with the threat of tears and her composure crumbled. "You wanted this, too," she whispered. "You did."

He did. He had. In his mind he could see himself kissing all the places he'd touched, sweetly, desperately, greedily. He could see her melting into his arms with a throaty gasp of surprise, her body limp and compliant, her mouth softened and yielding. He could see the fires of hell consuming him as for one transcendent moment he blindly found her lips and gave himself to the kiss.

"Jesus, please!" he groaned again, nearly convulsing this time. "Get out of here!" An unreasoning rage rose up inside him that kept him from saying the things he needed to say. All he could do was try to drive her out of his room, out of his life, before he lost control completely.

He turned away from her and fought the impulse to slam a fist into the stucco wall. "This isn't about my body," he told her. "It's about my soul. Wretched as it is, I offered it to God in exchange for the life I took. If you want a piece of it, you'll have to bargain with Him."

He heard her gasp and knew in the dim recesses of his rational mind that he had hurt her unforgivably, hurt her the way that other asshole had, the one who turned her into a cold, sarcastic tease.

He had to tell her he was sorry. He wanted to, but he couldn't find the words. And when he did turn, when the words were finally there—*I'm sorry, Blue, this is not about you, it's about me*—it was too late. She was gone.

14

Her calm felt unnatural. Neither her religious indoctrination nor her nurse's training could explain the silence that had taken hold of Mary Frances. It felt as if the master switch on her nervous system had been pulled and all the circuits turned off. In one way it made her feel strangely invincible, yet a part of her couldn't believe what she was about to do. Not a year out of the convent, and she was trying to bring down a criminal mastermind with the equivalent of a banana peel. Even the guy who hosted *Unsolved Mysteries* wouldn't have believed this. What was his name?

A sharp breath burned the question from her mind.

Her plan was wildly risky, but she was going through with it anyway. She'd laid out the bait where he couldn't fail to see it, then had slipped back into her nightgown, drawn the severed halves together and arranged herself on the brass daybed as if she'd never moved from the spot where Webb Calderon had left her. The handcuff was looped around her wrist but not locked, and she'd mussed up the bedspread, tenting it around her arm to hide what she'd done. Otherwise, she was resting against the pillows like one of Bluebeard's captive brides, awaiting a visit.

She was ready for him, as ready as she would ever be.

What she had in mind would take split-second timing. If Calderon hesitated or became suspicious, she was lost. And if he figured out what she was up to, she was dead. He would show no mercy, she was certain of that much. But she had to follow through for the sole reason that she might never get this chance again. It could be the only opportunity she would ever have to get at the truth of her sister's death.

Fortunately, Alejandro Cordes had long since left the party in his honor. She'd heard him storm from the house, probably still insisting his statue was a priceless artifact and a national treasure. The last guests were gone also, which meant Webb Calderon could return to the room at any time.

The bedroom door was locked from the outside, exactly as he'd left it. She'd discovered another door in the sitting room that connected to an adjoining guest room, and she'd used that for her earlier trip downstairs. It had seemed odd to her at the time that he'd neglected to lock it. A man like Calderon didn't miss things like second doors and loose bed rails. She'd wondered if it was part of another plan to trap her, but there was no way to know. Everything hinged on what happened when he entered the room. This room.

She had tried to plan for every possible contingency. There was only one other thing she had to remember to do now. Breathe.

And pray, she told herself.

Hail Marys. She touched the saint's medal at her breast and chanted them swiftly, mouthing the words silently

and losing count of how many. Prayers. Words. Moments. They all blurred together. She stopped only when
a noise alerted her that someone was at the door.

The room was dark. She'd left it that way so she could
watch what was happening without being seen. She held
the medal tightly and grew perfectly still, listening to the
soft slide and click of a metal cylinder. The key turned in
the lock and the knob slowly rotated until it clicked
again.

Hail, Mary, full of grace . . .

The words shivered like silvery chimes and went
silent.

Everything seemed to freeze as the door inched open,
even her thoughts. She closed her eyes, pretending to be
asleep, and heard the creaky sounds of someone tiptoeing
into the room. Common sense told her it could not be
Calderon. He would not tiptoe.

The creaking stopped and something touched her bare
foot.

Mary Frances relaxed her grip on the medal, only just
aware that she still held it. She was trying to stay calm, to
breathe as evenly as if she were asleep. But it was almost
impossible when she felt the phantom sensations of touch
climb higher. The intruder was now fingering the gold
chain around her ankle. And then the creaking started
again and the person seemed to be turning away from the
bed.

It wasn't Calderon. It was his housekeeper. Through
lowered lashes, Mary Frances watched the young woman
hesitate. She'd noticed an object lying on the carpet, and
she was kneeling to look at it.

Wild fear ripped through Mary Frances's heart. The
housekeeper was reaching for the antique scimitar that

lay exactly where Mary Frances had left it. The Serpent's Eye, Calderon's knife. Don't touch it!

The handcuff rasped as Mary Frances pressed back against the pillow. *Oh, please God, if you can hear my prayers, if you've ever heard them, don't let her touch the knife.*

"Traci?" It was Calderon's voice. His tone was soft, yet deadly, like the hiss of escaping gas. "What are you doing in here?"

The housekeeper jerked back and sprang to her feet. "I was walking by, Mr. Calderon. I thought I heard our houseguest call. I'm sorry, I really thought I heard her."

"She's asleep," Calderon said, his tone still chillingly calm as he glanced at Mary Frances. "How could she have called you?" He opened the door and made way for the housekeeper to leave. "Go to your room and stay there. We'll discuss this when I've finished here."

Any semblance of inner calm had vanished. Mary Frances was numb with dread as she watched Calderon usher the woman out and close the door behind her. She herself had pulled the dagger from its sheath and left both pieces on the floor, hoping he would wonder how they got that way and go straight to them and pick them up. But the odds of his hesitating and becoming suspicious had risen astronomically with the delay of dealing with the housekeeper.

A seagull's cry pierced her thoughts. The sharpness of it made her realize he'd opened the balcony doors. The breezes were laden with moisture, with salt and the pungent seaweedy smells of low tide. In another situation it might have calmed her. She'd always loved the smell of the sea in ebb, but tonight it was strong enough to sear the nostrils.

He moved soundlessly. It wasn't easy to track him as

he turned away from the open doors. He hesitated by the knife and she could hardly find the strength to breathe as he glanced up at her. Did he already know what she'd done?

She went as still as death as he knelt for a closer look. It felt as if her vital functions had come to a halt, as if even the blood in her veins had ceased flowing. Silently she watched him examine the case, apparently checking to see if the emerald eye had been tampered with. He picked up the dagger next and fingered the gems on its handle, then slid the blade into its macabre case. When it wouldn't completely sheathe, he hesitated and glanced up at her.

The point of the blade seemed to have penetrated something and stuck. He settled heavily on both knees, but wasn't able to free the thing. Suddenly his eyelids fluttered and he tilted dizzily.

Holy Mary, Mother of God— That was as far as Mary Frances got with her plea. Her conflict was so great at that moment, she wasn't at all sure what she was asking for.

The knife and case slipped from his fingers, and he looked up at her, his eyes narrowing to slashes. His breath had begun to rasp. She could hear it, but by then it was too late. Within mere seconds, he slumped to the floor, unconscious.

She pulled free of the cuff and rose from the bed, gathering her nightgown together as she cautiously approached him. She wanted to check his vital signs to make certain that he hadn't gotten too much of the Zin Quai, but she was still wary of traps.

The Chinese herb was a liquid solution that could be absorbed through the skin even after it had dried, and she had coated the sheath and dagger handle with it thoroughly to make sure he got enough to knock him out, even if he only handled them briefly. But there was nothing in her nurse's training that dealt with such exotic substances, and she had no idea of the drug's potency or absorption rate.

His hand was warm in hers as she picked it up, but she couldn't detect a pulse. She pressed harder, her fingertips turning white against the skin of his wrist as she scrutinized him for other signs. He didn't seem to be breathing. She held her fingers to the carotid artery in his neck and felt no response there either. Her mouth went dry with fear as she realized what that meant. No, this wasn't possible, she told herself. He couldn't have absorbed enough to kill him in only a few seconds, could he? His heart couldn't have stopped.

In the next moments she tried everything she could think of to bring him back. She had been trained in Basic Life Support, and though she had never had to use the emergency procedures to revive anyone, she went through them now automatically, numbly. The poison had been introduced through his bloodstream, so there was no need to induce vomiting. Artificial respiration was the first step, and if that failed, mouth-to-mouth.

Some frozen part of her seemed to step back and watch, astonished and gratified at how efficient she was. When the deep, rhythmic pressure of her palms on his chest didn't produce a response, she moved fluidly into the next phase. She bent his head back so that his tongue didn't block his throat and placed her mouth over his, blowing the oxygen heated by her own lungs into his in a steady forceful respiration, breathing her own life into him.

Breathe, she thought, gripping his face as she ministered to his body. Take my breath and use it. Breathe with me, *please*. Breathe *for* me! I don't know how else to save you. Dear God, I would give my own life to save you. Please, Webb, please.

She found herself caressing his face with her fingers, silently murmuring his name and gently beseeching him as she alternately forced air though his lips and drew back to check him for signs of respiration. But there was still no response. His head lolled back when she released him, and his neck muscles were slack in the cradle of her palm.

She was losing him. Perhaps she already had lost him.

No! Tears blurred her eyes and her neck muscles gripped. She was nearly immobilized with fear and remorse, but she went immediately to a closed heart massage, placing her hands midsternum and pressing down sharply on his chest to compress his heart. She did it once every second. She did it with a passion and fervor she hadn't felt since her earliest days in the convent, when she had believed she could save the world with faith alone.

Now all she wanted was to save him. Please, oh, *please.*

When she stopped the massage to check his pulse, he sighed once, deeply, a breath that lifted his sprawled body as if it were his last, and then he settled into a stillness that filled her heart with horror. He had no pulse. He wasn't breathing. This was clinical death. She had to take action immediately, drastic action, or even if they could revive him, he would be irreparably brain-damaged. She needed an ambulance, the paramedics, but she couldn't call for help. The hospital they took him to would do tests. They would discover the poison, and there would be a police investigation.

Her mind raced frantically until she remembered the service. Cherries! She would make contact with them,

tell them what had happened. They were the ones who
had told her to use the Zin Quai. They would know what
to do.

It took her several precious seconds to connect. *I can't
get a pulse!* she typed in. *I gave Calderon the Zin Quai
and his heart has stopped.*

The response was immediate and emphatic. "Leave the
premises NOW. Leave the way you were told and don't
speak to anyone, especially the police. We'll take care of
it." The message was signed by Wink, and a postscript
told Mary Frances to return to her apartment and await
further instructions.

But Mary Frances couldn't do it. She couldn't make
herself go, not with Webb Calderon's lifeless body on the
floor. She tried again to revive him. She went through
each procedure like an automaton, knowing full well that
it was hopeless, and when he didn't respond to her desperate efforts, and she was finally forced to admit there
was nothing left she could do, she bent over him and gave
way to her anguish. A horrible sound slipped out of her.
"Don't die. You *can't* die."

But he was dead and she had killed him. That was beyond her understanding. She simply couldn't grasp it, especially this man, who had seemed to exist outside the
mortal coil, beyond the reach of the frailties that preyed
on the rest of the race. Webb Calderon was invulnerable,
wasn't he? He couldn't be hurt or killed. He didn't even
feel pain.

When Mary Frances entered the cloister, she'd dedicated her life to healing the spirit. When she began
nurse's training, she'd dedicated herself to healing physical ills. And now she had taken a life? No, that couldn't
be. That was impossible. There was nothing in her experience past or present that could have prepared her for

something like this. She didn't take lives. She saved them. How would she ever make this right?

Finally, silent and drained by the ordeal, she sat alongside him for what seemed like hours. It was probably closer to moments, but whatever the time, she couldn't rouse herself to leave. Her body was as leaden and confused as her heart. The bond she felt with this man defied understanding. It was the darkest of ironies that she should feel these things, that she should feel *anything* for him, and yet she had from the very first. It was entirely possible that Webb Calderon had her sister killed. What *didn't* seem possible was that she could be mourning him when she couldn't mourn Brianna at all . . . but she was. She was.

The sea filled the room with its dark sounds and smells. Primordial, eternal, rank. Its heavy waves and lonely cries spoke of life and death tonight, and she could find no comfort there, or in anything that would normally have sustained her.

"Agnus dei, qui tollis peccata mundi, miserere," she recited, imbuing the plea with her sadness. "He who takes away the sins of the world, have mercy."

As she said the words she unclasped the St. Rita's medal and removed it from around her neck. His hands had fallen to his sides. She took the one that was scarred and placed her precious necklace there, in his palm, and then she pressed his fingers shut.

Her tears blurred the harsh beauty of his features.

"No," she whispered brokenly, *"no."*

Nothing could make it easier, not even the realization that he looked peaceful and serene in repose. At least death had given him that, she told herself. It had freed him of his demons, but it was small consolation. If her tears could have cleansed him, he would be free of the poison, too. If her pain could have saved him, he would be breathing now.

She still couldn't believe that he was gone. Any minute he would open his eyes and speak to her in his hushed cathedral voice. He had to. No man had ever said that she was all he would know of innocence. No man had ever looked at her the way he did, as if she were the most dangerously erotic creature he'd ever seen.

She had never considered herself dangerous in any way, but Webb Calderon had seen her as a threat to his very existence, and he had been right. She had been the one to stop him from whatever it was he was trying to do—and would ever do—but she'd never meant this to happen. Her plan had been to steal the real artifact and use it to barter with Cordes for information about her sister. Now she had to follow through. She had to know whether or not Webb was responsible for Brianna's death. It was the only way she'd ever have any peace.

In the dead of night, as Webb Calderon lay sprawled on the floor of the guest room, the fax phone began to ring in his office downstairs. There was no one in the house to receive the transmission, but the machine had a dedicated line, operational twenty-four hours a day. After four short bursts, it began to print.

The dateline indicated the fax was coming in from the Central American republic of San Carlos and the letter-head had the official government emblem in the left upper corner. The body of the transmission was encoded in language that only a trained cryptographer could understand, but the last two lines were in English.

I am surrounded by thieves and traitors. There is no

one I can trust in this gravest of matters but you. I await
further instructions.

It was not signed and the address box indicated the
sender by a code name only: *El Chacal*.

"You're the asshole, Caruso. She's not the one who took
the vows of celibacy, you are. She was just doing what
comes naturally."

Alone in the cramped office of the rectory, Rick
stood with his back to the door and his bare feet planted
solidly on the scarred wooden floor. As he faced the
cluttered desk he wanted to send everything on it flying, clear the unholy mess with one violent sweep of
his arm. He might have done it if he'd thought it would
help. But no matter what he said or did, he couldn't
quiet the rage he felt.

His Bible lay open to the passages he'd sought when
he'd been trying to find the words that would resolve his
turmoil. The computer screen burgeoned with kaleido-
scopic images of some asinine video game that had failed
utterly to distract him.

"A misstep," he said emphatically, "that's all it was. It
proves you're human." He *was* human. He was entitled
to a mistake now and then, even one with a woman. It
didn't mean he couldn't confess the sin, do whatever was
necessary to atone, and go back to his work with re-
newed fervor and dedication. It didn't mean he couldn't
go back to his life and to this parish, where so many people depended on him.

"There is nothing you can't overcome," he said,
echoing the words of advice he had so often given others. "Believing is the miracle. Anyone can start over,
start clean."

He sucked in a hard breath, determined to smother the last little flutter of sexual longing from his gut, to quash it with whatever means he had available to him. "A little faith, brother," he said, half groan, half threat. "You can do it. You *can*."

But the moan of despair in his chest told him otherwise. Some perverse fantasy had taken possession of his mind and his will. The images assailing his thoughts were even more passionate than what had happened between him and Blue, if that was possible. They started where he'd stopped, at the point where he'd told her to leave, only in his mind, he'd caught her at the door and they had done everything his body longed to do and more. There was no carnal desire they didn't indulge in, no act too forbidden. Their hunger for each other had been insatiable, their need as pure and cauterizing as fire.

He threw back his head, strangling the wild sound in his throat. His body *was* a battleground, and the war was going to destroy him. It was destroying him even now, and yet his lips still ached with the taste of her. He wanted her badly, more than anything, even more than he wanted to fulfill his vows. He *was* lost.

The violence he'd fought down flared out of control and he caught the desk by the edge and upended it. Papers sailed and glass shattered. A container of sharpened pencils flew like a quiver of arrows. Metal file boxes skated across the vertical surface and collided with the floor.

It should have been enough, this roaring act of mayhem, but it wasn't. There were plaques and pictures on the wall, each a proud, gleaming symbol of his deep commitment, each a part of his life, a piece of his heart.

He pulled them off the wall and smashed them one at a time. And when it was done, when the destruction was complete, he sank into the rubble of his own life, and wept.

15

Alejandro Cordes had the face of an angel and the soul of a B-movie monster. Irresistibly drawn by his dark good looks and charm, women saw only the bait and not the trap. His prowess was legendary. He was known as deadly in bed, the kind of man who ensnared women by introducing them to their own forbidden desires and needs. And though he wasn't averse to using whores for convenience, he preferred women of some virtue. His satisfaction came from making them love the pleasures they'd been taught to hate, carnal delights they associated with shame and degradation. He violated their natural boundaries and left them in breathless chaos, but by then it was too late. One taste of his powers and a woman no longer owned her own soul, or so it was said.

It was a further testament to Cordes's charisma that his perverse sexuality hadn't tarnished his social luster. He'd neatly avoided the bad press that followed his notorious dictator father by making sure it was widely known that he opposed his father on issues of civil liberties, workers' rights, and political reform—a liberal stance that made Alex not only politically correct but socially desirable.

He'd been linked in the tabloids with Hollywood A-list actresses and international supermodels. He routinely escorted socialites to charity functions and had more invitations to dinner parties than he could reasonably accept. Normally only the rich and infamous had access to Alex, but today was different. This morning he'd received an unexpected visitor in the library of his sumptuous suite at the Biltmore, and he was intrigued. Yes, her resourcefulness had intrigued him.

For one thing she was claiming to have killed Webb Calderon.

"It was a lethal overdose," she said, her hands clasped prayerlike over the red leather satchel in her lap. "A Chinese herb called Zin Quai . . . I only meant to induce unconsciousness."

Alex didn't know quite what to make of the situation. She'd seated herself in the fan-back chair nearest the door, and he recognized the case she held as Cherries paraphernalia, but he didn't recognize the woman, if he could even call her that. The black miniskirt, cropped jacket, and spiky heels she wore were cut to be sexy, but she looked more like somebody's kid sister who'd raided the closet.

The freckles dappling her nose like Scotch kisses made her skin appear luminously pale. Her eyes were the soft dark green of rain-forest ferns, the lush foliage of his own country, but their focus was surprisingly fierce, all of which conspired to give her the appearance of a child on a dangerous mission.

He couldn't imagine her killing an insect, much less a cold-blooded bastard like Calderon. Still, he was glad he'd sent both his aide and assistant out of the room. He wanted to be able to talk freely. The aide-de-camp was young, officious, and a Princeton MBA, none of which damned Luis Perez as much as Alex's suspicion that he had been sent along on the "art-buying trip" by Alex's father for the sole purpose of spying on Alex. At least the aide had proved to be meticulously well organized, an important consideration since he was guardian of the itinerary and social schedule for the entire U.S. trip.

Carmen had no such excuse. His assistant was twenty-five, slender, and a passionate, petulant Argentinean. She'd been hired to do whatever needed doing, including him, but she'd begun to take her duties too seriously. Lately, she'd become possessive and insecure, always fishing for compliments about her looks and seeking reassurance. The scene at Calderon's party was a perfect example, although to be fair, she was not entirely to blame for that debacle.

Still, Alex had little patience with such nonsense. It smacked of groveling and that reminded him of his early relationship with his father, and how he, Alex, had been forced to grovel. It might have been an unforgivable sin if Carmen hadn't been very good at what she did.

Would this one become possessive once she'd opened her legs for a man? he wondered, studying the severity with which his guest had forced her lush dark hair off her face and restrained it with a jade hairband that paled in comparison to her eyes. The drawn look to her features made him think of a beautiful young mourner at a funeral. Still, he sensed passion locked in her slim, stiff posture. Passion waiting to be freed.

"It was self-defense," she was telling him. She seemed to sense his skepticism. "Calderon accused me of breaking into his locked computer files and trying to steal confidential information. He drugged me with truth serum."

She brought her fingers to her throat, clearly expecting to find something there.

"And were you trying to steal information?"

"He killed my sister. I was looking for proof."

Her bluntness startled him. He couldn't tell if it was nerves or the lack of them, but perhaps he'd been too quick to presume her innocence. Looks could be deceiving, and there was that strange physical thrust to her eyes. "Did you find proof?" he asked.

"No, that's why I'm here." She'd already reclasped her hands and settled them on the case, tautly, as if they might spring back if she didn't. "My sister was Brianna Murphy. You knew her as Celeste."

Alex had been standing behind the desk by the window. Now he had to sit down. The floor was rolling beneath him, and he didn't want her to see how unsteady he was. This was Celeste's sister? He hadn't noticed the resemblance at first, but now that he looked—

Celeste's coloring had been very different. She was blond, blue-eyed, and perhaps more statuesque than delicate, or at least that's how she'd looked when she was with him. The Cherries escorts adopted different looks with different clients. But this one's features were similar to Celeste's, he had to admit, and they might look strikingly alike if she were dressed and made up like her sister. Celeste had had that same direct, forthright quality about her, too. Unfortunately, too much so for her own good. In Celeste, it had surfaced as bitchiness and defiance.

"You believe Webb Calderon killed her?" He sank into the leather swivel chair and dropped back, glad of its heaviness and solidity.

"Yes," she said earnestly, "and so do you. You as much as said so last night when you were in his workroom."

"Jesucristo—" The epithet exploded softly from his lips. If she'd been listening, then what else had she heard or seen? He reminded himself that she'd already given him enough rope to hang her. If she'd been telling the truth about Calderon, one call to the police would put her behind bars.

"I said I was having her death *investigated.* If you were there, then you know that."

Her quick nod barely acknowledged his comment. "Calderon was the last person with my sister the night she died. Who else could have done it?"

Interesting that she seemed to want him to confirm her suspicion that Calderon was the guilty party. Actually, the threat of investigation had been a way to jerk Calderon around a little and keep him off balance. Celeste's death had provided Alex with some unexpected leverage in his dealings with Calderon, a way to level the playing field. But his visitor didn't need to know that. Nor did she need to know that she'd blundered into the electronics espionage plot of the century. With Calderon dead, she would never know that the transaction had been anything more than a simple art deal.

Alex smiled, relaxing. He liked women, and he particularly liked this one. She was proving to be even more interesting than her sister. "Can I get you something?" he asked, absently wondering if her radiant gaze was going to burn right through him. "A drink? Coffee?"

"Calderon switched the statues on you," she announced with quiet intensity. "I know where the real one is."

"He *switched* the statues? How do you know that?"

"I was in the hallway. I saw it happen. He has a false panel in his worktable."

Alex sat forward, unable to stop himself. "Do you have

any idea what you're saying? That 'real' statue is a price-less Maya figurine."

She glanced down at her clasped hands and grew quiet, looking for all the world like a religious martyr taking comfort in her own unshakable faith. "I thought it might be valuable," she admitted. "That's why I'm here."

"And you know where it is now?"

"Yes, I have it. Not on me, of course. I left it some-where . . . safe."

A strange calm came over Alex as he realized he might be dealing with a worthy adversary. Either she didn't un-derstand that she'd yanked the sleeping lion's tail, or she knew and had done so deliberately. But even if her reso-lution came from naïveté, it was still impressive. "And you've come here to exchange it for something, am I right?" he asked. "What do you want? Money?"

"Information."

"About your sister?"

"Yes, about Celeste. I want to know who killed her and why."

"You already know." He rose from the chair and moved deeper into the room, not to confront her, simply to throw her off balance and scatter her forces, if that could be done. "Calderon was an art thief," he said. "You saw him steal the figurine with your own eyes. What did you say your sister's real name was? Brianna? She caught him in the act, too, only she wasn't as quick as you. He got to her first and silenced her. Permanently."

Her hands went pale first. Clasped tightly, they seemed to lose all their blood, and then the ashen quality crept up her face. "It was him? You're sure?"

"He sexually tortured your sister, and she wasn't the only one. He had an entire camera de tortura in the cellar of his hacienda. Talk to the other escorts if you like. They'll be happy to tell you how sick he is . . . *was*."

She closed her eyes and shuddered. She knew, he realized. Calderon had given her his "tour." "Absolutely sure," he said, "The driver of the car who hit her was overheard bragging that some wealthy art dealer had paid off the police on his behalf."

She lifted her head slowly to look at him. "You found the driver? Where is he? Will you give me his name?"

"Of course. But I'll need the statue first. You were planning on trading, weren't you? That is what this is all about?"

She wet her lips, nodded.

"Good. You said you left it somewhere safe?"

"Yes . . . safe. And public. You'll have to take me there, just the two of us"—she glanced at her watch, a worn Timex with a badly scratched face—"in about fifteen minutes."

Alex looked at his watch, too, an elegant twenty-four-karat Patek Philippe. He merely smiled, but he wanted to laugh with delight. In fifteen minutes it would be high noon. Any public place would be mobbed during the lunch hour. That would make it very difficult to dispose of her once he had the statue, especially since she was insisting they go alone—and giving him so little time to plan. He'd been right. She was worthy.

Exactly a quarter of an hour later, as Alex and his strange, silent visitor left the suite, he was still trying to decide whether or not to let her live, and the mere contemplation of such an irreversible decision was making his pulse erratic. He loved having the power of life and death in his hands. He thrilled to it.

•   •   •

Something was wrong. Blue hesitated on the steps of Our Lady Queen of Martyrs, torn. She'd wrenched herself from a troubled sleep with that chilling certainty nailing her body to the mattress. Something had happened and it involved Mary Frances, though she had no idea what beyond a gnawing sense of dread. The clock radio had said noon when Blue had finally broken free of the nightmares, and she'd known somehow that the time was important, too.

She'd thrown on her clothes, called a taxi, and now that she was here, she'd lost her courage. She had no proof anything was wrong, and she dreaded the inevitable confrontation with Rick. She couldn't imagine what she would say to him after what had happened between them. He would probably think she was making it up as an excuse to see him, and she couldn't bear to have him lash out at her again, or look at her with that withering contempt in his eyes.

Honestly, nothing could have brought her here today except the terrifying premonition about her friend. She'd wrestled with her conscience all night about her encounter with Rick Caruso. He hadn't accused her outright, but his eyes had laid all the blame at her feet, and she'd bought into it blindly, totally. She'd accepted the responsibility for initiating their angry passion, and she'd tormented herself for it . . . until she realized what he'd done to her. What every man she'd ever cared about had done to her.

Bitterness welled in her throat, hot and fiery.

It was fascinating how men always seemed to blame her for their own weaknesses. Her father had done so by his silence, and after that she hadn't really cared what anyone else thought. Her mother had slapped the label on her, and the rest of the world had seemed to agree. She was no good, a slut. Far be it from her to disappoint all of them. But maybe she hadn't expected that kind of callous treatment from a man of God. Maybe that's why she'd let herself care about Rick Caruso.

Mariana Delgado was in the rectory office when Blue entered. The Hispanic woman was staring helplessly at the rubble the room had been reduced to, tears rolling down her face. The desk had been upended and everything on it had crashed to the floor, including the computer, which had flown apart like a cheap child's toy and was clearly ruined. One wall had been stripped bare, every picture and plaque shattered.

"Look," she whispered to Blue, "look what they've done to Father Rick's office. Why? Who would do this to such a good man—" She knelt on the floor, searching through the debris until she found the phone.

"What are you doing?" Blue asked.

"Calling the police to report this vandalism."

"No, don't. . . ."

Mariana stared at her, bewildered. "Why not?"

Blue could only shake her head. "Not yet, please." She knew who had decimated the room, and it wasn't teenage vandals. It was Rick himself. He had done it because of her. She had caused this. She had driven a man to destroy his own office, to shatter his plaques and commendations, everything that was precious to him. Her mother's words struck at her like a whip, and this time she knew they were true. She was no good.

16

"You hid the figurine in *there*?" Alex Cordes was thunderstruck. The taxi they'd taken had just pulled up in front of the Bonaventure, a towering, futuristic monolith of a hotel set smack in the smog-banked heart of downtown Los Angeles, and Cordes was staring out the window of the cab in disbelief.

Mary Frances would have smiled if she could have managed the rigid muscles of her mouth. Apparently the prospect of his national treasure being stashed in the midst of the financial district, as the downtown area was called, made Cordes uneasy. She'd picked the Bonaventure, a busy, bustling showplace, for exactly that reason.

"We'll have to go inside," she told him. Her fingers tightened on the leather grips of the satchel in her lap.

"What are you trying to do, make a fool of me?" He turned abruptly from the window, his sensual mouth curling into a smile that rivaled a tooth-baring snarl for nastiness. "If you're fucking with me," he said, sotto voce, "they're going to find you in a million bloody pieces, stashed in Dumpsters all over town."

"I'm *not*," she assured him in an urgent whisper.

His hand dipped inside the lapel of his jacket, and he drew out an object just enough that she could see what it was—an automatic weapon with a silencer.

She registered the length of lethal steel and felt her skin begin to draw against her lips and her heart hesitate. Death poured off the weapon in waves, just as it did off him. She had thought Webb Calderon was evil incarnate, but this man was a human chamber of horrors. His smile was hideous, a death mask.

"You think I can't kill you once we're in there? You think I *won't*?" He nodded toward the hotel. "They won't even see me," he told her, breathing laughter. "They'll be too busy dealing with the woman who's fallen to the floor with a bullet through the base of her brain. I can't be prosecuted anyway. Even if I pulled the trigger in front of witnesses, they couldn't touch me. As the son of a foreign head of state, I have diplomatic immunity."

She reached toward her throat, and her hand curled into a fist as she remembered. Her medal was gone. Webb Calderon had needed its protection more than she had, but she didn't dare let herself think about that now. It would sap what meager strength she had left. It would shatter her.

Cordes's last threat probably wasn't true, she reasoned. It was unlikely San Carlos enjoyed diplomatic relations with the United States, but she wasn't prepared to argue the point, because she didn't doubt for an instant that he would follow through on the first threat.

He moved into the light from the windows. Horror trickled through her, frozen droplets of it, as she stared at the cold sheen of his eyes—and realized what he had planned.

Alex Cordes was going to kill her.

She tried to tell herself that was crazy. She hadn't eaten or slept in over forty-eight hours and she was suffering from shock and exhaustion. She could easily be delusional or hallucinating. Her thoughts had succumbed to confusion, even her vision was blurring. But the cosmic certainty of her fate gripped her like a garotte around the throat. It cut off her breathing for a moment. He *was* going to kill her. Even if she gave him the figurine, he was going to shatter her spine with a bullet. The deadly force would pierce her brain and extinguish her last thought, all her beliefs and dreams and hopes. Everything that was Mary Frances Murphy would be gone.

Fear assailed her throat like bitter bile. Insane. That was insane. He would never kill her in front of witnesses. She knew it was irrational to panic, but none of her arguments could quell the horrible premonition that she was about to die. As much as she had fought against yielding to superstition, she couldn't help but think how macabre and inevitable this all seemed. The curse that had haunted her family could only be fulfilled by her death. She would be the second of the Murphy daughters to die in one generation, but she was the ultimate sacrifice, not Brianna. Her sister was not the youngest, nor had she ever claimed to be anything but what she was, a hellion. Mary Frances was the pretender to sainthood. She had to die.

Impossible, her logical mind kept screaming. But she was too ill with exhaustion and guilt to fight off the fears. She couldn't drag her thoughts from the chaotic horror of everything that had happened in the last twenty-four hours.

"Wait here for me," Cordes told the cabdriver after he'd slipped the gun back into his coat.

A moment later he had Mary Frances out of the taxi and was hurrying her toward the entrance of the building, cuffing her upper arm with his hand as he steered her through the hotel's whirling doors.

She wasn't used to high heels, and the ones she wore were close to spikes, but even without them she would have been in trouble. Her legs were sticks. They were simply unmanageable. With Cordes at her back, all she could think about was the puncture sound of the bullet that would sever her spine. Would it be hot or cold, the pain?

The lobby of the hotel was a ten-story atrium surrounded by glass towers. The sense of brightness, of height and space, was disorienting to Mary Frances, and it took her a moment to get her bearings. There weren't the crowds she was hoping for, but a sizable group had gathered at one of the free-form ponds that wound through the lobby. Fortunately it was near the escalator, which was where she was headed.

"That way." She pointed past the registration area to the escalator that crawled toward the shops on the second floor. *Why did it move so slowly?*

Cordes gripped her arm as if to turn her around, but she couldn't have done it without falling. "Where's the figurine?" he demanded in a hushed voice. "This is as far as I go unless you tell me where it is."

"We have to go to the next level," she insisted. "There, the escalator!" She pulled against him, and a knee buckled underneath her. Her legs were going to give out, she knew. This was like living out some horrible nightmare where monsters chased you down and your legs wouldn't let you run. Her muscles were melting, aching, turning to ooze.

She stumbled as they reached the rolling tread of the escalator. It wasn't entirely an accident, but her ankles were so wobbly and her balance so impaired, it looked like one as the satchel slipped from her grasp. It fell to the hungry metal jaws of the machine and was swept from her. A sharp cry rang out as she lurched after it. "My case!"

Her heavy fall forced Cordes to release her. Stabbing pain shot up her arm as he tried to wrench her back and she landed hard on her knees. Bruises, she realized absently. She would be badly bruised. Sprawled on the lower steps, half off, half on the escalator, she fought to get up. The metal teeth raked at the bag, trying to devour it. Her fingers snagged the leather handles of the satchel before it climbed out of reach, and she yanked it back, gathering it into her midsection.

"Get up," Cordes ground out. He was trying to pull her to her feet, but they had begun to attract attention. Children were peering over the balustrade and a young couple had stopped to help.

"Miss? Are you all right?" the man asked.

"It's my wife," Cordes told them. "She stumbled. She's fine."

The commotion allowed Mary Frances a moment to dig in the satchel and find the object she needed, a moment to recover before Cordes knelt next to her.

"Get up or I'll kill you," he warned in whispers. He jerked her roughly to her feet before she could grab the case. "Where's the figurine?" he snarled in her ear.

A small gleaming ceramic object flashed brightly from the escalator. Mary Frances glanced up the metal stairway and pointed to it.

Cordes followed the trajectory of her gaze. *"Mio Dios!"* he ejaculated. "My God, no!"

The priceless and very fragile Maya icon was ascending the hungry conveyor on one of the treads and it was already close to the top. Mary Frances hadn't hidden it in the hotel as she'd told Cordes. It had been in the satchel all along. She'd lied to him and had done so with full consent of the will. Better to forfeit a small piece of her soul than lose the entire thing, she'd reasoned. She'd pulled the figurine from the case and set it on the step when she'd dropped to her knees, just as she'd once seen on *Real Stories of the FBI,* when an agent had been in hot pursuit of an art thief and was torn between catching the Ming vase the culprit had lobbed or apprehending him. The vase had won.

Cordes bolted up the escalator, and Mary Frances swayed on her feet, watching him dizzily and knowing she only had moments to make her escape. She had done the unforgivable. She had made a fool of Alex Cordes, and the public humiliation alone would drive him to find her and retaliate. She scooped up the satchel, turned, and bumped into the couple that had tried to help. "Miss?"

"I'm fine, thanks," she assured them, "but he may need your help." She waved toward the escalator and saw that the children had crowded onto it and were already scrambling up behind Cordes. He wouldn't be able to get back down, she realized as she turned and broke for the hotel entrance. That would give her more time, precious seconds at most. Somehow it had to be enough.

Rick? Father Rick!

Rick glanced up from his mug of beer, wondering if he'd had one too many. It sounded like someone was calling his name, but that wasn't possible. There couldn't have been more than two other customers in this hole-in-the-wall beer joint, and they were playing pool in the next room. Besides, she didn't call him *Father* Rick.

He grimaced as he caught his own reflection. The mirror behind the bar was cracked in so many places, he had a half-dozen faces, all of them broodingly morose. Not that he would have looked any more hospitable in an uncracked mirror. Not in his current mood. He couldn't remember the last time he'd seriously felt like tying one on, but Mojo's was the right place for it. He'd been in the murky bar a few times on missions of mercy—collecting inebriated husbands for their worried wives, counseling teenage gang members who hung out in the pool hall, clustered at the video games, and generally ministering to those who walked in the wilderness.

Today he was in the wilderness with them.

He was only on his second beer, but if he nursed another mug or two, he'd be just about loose enough to make a few more idiotic mistakes and finish the job on his moral character. He should have been on his knees, praying for forgiveness, begging for guidance, but instead he was holed up in a pool hall. Not much of a priest. Not much of a man.

As he sipped the acrid brew and contemplated the ruins of his life, he thought he heard her again, the woman calling his name. He shook off the notion and cradled the mug with both hands, but before he could get it to his lips, he felt a hand on his shoulder, and his heart lurched wildly.

He got another glimpse of himself in the funhouse mirror as he turned around. He looked like a rogues' gallery of wild-eyed men spinning on a top. He knew it was going to be Blue before he'd come around enough to see her, but he wasn't sure at that moment what he was going to do—push her away or pull her violently into his arms. Laughter roiled up into his throat. Who was he kidding?

"Rick" she said, "are you all right?"

He searched the woman's face, stunned. It wasn't Blue Brandenburg's blue-gray eyes he was staring into, it was Mary Frances Murphy's wild green ones. And something was very wrong.

"Come here," he said instantly, reaching for her as she stumbled toward him. She was carrying a red leather bag, and she seemed about to collapse as he rose and gathered her into his embrace. A heartbreaking sound caught in her throat, more moan than sob. The bag dropped to the sawdust-strewn floor as she sagged against him, forcing him to hold her fast. It felt good to touch someone, to give comfort, but she seemed so desperate she was frightening the hell out of him. She clutched his shirt with her hands, and a sharp shudder passed through her.

"What happened to you?" he asked, his alarm growing. "Where have you been?"

"I killed someone—"

"You *what*?" Now he was doubly glad the bar was empty. Aside from his shock, the only thing that kept him from interrogating her like a homicide detective was her condition. She was barely able to stand and clearly needed a strong shoulder and some time to catch her breath. He turned her into the crook of his shoulder and encouraged her to lean on him while he held the mug of beer to her lips. She drank eagerly, as though she were hungry more than thirsty—starving—and then she choked and had to stop.

"His name was Webb Calderon," she said when she could get the words out. With a deep, shaking breath, she poured out the whole story—how Blue had infiltrated an escort service to investigate Brianna's death and been caught, how Mary Frances had taken her place at Webb Calderon's party.

Rick was confounded, especially when she told him about her narrow escape from Alejandro Cordes. Blue had done an excellent job of throwing him off the track. He'd had no idea Mary Frances was playing detective with such deadly characters, although neither of the men was unknown to him. Unfortunately he wasn't at liberty to tell Mary Frances what he knew about Calderon and Cordes. He wasn't at liberty to tell anyone, otherwise he would have gone to the police himself—a long time ago.

His reasons for not bringing the authorities into what had happened were only indirectly related to Mary Frances's situation. It was a far bigger and much more complicated mess than she knew. There were others involved, and he had become an intermediary. He often questioned the wisdom of that now, but he'd given his word and would not go back on it.

The immediate problem was Mary Frances. He was worried about her safety. Even if she was free of Calderon, she wasn't of Cordes. He was still very much alive and probably wouldn't rest until he'd hunted her down and evened the score. From what she'd told him, she knew too much about Cordes's dealings with Calderon, and that alone could make her a threat. Rick didn't want to alarm her any more than he had to, but he couldn't let her go back to her apartment tonight.

"Mary Frances," he said gently as she fell against his chest, exhausted, her story told, "you've been through a grisly ordeal, and I don't think you should be alone right now. Why don't you come back with me to the church? You can stay at the rectory. You'll be safe there until we figure out what to do."

She sighed, her fingers searching for the saint's medal she usually wore on a chain around her neck. He wondered briefly where it was, but didn't ask. Instead, he caught her hand and held it in the warmth of his. She needed some support now, some rest.

"We have to find Blue," she insisted faintly. "She has to know what's happened, that it was Webb who had Brianna killed, that he's . . . dead."

She still looked weak enough to faint and terribly vulnerable. Rick drew her into his arms and hugged her fiercely. He was heartsick and conflicted and frightened for her, far more than he wanted her to know.

Mary Frances thought she'd never seen a more beautiful sight than Blue Brandenburg kneeling in prayer. She looked like a Madonna made of spun gold, her head hallowed by a blaze of votive candles. The nave of the small church was darker and more ethereal than Mary Frances remembered as she and Rick approached the altar, and it struck her how fragile Blue seemed, how softened and sad were her features as she raised her head and gazed at the glowing edifice.

Blue didn't notice them immediately, and when she did look around, she saw Rick first. The pain that flared through her expression as she looked at him made Mary Frances wonder if something had happened between them.

"Blue?" she ventured. She rested a hand on the back of the pew to steady herself.

"My God!" Blue sprang up from the padded kneeler, gaping at Mary Frances.

"I'm all right," Mary Frances assured her dizzily. But she wasn't. The high altar seemed to be moving and the darkened red and purples of the stained-glass windows had taken on a brooding menace. She needed to sit down. Otherwise, she was going to be ill.

"What do you mean 'all right'?" Blue demanded to know. "You look terrible!"

"I need—" But Blue was there before Mary Frances could ward her off, taking ahold of Mary Frances's shoulders in a stern maternal way. Not that she would have had the strength to ward Blue off, even if she were in the best of health.

"What happened?" Blue shook her gently. "Tell me."

"Webb Calderon is dead." Mary Frances managed that much haltingly and knew it was as far as she was going to get. She had spent all her reserve energy with Rick. She turned to him now. "Could you tell her for me? I can't go through it again. I need to sit down, or I'm going to fall down."

The candles flared suddenly, and the church reeked of their waxy smoke. Mary Frances wondered if the door had been opened, but she couldn't even make the effort to turn her head.

"What the hell happened?" Blue wanted to know. She was turning from one of them to the other, her voice rising. "Would *someone* tell me, please!"

Rick took over then. "She's had a rough time, but she's okay," he told Blue reassuringly as he helped Mary Frances to a seat farther down the aisle, out of the line of fire. He'd brought the Cherries satchel with him and he left it beside her on the pew.

"Don't worry," he whispered once he had her settled, "everything's going to be fine." But when he returned to Blue, Mary Frances saw the consternation in his profile, and she read the words on his lips. "Chill," he told the other woman under his breath, "it's bad, very bad."

The warning sobered Blue, but it barely registered on

Mary Frances's psyche. She was too numb with shock, too queasy with fatigue and hunger. The brilliance of the altar had begun to hurt her eyes, and the darkness of the nave to feel claustrophobic. Ceremonial incense from that day's service hung heavily in the air, mingling with the candle smoke and giving it the musty, stale quality of old cigar ashes. She turned and looked at the doors, wondering if she had the strength to make it outside.

Rick was still talking to Blue moments later as Mary Frances quietly let herself out of the church and wandered through the cool night toward the statue of St. Catherine. The barrio neighborhood was mostly quiet. A dog yapped in the distance, and a car backfired in some nearby alley. The air smelled faintly of gasoline fumes, spicy frying meat, and freshly picked flowers, a strange mix of perfumes, but much preferable to inside.

Daisies were strewn at the bare feet of the statue. Mary Frances knelt to pick one up and felt as if a heavy net had been thrown over her. Dizziness weighed her down so swiftly she couldn't get back up. Instead she tilted against the stone statue and sank down on its pedestal, resting her head against the saint's legs. It felt vaguely sacrilegious, but she couldn't help herself.

"God, make my life a little light within the world to glow," she murmured, recalling the prayer she'd said so fervently as a child. "A little flame to burn bright wherever I may go."

She didn't know whether to laugh or cry, but a strange calm came over her as she went on, continuing with one prayer after another, some of them silly, some poignant, all favorites from her convent-school days, and for the first time since Blue had reappeared in her life, she began to feel safe.

Blessed are they that mourn, she recited silently, *for they shall be comforted.* It was a line from the Beatitudes she'd never thought much about until now. And then softly she repeated the prayer she'd said for Webb. "He who takes away the sins of the world, have mercy. . . ."

As she murmured "Amen" a bright light enveloped both her and the statue from behind. Rick and Blue had found her, she imagined. They'd thrown open the doors of the church, allowing the blaze of candlefire to escape. She turned slowly, prepared to be harangued for frightening them, and instead she saw a solitary figure coming toward her.

The dark silhouette seemed to be materializing out of an inferno of light. The radiance of the image made her want to hide her eyes, and the strange force with which it moved was vaguely sinister. Her scalp pulled tight across her head, and the skin of her face began to draw and tingle painfully. Her heart was silent, eerily silent, as if listening.

Mary Frances rose up, her dizziness gone. Apprehension braced her shoulders and stiffened her spine. She couldn't see who it was, but she could feel the impending threat as if it were crawling up her spine. Her body reacted as it always had when she was in the presence of evil.

Whoever it was, he'd come for her. Cordes had tracked her down or sent one of his aides. It might even be someone from the escort service, she realized, startled at the prospect. The anonymous party who sent her E-mail orders. As the figure moved out of the blinding halo and into a pale patch of light, his features were partially revealed, but Mary Frances still couldn't be sure.

"Who is it?" she asked.

He raised his hand and turned it to the moonlight. A saint's medal glowed luminously in his palm.

"No," she breathed, and fainted dead away.

17

"Packed your bags yet, Luis?"

The aide de camp glanced up from the correspondence he'd been answering. His obvious surprise might have pleased Alex if Alex hadn't been in such a murderous mood. He'd been made to look an ass today, and Alex didn't like looking foolish. It pried open the locked closet of childhood humiliations and tortured him with the fears, the rage and shame he'd had to endure. Mostly shame, the emotion he abhorred above all others.

"My bags?" Luis set his pen down. "What do you mean? Are we leaving?"

"No, *you're* leaving. I want you on the next plane to San Carlos."

"I'm sorry . . . I don't understand."

"It's not important that you understand, it's important that you leave." Alex reached inside his coat and pulled out the automatic weapon he'd taken to the Bonaventure that afternoon, aware that the silencer made it look doubly deadly.

Luis rose from the desk, gaping at the gun.

Cheated, Alex thought, aware of the satisfaction he would have taken from this situation under other circumstances. He was being cheated. Again. He'd always been fascinated by the transformation from shock to abject fear. Not that it was any great challenge with this one. Ducks in a shooting range, he thought. But Luis was the only target he had at the moment, and given Alex's state of mind, someone had to suffer.

The figurine had been saved, but at great cost to Alex's cosmopolitan image. Not even priceless artifacts were worth the loss of face, the savaging of his dignity. The woman who'd done it to him wasn't around, so this duplicitous aide would have to do.

"I'll pack," Luis said. "I'll be out of here in fifteen minutes."

"Fuck packing, get out now."

"Without my things?" Luis glanced down at his stockinged feet. "My shoes?"

An ominous click sent the aide scurrying for the library door. Alex had released the gun's safety. "Wait a minute!" he shouted as Luis attempted to make good his vanishing act.

The young man halted on the threshold and turned slowly. His lips were trembling, his eyes pinpricks of terror. He couldn't take them off the gun, which he clearly now understood would be the instrument of his undoing, unless Alex decided to be generous and show mercy.

Alex felt a mix of sympathy and disgust for his victim. He understood the impulse to survive at any cost. He had experienced enough of it at the hands of his parental figures. But he would have expected more than this, even from Luis.

Alex knew at that very moment that he would not surround himself with cowards and incompetents again. He would hire real professionals from now on—a bodyguard who could also function as his assistant, a personal security force—not children, not his father's *minions*.

Luis was waiting to learn his fate, but Alex hadn't quite decided what that would be yet. "Where is Carmen?" he asked.

"I—I don't know; out, I think, shopping."

The boy was a hopeless liar. "Where the *fuck* is Carmen?"

Luis nodded down the hallway, his Adam's apple bobbing like a lottery ball in the hopper. "She's in her bedroom, on the phone."

"Stay where you are," Alex commanded. He stormed to the desk and soundlessly plucked the receiver from its cradle. Smothering the mouthpiece with his hand, he brought the phone to his ear.

"Ah, Señor Jackal," a female voice crooned seductively. "You will eat this little pussycat up when she gets back, no? The big bad doggie will lap her up. He will nibble his Carmen to death, no?"

"*Sí,* the jackal, he will eat you alive, *cara*—"

If Alex had had the physical strength to crush the phone in his hand, it would have been nothing but wires and plastic dust. Blind fury bleached the color from his world and left him scattered for reeling seconds, precious seconds. Everything was white noise. He couldn't think what to do. He had recognized the raspy male voice on the phone the instant he heard it.

"Can I—can I go?"

Fear. Another kind of rasp. The sound of Luis's pleading fear soothed Alex fractionally. He replaced the receiver with hands that shook. "Not yet," he said, knowing exactly what he must do. The calm that had descended upon him in the last seconds told him that he was completely justified in his ambitions to revolutionize the Republic of San Carlos, that he was right in everything he intended to do.

He brought his hands to his mouth, prayerlike, and pulled hard on the air in the room, filling his nostrils with it.

"Perhaps you'll give my father a message for me, Luis," he said, glancing up at the aide. Luis was almost an afterthought now. Alex cared nothing about what happened to him beyond this one last task.

"I would have told Ruben myself just now," Alex explained, his voice dropping to something soft, a whisper, "but I didn't want to interrupt the *conversation,* you understand. So you tell him for me, Luis. Tell him she's dead."

Luis's hand flew to his mouth. The aide stepped back as Alex dismissed him with a nod, and then Luis bolted down the hallway to freedom.

Alex was not in any way concerned that Luis would contact the American police. In his country, people in terror of their lives did exactly as they were told. It was the only way to survive the death squads, whose existence Alex roundly denounced, of course. Luis wouldn't even think to stop and call ahead. He would go straight to Ruben with the message and probably be executed for his trouble.

Alex checked the ammunition clip, assuring himself the weapon was ready for use. His short trip down the hall took him in the opposite direction from Luis's flight. The presidential suite had two guest bedrooms. When he reached the one he wanted, he tested the door, found it unlocked, and eased it open.

Carmen was curled up on the Persian carpet in a

brightly flowered kimono. The robe's ties were flung in either direction and the front hung open, exposing her lithe nakedness. Her eyes were closed, her head lolling back against the armoire where her shoulders rested. Slender fingers purled her inner thigh, creeping higher as she talked to her lover, his father.

Alex took aim, his hand as steady as glass. He'd already released the safety, so there was no click, just the sudden hiss of deadly force as he squeezed the trigger. The first bullet embedded itself in the cherrywood next to her head. The second found its target.

The phone receiver dropped to the carpet, splattered with the most vibrant crimson Alex had ever seen. Life, he thought. Her life. Her strange, tiny squeal filled him with wonder. It brought tears to his eyes.

Mary Frances was shaking. Everywhere. Every part of her was uncontrollably alive. Fine perturbations thundered and droned. They sizzled in her skull, zoomed the length of her spine, and shot like sparks to her toes. She could feel the buzz in her throat and her tailbone. Even her lips trembled slightly.

The surface she lay on was vibrating, too.

Noise. There was so much noise.

A pungent smell permeated her nostrils. Gasoline?

Her eyelids fluttered. She wanted to open them, only something told her not to, that she was safer in the gray oblivion of sleep. The warning registered fleetingly and was gone, drowned out by the low roar of engines, the smoky combustion of diesel oil and the musk of damp canvas.

Her lids had already drifted open, and the shadowy gloom that lay beyond them was a dark landscape that made her strain to remember what had happened to her

. . . remember the prayers whispered at St. Catherine's feet, the drenching darkness, broken by a blaze of light and the black form coming toward her, materializing from the brilliance.

Remember the raised hand glowing with her saint's medal.

The man she'd left for dead . . .

The confusion that tore from her throat was his name. "Webb Calderon?"

The darkness was disorienting. She tried to sit up and felt hands grip her shoulders and hold her down. Someone had moved over her and was pressing her into the bed, bearing down with a weight so heavy she couldn't fight it.

"Stay down," he warned.

She couldn't see him, but she croaked his name again, still disbelieving. "You were dead. I couldn't revive you—"

"Stay down or I'll have to restrain you."

His voice echoed inside her head. It rumbled and roared, a temblor from somewhere beyond the earth. She could feel it moving through her like the vibrations, buzzing, jumping. She had never felt so helpless, even when he injected her with the drug. At least then she'd been unconscious. What was this unearthly trembling?

"You weren't breathing. Your heart—"

"Zin Quai paralyzes the muscles," he said, "including the heart and lungs. Your efforts to revive me brought back enough cardiovascular function to keep me alive. If you'd checked again before you left, you would have realized I was breathing. I was conscious the whole time, too. I just couldn't move or speak."

"Conscious?" Did that mean he knew everything she'd done, including the tears she'd cried over him? She was aware of a drug with similar properties from her nurse's training. It was a neuromuscular paralyzing agent used in trauma cases to stop tremors or excessive movement. It also stopped respiration unless there was intervention.

"Then I . . . saved your life?" She was trying to get it straight.

The weight lifted from her shoulders, but she made no attempt to move. She still couldn't see well enough to know where she was, or which way to go if she were to try and escape. She was just beginning to be able to make out the details of his features, which were in no way reassuring. Formed and hollowed by the shadows, they were even more hauntingly sinister than she remembered. If a man's face could elicit fear and erotic fantasies at the same time, his did. Cold, cruel beauty. And those eyes, God, those torture-chamber eyes. She could almost believe he'd risen from the dead and come back to claim her.

"That's one way of looking at it," he conceded, his smile bleak. "However, you wouldn't have had to save me if you hadn't drugged me."

The bed she lay on moved beneath her as if it were on rollers. Nausea surged in her throat and gripped the base of her skull. Her stomach rumbled as loudly as the engine noise. "Where am I?" She'd lost track of how long it had been since she'd eaten.

"You're on a boat out of Miami, heading for the Bahamas."

The Bahamas? That was the other side of the world from Santa Ana, California. "Why?"

"Because that's where I'm taking you."

"Don't!" she cried dizzily as she felt her hands being drawn together, her wrists looped with rope. "Why are you tying me up? I haven't moved."

"I play dirty. Or did you forget?"

A rage of indignation swept through her. It burned high in her veins, heating her throat and face. The lingering odor of diesel fuel had sensitized her nostrils. Now it seared them and made her even queasier. "How could I?" she retorted bitterly. "You make every moment so memorable."

Her anger wasn't just at him, she realized. She felt as if she were being tested by the heavens. Even though she'd been a model student, she had never truly succeeded in confining her will or mortifying her flesh in the convent. Mary Frances Murphy had "impediments." That was what they'd said about her. No matter how hard she tried, she wasn't quite modest, deferential, or humble enough. She had never learned to be properly obedient, certainly not compared with the other postulants who'd been called to their vocation by their hearts. She had battled with her own nature and denied her true feelings for so long she didn't realize how deeply she resented anything to do with submission.

She understood the higher reasons. The body was confined in order to free the spirit. The human will was subdued in order to better receive the divine will. The greatest part of her education and training had been designed to help her overcome earthly desires so that she could embrace spiritual ones. It was a worthy effort and a glorious calling for some, but she'd been a resounding failure. It was the reason she'd been asked to leave. That was the real sin in the mistress of postulants' eyes, even more unforgivable than her sins of impurity.

"There's no need," she told him, hating the desperation that had sneaked into her voice, and hating him for bringing her to this point of nakedness. "I won't try to escape. I can't swim anyway."

"I'll remember that," he promised.

He tied her feet, too, and though the ropes were loose, their coarseness burned the tender skin of her ankles.

When he was done, a light flashed on, and she saw that they were in what must be a forward stateroom. It was small, but elegantly appointed in teal fabrics and varnished teak. The bed she lay on was flush against the wall, and he stood across the room, regarding her dispassionately, one of the golden immortals, terrifying in his ability to reduce mere flesh and blood to dust. His face had no softness. None, anywhere. The bones could cut. The eyes were diamond drill bits, and his expression was frozen over with a mask that she could only have described as indifference. Brutal indifference.

She could hardly make herself believe it was the same man she'd left for dead. She had wept over him and offered up her aching tears as penance. She'd even tucked her medal in his hand in a confused moment of guilt and longing.

It pained her now the way his marbled gaze shone with coldness, as if he had no earthly ability to feel anything for her at all, even compassion, as if she were hardly worth the effort he'd expended to get her here. Once she had seen agony seep into those same eyes, just a flicker before it died a cold death, but she had wanted to believe that something in her had touched it, some need he hungered for that only she could meet. Obviously that had been the most pathetic kind of wishful thinking on her part, just as she must have imagined that ridiculous reference to her innocence.

Why did she let herself think those things? What was this romantic failing of hers that she had to imagine a man tortured with some poetic need of her? Any man. *Him.* She'd been cursed since childhood with fantasies of dark souls that needed saving, only she hadn't been dreaming about religious conversion then.

She was staring directly at him. She had been for several moments, searching for evidence of who he was, wanting to believe that she had not squandered herself on an unfeeling bastard, that he was worth her grief. She drew back instantly. It was dangerous staring at him. It felt as if she were looking at the sun without protection and could burn her retinas. Custody of the eyes, she told herself.

He spoke, quietly. "Where do you go when you do that?"

She knew what he was asking. She had always assumed everyone had a place inside that they retreated to, an unassailable haven where nothing could touch them, not even the monsters of their nightmares, not even men like him.

"Nowhere . . ." Silent a moment, she reluctantly admitted, "Away. I go away."

"Is it like the book? That child's book? *The Secret Garden*? Do you have a place like that where you hide?"

She didn't answer. Yes, it was exactly like that. How did he know? The boat rolled as if it were turning, and she leaned toward the wall, not wanting to topple off the bed. The instinctive impulse to protect herself told her how much she wanted to hide from him, stay curled against the wall and hide.

"Look at me," he said once the boat had settled. "Wherever it is you go. I don't want you to have that safety now."

She came around reluctantly, but refused to look at him. He would have to force her to do that. He needn't have worried, however. She couldn't seem to find the safe place anymore, even now when she truly needed it.

There was nowhere to hide, nowhere to avoid him. She wasn't looking at him, but she couldn't escape his voice. It was everywhere.

"Your attempt to kill me was the least of it, Irish," he told her. "If that were the extent of it, I wouldn't be going to all this trouble. You triggered a disastrous chain of events. Alex Cordes was *supposed* to get the fake Maya figurine. That was the deal."

There was a moment's hesitation before all thought of avoiding him vanished. She simply couldn't imagine what he was talking about. "Why would anyone want a fake? The real figurine was priceless, wasn't it?"

He settled himself on a console, as if contemplating how much he should tell her. "The real figurine was payment for a prototype microchip that was hidden in the fake," he explained. "And since you stole it from me, you're going to steal it back."

The stateroom shuddered violently, as if the boat had hit some rough water. Somewhere below them engines roared, struggling against the elements. "Steal it back?" she said as soon as she could be heard.

Webb had caught hold of a chrome safety rail to brace himself, and his powerful biceps bulged with the strain. He was wearing linen slacks and a black silk shirt that draped his frame like water would have if it had been a fabric. His physique was long and burnished gold, wiry strong, but his true strength was his diabolical intelligence, she knew. She'd already made the deadly mistake of underestimating him.

"Exactly," he said, "from Cordes, the man you gave it to."

Mary Frances couldn't believe he was serious. She wanted to laugh, but he wasn't even smiling. "How am I supposed to do that?" she asked.

"I'll tell you when we get to our destination." The
smile she'd been looking for appeared now, faint, mysterious. "A small island off the coast of Nassau. It's called
Paradise."

It took a supreme effort to get herself to a sitting position. Her stomach lurched every time the boat did, and
her brain burned with an exhaustion that felt as if it were
poisoning her entire body. She managed by using her
knees and tied feet as levers, but not without dangerously
depleting her scant energy stores.

"That's absurd," she protested weakly. "I won't do it."

"You will if you care about what happens to your
friends."

"My friends?" He could only mean Blue and Rick.
"Where are they?"

"I left them bound and gagged in a storeroom in the
church. No one will find them, or even look there. Someone vandalized the rectory before I got there, so all I had
to do was leave a ransom note saying the priest had been
kidnapped. I made it sound like a gang member, high on
drugs, ranting about how the Roman Catholic Church
should 'share the wealth.' "

The look on her face must have been one of sheer disbelief. "What are you saying? That you'll kill them?"

"If you're thinking I'd hesitate, think again," he
warned. "The men who supplied the prototype chip are
expecting the real figurine as payment. If they don't get
it, they'll retaliate, and their methods are more barbaric
than anything you saw in my humble little torture chamber. They wouldn't blink at hacking off my vitals and
forcing me to eat them for an appetizer, raw and bleeding.
Then they'd butcher the rest of me, piece by piece, and
feed that to me, too, while I was still alive, of course."

He released the rail and automatically flexed his arm.

It seemed an attempt to work out the biceps more than any desire to demonstrate his physical superiority, although it managed to accomplish both. "They'd have even more fun with you," he mused, a pointed afterthought.

It was sick exhaustion that made Mary Frances convulse, or so she told herself. She drew her legs up in a huddle with the certain knowledge that Webb Calderon was evil, and that there really was only one way to deal with evil and not be destroyed by it. You had to smother it within your own spirit, let your heart stop it like a spear.

It was possible she could have done that once, but not anymore, she realized. Something had changed in her relationship with him. It had happened as she bent over his dead body and wept. Her tears were more than guilt and regret. They were tears of loss. He might have been a monster, but that didn't matter. She'd opened her heart to him. She'd allowed herself to care, and that had made her vulnerable. It made her vulnerable now. She couldn't survive his evil any more than she could stop a sword with her heart. Either would kill her. She no longer had the grace.

As she rolled to her side, facing the wall, she realized that all her protections were gone . . . her medal, even the sanctuary within. She closed her eyes and a wave of fatigue overtook her. Would that be her way out? she wondered. Oblivion?

Sometime later, groggy with exhaustion, she felt him untying her ankles. "What are you doing?" she asked.

"Removing the bracelet. You don't need it anymore."

She turned listlessly, watching as he sat down on the bed and cradled her foot in his lap. He undid the clasp with a tiny screwdriverlike tool.

"Why did I ever need it?" she asked, hardly caring.

What more could he tell her? It was all so incomprehensible, no one would believe it anyway. She tried to imagine herself telling Maury Povich or one of those other talk-show hosts what had happened to her the last few days, and wanted to laugh.

"The tattoo inside your ankle is implanted with a listening device—"

Her head came up, but she was too dizzy to control its weight. "There's something in my ankle?"

He nodded, busy with the screwdriver. "Under the skin. It was implanted when you got the tattoo."

"Why?"

"That's how Cherries keeps tabs on their escorts and monitors their various activities."

"They listen in to the escorts having—"

"Sex? No, that's not what they're interested in. Well, not entirely."

She couldn't stop the laughter now, though she knew it must be hysteria foaming into her throat. A bug? In her body? She ought to have been appalled. She probably was, and yet this seemed like just one more atrocity added to the laundry list. They'd been listening to her the entire time, to everything she said?

He freed the gold chain and held it up. "This little gadget blocks the signals, which is why I put it on you. I didn't want the service spying on me through you. The implant is the latest technology, but its power is limited to a ten-mile radius, and we're well out of range now."

This was all beginning to make some kind of bizarre sense, she realized, though the idea of a master plan disturbed her even more. "What do you mean by *their* activities?" She had the feeling he was about to confirm Blue's suspicions that the service was a front for white collar-crime.

"They're into everything—industrial espionage, information smuggling, microchips, fine art. The only thing they avoid is drugs. Too upmarket for that. Don't tell me you didn't know."

He gazed up at her in the probing way that made Mary Frances feel like she needed several extra layers of clothing. She could have sworn he could see every flaw and blemish, even the ones that weren't on her body. But it was the fleeting evidence of a smile that had her most concerned. There was a darkness hidden in the sensual curve of his lips that told her it wasn't over yet. He had something more in store for her.

"Please," she implored him, "let me rest. I'm exhausted."

He dropped the chain in the breast pocket of his shirt, settled her foot back on the bed, and rose without retying her ankles. "Your wish is my command," he said, without a trace of sarcasm. "Get some sleep. I'll have food brought down for you, and some fresh clothes. You're only going to get a nap, I'm afraid. The big event's at dawn."

Her heart froze. "Dawn? You're expecting me to steal back the statue at dawn?"

"No, that will have to wait until Cordes meets with his buyers, which should be sometime in the next forty-eight hours. The sun's going to rise on an even more special occasion, a wedding ceremony. My first. How about you?"

The flash of amusement in his eyes caught her off guard. "Who's . . . getting married?" she asked.

"We are."

She shook her head in confusion.

"I'm afraid so." He braced himself as the boat began to buck and surge again. "You and I, Mary Frances. I've taken care of everything. Should be a lovely ceremony."

Nausea surged into her throat, and she rolled to her side, afraid she was going to vomit. "Are you insane?"

"Very possibly."

She closed her eyes, but the soft precision of his voice pierced her more efficiently than a surgical instrument could have. She couldn't escape him, not even in the remotest recesses of her mind. "Why?"

"I have this thing about virginity. About innocence. Didn't anybody tell you?"

"Why are you doing this?" she persisted, and then her voice changed. It implored him. "Don't do this. Don't."

He startled her by walking over and sitting down on the bed. He even seemed faintly amused when she scuttled away from him.

"It won't be that bad, Irish. I'm not an ogre, really. I don't gobble women up as snacks, unless that's what they want. This Bluebeard guy you keep mumbling about. He made his wives very happy, didn't he?"

"*Before* he killed them!"

His eyes had changed. They were searingly soft now and almost painful to look at. "Why don't we concentrate on the other part?" he suggested.

"You mean where he locks them up and keeps them captive to his desires, prisoners in a garden of sensual delight?"

"Sounds like more fun than *your* garden."

He obviously had no idea how erotic her garden was . . . or maybe he did. Either way she didn't want to talk about this with him. She didn't want to discuss the relative merits of dying with a smile on your face, which he seemed to be suggesting was the case with Bluebeard's hapless brides.

"You didn't answer my question," she reminded him. "You didn't tell me why you're doing this."

He went silent for a moment. "It's a safety precaution," he explained. "You don't mind, do you? According to my sources, Cordes has taken steps to ensure himself against retaliation by the Asian Mafia. He's notified his country's consulate and the U.S. Treasury Department of the theft of the figurine, and he's framed me for the crime. Since Cordes believes I'm dead, the authorities now have an APB out for you, Mary Frances. He named you as an eyewitness."

She understood now. "You're making sure that I can't testify against you if we get caught."

"You're quick. That's good. You'll need to be."

She found enough energy to look at him again, to focus all her enmity into one aching glare. "You'd marry me," she said, "and then throw me to the wolves, to Cordes?"

"You stole the statue, love. It's only fair that you return it to me."

"But if Cordes catches me, he'll kill me."

His voice took on an edge the sarcasm couldn't quite cover. "Don't let him catch you."

"But he *would* kill me?"

"Yes, undoubtedly, but not right away. He'd torture you first."

"Like you," she lashed out, astonished that he could be so callous. "The way you torture women?"

"There's a difference. I don't do it for pleasure."

What about my sister's diary? she wanted to shout at him. *What about the way you ensnared Brianna and nearly drove her insane?* He'd split her sister off from herself and turned her into a "wanton, hedonistic crea-ture" by her own words.

In fact, she could remember the *exact* words. She could feel the emotion and excitement, the near rapture with which they were written. He'd made Brianna care about nothing but her own flesh and the pleasure it could give her. That was as frightening as it was disgusting. No one should be able to wield that kind of power over another human being. The later entries were even more erotic and then Brianna had begun to hint at darker things, dangerous things, but she'd never said what they were before the entries stopped altogether.

Webb Calderon had done all that to her sister. And now he was studying Mary Frances with a look of such cool, calm deliberation that she knew she was next. He was going to marry her. And then he was going to sacrifice her. She *was* to be one of Bluebeard's wives after all.

A fly, he thought. He could squash her like a fly without even trying. Could and should. She'd stolen his statue, jeopardized his mission, and tried to kill him. He'd retaliated against "friends" for less. Much less. Still, he'd been wrong to brand her an enemy. She was a child when it came to rough games, no match for him. That was obvious tonight. He'd put crack after crack in her facade of serenity. He'd had her close to the breaking point, using nothing more than words as his weapons. A touch would have done it. Nothing too intimate, just a light feathering of her lips to remind her of all the other tender places he could touch while she was bound and helpless. He would love to have done that, love to have felt her trembling beneath his hands.

So why hadn't he?

He turned into the wind and let the stinging salt spray whip his face as the ship churned through windroughened waters.

The answer was obvious. What good would she have been to him broken? He needed her alive and as luminous as a votive candle, the embodiment of sweet vulnerabil-

ity, the perfect lure for Alejandro Cordes. According to
Webb's sources, she'd beat the South American at his
own game, humiliated him. Being the man that he was,
Cordes would want his pound of flesh, and she was the
kind of flesh he liked best—pink and sweet and virginal.

Ironically her interference had created a once-in-a-
lifetime opportunity to catch Cordes in the act. So, instead of squashing her, Webb was going to use her in a
way that had made him think the concept of destiny
might not be outmoded. He was going to sacrifice her
for the cause. Yes, it felt like fate. But before he did
that, before he let her go, he was going to surrender to
one last dangerous impulse and walk in her cool, dark
garden. He would lose himself in the fern grottoes of
her untouched flesh, bathe in her virginal springs.
Cordes would not have her innocence. Only Webb
Calderon could have that, and only after a ritual that
would bind her to him in every way. Marriage, a ceremony he detested, but she undoubtedly considered sacred. That ritual would make her his . . . simply
because she believed in it.

It was a brilliant plan all the way around.

So why couldn't he do it? Why couldn't he?

He turned his hand and opened his palm, exposing the
religious medal she'd left with him the night she believed
him dead. He'd investigated the mysterious images—a
single rose abloom in a bitter winter landscape—and discovered they were the symbols of Rita of Cascia, the patron saint of impossible causes, the rose that blooms in
winter. It was a beautiful, delicate thing, her pendant, yet
he knew if he closed his hand over it, it would pierce him
and make him bleed. It would restore all the feelings he

was missing, the pain, the agony. It would bring him
flooding back to life like a mountain river in spring thaw.

He knew that. Wanted it. So why couldn't he do it?

Because something had changed. She was a child at
rough games.

18

By some cruel quirk of fate, Blue Brandenburg had ended up with exactly what she wished for. Rick Caruso couldn't escape her now if he wanted to. They were bound hand and foot to each other. An assailant, who could only have been Webb Calderon by his haunting voice and his threat to make Mary Frances permanently disappear if they went to the police—had taken them hostage at gunpoint and ordered them to disrobe. Blue had never managed a good look at him, but the sheer perversity of his demands alone told her it was Calderon.

Who else would tie up a priest and prostitute naked?

Once he'd had them strip to their underwear, he'd ordered them to the floor of the storage room, positioned them back-to-back, lashed them together with cinctures, the cords used to secure liturgical robes, and gagged them with linen altar cloths. At least he hadn't tied them face-to-face. That much mercy he'd shown.

"Icamuuuv," Blue mumbled, "ca-uuu?" She'd loosened the wad of material in her mouth by twisting her head back and forth, but still wasn't able to make herself understood.

Whatever Rick mumbled back, she didn't catch a word of it. But she caught every twitch of his back, pressed ramrod stiff against hers in several pertinent places. He seemed afraid to move, and given their last encounter, she understood why. Each bodily point of contact felt like a live land mine, designed to explode with the wrong kind of pressure, which was basically *any* kind of pressure.

He was probably thinking about it, too, she realized, the wildness that had erupted between them. She'd never seen such passion in her life. They'd both been nearly torn apart by it. More than anything, it was his ability to hold back that had confounded her, especially when the desire flaring in his eyes had been hot enough to scorch everything in its path. She had been burned by the blue flame in Rick Caruso's gaze. She could feel it burning her still. Yet she'd never done less—and wanted to more—in her life.

Playing statue seemed the only safe course now, but Blue wasn't the cautious sort, especially when she'd been hours in one position. She couldn't know for sure how long it had been, but her legs were nearly numb from lack of circulation, and that was long enough for her. Whether they were trussed up like holiday turkeys or not, half-naked or not, *burning flames or not,* something had to be done.

"Yewmove?" she asked.

"Dmmuunnlltuurnnyewmumuu . . ."

"Huh?" She felt activity almost immediately and realized that he was trying to turn. As much as she wanted to be liberated from the cinctures, she suddenly wasn't sure that was a good idea, especially the way he was rotating against her. He probably couldn't do anything but bumps and grinds because of the grip of the cords, but it felt like his behind was getting awfully familiar, and there wasn't anything back there for it to get familiar with but hers.

She'd been surprised by his skimpy Calvin Klein briefs when he undressed. She hadn't been surprised by his long, muscled legs. She'd already had the pleasure. Of looking anyway. His jeans had worn through and ripped in some interesting places.

"Hooostlllnnlemmemuvv."

"Wha?" Was he telling her to hold still? She wasn't moving. He definitely was, however. The cords yanked tight around her breasts and shoulders. They abraded her naked thighs like sandpaper. "Owwww!" she yelped. "Stoptha!"

The pressure intensified, and she realized he wasn't going to stop—either mumbling or moving. He was trying to direct her in some way, probably to make the ordeal easier, but she still couldn't understand him. If he kept this up, she could open up her own curiosity shop and be the featured piece—Madame Blue's House of Ropeburn.

"Shiiii!" The ropes bit into her shins and she kicked at him, trying to get him to ease up. She'd only had a half-dozen "dates" during her brief time with Cherries, but one of the kinkier souls had wanted her to try something like this. She'd said no then, and there'd been big money involved.

Rick was muttering again, more instructions she couldn't understand. She could feel him coiling like a spring, though she couldn't imagine what he hoped to accomplish. A sudden force jerked her around and upward. He was trying to flip them like pancakes! She realized the ropes must be shredding her flesh to the consistency of cross-stitching. She could feel almost nothing below the knees anymore, which probably meant she was going to get gangrene or something equally horrible and die.

Her keening shrieks did the trick. She let go of one after another, not stopping until he did, which was abruptly.

They went back to being statues again in the pulsing moments that followed. Only it wasn't quite the same. Body heat rolled off him in frustrated waves and his breathing made her think of flared nostrils and fiery dragons. As tense as she was abraded, Blue figuratively licked her wounds in whimpering silence. If she was going to die, at least she could be allowed a little dignity. But it wasn't her own life she saw flashing before her eyes. It was Cardinal Fang's. What would happen to the cat if she died? He would starve on the meager rations in Mary Frances's place.

She was planning the double funeral, a Native American motif with a canoe drifting down the river and Fang nestled in her arms, when she felt Rick moving again. Apparently he'd given up on brute strength and was now trying some kind of rhythmic rocking motion. He was moving as if he'd decided to coax the ropes rather than force them, and as unbridled as their encounter had been the night before, Blue couldn't stop herself from wondering if this would be his preferred approach with a woman—wonderfully slow and seductive. Works for me, she thought, her response instantaneous. The longing in her belly felt like fiery little darts of light. It flared into her thighs and left her weak. She didn't want to think about what was happening to the cotton crotch of her panties.

She could actually feel the ropes begin to give as he shifted and shimmied, but she despaired that he would ever get them free. God, he had to! Otherwise she had visions of being transformed into the human equivalent of a leaky faucet—trickling warm female juices and lubricating the storage-room floor. Damn Webb Calderon! It wasn't even them he was after. It was Mary Frances. He'd threatened dire consequences when they wouldn't tell him where she was. But they couldn't have if they'd wanted to. She'd left the church, and neither one of them had seen her go.

Blue hadn't crossed herself since Catholic school, but if she could have at that moment, she would have. There was almost no chance Calderon hadn't caught up with Mary Frances, and she hated to think about what he did to people who messed with him, even women. As nasty a character as he was? Gorgeous, okay, but that slitty stare, please! It was crawling with demonic energy.

"Whoa," she cried. This time Rick had dipped under her and raised her right up off the floor. "Whazzat?" He seemed to be trying to reposition both of them at once, and she could only wonder if his methods were having the same effect on him as they were on her. Were his insides liquefying like oranges in a juicer? Was he melting to warm trickles of sensation like she was?

At least she could talk. In all of her twisting and turning, the gag had slipped from between her teeth. It was still covering her mouth, but not so tightly that she couldn't make herself understood.

She'd been trying to block out his gyrations, but he seemed to be turned about halfway around. His shoulder was jutting into the curve between hers, and his hipbone was nestled lower, in the lush cleft another Cherries escort had affectionately referred to as the Continental Divide.

"Wouldn't it be easier to chew through the ropes with

our teeth?" she sincerely wanted to know. "And less painful?"

His only comment was a sensual warning growl.

It took considerably more maneuvering for him to get where he was going, which included a great deal of bumping and rubbing against each other as they inched their way over to a rusty file cabinet, where he hooked his gag on the handle and pulled the material out of his mouth. By that time, Blue was hypersensitive to his every twitch. This was the way lovers' lay, *afterward,* she thought, aware of his breath on the back of her neck and his body heat everywhere else. Their bodies were curved and cupped like the proverbial spoons. He wasn't oblivious to the unavoidable intimacy involved either. Unless she was mistaken, certain of his body parts were already responding. Given the way her hands were tied behind her back, she would soon know for sure.

"What now?" she asked, trying to figure out how one found one's comfort zone in a situation like this. Her shins and shoulders were still smarting from the ropes, and her hip ached against the floorboards. But none of that bothered her nearly as much as the brand-new interloper in her nether parts. She blushed hotly as he shifted his hips and the pressure deepened. Some part of him was all but penetrating her. The question was: which part?

His voice was thick and husky. "I was hoping we could work our way over to that shelf where the scissors are."

I'll bet you were, she thought. "What scissors?"

She looked around the tiny room, convinced they were locked in the storage bin that time forgot. There were dented canned goods with peeling labels, stacks of yellowing linen surplices and black cassocks, all neatly folded, boxes of votive candles, and tarnished brass urns.

Finally Blue spotted a pair of rusty shears abandoned near a threadbare kneeler pad. Hope surged in her chest.

"And how do we get over there?" she asked, only half sarcastically. "Stand up and hop?"

"We could either scoot . . . or roll."

"I'm all scooted out, thanks. Let's roll."

They didn't even make it a half revolution before she called it off. "I can't do this," she gasped as they rocked back to their original position. "You have an erection!"

Silence crashed around them. The place might as well have collapsed into dust, it was so vibrantly still.

"No kidding," he breathed finally, and then heaved a sigh. "I don't guess it's the first time you've come into contact with one of those."

"Maybe not, but it wasn't attached to a priest. This time you *should* have checked it at the door."

"Yeah," he agreed heavily, "maybe so."

She began to shimmy and twist in an attempt to re-arrange herself. Her shoulder bumped his chin and her hip nudged his thigh. Either the ropes had loosened or she was one desperate cookie, but she was clearly the more agile of the two. She was slippery as a netted fish, wriggling around and squirming to get to a position where it didn't feel as if they were about to mate in the way of forest animals.

"What are you doing?" he demanded to know.

"I can't stay this way."

"You have to!"

"I can't—"

"You're only making it worse, Blue."

"It couldn't *be* worse," she cried. But it could. As she twisted around she heard him moan and felt the sound of it shiver through her like the icy swell of some certain, yet unknowable truth. It affected her exactly the way the evening bells at St. Joseph's had, the church near her childhood home. It made her throat tighten with hope. God, it made her nearly sick with hope.

As a romantic kid, she'd associated the bells with a perfect union, the meeting of soul mates. Corny stuff, but that was the kind of kid she'd been, a sentimental ninny, and there was no helping it. In her mind she'd seen fingertips touching, and the vision had always seemed to promise the one true love who was waiting for her somewhere out there, if she could only find him.

It pulled at something deep within her even now, but instead of stopping her turn in midrevolution, it spurred her on uncontrollably. If not for his throaty moan, she might have hesitated halfway, facing the ceiling instead of him. She might not have gasped softly and put every ounce of her strength into seeking the source of that moan.

"I have to," she acknowledged, breathing the words. She struggled around to face him, and when she did she saw what she'd been waiting to see since the day she met him, the heart-stealing hunger of a man who wanted her. His features shimmered with need. The effort to contain it made his jaw jut and his olive skin pull hard at the corners of his mouth. He looked beautiful, sensual. He looked ravaged with conflict.

"Didn't I tell you?" He searched her gaze, his own colored with irony and pain. "Worse, huh?"

"Yes . . . oh, yes, much worse . . . so much." Her lashes stung suddenly and she blinked away a sparkle of tears. Her own rising pain was mirrored in his eyes. "I could just die it's so much worse."

She laughed weakly, fully aware that he hadn't wanted her to see this, his utter helplessness in the face of his own bodily desires. Such sweet wild desires. But she had needed to see it more than she ever could have expressed, even the suffering he was going through, because she was suffering, too. Now there was only one reason to get out of their bonds and that was to make love. She knew it. He knew it.

She lifted up to kiss him, and as their lips brushed, a heartbreaking realization slipped out of her. "Oh, God," she groaned softly, desperately, "I love you."

"No—don't say that." He pulled back for an instant, then closed his eyes and shuddered. She knew then that he was going to surrender to what was happening inside him, the uncontrollable passion. He was hers. She'd won. He was going to make love to her, perhaps even change his entire life for her. She knew all that even if he didn't.

"Ah, Blue . . ."

His voice dropped to nothing, but she had never heard anyone say her name like that. It was a prayer. She should have been enthralled, but a terrible sadness came over her as she searched his face. Another shudder racked him, and she knew this was more than passion. It was pain. And not just the pain of desire. It was agony. Wanting her was killing him. Ultimately it would destroy him completely.

She strained to touch him. Just once she wanted to touch him, but she couldn't with her hands bound. "Wait, please," she said as he bent to kiss her.

He blinked, stared at her. "Why?"

"We can't do this. It's not right." The tears stung her lids again, nipping like angry bees. "I do love you, too much to let this happen."

"What do you mean?"

"You'd hate yourself afterward. I know that's supposed to be the guy's line, but it's true. You'd hate me as well."

His smile was crooked and unbearably sad.

By now her eyes were full of tears, flooding with them. "We can't do this. We just can't." It wasn't too late, she told herself. She could probably have taken advantage of the situation even at this point. Her body was still throbbing and bemoaning its unsatisfied urges, and it almost seemed as if he wanted her to lead him into temptation. But she'd been right about the havoc that would wreak. It would destroy him. And she couldn't do that. She would rather die than do that. He was a good and honorable man.

Hope. Sucker that she was, she always fell like a ton of bricks at the first glimmer of it. Her heart seemed to feed on hope, but by now her head should have known better. Yielding had almost never failed to bring her pain. Her throat was wiry and hot. Her eyes were swimming. And yet she clung to the small satisfaction of knowing that this was right. It was the best thing she'd ever done. Not loving him. Letting him go.

What made it so painful was that she did love him. It was a fine, fierce love, as free of dishonesty as anything she'd ever felt, and at least she could hold that knowledge close to her heart. She would know that once she had cared about someone more than she had cared about herself, and that would get her through. It was her first totally selfless act. It was also a lesson she would never forget. There were things more important in life than Blue Brandenburg's emotional needs.

He peered at her through the eyes of a man who was mystified and anguished and a victim of hope himself. "What is it you want, Blue? What in God's name do you want?"

"I want to get those shears," she announced hoarsely. Smiling was no easy feat when your heart was breaking in two, but she made a valiant effort. "Roll or scoot?"

• • •

Had she stayed in the convent, Mary Frances would have been having a very *different* wedding. She would have been dressed in the whitest of whites, wreathed in a veil of antique Irish lace and carrying a single red rose, the symbol of her patron saint. She would have been a bride of Christ, the blushing consort to the perfect Bridegroom. Instead she was marrying Lucifer himself. The perfect fiend.

At least she was appropriately dressed. Her groom's idea of a bridal gown was a little black number more suited to a cocktail party. Or a wake. Her high heels were dangerous weapons, the same black stilettos she'd worn for her meeting with Alex Cordes. Fortunately, she'd been provided with a fresh pair of nylons, black, of course. And then there was her hair. She couldn't have tamed it with a whip!

She couldn't begin to manage the style Blue had created, but she hadn't been able to wrestle it into the familiar braids and coils either, and the result was a scatter of wine-dark wisps and spirals that would have induced even Orphan Annie to put a bag over her head. Maybe it was the humidity.

Maybe it was the heavens. She'd tempted them, obviously.

"Marriage is the most solemn of commitments between two people to honor, cherish, and respect. . . ."

How can this be? Mary Frances thought, standing stiffly next to Webb Calderon while the ship's captain officiated in the main salon. The vessel had been swaying ominously since they started, but that was nothing compared with cruel cosmic forces that had conspired to bring about this ghastly state of affairs.

Michael Benjamin Murphy, her long-suffering and

devout-to-the-very-last-breath father, would have been writhing in his grave if he knew. And every one of her ancestors as well. Writhing and howling. She'd felt great guilt over the possibility that the Murphy family curse might have been fulfilled by Brianna's death. Anguish no more, Mary Frances Murphy, soon-to-be Calderon, she thought. This has to be the curse in action, and it wants you.

"Do you take this woman . . . ?"

The youngish, deeply tanned captain looked up just long enough to catch Webb's nod, then hastily mumbled through the rest of the civil service, glancing back and forth between them as he posed the questions that would make them man and wife. At no point did he wait for Mary Frances to answer, and his furtive manner made her wonder if he knew that by performing this foul ceremony, he was marrying a virginal hostage just barely out of the convent to the foulest of men and for the foulest of reasons. No doubt he was being paid well enough for his services that he wouldn't have cared if she'd been thirteen, in pigtails and sucking on a lollipop.

The only other people involved with the ceremony besides the captain were the witnesses. Both were women and possibly on the galley staff, although as far as Mary Frances knew, they could be running the ship when they weren't standing up at weddings and gawking at Webb Calderon. He did look incredible in his blousy, ivory-white shirt, baggy linen pants, and sandals. Not exactly dressed for a wedding, more like a holiday in Spain. But you'd have thought he was that guy who posed for romance-novel covers the way they were making cow eyes.

"By the power vested in me—"

The ship came up and slammed down hard. Mary

Frances felt her stomach go with it. She swayed forward, but something jerked her back as the entire vessel listed sharply. Webb had caught her by the wrist, and he was tugging her toward him. She tried to resist, but when the ship rolled back, she lost her balance altogether. Vertigo made her tumble into his open arms, and weakness kept her there.

"Are you all right?" he asked in his beautiful, sonorous, *sickening* voice.

"No, I'm not! I'm going to be ill all over this boat!" Oh, please, she thought, let it be true! Let me be sick, right here. Right now. On him. What a fitting ending to this disgusting ceremony. I'll soil his pretty white shirt and make him stink.

The boat continued to roll, but Webb didn't seem too concerned with her dire threats. He held her as possessively as if he never intended to release her, and then he breathed a threat of his own in the hair at her crown.

"You're no good at rough games, Irish. Give it up, sweetness. You can't win."

Everything in her screamed no, but the floor was rolling beneath her feet, and he was the only solid thing in her environment, the only anchor. Her legs were as flimsy as thread, but her neck muscles were taut as he delved into the thick of her raven hair with shocking intimacy and caressed the cords of her nape. By wearing her hair up, she had unintentionally made herself very vulnerable. Was that why men liked women with long hair? she wondered. The mystery of having it long and concealing? The exposure of wearing it up? It was almost as though she'd stripped for him.

"Get us married," he growled at the captain. "And do it now!"

The roughness in his voice startled Mary Frances. Really

startled her. The gyration her stomach did was close to a
somersault. She clutched her hands there, but it did no
good. Something about his demand had caught her off
guard. It had thrilled her, she realized, though she was loath
to admit it. And everyone else, too, apparently.

The younger man was flattened against the forward
bulkhead and the two women were holding on to a teak
sideboard for dear life. "I now pronounce you husband
and wife," the captain blurted. He tossed the groom a
nod. "You may," he said.

Mary Frances stiffened, but Webb didn't seem in any
hurry to follow the captain's instructions. He turned toward the woman he'd just pledged to honor, respect, and
cherish and let it be known, by the way his gaze drifted
to her mouth and lingered, that he didn't intend to do any
of those things. But he did intend to kiss her.

"And I will," he said softly, "later."

Later? She could tell by the press of his body along the
length of hers that the thing he was saving for later was
coming much too soon to suit her. Her new husband was
ready for a honeymoon on the high seas.

"Champagne?" Webb held up a bottle of Dom Pérignon
and a crystal flute that flashed in the candlelight, dancing
rainbows around the room. They'd retired to the master
suite of the yacht, where apparently the honeymoon fes-
tivities were to take place. Either that or she was to be tortured again.

Same thing, she thought, smiling ruefully.

"Only if I can hit the groom over the head with it," she
muttered under her breath. She gave him a look and took
the bottle anyway, barely able to disguise her contempt.
She wasn't passing up perfectly good wine just to thwart
him. She'd developed rather a taste for the stuff at St.

Gertrude's, the plum and dandelion varieties in particular. Besides, if she got drunk enough, then perhaps she would upchuck—

She shuddered, wondering at her preoccupation with regurgitation. Her new husband surely brought out the worst in her.

"Black was the wrong choice for you," he said, apparently meaning her dress. "It's too severe."

"Lucky I'm not a nun," she murmured.

"Yes, isn't it."

She arranged the neckline, which was cut in a wide deep V with black pearl buttons to the waist, and would have made even the most waiflike of supermodels look busty. It certainly did Mary Frances, who had never thought of herself as full-breasted. The all-occasion sheath, she decided sardonically, a blushing bride could wear it to both wedding and funeral—undoubtedly her own if Webb Calderon had anything to do with it. Actually, it would have been perfect for one of Bluebeard's wives, she decided.

He smiled and raised his glass to toast her. The champagne glowed in the light, pale white fire, as hypnotic as his eyes. "I'm serious. You're too delicate for black. Your skin is like eggshells. It's beautiful," he added in a low voice.

Not as beautiful as you, she thought impulsively, hating herself for the admission. She couldn't decide if his faintly tortured aspect reminded her more of a martyr or a saint. But now, gazing at his mouth, she could feel her insides respond in that deep, strange way, like an oar taking strokes in the water. It was hard for her to believe that she could feel these things for him, that her reactions to him could be so confused with repulsion and attraction. Mostly attraction, unfortunately.

He'd dressed in a totally casual way for the wedding. The blousy shirt, baggy linen pants, and woven sandals were a European look and a startling contrast to the caramelized gold of his tan and the whitened highlights in his dark blond hair. The sun had bleached all the color from the wisps that curled at his temples and the shimmers lighting his crown.

The contrasts were as vivid as ever, but as always, it was his face that fascinated her the most, the duality in his features. The extreme sensitivity in the lines of his mouth, the lurking cruelty. She couldn't help but wonder if that was part of the attraction, that he was capable of both. Her pulse fluttered suddenly, wildly. He had shown her the cruelty. He had touched her with that part of him. If he ever touched her with the sensitivity, she would be lost.

Pain stabbed, and she realized she was squeezing the champagne glass so tightly that its crystal facets were digging into her thumb. As long as she was torn between her feelings for this man, as long as she fought them, he had her. And he knew it. If she could find that quiet place, that interior silence where he couldn't reach her, she would be safe from him.

What is the strongest of all things?

The question flashed out of nowhere.

What was? she asked herself. The refuge of her mind?

19

She was going to polish off the whole damn bottle, Webb observed dryly. All by herself. Not only was his brand-new bride working on her third glass of champagne with the dedication of a confirmed wino, but she had a stranglehold on the bottle itself. She'd gripped it by the neck in one of her delicate "eggshell" hands and would probably be drinking straight from it when she'd polished off the glass. Joan of Arc on a toot, he thought, wondering how she managed to get sloshed and look saintly at the same time.

"More champagne?" he asked, unable to resist. He was reasonably sure she would have broken his arm before she'd let him do the gentlemanly thing and pour for her. Nobody was going to get that bottle away from her. Not and live.

She cut him a look that said, *What are you trying to do, get me drunk, buster?*—then announced, inexplicably, "I've had plenty, thanks," and went right on drinking.

Webb felt the heat of a smile in his throat. She was a

mouthy little lush. He'd been quietly observing her from
across the master bedroom for three quarters of an hour
now, amused by her slow but determined descent into the
bottle. She'd been boozing this way ever since he suggested they retire to the room and drink a toast, and by
now he was more curious than anything else. He was
waiting for the moment when she tipped over and fell on
her adorable retroussé nose.

He knew what she was doing, which was why he hadn't
stopped her. Watching someone dig their own grave was
always more entertaining than doing the excavating yourself. And one hardly had to look at her to see the mental
shovels flying. She was searching for some way to reclaim
the distance that allowed her to hide. She needed the safety
of her secret place, but unfortunately for her, she'd been
locked out of her garden. She'd sneaked out to have a look
at the big, bad world, and the door had slammed shut behind her. She didn't have a key. She couldn't get back in.
She was his.

"Did all your wives get to wear this black Ace bandage?" she grumbled, tugging at the clingy spandex skirt
of her dress.

"All my wives?" She was talking in riddles. Earlier
she'd asked him something about the strongest thing of
all. She'd also made another oblique reference to Bluebeard and his penchant for "uxoricide," which she clearly
wasn't disposed to explain. She *was* a strange little thing.
He couldn't decide whether she'd been in the convent too
long, or not long enough.

It was humid in the room, despite the early hour and
the air-conditioning. He could feel the dampness at the
back of his own neck, but the effect on her was far more
interesting. Dark scatterings of corkscrew curls had come
loose from their pins, and her cheeks bloomed like hot-

house flowers. The dampness above her upper lip fascinated him, too. Completely.

"To be married in a hand-me-down wet suit to the Marquis de Sade of the Bahamas. Isn't that every girl's dream?" Her tone oozed sweet acrimony.

The smile flared into his jaw. Despite the ache, Webb continued to suppress it. He was enjoying this, biding his time, savoring the sight of her the way any hungry predator might . . . the spider watching the fly struggle and ensnare herself more inescapably with every stroke of her silky wings.

A damselfly, he thought. Spindly, yet graceful, trembling at the prospect of the spider's deadly embrace. The black dress he'd chosen for her was stark, yet ultrafeminine on a woman of her coloring. Cut wide and deep at the bosom, it barely touched her pale shoulders, but concealed her slender arms to the wrist. Her breasts were pink-tinged puff clouds, rising like drifts in a dark valley. Plump and pale, they made him think of cotton candy and other delectable things.

Hell, they made his mouth water.

He settled his own champagne glass on the silver tray next to the ice bucket, aware of the warmth pooling in his fingers. He didn't need champagne. His blood was already stirring. He could remember emptying a champagne glass in one swallow and then laying the crystal out against a fireplace just to hear it shatter. The explosions rarely did more than send a faint shiver across his shoulder blades and remind him he had a functioning nervous system.

Nothing like her effect on him.

Something had changed inside him when he'd touched her throat during the ceremony and felt the wildness of her pulse. Some latent appetite had awakened and quivered to life. His own flesh had responded involuntarily. Juices rose, fibers thickened, all in some quest of their own. That was why he had to be careful. Hunger was dangerous. It created its own demand, a need that had to be filled. It made you do things, take risks.

"Shouldn't you have something to eat?" It wasn't what he wanted to ask her. There was a much more interesting question on his mind. *Are you really as virginal as you look?*

Maybe it was the freckles or her wobbly claim on the high heels, but she looked like a kid on her first date. The escort service provided bios that were more fantasy than fact. Hers had said she was in her mid-twenties, which was well past the age of consent for most women. Still, she'd only been masquerading as an escort and he doubted she was out of the convent much more than a year, so it seemed possible she'd never been with a man.

"Plenty, thanks," she murmured.

He had no idea what that meant. She'd had plenty? She wanted plenty? The staff had supplied a tray of hors d'oeuvres in addition to the champagne. He picked them up from the occasional table and walked to her.

She shook her head as if she'd seen him coming, then glanced up as he reached her. It was just a fleeting thing, a way to judge the situation and assess her safety. After all, a spider offering food? What did that mean?

He could have insisted. She may well have eaten what they'd brought her earlier, but that wasn't the point. He'd only wanted a reason to approach her without putting her too much on guard. She'd stopped drinking and was determinedly staring at the bubbles exploding in her glass. Were there bubbles self-destructing inside her, too? Was excitement any part of her response, or was it all just nerves and fear and loathing? Suddenly he wanted to know if that was how she felt. If she loathed him.

There was a console behind her. By the time he'd set the tray down, she'd turned away from him, which somehow made her all the more tempting. Where to touch her? That was the question in his mind. Her arm was the obvious place, but not nearly as interesting as her nape. With her head tilted down, the slight strain on her spine raised delicate bones. The slope of her throat was tempting, too, but if he came into contact with that pulse again, it could be dangerous for both of them.

The *Hatteras* rolled beneath his feet. He grasped her arm, more to steady her than anything else, but she flinched and lost her grip on the bottle. It fell to the floor and rolled across the room, gushing champagne like a fire hose.

A moan rose in her throat, the sound of abject distress. "Let me have the glass," he said as he pulled her out of the spray. But she clutched it to her bosom as if it were her child and he a kidnapper. Fortunately there wasn't much champagne left in it. What was there foamed over her breasts and sheened them with sparkling lights.

The yacht rolled back and settled almost immediately, but Webb didn't let go of her. Releasing her was the last thing on his mind and hers too, apparently. There seemed to be little either one of them could do but stare at the beautiful mess she'd made of herself. Her breasts shivered and glittered like crystals. They trembled with each heave of her shoulders, but the lights in her eyes made the gems seem pale as she looked up at him. Her eyes were falling stars.

It was all there in her defenseless gaze, the naked truth.

Her garden sanctuary was a sensual Eden, lush and fertile. Nature had created burgeoning erotic life within her, and she was compelled to give expression to it, to relieve the building pressure. It was only fear holding her back—fear and shame.

What *was* her sin of impurity? he wondered.

Her eyes beseeched him and held him off at the same time. He'd never seen anything quite like it. Her conflict almost evoked the sympathy she was searching for. She was frightened, and had a right to be. If she'd known what was going on inside him, felt his rising hunger, tasted his need, she would have been shaking.

"You're going to break that glass," he warned her.

She had crushed the fragile flute in the cleft between her breasts and the stem looked about to snap.

"Let me have it," he said with quiet force. But she refused to relinquish it, and he had a vision of glass shards stabbing her tender flesh that nearly made him sick.

She defied him with a fierce look as he reached for the glass, and her grip on the stem forced him to delve beneath her fingers and into her cleavage. Her body's response was exquisite. Her heart was maniacal. Her breasts felt as if they were pulsing and swelling against his knuckles, and the moan in her throat told him everything he needed to know.

She *was* his.

The fly was already entangled too deeply to get free. Everything she'd done to protect herself had only ensnared her more. The struggle with her inner urges had driven her further and further from that unassailable place of silence. The champagne that was supposed to fortify her had lowered her inhibitions and made her more susceptible.

She was lost. She knew it, too.

A hard little shudder went through her now, untying every last knot of resistance in her spine. If he were to draw her to him, she would come without a fight. If he were to caress the underside of her chin and brush her lips with his, she would respond helplessly. The softness that quivered against his knuckles might as well have belonged to him. It did belong to him.

Webb understood all that with the instinct of a hunter, but knowing would have to be enough, he told himself. As much as he wanted it to be, this wasn't the time. There was still horror glittering in her eyes, and though it made her luminously beautiful and nearly drove him mad with lust, it wasn't the response he wanted.

Fear incited the predator to action. It was the universal scent that aroused animal hunger and even savagery, and fear was rising from her skin like sweet perfume. Every primitive urge known to man was churning inside him right now, and probably a few known only to the animals. Her vulnerability was an undeniable aphrodisiac. It made him wild, and he hadn't felt wild in years, not like this. But he wanted more than simple fear. He wanted to see desire in her eyes, the white-hot spark of life. He wanted it to sear away everything else, even the fear, and consume her.

"Let me have it," he said. His voice was harsh, but she knew what he meant.

Her fingers opened, and the glass slipped through her hands.

Webb caught it before it hit the floor. Cradling the crystal in his palm, he was aware of her radiant reflection in its surface and the warmth of her breasts on the stem. He returned the glass to the tray, but found he didn't like taking his eyes off her, even for that long.

"I could order coffee," he suggested, turning back to her. "Or we could just get on with the honeymoon."

He'd meant it half humorously, but she reacted as if she were about to be ill, cringing away as he approached her. It surprised him how much her reaction disturbed him. "Apparently you'd rather *not* get on with the honeymoon. Apparently you think I'm some kind of a monster."

"Aren't you?"

"Some people might say I've done monstrous things."

She brought her fingers to her throat, reaching for something. Her hand made a quick fist when she didn't find it. "I *know* what you've done," she said. "I read Brianna's diary."

Her *sister's* diary? She'd found it then, on his computer.

"You turned her into some kind of sex fiend." Her voice was soft but vehement. "That's all she wrote about—her 'carnal desires'—and how you subjugated her until she could think of nothing but her own flesh and the pleasure you gave her. Those were her words, almost exactly."

He wanted to smile. "Doesn't sound like a crime to me."

Anger whitened her jaw. "You introduced her to bondage and whips and God knows what else," she hissed. " 'Slender silken whips that sting like bees, yet drip with honey so sweet it makes your throat tighten with longing.' My sister didn't even know who she was when you got through with her."

Interesting that she knew the diary word for word, he observed. She might be in terrible conflict, but the quake in her voice told him more than she wanted him to know.

This had as much to do with her own fantasies as it did her sister's.

"Are you concerned because your sister liked that sort of thing? Or because you think *you* might?" He let his gaze drift downward, studying the hand fisted in the warmth of her flesh. It did seem to be a favorite place of hers. Understandable, he thought.

What was less understandable was what she did to him. The sex-fiend reference wasn't too far off. He found it hard to tear his gaze from the flush that started where her fist was tucked and flared upward, warming her throat. He found it even harder not to work his way down from that same place, button by button. And hardest of all was the tension that was taking shape in his gut, a coil spring of tensile steel that only promised to get tighter and tighter. Desire.

"I'm concerned because she's *dead*." Her secret-garden eyes were blazing now. With fire and brimstone. They accused him of everything from sexual enslavement to murder.

He took a deep breath. "If I told you that I had nothing to do with your sister's death, would you believe me?"

"No!" The boat swayed from side to side, and she leaned against the console rather than risk any more contact with him.

Fine vibrations permeated the room, the ship, as it surged through the water. Webb could feel them in his fingers as he adjusted the leather strap of his tank watch. "What if I told you I don't know anything about the diary or how it got on my hard drive, that I discovered it after some routine computer maintenance was done by someone claiming to be a repair person?"

She stared at him suspiciously, her hands braced behind her. "Why would someone do that?"

"Perhaps to implicate me in Brianna's death?"

"The investigation was closed. Her death was ruled an accident."

"But you don't believe that, do you?"

"No, I don't believe it. I think *you* did it. You had a motive. Brianna found a pre-Colombian relic in a suitcase she was supposed to deliver to you."

"Cherries' clients are among the most powerful business moguls in the world. They don't have to deal with couriers who steal contraband. The service itself handles that. You're on the wrong trail, Mary Frances." Try as she might to hide, he thought, it was all right there in her expressive features—doubt, anxiety, frustration. She clearly didn't know what to believe.

"You're saying it wasn't you? You had nothing to do with it?"

"Nothing." Fortunately, he didn't share her qualms about lying.

Her fist was still pressed to her chest, and he knew what she wanted. He magically produced her saint's medal from the pocket of his linen pants. The chain laced his fingers and the antique pendant was cradled in his palm. "Is this what you're looking for?"

"My medal!" Her face lit up as he held it out.

He knew why she wanted the medal so desperately. It was her protection, the key that would let her back into the garden.

"Thank you," she breathed, and started toward him.

He watched her sway as the yacht made a slight correction. She looked dizzy, eager, and his chest tightened as he made a decision. He wasn't going to give it back to her. Not yet. He needed her this way, vulnerable. If she found that calm place again, she would vanish and never come out.

He closed his hand, and she stopped in confusion, not even two feet from him. "You're not going to give it to me?"

Irish, Irish, he thought, almost sadly, have you forgotten? I play dirty. You can forget all the rest of it, but don't ever forget that. *Don't ever forget what a bastard I am.* He sifted the chain through his fingers, remembering the trembling passion with which she'd brushed her lips over it. At the time he'd thought he could die happy if she ever brushed her lips over his that way, with such pure passion it could burn the soul.

"Maybe." he said slowly. "What's it worth to you?"

She flushed and shook her head, sending tendrils of raven hair flying. He was close enough to touch her and the urge rocked him almost painfully. Jesus, he hadn't felt his guts clench with this much force since childhood, not since before the massacre that took his entire family. Webb Calderon's own personal holocaust.

Her chin was tilted down and the shadow of her lashes fanned across her cheeks like the points of a star. Golden freckles danced like sunshine across the bridge of her nose, bringing the luminosity of her skin into sharp relief. As he scrutinized her features in profile another woman came to mind.

"God, you're so much like her." A touch to Mary Frances's chin brought her face up.

Confusion, and then: ". . . Brianna?"

"No, a painting of mine." In reality her features were nothing like the woman's in *Blush*, but in unguarded moments like this one he could see fascinating similarities. There was a quality of expectation in her green eyes, of erotic longing that was identical.

"A painting of what?" she asked.

"A woman . . . kissing her own reflection in a mirror."

"How odd, kissing herself?"

"I always thought she was practicing."

Her gaze darkened sensually and it registered on Webb's nervous system like a blow to the midsection. "For a man?" she wanted to know in a tone that was throaty and soft.

He didn't answer the question. It would have been far too dangerous, for her. "I'm not the kind of guy you should be looking at that way," he warned.

"What way am I looking?"

"Like I'm the man who can save you." *Like I'm what you need—tonight, tomorrow, forever.* Something moved in the depths of her eyes, and he was aware of changes in his own respiration, of the need to breathe deeply through his mouth. They were in the most extreme of conditions, and yet at their most essential, still just a man and a woman.

"Aren't you?" The question caught in her throat.

Power. What did a man do when he knew he had power over a woman? This one was helpless without the saint's medal, or at least she believed she was. It was a tantalizing prospect. If he were to make love to her now, she would be emotionally naked, unable to protect herself. She would give up everything—her pristine body, her virgin mind, even the part of her spirit that was untouched and inviolable. He wanted that. He wanted her soul, but if she surrendered it, he knew instinctively that he would be lost, too. Why? Because then he would have to love her, and love would destroy him.

His hand contracted into a fist and pain stabbed him. Sweet fiery pain.

"Aren't you that man?" She pulled a breath, hot and shaky. Her body swayed toward his. He wondered if she were about to do something rash, and he felt the steel inside him tightening. She hesitated, too, then reached out to touch him, and he felt a surge of desire. It rushed into the void left by all those years of emptiness. It threatened to engulf him.

He hadn't felt desire for anything but the taste of Ruben Cordes's blood since he was a child. Yet what he felt now, for her, was the real soul-shaking desire of a man for a woman. Wanting her had brought him back from emotional death. It had brought him so painfully alive he was almost afraid to act on it.

Her fingers grazed his cheek like silky wings and were gone, a damselfly daring to tempt the spider. He searched her expression and wondered if she knew what she was doing, if she wanted him to devour her.

The low rumble of the charter's engines permeated the room. Champagne and ocean brine and searing traces of diesel fuel mingled in a potent brew.

Mary Frances breathed in the fumes so deeply it made her light-headed. In every fiber of her being she was aware of Webb Calderon's brooding fixation on her. The last thing she should have done was to return it, but she couldn't help herself. The pull was deep and elemental. Like the churn and suck of the sea beneath them, like the oars battling deep currents. Despite everything, or perhaps because of it, she couldn't shake the feeling that this was the experience she'd been waiting for her entire life, that he was the man.

He looked at her as if he knew everything there was to know about her secret needs, and she was beginning to have that same sense of him, that she could peer into his soul just by looking at him. A man couldn't concentrate on a woman this deeply without opening and revealing something of himself. There were moments, like now, when she saw the sorrow of a saint, the rage of a martyr, in his eyes. Did he weep, too? The thought pierced her.

He bent toward her, and instead of shrinking away, she rose to meet him. It wasn't a deliberate act. She hadn't consciously decided to kiss him, and yet there didn't seem to be any other choice. She had to taste and be tasted. Touch and be touched. She had to know. So much to know. Even if it was dangerous. Even if he didn't love her. Even if he killed her.

Love her? What did that mean? She didn't know where that reference had come from, but it had flowed out of her with the naturalness of a river. The same strange and wild river that was rippling through her. Tears stung her lids and wet her lashes. Please don't hurt me, she thought. Love me instead.

She curled her fingers in the cords of his shirt and her lashes lowered as she sought his lips. Startled, she felt something jerk her head back and realized that he had claimed her in the most primitive and symbolic of ways, with a handful of hair at her nape. He held her that way, the muscles of his face jutting and hard. His lips parted as if he might speak, but all he did was breathe, flooding her with his rising sexual heat.

The river swirled higher as his lips hovered near hers. She was swept with sensations that made her feel ensnared by anticipation as much as by the man. But he hadn't kissed her yet, and in some silent, remote part of her being, she knew there was still a choice, a question to be answered. Did she give herself over to the riptide and let it take her under? Did she willingly let herself drown?

Webb was on the brink of going under himself. Drowning in sensation. The feel of her, the sound of her, the smell of her—all of that washed over him, arousing him, inciting the predator. His hand was buried in her hair—

rich raven curls that somehow reminded him of ginger-bread, or maybe it was the subtly spiced scent his delving fingers had released from her tresses. Cinnamon? What-ever it was, it made his jaws ache.

He brushed her mouth and hissed with surprise. It was as sweet as he'd imagined. Sweeter. She was as succulent as anything he'd ever tasted. He wanted to eat her alive. His entire being quickened with ravenous excitement, ris-ing and responding to the urge to consume. Within sec-onds her lips were soft and swollen with stimulation, pink from his little nips. Mouthwatering. He sampled her chin and cheeks and throat with eating, sucking, nibbling kisses. He fed on her exquisite flesh with a lust that sprang from ancient hungers. He ached in every fiber, ached with the promise of satisfaction. His body cried out for it.

The spider was feasting on the damselfly, devouring her mouthful by tender mouthful.

"Tender prey," he whispered near her ear, "mine for the taking. All mine."

The ship rolled beneath them, pressing their bodies together. Her breasts melted against his chest and her hips bumped his with every swing and sway of the ocean. She felt as languid as the currents that rocked beneath them. His hand tightened in her hair and the sound that slipped out of her was the sweetest of whim-pers, a mating call.

He nipped her too hard. She moaned and struggled, then shuddered with a sigh. "Please love me," she whis-pered.

Love her? Webb's reaction was strangely delayed. Her voice was so soft he wondered if he'd imagined it. It didn't seem possible she'd said those words, and then he knew. With slow-dawning certainty, he knew that she had. *Please,* she'd said, *please love me.*

The realization seemed to paralyze his senses for a moment. He couldn't make himself understand why she'd said it, what it had meant—and how he felt. It seemed incomprehensible to him that someone could love him, given who he was, *what* he was. And even if she was saint enough to find something worth loving in him, he couldn't love her back. He couldn't love anything. He'd lost that ability when he was a child. He couldn't even feel. He was barely human, for God's sake.

He felt as if a fist had reached into his gut and was going to crush his vitals. The slow twisting force of it held him motionless while he fought to understand what was happening. Pain was making a liar out of him. Agonizing pain. He was as human and vulnerable and subject to torment as anyone. More. God, so much more. It was his hand throbbing now. It was his heart. Something was ripping him apart.

He released her and opened his palm, aware that she was staring at him. The sharply filigreed edges of her saint's medal had cut into him, sliced through scar tissue and pierced to the bone. Blood pooled in the cradle of his hand.

A scream was strangled off somewhere inside him. He barely recognized the sound as his own. Pain. Mangled flesh. Broken bodies and a little girl's song. How could he have forgotten this? This was what happened when you let yourself feel. You bled to death.

"Are you all right?"

She touched him, trying to get through, but his mind was already lost in the carnage. It wasn't the pain he feared. It was the memories. They'd been encased in steel his whole life, walled off so thickly he'd been able to control them. Whenever he wanted to remember, to wake his sleeping rage, he brought them out selectively, viewed them as if from a distance, through the prism lens of time. He could deal with the fragments. But this was different. It was dangerous. He no longer had that wall. Memories were rushing out of the void, wailing at him like banshees, threatening to swamp him.

"I know how you got the scar," she said softly. "I know everything. If you want to talk about it—"

He turned away from her, raised his hand to stop her.

"It might help," she pressed, clearly meaning well. "I know what happened, Webb, to your family, the torture."

"No—" He was shouting at the images as much as he was shouting at her. With merciless clarity, he could see his stepfather being shot through the head in front of him, his mother stripped and repeatedly raped by a gang of insurgents, crazed with bloodlust. Lucinda Calderon had pressed her antique ruby cross into her nine-year-old son's hand before they dragged her in front of the tribunal and savaged her like a pack of mad dogs. When they were done with her, they put a bullet between her eyes, their one merciful act, and allowed her to join her husband.

Webb had crushed the cross in his hand with such pressure it had embedded itself in his flesh. Years later, after his escape from prison, he'd had to have it surgically removed.

"You were forced to watch," she said, breaking into his thoughts again. "I know what that must have done to you—"

No, you don't, his mind roared. *You couldn't possibly know.*

"Your mother, your stepfather . . ."

My sister. Isabella. Her name brought such exquisite

pain, Webb could barely allow it into his conscious mind. Nothing compared with the tormenting memories of his courageous eight-year-old sister. She'd sung a hymn throughout the devastation, a frail, terrified child clinging to her sanity by singing softly through the horror of her parents' slaughter, singing even while she herself was being violated.

When they couldn't break her, couldn't stop a dry-eyed eight-year-old from singing, they slit her throat and left her to bleed to death, slowly. Interminably. Webb had known that she might not die for hours. Driven by blind rage, he'd attacked one of the soldiers as they came for him. He'd ripped the man's gun from his shoulder holster and saved his sister with a bullet, but nothing could save Webb from her song. He couldn't remember the hymn or the words. All he could remember was the piercing clarity of her voice, playing night after night in his head until he had found a way to shut it off. Shut everything off.

"Webb? Webb, please! What's wrong?"

He felt a hand on his arm and was suddenly aware that he was on the other side of the cabin, his body rigid enough to crack. He didn't remember walking there. "Nothing's wrong," he said, his voice empty, blast-frozen of emotion. "Not a thing. It's all perfect."

She went quiet and he realized, absently, that she had never been more in danger from him than she was now. He was cold enough to do anything, to hurt anyone. No one was safe from him now.

"If only you'd let me help. I was trained for this, trained to comfort and counsel. I know I could help."

He opened his palm, stared at the bloody eruption that had once been scar tissue, at her medal. "It's not possible to help me." She had to stop. She had to. *Stop.*

"At least let me dress the injury, then. It's broken open the scar—"

I know how you got the scar. I know everything.

He whirled on her, a snarl rattling in his throat. "How do you know about the scar? How do you know about any of this? Who the hell are you?"

"I stole your file from the escort service." She hesitated, reached for the medal at her throat, the medal that had made him bleed. It wasn't there, but she couldn't help herself. It was a reflex. She needed protection. She was lying.

"Whatever happened to you, Webb, it can't possibly help anything to seek vengeance after all this time—"

"What the fuck do you know about vengeance?"

"I know my sister's dead."

"Exactly—and you're here because you think I killed her."

"But I'm not seeking vengeance, I'm seeking understanding. And justice. I don't want her death to have been in vain."

Her piety made him ill. She wanted him to reduce the brutal slaughter of his entire family to a quest for understanding? There *was* no fucking justice in San Carlos, and Cordes couldn't be prosecuted anywhere else.

Webb's hand closed over the medal in his palm, shutting out everything but the ice storm that raged through his veins. He was cold, so blessedly cold he would never be warm again. Pain was not a gift. Pain was his enemy. She was his enemy.

Fuck societal justice. There was no such thing. Did she know how badly he wanted to kill someone, anyone, how badly he *wanted* blood on his hands? Did she know that anyone who got in the way of his vendetta this time was going to die, too? And right now that was her. Did she *understand* any of that?

She was about to find out.

20

Mary Frances knew she should say nothing more to provoke him. Nothing. Not one word. But she could feel his pain as sharply as if she were bleeding instead of him, and it was deeply rooted in her nature to be nurturing and compassionate. She had left the order, but it was still part of who she was and always would be. Comforting the afflicted and counseling the troubled were to have been her life's calling. They were two of the Seven Acts of Mercy, and this man cried out for mercy.

The ship groaned with the pressures surging against its massive hull. The sound was heavy and mournful, a funeral dirge.

In a voice so soft she wasn't sure he could hear her across the room, she said. "You're right, I don't know what you went through. I can only imagine the horror, but that doesn't mean I have nothing to offer."

"What do you know about my background?" he demanded to know. "And how did you find out?"

She clasped her hands at her waist. When you lied to

protect someone else, was it as serious a transgression as lying to protect yourself? she wondered. Did it still take a piece of your soul as its price? It was possible he already knew about Blue's involvement and was testing her. Mary Frances would be lying for nothing. But she couldn't take the chance.

"I stole your dossier from the service's files," she said. "I wanted to know everything I could about you, and I was hoping to find some background information."

"And did you?"

"Yes." She could hardly fathom the difference in him, or the speed with which he'd changed. It didn't seem possible this was the man whose kiss had reduced her to sweet, clawing shock. That she had barely been able to stand on her feet. She could still feel his breath whispering near her ear, and it might as well have been made of fire instead of oxygen. Only now everything was different. His voice had gone as terrifyingly cold as his heart.

She didn't know how to reach him, but she had to try. "It said that your family was murdered during a military coup in San Carlos, and you were forced to watch their executions."

"What else?" The calmness with which he adjusted the leather strap of his tank watch disturbed her. She'd seen the agony in his eyes, but it was gone now. If he was in conflict, the outward signs had vanished.

"You were imprisoned and tortured in monstrous ways. They did everything but kill you with some ghoulish combination of water baths and electrical voltage." She shuddered thinking about it, shuddered for him.

"Did it mention my parents?" he said tonelessly. "Did it say how they shot my stepfather through the head and raped my mother before they executed her?"

"Yes, but I'd rather not—"

He was tightening the watch too much. His skin was white against the leather strap. "Did it say what they did to my sister?"

The ice cracked open and a hiss of pain escaped. She could hear it in his voice, raw and constricted. This was the wound that wouldn't heal. Mary Frances knew the girl had been sacrificed along with her parents, and there'd been something said about a mercy killing, but she hadn't thought Webb— No, he couldn't have done it. Not at nine!

Mary Frances was well schooled in the gruesome aspects of torture. Most of the Catholic saints and martyrs had been horrifically persecuted, but that was far removed from her experience. This was as immediate in her mind as if she'd witnessed it, too. A nine-year-old child had watched his family being butchered, and God only knew what else.

She'd hoped to encourage him to open up and talk so that it might help free him from the bondage, and he *was* in bondage of the worst kind. He'd been imprisoned by his own dark drives for decades. For herself, she'd hoped he might ultimately change his mind about his plans for her and Alex Cordes. She'd meant to forge a bond with him, but instead she'd reminded him of these atrocities.

He was staring at the pendant in his hand as he moved toward the tray with the ice bucket. Eyeing the necklace nervously, Mary Frances wondered if he meant to set it there. How she wanted it back! Was this his way of returning it to her?

"They killed her," he said tonelessly. "They cut her throat to stop her from singing."

Her necklace hit the tray with a sharp clack. He grabbed a napkin and wadded it in his fist. For the blood, she imagined.

Mary Frances knew better than to ask him to explain.
Webb Calderon's will and the force it contained were
massive—a superstructure like one of the great dams. But
paradoxically, such things were vulnerable. The more
massive the structure, the more vulnerable it was, because even the tiniest of fissures could imperil it. And
that was what was happening now, she realized. There
was a crack.

He'd moved into the shadows of the small stateroom,
and she didn't know how to reach him. "Maybe it's time
to let go of the past," she suggested, knowing how sim-
plistic that must have sounded.

He didn't give her the chance to say anything more. He
whirled on her with glacial fury. His mouth curled in a
beautiful, frightening snarl. "Let go of the past? Christ,
you'll be quoting the Golden Rule next. You read some
words in a dossier and that makes you an expert on my
past?"

Her impulse was to edge back, away from him, but
there was nowhere to go. His eyes burned cold, an ice
fire. If she hadn't been clutching her arms, the glare
would have frozen her through to her spine. "I know
vengeance resolves nothing. It only hurts more people. I
know that no one can really heal until they forgive and let
go—"

"*Forgive?* Are you insane? I would destroy *myself*
first. I would cut out my own heart before I'd forgive
those murdering animals."

She was too shocked to respond. His contempt was
scathing, but it was the change in his appearance that
truly frightened her. He might as well have had an aura,
he seemed so charged with destructive potential. Even
the pale streaks in his hair were iced by lightning. The
moment had an explosive feel to it, but she couldn't help

herself. She *believed* in forgiveness, in mercy, even for crimes as heinous as these. "You can't help your mother and sister now. You can't play God."

"Why not?" His voice had dropped to a terrifying whisper. "I do it every day."

The boat groaned pleadingly. It was the sound of souls trapped in purgatory. And Webb Calderon's sightless glare was death itself.

Something was desperately wrong. She could feel it. In her floundering attempt to help, she had pushed him too far and unleashed a murderous rage. She began to inch toward the door, then abruptly pivoted to make a break for it. The rug slipped out from under her feet, and she lurched forward, flailing to catch her balance.

She let out a wild cry of relief as her fingers grazed the doorknob. She'd stumbled toward the door! She had it open, the knob in her grasp, when he slammed the door shut and pulled her away. Her high heels were impossible to manage. They slipped out from under her as she tried to free herself.

With a savage grunt, he clamped an arm around her waist, lifted her into the air, and heaved her onto the bed. The softness of the down comforter cushioned her fall, but the swiftness of his assault left her reeling.

Violence flared through him as he dropped down, looming over her. "Now let's talk about forgiveness," he said. "Let's talk about how those pigs forced themselves on my mother and sister, assaulted and raped them. Do you know what that's like? Have you ever had a man force himself on you?"

She couldn't find her voice, but he wouldn't have listened anyway. He studied her terror for a moment, and then dismissed it, claiming her mouth with a soft snarl. His hands pressed her body to the bed with imprisoning weight. His kiss cut through her like knives. It bruised and beat at her soul. There was no mercy, even in its brutal hunger, its hissing heat. His mouth was a weapon and he was using it to punish her for the way she'd carelessly broken open his wounds.

I didn't understand the depth of your pain, she cried silently, imploring him. *I only meant to help!*

She heaved and struggled, knowing it was useless. He was superhuman in his quest for justice. Any kind of justice, even this. He had lashed out with the need to wound, and somehow she had become his symbolic enemy. She couldn't fight him. He wanted that! He wanted her to struggle so he could feel justified in his own destructive impulses. He wanted violence to match his own, and crazed as he was by pain, he wanted to conquer and lay waste to anything that reminded him he was human.

Take it then, she thought. Take your justice. Take it from me if that will appease you. What triumph could there be in the unconditional surrender of your enemy? she asked herself. She would rob him of that at least. He couldn't win if she capitulated. She would offer herself like the martyrs did, a sacrifice to the cause of one man's blood justice. Blinded and beheaded for their beliefs, those women had triumphed over every attempt by their persecutors to break them. Rita of Cascia herself, saint of the impossible, had triumphed over her tyrant of a husband.

Mary Frances knew a fiery surge of resolve. Let him tear her apart. Let him inflict his wounds and leave her bleeding. Maybe this was the most that could ever come of a relationship with him—bitter hatred and heartbreak.

Tears welled in her eyes. She sighed against his angry mouth and felt a shudder rack him. "Don't do that," he whispered raggedly. "Don't make me care what happens to you. Not when I want you dead and gone, out of my life."

"But you do," she told him, broken-voiced. "You do care. That's why you're doing this."

She couldn't fight, not him or the tears. They soaked her face and wet his lips with salt and sorrow.

A horrible sound choked out of him, and he pressed her into the bed with resurgent fury. He seemed determined to destroy every shred of emotion, even if it meant destroying her in the process. But his body defied him. It shook with emotion, shook with rage at his lack of control.

"Can you forgive this?" His hips ground against hers, and his tongue speared deeply into the womb of her startled mouth, violating it. Angry hands plowed into her hair and scooped up thick raven fistfuls. Powerful knees forced her legs apart until he could wedge his way inside them, and when he was there, between her thighs, pressed high and hard against her pubis, the most intimate of bones, he took her mouth again. Roughly. Hungrily. Trembling with passion.

The raw power of it scalded her.

"Or this?" he whispered, claiming her breast. He slid his hand inside the bodice of her dress, molding her to his palm with shocking insolence. His manhandling was possessive and crude. But the sound of his voice was different now. There was pain. It was visceral.

"Leering pigs, touching you like this?"

Shock rolled over her, protecting her with its eerie, insulating veil. Her mind was trying to detach, to separate her from what was happening, but her body was responding in ways that defied explanation. Muscles had knotted. Nerves quivered brilliantly. They lit her from within like lightning. Her flesh would not let her detach.

This man who was determined to make her feel his pain was not a stranger. She loved him.

He rose up and ripped open her dress with his free hand. Black pearl buttons popped like Styrofoam bubbles, flying everywhere. He had her naked now, her breasts bared and trembling, but instead of touching her, he reared back as if to swing off her. He had meant to stop, she realized. He was going to leave her that way, exposed and humiliated. That was his plan, but he couldn't do it. The sight of her made him flinch.

"Jesus," he whispered.

There was something else driving him now. Not conflict, need. He bent and took her breast in his mouth, drawing on her flesh deeply. Some strange tenderness overtook him and it made him rage even more. He didn't want to need her. He hated himself for it.

Dizziness swept over Mary Frances. She was sinking, spiraling downward, and afraid she might faint. This was too much. This wild confusion and excitement was too much. His mouth was her only contact with reality. It tugged on her so vibrantly she almost didn't want him to stop, and then suddenly he had stopped, and he was looming above her again, leaving her nipple naked and aroused.

She could hardly fathom what he'd done, that he was upright, yet still on his knees. He could have been kneeling in prayer, except that one of his hands braced his thigh, and she could see the source of his conflict now. The material of his pants strained to contain massively swollen flesh. He was burgeoning with lust and pain and the primal need he could no longer deny.

"Unzip me." His voice had gone cold and harsh, all the passion stripped from it. "Do it."

He'd already accused her of madness. To refuse would

have proven him right. But that wasn't the reason Mary Frances responded the way she did. She wasn't aware of any conscious choice, that any decision had been made, but it couldn't have been fear alone that made her touch him. She was too caught up in the strange wonder of her own reaction to the sight of him, of the involuntary trembling of her hand, her fingertips, as she traced them over the living thing that throbbed beneath the cool linen material of his pants.

He jerked at the first contact, jerked and turned to molten stone beneath her fingers. Now there was fear, but it was fear of the unknown. It was confusion. She'd had no experience with the power of this thing that was transforming his body.

She couldn't manage the zipper. Not at all. It would have taken her years. He stayed her hand with a groan of utter despair and did it himself. Dark and engorged, the starving muscle thrust from his clothing as he fell over her. His hips wedged her open, enveloping her with his hunger. Only her panties prevented him from penetrating her.

"Can you forgive this?" He drove against her, letting his body speak for him. "Can you?"

She shook her head helplessly and blinked away tears. As she reached up to touch his face she felt the moisture there and realized only belatedly that his eyes were glittery, too. Could diamonds weep? Her heart twisted at the thought. How much devastation must it take to bring a man like this to tears?

Still, he was merciless in his violations, one after the other, numbing her with such astonishment she couldn't scream, couldn't even speak. His hands raked over her, ravenous. He was going to breach every barrier if she didn't stop him.

She whispered that, told him he must stop, implored
him, but it did no good. She couldn't make herself heard,
and what was infinitely worse, she couldn't make herself
stop. There was something in his passion she responded
to involuntarily. She didn't know what it could be, other
than the depth of his pain, but whatever it was, her entire
being was caught up in it, caught up in shock waves of
sensation. Her body was an earthquake. Her heart was
wild, her belly clenched.

It was more than pain, she realized, it was need. He
didn't want to hurt her any more than she wanted to be
hurt. He wanted to love her and couldn't let himself. She
knew that as surely as she knew the need that racked him
was in her, too. Only she couldn't deny it. She didn't
want to deny it. Maybe she had gone mad, but it felt as if
she were here, in this place, for that reason and no other,
to join with this man and make it beautiful instead of
tragic, to make love out of hate and life where only death
existed.

"Please," she whispered, trying to make him understand, "I've never been with a man before. You have to be
gentle."

Another violent shudder passed through him, and his
hands tightened in her hair. Somehow they both understood that he was beyond gentleness. But he wasn't beyond everything human. He stopped when he discovered
she was telling the truth—that she really had never been
with a man. The same fingers that had probed every other
tender orifice had finally come up against an impassable
barrier. Her body's natural limits had protected her when
she herself could not.

"Christ," he whispered, searching her face, touching
her mouth as if to assure himself that she was real, "you
are a virgin."

The tears she'd thought she felt earlier sprang to his eyes, and the chaos of his heartbeat shuddered in his fingers. He stared at her as if he wanted to heal every place he'd hurt, to beg her forgiveness. His face clenched with the pain of what he'd nearly done to her. His mouth twisted.

But some frightening thing happened to him as he looked away from her and a sickening knowledge took hold of him. A moment later he was off the bed, moving through the cabin, a caged animal. His voice was an open wound. "Cordes will love that," he said, breathing pain. *"Jesus, the bastard will love that."*

"Cordes?" For a moment Mary Frances wasn't sure what she'd heard, and then something in her went deathly silent in the attempt to understand. He was going through with it? He was going to throw her to the wolves, even after this? That didn't seem possible. He couldn't mean it. But if he did, then what he must be saying was that she'd been wrong, completely wrong. He didn't love her. He didn't return her feelings in any way. The turmoil they'd just been through wasn't about his need for her, it was about his obsession with his past.

Numbed, she rolled into herself and pulled her dress down around her knees. She heard him say something, her name perhaps, but she didn't respond. She was barely aware of him leaving, but as the door shut and the lock clicked into place, she stirred.

Sometime later she remembered and sprang up. Urgency took her to the silver tray, but her medal was gone. He'd taken it. The only evidence that it had ever been there were the crimson drops of his blood.

Alex Cordes stood on the balcony of his Paradise Island villa, a crystal flute of champagne cradled in his hands as

he savored the jeweled hues of twilight. Mother Nature
had been in a generous, even decadent mood when she
accessorized this part of the globe, he mused. The Bahamas had always made him think of a treasure chest,
dripping with sapphires and emeralds, heaped with gold.

The secluded cove just below his villa was a gemstone
nestled in coral reefs, the water as clear and faceted as a
marquise-cut turquoise. The beaches were pink and gold,
the banyan forest maidenhair green. It was as lush as anything he'd ever seen in San Carlos's misty jungles. Or
Tiffany's private rooms.

He lifted the flute in a silent, triumphant toast and
touched the gold rim to his lips before sipping the bubbly
froth. His father would have told him it was premature to
celebrate, but Ruben Cordes had never been a man of vision.

Intoxicated with thoughts of the evening ahead, Alex
took a swallow and then laughed aloud, champagne
spuming in his throat. His plan for the microchip was daring and wildly ambitious. The sheer brilliance of it enthralled him. If the businessmen he'd proposed it to—a
small, select consortium who traded in both information
and technology—were equally ambitious, he would be
vastly wealthy. If they agreed with his vision, he would
wield unassailable power and influence. He would be a
hero, the undisputed savior of his people.

"Excuse me, Mr. Cordes—"

"What?" Alex spun around, champagne flying. He'd
recognized his bodyguard's voice, but he was incensed at
the Neanderthal's insensitivity. He was being paid to provide personal protection and to secure the villa, but that
didn't give him the right to intrude on a private moment.
Even Carmen and Luis would have known better!

Well, perhaps not Carmen, Alex amended, faintly bemused. She had turned out to be a profound disappointment, but he regretted now what he'd done in a moment of rage at his father. The wrong person had died, he realized.

The tight-eyed, butch-cut former marine was quick to apologize. "Sorry, sir, but if you want the back entrance covered, I'll need to put another man on it."

"*Of course,* I want the back entrance covered. I want every possible point of entry covered, even windows."

"That won't really be necessary, sir, now that the alarm system's been installed."

"Nevertheless, I want someone at both doors, do you understand?" Exasperated, Alex set the flute on a glass patio table. Why was he having to tell a hired security expert his business? "I want someone physically there."

"Of course, I'll take care of it."

The man did everything but bow before he made a quick exit. Alex wasn't mollified. He'd waited too long to bring in professional security and wished now he'd given it more thought. The bodyguard had been recommended by contacts Alex had used before, but so far he'd done little to inspire confidence. Perhaps it was just nerves, Alex allowed. His own nerves. Tonight was so fucking important.

He turned back to the sunset, surprised to see a woman walking along the water's edge. She was wearing black, a sheer sundress affair that opened up the front and swirled around her legs as she walked. Her hair was a long, rich ocean of goldenrod yellow, streaked silver by the sun and rippling in the gentle breezes.

Alex watched her a moment, frozen with disbelief. As she reached up to gather her flying mane in her hands and drape it over one shoulder, he gasped softly. "Celeste?"

The shock of seeing her nearly brought him to his

knees. It couldn't be. Celeste was dead. She'd been taken
in a violent, senseless way that he deplored all the more
because of all the other horrors that had been done to
her—and because of the responsibility he bore in all of it.
Her death had been the final degradation, the most mean-
ingless act of all, and it had left him with a crushing burden of guilt.

It was the falling light, he told himself, watching
closely as she lifted her skirts. A wave swept up, covering her bare feet in foam. She scooped her skirt into her
lap and crouched, a golden sea nymph, entranced by the
water as it swirled and eddied round her. A coincidence?
It had to be, and yet how many times had he seen Celeste
do just that? Right here on this beach? A crazy notion
took hold of him as he contemplated going after her. Was
he being given a second chance? Everything about this
night felt crazy, and destined.

He had to know who this woman was.

Balcony steps led to the terrace below, where there was
another flight that led to the beach. His descent was quick
and soundless. He hadn't bothered to tell the guard he
was going, and he didn't want the woman to hear him approach, though there was little chance of that. By the time
he reached the sand, she was well down the beach, a
black silhouette floating against the pink sky.

A sense of panic overtook him as he began to jog
through the warm drifts. He sank to his ankles, but even
the deep drag of the powdery coral couldn't slow him
down. If he didn't get to her before she disappeared, he
was sure he would never see her again. He still thought
she must be some kind of hallucination.

Within moments he was laboring to breathe and wondering if he'd gone mad. He'd suffered from asthma as a
child and his lung capacity was limited. But more signif-

icantly, some of the most consequential men in the world would be arriving within the hour. Titans all, they were ready to do business with him, *anxious* to do business with him, and he was jogging down the beach, chasing mermaids.

Tonight's deal would bring him more power and glory than he'd ever dared to dream of. It would satisfy the terrible lust for respect his father had always denied him. But even that wouldn't hold him forever. Something essential was missing. It always had been, some fundamental need, deep and painful. Nothing had ever filled it. Only one woman had relieved it, but he hadn't really appreciated how crucial she was to his well-being until she was gone.

God, how he regretted the violence he'd done to her, genuinely regretted it. Maybe it wasn't too late.

She was still walking at a leisurely pace, and now she couldn't be more than a hundred yards away. He'd gained some ground on her, but he was laboring. The briny air burned his throat and lungs and his legs ached with fatigue. He wanted to call out, but couldn't risk it. Without the element of surprise, he couldn't be assured of catching her.

She hesitated as he pulled even closer, then glanced over her shoulder. He heard her gasp and recognized it as terror. "Celeste, no!" he called as she began to run.

It was all he could physically do to catch her. He was gasping for air as he snagged the hem of her skirt and jerked her backward. She stumbled into his arms and they both dropped to the sand.

He crawled on top of her prone body and nuzzled his face in her sweet yellow hair, holding her, bruising her he gripped her so hard. Her scent aroused him. Everything about her aroused him. "I'm sorry, Celeste," he said, overcome by emotion.

But when he rolled her over and saw her face, he could do nothing but gape. *"Cristo,"* he whispered, bewildered.

Rage shuddered through him with the suddenness of an explosion. Stricken, he reared back and cracked her hard across the mouth. This wasn't Celeste at all. It was her sister, the bitch who'd tricked him at the hotel and sent him scrambling up the escalator like a fool. There weren't too many people who got the chance to make a fool of him twice. She never would again.

21

"No police." Blue sat slouched on the edge of the fifties-style dinette set in the rectory kitchen, dangling her rope-burned legs and gingerly holding the steaming cup of coffee Rick had brewed. "We can't bring the law in on this."

Rick was across the room, leaning heavily against the stove, his arms folded over his chest. "No argument there, but there has to be something we can do. Hell, I'd go after Calderon myself if I had any idea where he was taking her."

"And I'd go with you, but we'd have a better chance of finding Jimmy Hoffa than Webb Calderon, who undoubtedly has hidey-holes all over the globe."

Blue had been expecting an argument, but she was too preoccupied to ponder why Rick hadn't insisted on calling the police. Mary Frances had been kidnapped and the obvious thing to do was call 911, only she feared that would solve nothing and complicate everything. Several arms of law enforcement would be involved, including the FBI.

Blue now had the weight of Mary Frances's welfare, as well as Brianna's death, on her shoulders. It was a terrible burden, one she'd love to hand over to the authorities, but she knew intuitively that would be a mistake. There was some other way to handle this disaster. She just had to figure out what it was.

Trouble was she couldn't concentrate long enough to sustain an intelligent thought. The incessant drip of a leaky faucet in the kitchen's cracked and yellowed porcelain sink was the equivalent of Chinese water torture. But it wasn't even close to the torment she was staring at.

Speaking of disasters. He was the most beautiful mess she'd ever seen. Shirttails untucked and the knees of his embattled jeans ripped to ribbons, Rick Caruso gazed at her with the forbearance of exactly what he was, a priest. Outrageously sexy and sweet, but a priest nonetheless.

"Any ideas?" he asked.

Oh, yes, she thought. Many. All of them road signs leading straight down the Heartbreak Trail. Lucky for her he was dressed.

A huge achy sigh welled inside her. It was all she could do to contain it. Her chest felt like a balloon that had overinflated and was pressing heavily on her heart. It might even crush her if she couldn't find a way to relieve the pressure.

Of all the men, she thought wistfully.

Snap out of it, Blue, she told herself emphatically. Rope burns and broken hearts were not the point. Her friend had been kidnapped. There was a life at stake.

She took a sip of coffee and grimaced. Even that sucked. "Thank God," she muttered, scowling at him. "You're not perfect. You make putrid coffee."

He pretended to be hurt. "If I'd known it was a priority, I'd have perked it to the softball stage."

She laughed, unable to help herself. They both did, and in the aftermath—in the rising silence of their awareness—they locked gazes and simply looked at each other for what seemed like several moments. The longing that stretched between them must have been a tangible thing, Blue imagined. Anyone watching would surely have been able to see the arc of a rainbow, tinged with the hues of sweet, sweet hurting.

The infinite sadness in his smile pulled at her heart.

"Are you going to be all right?" she asked him. Maybe she was trying to distract herself from her own misery by focusing on him, but she was honestly worried that their fatal attraction might have brought on a crisis of faith or some other debilitating internal struggle. She should never have given in to her desire for him. Some things were sacred, she was learning.

"I think so," he said softly. "You?"

"It's not the same for me. I haven't taken any vows."

The faucet's steady leaking gave way to a noisy crescendo of dribbles. It could have been a drum solo, each trickle of water magnified to the ratatatat of tom-toms. Rick walked over and gave the cruddy spigot a hard crank. Several more drops oozed out, as if to confirm that it was a hopeless mission. Love and kidnappings and leaky faucets were not under the immediate control of the will.

He returned to the stove, bemused, and gave her a grin. "Now that you mention it, confession's going to be a bitch, especially when I get to the part about how a woman named Blue saved me from myself."

A smile bubbled. "Better than a boy named Sue."

She hung her head in shame at his pained expression. It had just popped out of her, and the goofiness of it made her want to groan. Still, she felt the teensiest little bit better. Being asinine always seemed to reduce stress. She'd often thought people ought to indulge more.

"You and I are going to survive this," he pointed out gently. "It might not feel like it right now, but we will. I'm not a hundred percent yet, but I think we're doing what's right, Blue. And God knows it's your strength that's making it possible, not mine. You are a tough peach. . . ."

He made a valiant effort but couldn't plane the throaty catch from his voice. "We *will* survive, you and I. But Mary Frances might not. Calderon's back from the dead, and she tried to kill him. She's the one who's in trouble."

At least Blue could agree wholeheartedly on that. "He must want the statue back, and he's going to use her to get it."

She tapped her coffee cup absently. Her thoughts had already veered off in another direction. "How about a private eye—a missing-persons expert?"

"I don't think so. I think we're overlooking the obvious. What about the escort service?"

"Cherries? What about them?"

"Mary Frances told me it was the service that suggested she give Calderon a lethal overdose. They've already got a stake in this. We just don't know what it is."

Blue still didn't see where he was going. "I doubt if they're going to volunteer the information."

"They don't have to." He pushed up the sleeves of his shirt, bunching the material around his biceps with get-down-to-business force. "We've got a pretty good idea whose side they're on, and it's not Calderon's. They might even be able to find Mary Frances for us."

Blue stared at him, startled. Her pulse quickened as she

began to see the possibilities in what he was saying. "You're right."

She abandoned the coffee cup, slopping some of it as she slid off the table. After she and Rick had cut themselves free in the storeroom, she'd remembered the red satchel. It had still been sitting on the pew where he'd left it next to Mary Frances, and Blue had rescued it and brought it into the kitchen with them.

"What are you doing?" Rick asked as she dropped to the peeling linoleum floor and began to rummage through the case.

"Looking for the computer. I'm going to check my E-mail for messages." Panicked gripped her when she couldn't find the small portable unit in the jumble of lingerie and sex toys. Anyone could have filched it, she realized, including the young homeless guy who slept in the back pew of the church.

She tipped the satchel upside down and dumped everything on the floor. Among other things, a gleaming ebony vibrator of sizable proportions rolled out, along with a set of cherry-red plastic nipple clamps, and finally, her cell phone.

"Thank God," she whispered, spotting the computer under a black satin bustier. She haphazardly stuffed the lingerie back into the satchel and abandoned the cleanup effort.

Rick crouched next to her as she settled herself on the floor with the machine on her lap. Within moments she'd brought up her Internet mail box and scrolled through dozens of messages from the service, all demanding to know Blue's whereabouts.

"I'm in grave danger," she murmured, typing the words on the screen and waiting to see what the reaction would be.

What kind of danger? came the almost instantaneous reply.

The keys clicked noisily as she started typing again.

Rick had moved behind her to read the screen over her shoulder. "Mind telling me what you're doing?" he asked.

"I'm going to throw them a little bait, namely the risen Webb Calderon."

Her fingers flew as she keyed in that she'd been abducted by Calderon, who was in pursuit of Alejandro Cordes. "Let's hope they know how to find Cordes," she said. "And that it leads them to Calderon and Mary Frances."

Again the reply was instantaneous: *Are you on your way to the Bahamas?*

Blue glanced around at Rick, unsure what to do next.

"Tell them you don't know where you are," he suggested. "Say you were drugged and you just came to."

"You're good at this." She did as he said, released a taut sigh, and waited.

The reaction they got astonished both of them.

The words flashed on the screen as if they'd been uploaded from the sender's mind:

STAY OUT OF THIS. YOU CAN'T SAVE MARY FRANCES MURPHY. IF YOU CONTACT THE MEDIA OR THE AUTHORITIES, SHE'S A DEAD WOMAN. STAY OUT OF THIS IF YOU WANT HER BACK ALIVE.

Blue stared at the screen, frozen. The other messages had all been signed "Wink" with a corresponding emoticon. This one was unsigned. Blue's voice dropped to a whisper. "They know who Mary Frances is. They know Calderon has her and not me."

Blue might not have been quite so confounded if she'd had any idea whom she was dealing with. The only contact she'd had with the service was through the computer. There was an office on Wilshire where she'd met with the retired judge the day she and Brianna had been interviewed, but since then, there'd never been anyone there but a receptionist. It was like interacting with a disembodied mind.

When she looked up at Rick, he was standing at the stove, his back to her. His head was bowed and his hands were tucked into his jeans pockets.

"What are we going to do?" she asked.

"Nothing." He turned slowly, and she could see by the look on his face that he meant it. She had never seen him as grave or as determined. "We're not going to do anything. She's dead if we try, that's what they said."

"But we don't even know who *they* are—"

"I have an idea who they are, Blue."

"What? You know who's E-mailing me? How could you?" She set the machine aside and struggled to her feet, using one of the metal dinette chairs as a crutch. "If you know, then tell me, Rick. Who is it?"

"I can't. I'm sorry, Blue, I really am, but there's nothing more I can say. The information came to me through someone's confession and that makes it privileged. But even if it wasn't, I promised I'd never reveal what I was told, and I can't break that vow." His chest filled with a deep breath. "I can tell you that it isn't just Mary Frances who's at risk. There are others involved in this, too. Lives would be destroyed."

"Then I should have called the police. I still can."

"No—" His hands ripped out of his pockets as if to make his point. "That would only blow things wide open. The authorities would have less chance of getting her

back than you or I would, and once they're involved,
nothing is sacred and no one is protected. We've done the
only thing we can."

"By contacting the service?"

"Yes, trust me on this."

It wasn't just the tone of his voice that cautioned Blue
not to argue with him, it was her own experience with
him. But if he was attempting to reassure her, he hadn't.
She was more frightened for Mary Frances than ever and
plagued with questions. Curiosity consumed her. It
burned as brightly as her concern for her friend, and yet
somehow she did trust him, in ways that she'd never
trusted anyone else.

It felt as if his blue eyes were touching her from
across the room, and that ironic awareness brought a
resigned sigh to her lips. If anyone should have known
how he felt about vows, it was her. She couldn't ask
him to violate this one any more than she could the others. "Just tell me this, then. Is Mary Frances going to be
all right?"

"I don't know, but maybe there is one more thing I can
do." He glanced at his watch, a conviction in his tone that
startled her. But what startled her even more was what he
did next. He began to unbutton his shirt.

Her cries cut at Webb like razor blades, flashing and
slashing, threatening to leave him in ribbons. He should
have been writhing in pain, yet he felt nothing. He did
nothing.

The needle jumped wildly on his recording equipment,
spiking with every rasp and shudder of sound. He
watched it with preternatural stillness and no more response to its flailings than an eyeblink. But from the center of the deathlike silence that was Webb Calderon's

world came an answering shriek. Some exiled part of him *was* writhing. It was being cut to ribbons.

The surveillance equipment had become his nervous system. Each spike and dip of the needle reminded him how he would have responded, *if* he were capable of responding. The phosphorescent orange glow of the digital readout displays held him hypnotically. His headphones registered her every ragged breath and strangled moan.

The chase was over. Cordes had caught her. He'd brought her down. The man's heaving gasps muffled what he was saying, but his sharp intake of air told Webb he'd just discovered the identity of his hostage. The sudden crack of sound told Webb that Cordes had retaliated. He'd hit her.

Somewhere in the recesses of Webb's brain, buried in the center for rage, a nerve fired. His field of vision went ice white, and for a split second he was blinded by an emotion he couldn't feel. Nausea foamed into his throat. He could taste it, smell it, and the stench should have repulsed him. He was violently close to losing the contents of his stomach, but it might as well have been another man's gut that was convulsing. It might as well have been another man sitting in the chair, staring at jumping needles and irradiated numbers. He felt nothing. Did nothing.

A ghost loomed in the black mirror of the readout display. It stared with hollowed eyes and a sorrowing mouth, and Webb knew he was in the presence of his own soul. It resided in a void that was cold and black and vast. No-man's-land. This was where Webb Calderon lived. He understood that now with more clarity than he ever had before. He could see the dark, bleak tundra in his mind. It was hell. It was home.

He pulled off the headphones and freed them from the

recorder at the same time, letting the sounds of Mary Frances's ordeal fill the spacious room. Magnified in the unfurnished space, her harsh breaths came alive with anguish. Their vibrance brought his own deadened reality into sharp contrast.

He left the table full of surveillance equipment, but she was everywhere, gasping and sighing, a child locked out of her secret garden. The two-story Mediterrean villa he'd rented fronted the ocean with a window that ran the length of the living room. It was an exercise in futility, Webb knew. There was no chance of seeing her, but he found himself at the window anyway, searching the beach, figuratively sifting every grain of sand.

The real-estate agent had promised an ocean view. As it turned out, Cordes's beach was obscured by a small forest of banyans, but Webb's only concern at the time had been proximity. He'd rented the place next to Cordes's to ensure that his equipment would pick up the frequency from the implant in Mary Frances's ankle. That was the real reason he'd removed the bracelet, to reactivate the listening device to record the meeting between Alex and his business associates.

Brilliant bastard that he was, his plan was working perfectly. Except that in his obsession with bringing down Alex Cordes, he had missed the fatal flaw in his strategy. His listening device had become a torture device.

She was thrashing and kicking. He could hear her.

Don't fight, he thought. *God, don't.* Cordes gets off on that.

The blades that lived in his vitals whirled and sliced viciously, cleaving like a thresher. They would eviscerate him if anything happened to her. There would be nothing left. He would cease to exist. At some point he had shut every thought of danger to her out of his mind, destroyed every doubt as if it were a mutating cancer. He couldn't have gone through with this otherwise, and he'd had to go through with it. There was no other way to live with what they'd done to his family, what *he'd* done to his sister.

By stealing his revenge, Mary Frances Murphy had given him the perfect shot at Cordes. Her resemblance to Brianna alone should have made her irresistible to Cordes. And it had. Webb had known nothing about Cordes's blood hatred for Mary Frances, but that only made him want the bastard more, if that was humanly possible. Webb's plan was far more complicated than simple payback. He wanted the guilty ones to be their own executioners, to turn their greed and bloodlust against themselves in one poetic moment of self-destruction. Small wonder he'd thought she was sent to him for that purpose, the perfect bait for his trap.

But somehow she had touched him and drawn warmth. She had found a place that wasn't dead, and he had responded helplessly to a spirit as unlike his own as anything could possibly be. It wasn't difficult to understand the attraction. She was everything he wasn't—serene and innocent, an impassioned soul with a penitent's gift for surrender. She'd made him feel things he thought he'd killed off years ago.

But if she'd drawn warmth, she'd also drawn blood. She had proved to be as dangerous as he'd known she would. His first instinct about her had been right. She was the perfect bait. But not for Alex Cordes. For Webb Calderon himself.

A low buzz emanated from the surveillance equipment.

Webb returned to the recorder, expecting to hear the sounds of her struggle, but there was nothing except the low drone that had drawn his attention, normal electronic feedback.

Had she given up, then? That would buy her some time. It would buy *him* some time. It might be possible to get what he needed and get her out of there, too. But he couldn't let himself think about that yet. Ruthlessly forcing his focus back to the plan, he adjusted equipment with the cold efficiency of an automaton, caressing toggle switches and levers.

He'd allowed her to think she was going to lure Cordes away from the villa so Webb could capture him, but the real plan was quite different. He wanted Cordes to take her back to the villa. The implant in her ankle was state-of-the-art. She could be in the next room when Cordes's deal was being cut and still pick up the transaction. And once Webb had that transaction on tape, he would have the evidence he needed to follow through with his plan.

"What the fuck is your game, bitch?"

Cordes's voice burst through the microphone.

Webb went animal still. Nerves fired blindingly at the base of his brain. Another man would have been snarling with rage, but Webb was barely breathing. Every cell was focused on the voice, the noise. On her. He could hear scraping and shuffling. It sounded as if she were being pulled to her feet.

The static escalated, making it difficult to hear what was being said, but she seemed to be moving through the sand, or perhaps Cordes was dragging her. Webb could just make out his muffled threats. Cordes was demanding to know why she was wearing a wig and dressed like her sister. Her silence said she wasn't going to implicate Webb or reveal that she'd been forced, but it also triggered Cordes to more belligerence. "You're going to be the entertainment tonight," he warned her, his voice blaring in and out. "And you'd better fucking well be good."

Feedback crackled and spat like firecrackers. The audio distortion should have been painful, but Webb remained frozen at the machine. Sand, he told himself, the grainy sand they were walking through was fouling the transmission. It had to be that. Cordes hadn't hurt her. Not yet. He needed her. He wasn't done salving his damaged ego.

Webb needed her, too. Alive. *He needed her.*

They were cutting him to pieces. Razor blades. Flashing and slashing. They'd used them on him as a child, scoring him like raw meat and leaving him for the rats to feed on. A long-delayed echo of that excruciating horror cried out now. A nerve in his cheek stabbed hotly, but his fingers didn't move from their resting place on the knob and his breathing never wavered from its preternatural stillness.

He had witnessed the slaughter of his stepfather and mother. He had executed his own sister. Everything since then had been child's play. Even this.

"Father Rick!" Mariana Delgado bundled into the rectory kitchen, her arms full of his ecclesiastical garments. "What are you doing in here? I been looking everywhere for you. Jesse is out there already, lighting the candles. You're late for mass!"

Mass, Blue thought, watching Rick fumble with the placket on his shirt. That must be what he was doing. For a moment she'd thought—

"I'm going as fast as I can, Mariana." His determined housekeeper got the benefit of an adorably helpless smile. "These buttons must be possessed by demons today."

Mariana scoffed. Demons were no match for her. She had only one mission. "Get those clothes off, or I'll have to do it for you," she warned him. "Jesse will make sure the candles don't get lit until you show up. What can he do, poor kid? There's a breeze in the nave this morning, and it keeps blowing those damn candles out."

She grinned mischievously, seemingly delighted with herself. "Come on," she urged Rick. "Strip! We don't care, do we, Blue? Whatever he's got, we've seen it before."

Sure have, Blue thought. Up close and personal.

As Rick began to pull his clothes off, Mariana draped the vestments over the dinette chair and turned to give Blue a hug. The ridged vibrator in all its gleaming ebony-black glory lay at the housekeeper's feet, along with some of the other paraphernalia that was still scattered around.

"What's this?" She nudged the vibrator with the toe of her shoe. "Looks like one of the gardener's tools, yes?"

Blue bit her lip, not trusting herself to say a word.

"That man is getting so careless," Mariana confided. "Do you know what? The other day I found his weed whacker in my panties, er—I mean *pantry.*"

They both laughed and Blue made a comment about men and their midlife crises. Mariana dismissed the vibrator with a tsking sound. Fortunately she was more interested in Blue at that moment than she was in garden tools.

"I'm glad you're here," she whispered as she reached Blue. Her expressive brown eyes sparkled with tears. "I just want you to know. Jesse told my husband how he met you and gave you the flowers, and when Armando found out that his son had been praying to St. Catherine, it made him cry. *Sí,* it did. He cried, and then we talked, Armando and I, and I think it's going to be all right. His own pain, it was blinding him to the pain he was causing his family."

She brightened with a smile. "He's coming to mass today, and then he's going job hunting."

Blue stepped into Mariana's outstretched arms and hugged her soundly, grateful she'd been able to help someone, although she knew her part in it was mostly co-incidental. Maybe Catherine of Siena had come through? "I'm happy for you, Mariana. I really am."

"And my boy, Jesse," Mariana said as they released each other, "he thinks they should put a statue of you up in front of the church. He thinks you're a saint, too."

"You tell him the feeling is mutual. I only wish he were twenty years older."

They caught hands for a moment before Mariana went to help Rick finish dressing. He'd managed to get his shirt off and now he was fumbling with the various robes and garments, trying to get them arranged. As Mariana began doing up hooks and tying sashes, Rick looked over at Blue and winked.

"A sorry sight, huh? Some poor-slob priest who's late for morning mass and can't even get himself dressed."

Poor slob? Never. But that's the only thing she was sure of. She couldn't imagine how he was involved in this situation with Mary Frances, or what he knew that he couldn't tell her, but he'd asked her to trust him and there was little else she could do. She had no one else to turn to.

Rick Caruso, whose secrets are you keeping?

She knew that question would plague her until the end of time, or until she had an answer, whichever came first. But answers would have to wait. Right now she was going to attend mass for the first time in years and years. Someone she knew desperately needed her prayers.

22

"No one makes a fool of me twice."

Mary Frances fought not to gasp as Alex Cordes gouged her hip through the filmy material of her dress, twisting the flesh painfully. The whispered warning jetted moist heat up the back of her neck. *"No one."* He stood behind her, facing a wall of mirrors, his image partially blocked by hers.

His reflection was a mask of cool, steamy menace. All of his earlier outrage had funneled itself into a strange, humid calm that made her think of the one terrible, pregnant moment before a storm broke.

Mary Frances knew what happened to men when their emotions turned cold and focused. They were ruthless. Killing was too merciful. They wanted to inflict damage first. Cordes's brainchild was to publicly humiliate her as she had him. He was going to make her the lounge act for his consortium of smugglers and thieves.

She held out no hope of escape. He wasn't a big man, probably not even six feet to her five feet five, but he would have forgone his need for perfect vengeance and killed her instantly if she'd made a wrong move. Maybe she was lucky he had such a refined taste for humiliation. At least it would give her some time to think.

"Make yourself presentable," he said, distaste in his voice as he surveyed her dishevelment. "You look like something out of a Dickens novel. I want a femme fatale, not a ragpicker."

When he'd brought her up from the beach to his palatial pink-and-white villa, he'd locked her in one of the bedrooms—a place where she seemed to be spending most of her time lately—and told her he'd be back for her when his guests arrived. He'd also issued a deadly ultimatum: If the deal went through, she would die mercifully. If it didn't, hideously.

He'd returned to the room moments ago to announce that the party was under way in the music room, where the men were having drinks. He'd described them as international powerbrokers, hinting proudly that one of them was an American CIA operative, but would say nothing beyond that.

"Get them in the mood to hawk their souls," he told her now, "and I may do you a favor before I turn you over to my hired guns." His hand caressed the tender bruise on her hip, then snaked down to fondle her buttock.

"Instead of a last meal, one last ride on the pony, eh? I'll even let you get down on your knees. I hear ex-nuns prefer it that way."

Mary Frances's throat tightened with revulsion. She would rather die hideously, whatever that meant, than be forced to service this man sexually. She could barely tolerate his breathing on her. His tawny sensuality was repugnant to her now that she knew what it concealed—the ugliest of souls. She couldn't imagine any woman willingly putting up with his abuse, including Brianna, though she wondered if her sister might have had a secret need for punishment, given her troubled relationship with their father, who openly accused her of "whoring" on more than one occasion.

"Do something with this," Cordes said, referring to her hair. Her blond wig had come off during their struggle on the beach, leaving her with a matted, stringy headful of ringlets and spikes. "Shake it out or something."

She tried. She shook the heavy mop and raked her fingers through it, but there was little she could do. Sand and humidity were the least of it. Fighting for her life had taken its toll on her entire body. Her eyes were darkly shadowed and her skin was the color of dishwater.

Cordes let out a sound of disgust as she moistened her fingers and began to rub at the smudge on her face.

"Forget it," he said. "For your sake, let's hope there's a pedophile among the bunch who likes dirty little girls." Pain flared as he assaulted the hip he'd already bruised. "Let's go." His fingers dug into her flesh, impelling her toward the bedroom door.

A moment later he was directing her down an elegantly appointed hallway to the next room. She was no expert, but the walls were studded with art that looked old and expensive, as did the furnishings. Taking it all in, she found herself wondering if Cordes owned the sumptuous place, and if Brianna had stayed here. Disturbing as the prospect was, it seemed her sister might have been involved with both men, Calderon and Cordes.

Mary Frances knew more than she wanted to about her sister's relationship with Calderon from the diary, but she couldn't make sense of her involvement with the other man. His apologies on the beach were either the outpourings of a heartbroken suitor or a terribly guilty one. She had assumed it was Calderon who had wanted Brianna out of the way. All the evidence pointed to him, including the information from Cordes himself. Calderon had denied it, of course, as even a guilty man might, but it seemed possible now that he was telling the truth.

An arched doorway gave Mary Frances a glimpse of the villa's music room as they approached it. The salon was a showplace of mirrored marble and sweeping palms with shell-pink overstuffed furniture. A series of graceful glass doors opened onto a terrace of snow-white rock, and the wet bar where some of Cordes's guests had congregated was a dazzling mix of mirrors and white lacquer.

Mary Frances quickly rubbed away the smudge on her face and straightened her dress. For some reason it was suddenly important not to look like a "dirty little girl." She didn't want to be vulnerable to these men in any way. She wanted to be as cool and aloof as Blue would have been, as fearless as Brianna.

She drew in a breath, searching for something, for whatever was missing. It felt like there was a gaping void in the middle of her being. The things that defined her had all been taken from her—her vocation, her medal, her quest to solve the mystery of Brianna's death, even the painful bond she felt with Webb Calderon had been ripped away. There was nothing left. This moment was about surviving, about protecting Mary Frances Murphy above everything else. It was imperative that she put her own welfare first, and she didn't know how to do that.

She would have to be Brianna . . . cool, aloof, fearless. Her sister was all those things. But most of all, Brianna had been the center of her own universe. She had always put herself first. Five men in a music room would have been too small an audience for Brianna. She would have been more at home in the Roman Colosseum with the lions eating out of her hand.

It was a nice fantasy, but the reality was something far different, Mary Frances discovered. Every one of the five men turned to look at her when she entered the room, and for the first time in her life she understood the true meaning of the term *sex object*. It was no longer an abstract concept for her, defined by *Webster's Ninth* as an "object of sexual interest." The men's narrowed gazes did more than undress her, they reduced her to a chart of secondary sexual characteristics. She felt like body parts arranged on a female frame, one of the "nudie" pictures in anatomy-and-physiology textbooks.

She hesitated in the arched doorway, and this time Cordes grabbed the flesh of her arm, squeezing until the pain made her move. Her sucked-in gasp brought a fleeting smile to the face of the man nearest her, a lean, graying Eastern European type by his looks, with round metal glasses and a seemingly perpetual sneer. He was lounging in one of the overstuffed chairs, drinking vodka from a hoar-frosted tube glass and observing her discomfort with thinly disguised pleasure.

Mary Frances knew a moment of cold terror. Sweet God, she thought, these men weren't going to be content with watching, no matter what she did. She'd heard about what could happen to males in groups in this kind of situation. Even innocent bachelor parties could escalate into assaults when the participants were drunk and sexually aroused, and this was no bachelor party. Whatever hope she might have had of getting help from these men was lost. With the exception of an Asian man, who seemed transfixed by the pale depths of his wineglass, they were looking her up and down as if she were a new car they might want to test-drive. Or a piece of prime meat for the

grill that night. Fortunately, Cordes didn't seem to have
pets or they probably would have requested that she
"companion" the animals.

"Gentlemen," Cordes said, stepping in front of her like
the master of ceremonies at a gala entertainment, "I mentioned something special, and here she is. Rather nice,
wouldn't you say?"

They murmured appreciatively, and he nodded his
agreement, obviously pleased with himself.

Nice was not the word Mary Frances would have used.
She still felt like a soiled waif in her crumpled black dress
and uncombed hair. But as she spotted her reflection in
the mirrors, she began to see what the men were admiring. She looked more wanton than waifish. The wild dis-
array of her dark hair and the low-cut tatters of her dress
were reminiscent of the old westerns where the women
were earthy and sensual and in perpetual danger of being
ambushed by Indians. Mary Frances had watched them
when she couldn't sleep, and to her way of thinking, the
woman in the mirror bore more than a passing resemblance to a heroine in a Sergio Leone film.

And the men were admiring her. Even as their eyes
crawled all over her and they played out their secret fantasies, they were seeing the same strange, wild beauty,
the same fey sensuality that she saw.

Cordes signalled Mary Frances to join him, and when
she didn't, he caught her by the wrist and forcibly
brought her to his side. It was a show of male dominance.
He was performing for the boys, and she knew resisting
would only make it worse. He would feel compelled to
do whatever was necessary to control her in order to save
face.

"What's your specialty, sugar?" one of the men called
out. "Every Cherries escort has a specialty, doesn't she?"

"Yes, of course—" But what's mine? Mary Frances thought. She should have known these men used the escort service. It seemed to be a clearinghouse for international espionage. Mary Frances didn't have to wonder what one of the martyrs she'd studied would have done in this situation. They were schooled in the belief that there was no heroism in religious life. Rita would have begun to pray, for the men as well as herself, all the while stoically accepting her fate with the faith that if it wasn't her time, divine intervention would be forthcoming.

Which was exactly why Mary Frances wasn't a nun. And why she wasn't going to be a martyr either, if there was any way to help it. Somewhere along the line she had lost her ability to surrender her will that way. St. Rita would have given herself up to the situation, not knowing if she was going to be eaten alive by marauding men or ravenous lions. Her faith and charity were equaled only by the austerity of her life. Her specialty was patient obedience, and as much as Mary Frances might have admired that, she knew now that it was not, could not, and would not ever be her specialty.

She touched her throat, reaching for the medal that wasn't there, and was surprised at how resolved she felt, even in this situation, even without the medal. It had brought her strength and comfort when she needed it most, but perhaps she was reaching somewhere else for that strength now, within herself. As she scanned the leering male faces she suddenly realized what her specialty was.

Alex Cordes was smarter than Webb had given him credit for. He was going to use Mary Frances to loosen up his business cohorts, pass her around like a box of truffles, and then, afterward, during the bragging and male bond-

ing that followed such tribal rituals, he was going to cut
the deal of all time. If she were privy to the business
transactions, and it looked like she would be, the odds of
her getting out alive were virtually nil. Cordes would
hardly allow her to walk away knowing such explosive
information.

Webb sat in the darkened room, staring out at the tropical night, his right arm bathed in the machinery's amber
glow.

She'd just been asked what her specialty was.

He could have told them. She specialized in truth and
innocence and destroying full-grown men. Maybe he
should have warned them. He slipped his hand into the
pocket of his pants and fished out her medal. The lacy
gold chain drooped through his fingers as he rubbed his
thumb pad over the pendant's spiky edges. Yes, those
were her specialties, and love, too. She had found something to love in the least worthy of men.

Webb had not counted on this. He had thought Cordes
would lock her up somewhere, with luck in a room close
enough to the business dealings that the implant would
pick them up. The risk would come after the meeting,
when Cordes confronted her. But that would have given
Webb time to act, to get her out of there.

He forced his thoughts back to Cordes's associates, to
their conversation. The implant was designed to pick up
signals through walls, and he'd been able to record the
meeting from the beginning. Names had not been used,
but he'd recognized some of the voices from his own
business dealings, both above and below the board. The
value of the microchip didn't seem to be in dispute.
Money hadn't been mentioned, which told him the price
had been prearranged. It was Cordes's other demands that
had brought the negotiations to a halt.

"My country needs new industry," he'd told them rather grandly. "My people must profit, too."

He'd wanted guarantees that the chips would be manufactured in San Carlos, but so far none of his prospective partners was convinced it could be done. Webb himself doubted the country had the resources necessary to train the labor. At that point Cordes had wisely suggested they take a break, and he'd brought out the "entertainment."

Mary Frances Murphy. Webb closed his hand over her medal and felt the prick of its edges. He tried to envision her, and what he saw beneath the stoic strength he remembered was the wariness of a trapped animal. She was totally outnumbered. It was several men against one woman, the stuff of which gang rapes are made. She must be terrified, but if she showed it and the jackals smelled fear, it would go worse for her.

"Fuck—" The obscenity slipped through teeth he hadn't realized were clenched. *She'd never been with a man before. Possibly never even been kissed until he himself had kissed her. She was the authentic vestal virgin being led to the altar, and it was a half-dozen brute males who were going to sacrifice her.*

He rose from the chair, aware of the charge that was locked up in his muscles, the fisted energy. His legs were as tight as his spine. He'd left the entrance-hallway light on, but the rest of the living room was cloaked in shadows. Something was different now, he realized, but it had nothing to do with the room. The preternatural stillness. He wasn't frozen in space, senses pricking. He needed to move, release the tension. That hot white light at the base of his brain was firing, and his entire body burned to respond.

He came back around, staring at the silent microphone

and wondering why everyone had gone quiet. And then he heard her voice, soft and seductive.

"Anything special you gentlemen would like?" she purred. "I'm good at reducing stress. Maybe a shoulder rub?"

"I could use something rubbed," one of them said with a laugh.

"You can *start* with my shoulder," another assured her.

Webb hesitated, confused. What was she doing? Everything about her voice was different, its tone, its breathy sensuality. If he hadn't known who it was, no one would have been able to convince him. She didn't sound frightened. Christ, she sounded like a professional hooker, plying her trade.

"Cara mia," Cordes said, his voice dropping low and becoming guttural, "you never told us your specialty."

"I'd prefer to surprise you," she told them. "But if you insist."

Webb's imagination went into fifth gear as the men began to buzz and laugh. What was she doing? Smiling, touching herself? He could bet the bastard's dicks were getting stiff already.

"What is it?" one of them asked eagerly.

She laughed, too, and the sound of it made him think of water cascading, the soft splash of raindrops. "My specialty, gentlemen, is the Golden Needles of Ecstasy," she said. "Any volunteers?"

She'd described the technique when Webb had interviewed her on the Internet. As he remembered, it involved a variation on acupuncture that was designed to do the exact opposite of relieving stress. It was designed to turn a man into a fucking telephone pole.

A chair scraped across the floor, as if one of the men were rising to volunteer. "Why don't you give me a private demonstration?" he suggested, his heavily accented voice thickening with desire.

Alex Cordes laughed nervously. "And deprive the rest of us of her talent, Otto? Surely you can wait long enough to let her perform her specialty, then she's all yours."

Otto Lazlinko. Webb knew him as an eastern-bloc operative during the years of the cold war. Since then he'd gone into the technology business and become wealthy developing nonmilitary applications, most of which had been stolen from the beleaguered American defense industry.

Lazlinko was a trained assassin. He was also a sadist. Routine sex didn't begin to satisfy him. He needed sound effects—screams and sobs that had nothing to do with pleasure.

More laughter bubbled—hers—only this time there was a delighted quality to it. "My, oh my," she breathed sensually, apparently reacting to Otto's interest. "I love an eager man, Otto, but you take my breath away. Can you hold those horses a moment or two? Hmmmm? I'll make it worth your while."

"Yes, you will," Lazlinko assured her coldly. "But be warned, I'm a hard man to please."

"Really, Otto? You, a *hard* man? I can barely wait."

A sound rose up in Webb's throat, the vestiges of a primordial snarl. Even physical torture hadn't sickened him the way this did. He couldn't stand the thought of some other man touching her, being touched by her—

Christ! He'd never felt such turmoil in his life. He'd thought nothing could exceed the bloody ravages of his childhood, but this was indescribable, a new and improved personal hell. If he intervened now, he'd lose everything. The opportunity to bring down the Cordes family and their reign of terror would be gone, and there would never be another. How else would he give meaning to the senseless slaughter of his entire family? Or silence the men who had silenced his sister?

He had made a vow to himself when he pulled that trigger, and yet if he didn't intervene now, he would be forced to listen to a woman being brutalized by a sadist—emotionally, mentally, and physically violated. History would repeat itself, and he would be witness to the slaughter of innocents all over again. *There was no way to win.*

There was virtually nothing in Mary Frances's background that could have prepared her to be the main show for six leering international profiteers, not even imagining how Brianna would have handled them. This performance had to come from her, from the wild heart of Mary Frances Murphy, and surely there was that kind of boldness and daring in her somewhere, because a terrifyingly simple idea had come to her when she'd excused herself briefly, pleading the need to use the bathroom to ready herself. Fortunately, a tray of toiletries on the countertop had produced exactly what she needed in the way of props—a fancy sewing kit.

"My, is it hot in here?" she asked, undulating her shoulders as she toyed with the straps of her sundress. She had never felt more awkward and less seductive, but she couldn't let that show, not a hint of the cold panic that lived inside her, ready to seize her if she let it. If she could find the female instinct that understood what men like this wanted, she might be able to pull this off. If not, there wasn't a prayer. She had to distract them, because her deceptively simple plan was also deadly.

Most of the men were still sitting at the wet bar and the rest were milling about the terrace doors. But they'd all been waiting like a pack of wolves for their dinner when she came out of the bathroom. And they were watching her avidly now, including Cordes, who was probably wondering if he'd made a mistake having her around. All interest in his microchip had vanished.

Mary Frances had requested rock music, hoping the volume alone would cover a multitude of sins, but the selection of tunes was limited to softer fare. Nevertheless she managed a flirty, come-hither smile as she strolled around the center of the room, swinging her shoulders to the languid sexiness of "A Taste of Honey."

She hadn't a clue how to simulate a striptease. They didn't often do those in the old westerns. Fortunately, the female awareness she sought was beginning to stir. It existed even within her, and it was responding to something, most likely the desperation of her situation. But the sensual music was having its effect, too, if not on her, then certainly on them. The sultry number saturated the room with its low, throbbing promises of pleasure—and saturated their libidos as well, she imagined. There was no mystery to what these men wanted, she realized. She knew exactly what it was, and part of her plan had to involve making them think she was going to deliver.

Undoing buttons seemed like a good way to begin. She freed the first one and held the material open suggestively to slow nods and appreciative murmurs. She'd read an article about women who danced in clubs and the command they felt over their male audience. They'd described it as heady and intoxicating, a power trip. If she could concentrate on that, it would help her brazen this out. But one of the men in her audience was drinking a little too heavily to suit her and his hungering stares warned her he wouldn't be content to watch for long.

It wasn't Lazlinko. The industrialist hadn't moved

from his impassive pose. This was an American, a Silicon Valley electronics mogul, and as he rose to replenish his drink he lifted his glass in a salute to Mary Frances. There was a telltale sway in his posture. She picked up on it immediately, and her instincts quickened as she realized he might be just the distraction she needed. Knowing full well how dangerous it was, she winked at him.

"Go for it, baby," he said, his drawl thickened by the expensive fifty-year-old Scotch he was drinking.

Mary Frances's only response was a smile. Her dress wasn't made to be worn with a bra, a deficiency she hoped would keep the men visually entranced while she undid herself. With another coy, come-hither look, she turned away from them and rotated her hips, secretly amazed that she could do such a thing. Someone whistled, a low throaty, wolfish sound, and she was sure it must be the American.

His comments grew bolder, and Mary Frances's smile felt frozen solid. As unsavory as the prospect was—as frightening as it was—she needed to provoke him into something rash or clumsy. Even a spilled drink might work if it created enough of a diversion.

"Take it off," someone chanted. "Take it *all* off."

She'd unbuttoned the dress nearly to her waist and let the placket fall open seductively, and though no one would have called her voluptuously endowed, the light and shadows conspired to create rather spectacular cleavage as she turned back to the men.

"Baby, baby," the American moaned.

Mary Frances felt an odd little thrill at the raw need in his voice. She'd never aroused that sort of reaction in a man before, and it *was* a strangely heady experience. She knew why he was moaning, but she couldn't quite fathom what she'd done to provoke it, especially since he sounded as if he were in abject pain. There was no doubt Webb Calderon had been in pain when they were together, but that seemed to have as much to do with his past as it had to do with being with her. This man was turned on by the woman swaying seductively in front of him and that woman happened to be Mary Frances Murphy. It was an alarming new reality.

"Nobody wants to volunteer for the Golden Needles?" she asked, pretending to pout. "Then I'll just have to demonstrate on myself." She slipped her hand inside the bodice of her dress and began to stroke her skin.

"How about me?" The American set his glass down on the bar as if he were going to join her.

Lazlinko rose slowly and Alex Cordes came alert, apparently ready to intervene if necessary. This was the diversion Mary Frances had wanted, but it was coming much too soon. She wasn't ready.

"Sorry, gentlemen," she told them all breathlessly. "I don't perform with groups. If you want to see my specialty—and trust me, you do—then sit down and let me finish." She ran her tongue over her lips, hoping to tantalize them. "There will be plenty of time for private demonstrations later."

The American nodded reluctantly, and Mary Frances realized she had to act fast. Her dress had a pocket in the skirt and she reached teasingly into it. The gold-plated needle was there, stuck in the paper cover of the sewing kit. She drew the needle out and let it flash in the low light, then laughed softly. The sound gurgled in her throat as she ran the needle across her tongue to wet it.

Her ploy was having the effect she wanted. They were all watching expectantly as she began to play with her lower lip, pricking it ever so slightly and making soft moany little noises.

"A woman's lips are ultrasensitive," she paused to explain in a throaty voice, "much like her nipples. The membranes of both are nerve-rich and very responsive . . . as I'm sure you gentlemen know."

"Don't prick yourself, sugar," the American said. "Let me do that."

The laughter that swelled around her had a rumbling male quality to it, urgent yet powerful. There was something rank and primitive about the energy these men exuded, she realized, as if their responses were surging up from somewhere ancient and ungovernable, that seat of all animal behavior, the base of the brain. The rising level of excitement was contagious. Even her own heart was pounding, though she knew it was from anxiety. Still, she had to be careful not to let the room's potent chemistry get to her. She had to stay in control.

She drew the needle down her chin, pleating the softness just beneath it. Several quick touches of the point prickled her flesh, but one bit too hard, and the little sound that came out of her was completely spontaneous. Half gasp, half sigh, it was laced with pain and utterly sensuous.

The American's low oath was unintelligible.

"The Golden Needles can be very dangerous," she cautioned, "The erogenous zones are rich with veins and arteries as well as nerves. If you lose control, even in ecstasy, and puncture a vessel, you could bleed to death."

She drew open the bodice of her dress as if she were about to reveal one delicately rounded breast and found the act too bold to fake. She couldn't hide the modesty she felt, or the sudden, painful pride in her own body. She didn't want these men to see her this way. She didn't want any man but one to see her this way. It astonished her that she could feel so strongly—that she could feel anything at all after what Webb Calderon had done—but she couldn't deny that her hand was locked in a fist or the hot flush of confusion that was creeping up her throat.

"What's wrong with her, Cordes?" someone asked.

"Nothing, give her a moment." Cordes raised his hands as if to quiet any concerns, but his dark glare told Mary Frances her death would be hideous if she didn't go through with it.

"Nothing's wrong," she insisted. The laughter that caught in her throat had a choked, hysterical quality she couldn't control. "You've seen an aroused woman before, haven't you?"

Her hand was unsteady as she traced the point of the needle down the fullness next to her cleavage, leaving a bright pink mark on her porcelain skin. "See how my body responds? And the inside of the wrist is even more sensitive."

Pressing hard, she raised several rosy streaks on the blue-veined surface. A quick jab drew a drop of blood. The moan she let out was sharply wanton, but there was calculation in it, too. "I want someone to touch me," she said urgently. "Now, now—"

The American's drink hit the bar with a clunk.

"Hurry!" Mary Frances pleaded. Lazlinko rose to block the American, a signal that she had to move quickly. A confrontation between the two men was imminent, and as the group's attention swung to them she carried out her plan. Thanking God for her nurse's training, she forced the point into the artery in her forearm and released her clenched fist. The blood began to spurt in a crimson arc. Within seconds she was splattered with it, and the scene looked like a grisly car accident.

Cordes was the first to notice what had happened.

"Stay away from her!" he shouted as the men sprang to their feet. "Stay away! She's been hurt. She's *bleeding.*"

Mary Frances slumped to the floor. She knew how to stop the bleeding, but she couldn't let them see that. "Get me to a hospital," she rasped, digging her thumb into an arterial pressure point. "Quickly."

Cordes shouted for the guards. He tossed his car keys to the first one who raced into the room. "There's a clinic on Nassau. Shirley Street," he instructed the man. "Tell them it was an accident, and make sure she doesn't say anything different. The doctor knows me. If you have any problems, have him call me."

The guard apparently thought he knew first aid because he pulled off his belt, dropped down next to her, wrapped it around her upper arm, and pulled it tight. But not nearly tight enough. He seemed afraid of hurting her, and Mary Frances didn't dare tell him what he'd done wrong. If she let go of her arm, she would start gushing again. She would bleed to death. She told herself to stay awake, as soon as they were outside she would deal with it, but the sickening dizziness that swept over her made her realize she might not last that long.

She swayed backward and felt herself being lifted, carried toward the door. Her one thought was to get outside, to breathe in the fragrant night air, to feel the breezes of the tropics blow across her face and smell the sweet scent of freedom. She had to stay conscious. It was her last thought.

23

Our Lady glowed with ethereal beauty. The small church's cracked and peeling edifice blushed like a cinder girl dressed for a prince's ball. She looked as if the heavens had opened and sent rainbows to gown her in. The fulgent reds and fuchsias and blues of the stained-glass windows swam with sunlight so rich it appeared to have substance. Dust motes shimmered like gossamer veils.

It was almost possible to believe that God was listening as Father Rick Caruso spoke from the pulpit about the trials and tribulations of Job.

"'Yet when I hoped for good,'" he said, quoting from the Bible, "'evil came. When I looked for light, then came darkness. . . .'"

He was speaking of the necessity to believe, even through the most severe tests of faith, and from her vantage point in a pew near the middle of the nave, Blue wondered how she could ever have thought him unsuited for the clergy. He was not only convincing in his white robes and his black cassock, he was commanding and charismatic. His "street" edges enhanced the effect, giving the message an earthy sincerity.

The scriptural passages were not selected at random in a Catholic mass. There was a preestablished order to them that ran throughout the year. Still, he couldn't have had much time, if any, to prepare his sermon, and yet he'd beautifully dovetailed his message to the crisis with Mary Frances.

"When's the last time you saw a mountain moved by faith?" he asked the crowd. "I'm not going to lie to you. I never have and don't expect to. Yet without faith, we couldn't get from one moment to the next. Everything is an act of faith, even breathing. But faith is a choice, too. When things get rough, it lets us curl up and take a little nap in God's palm. We rest. We trust. We heal. . . ."

Whether he was determined to convince his flock or himself that believing was a powerful thing, Blue didn't know. But it was working. She was impressed. She hadn't wanted to be, not in her current state of confusion about Rick Caruso. But if she'd ever doubted that he was cut out to be a priest, she didn't anymore. He was good at it. He brought a personal magnetism to the role that lent sincerity and weight to everything he said. And his congregation adored him. It showed in their rapt expressions and their hushed responses during the reading of the Psalms.

She held the prayer book tightly, confusion forcing a sigh. Brianna was dead. Her friend's sister had been kidnapped, and now this man, whom she was still half in love with, was involved in some way he couldn't reveal.

Glancing up, she caught the intimacy of Rick's quick smile and felt a pang that it wasn't directed at her. She searched the heads in the front row and realized he'd taken a moment to nod at his altar boy, at Jesse. Blue had slipped out of the kitchen while Mariana was helping Rick dress because she'd wanted to watch Jesse light the candles. She was glad now that she had.

The youngster had performed his duties with such solemnity Blue'd had to mangle her lower lip to keep from losing her cool. He took an inordinately long time, and Blue remembered what Mariana had said, that Jesse would stall for time until Rick was ready. But Blue doubted the child was stalling. The braced leg seemed to genuinely hamper him as he fought for the steadiness to light the candles, and yet he kept at it laboriously, clearly proud to have been chosen for the duty and willing to go to any lengths to perform it. Tattered blue jeans peeked from beneath his crisp white robes and his scruffy hair made him look like a street urchin, but Blue had never seen such grace of spirit.

Her heart swelled with an emotion she could only imagine was wonder. If she'd ever needed evidence that there was still good in the world, Jesse was it. Living proof.

"If you'll all pray with me now for a special friend," Rick asked the congregation. The small group bowed their heads, and he led them in an intercessory prayer for a young woman he never mentioned by name. By the time he was done, his voice was harsh with sadness and in danger of breaking.

"Preserve and protect her through this ordeal," he said, his entreaty burningly soft. "If a task force of angels is what it takes to bring her back to us, then send them, Father, please. She's one of the good guys. . . ."

Blue held on to the missal so tightly her fingernails drained of blood. As the crowd murmured their amens she remembered a prayer from convent school, one that

had brought her and Brianna into close personal contact
with a willow switch on several occasions for "messing"
with the words.

*God, send a boy to light my fire and make my privates
glow—*

She smiled ruefully. They'd fiendishly come up with
substitute words for privates like "lamp of love", "butter
boat," and the obvious animal-world references. Blue
could recall all that with perfect clarity, but the actual
wording of the prayer had escaped her over the years.
Today it came to her in one lucid flash. *God, make my life
a little light within the world to glow. A little flame to
burn bright, wherever I may go.*

As a kid she'd thought it excruciatingly corny and was
embarrassed to be heard repeating it. But Mary Frances
hadn't. Her eyes had lit softly from within, and she'd said
that sappy prayer with the quiet passion of a true believer.
She wouldn't have dreamed of messing with the words.
Rick was right. She was one of the good guys. It should
have been me, Blue thought. If anyone deserves this
nightmare, it's me, not her.

Perhaps Blue was smiling sadly as she looked up and
noticed Rick's gaze on her. Later she would wonder if
that had been the case, because it was one of the only ex-
planations that made sense when he smiled back at her.
He nodded as if he understood what she was going
through—everything—as if he were reassuring her that it
was going to be all right. Or at least that *she* was going to
be all right.

A calm came over her as she felt the comforting reassurance of his prediction. Perhaps she could allow herself
to believe it because she had the strongest feeling that he
wasn't seeing the physical Blue Brandenburg at all. He
was looking directly into her heart, and whatever he saw

there, it brought him the sweetest kind of anguish. But more than that, she sensed that it would reinforce him in his decision and give him the strength to go on and accomplish the great things he was capable of. He had given up a lot for his calling. Now he would make that choice mean something.

She also knew, even if he didn't, that he was saying good-bye. The only thing holding them now was their mutual concern for Mary Frances. They had separate lives to reclaim, individual futures. He would go on with his work, struggling to make a difference in the lives of disadvantaged kids, even though he had little to offer that could compete with the material lure of drug money or the adrenaline rush of gang warfare. But that wouldn't stop him. He was too determined a man, and she wished him well. With all her heart, she wished him well.

Godspeed, Rick Caruso, she thought, returning his smile. You can do it. The tears that sprang to her eyes told her she wasn't ready to say good-bye yet, and as he resumed his sermon, she scooped up the red case that sat on the pew next to her and quietly slipped out of the church.

Her vision was hopelessly blured as she stopped for a moment at the crumbling statue. She regretted not having flowers to lay at St. Catherine's feet, one for everyone who needed a blessing today, including her. But there were so many more people in her life now, it would have taken a bouquet she realized. She did have that to be grateful for. New friends. And even though her heart felt as if it might break apart as she stood there, she forced her concerns to one of those friends, scruffy marmalade tom who hadn't been fed since yesterday.

A huge city bus came lumbering down the street as Blue reached the curb. She had the feeling it was going to stop at the corner, and if it did, she might just get on it.

Somehow she knew that wherever it was going, it would take her home, and there was someone she was hoping to find there. A little girl named Amanda.

It had to be a hospital room. Everything was white. Flowing, fluttering, snowfall white.

Mary Frances opened her eyes to a wonderland of gossamer. A canopy of sheer, cloud-like veils enveloped the bed she laid on. Silken netting dipped from above her, ruffling as if blown by heavenly breezes. Angel wings, she thought. That's what the veils reminded her of.

She looked around, but made no attempt to sit up. The layers of transparent film kept her from seeing anything but nebulous images beyond the canopy. Were those people moving around her bed? Ghosts? Or only shadows?

She couldn't imagine where she was, couldn't even remember where she'd been. Her mind was as white and transparent as the veils. There were bruises on one forearm and an adhesive bandage on the other. She didn't notice any other injuries, but the effort it took to sit up told her she was in a weakened condition. She'd suffered some kind of physical trauma, though she had no idea what or how severe.

Even more bewildering, she was wearing a man's shirt. The huge, blousy sleeve engulfed her hand as she reached over to open the curtains. It seemed to be of the artist's-smock variety, with a deep fly front that would have fallen open all the way to her navel if it weren't for the string ties. There was something vaguely familiar about the gathering and stitching, but she couldn't come up with any particulars. What was she doing in this strange bed, wearing nothing but a man's shirt? As much as that question perplexed her, it was swept away as she drew back the folds of her tent.

She shrank back to shade her eyes, but pain struck her pupils like needles. The bedroom was all glass, and the dazzling blue landscape outside the windows was too vibrant to stare at with unprotected eyes. She'd never seen anything so bright and dense at the same time. But was it the sky or the sea? She could hardly breathe from the intensity. But it wasn't just the color, it was the scene, too.

She'd been here before. Patio doors opened onto a dazzling panorama of white stonework and cerulean-blue water. A huge circular swimming pool had marble steps that spanned the entire circumference and alabaster Greek statuary at each point of the compass. Ultramodern pool furniture and striped umbrellas were a dramatic contrast to the black cliffs that dropped to the sea below and then rose again, miles offshore, in a jagged island of rocks, silhouetted against the horizon.

Yes, she'd been here. She'd stood near enough the cliffs that she'd felt their power and majesty. She'd been blinded by the sun and felt the caress of the breeze on naked skin, her silken kimono lying around her feet. But what she remembered most vividly was the thrill—and fear—of being visually stalked by a phantom. Her backbone had arched sharply under his gaze. She had trembled inside.

Where was he now?

She stepped out of the filmy tent, naked again except for the shirt—and trembling before her feet ever touched the floor. She still had no idea how she'd come to be here, but she did remember where she'd seen the shirt. Webb Calderon was wearing it the night they got married, the night he forced her down onto the bed and stopped only because she'd never been with a man before.

Dizziness gripped her. She reached for a bedpost to steady herself, but all she found were veils. There seemed to be no end to them, an infinity of gossamer. The black marble floor tiles were a sheet of ice beneath her feet and their whitened surface sent her reflection rocketing across the room. But it wasn't just the physical stimuli disorienting her, it was the awareness of something missing, chunks of time gone. It seemed as if her memory were tricking her, purposely holding things back. All she could remember with any clarity was what happened here, and yet she'd never been here, except in her head. . . .

She'd been wearing a kimono. She couldn't even remember the color now, but he'd told her to take it off. She did remember that. She'd resisted with all of her mental strength, but the woman on the screen had acquiesced with the shy grace of a dream creature. She'd drawn the silky robe from her shoulders and let it drop to her elbows, exposing herself as if the only desire she had in life at that moment was to give herself to this bright day, to this dark man. She had wanted him to look at her, to find her pleasing, to desire her with the same quaking passion she felt.

Mary Frances had been so appalled she'd wanted to scream at the woman to cover herself and turn her back on him. She'd been stricken with shame and embarrassment, and the turmoil hadn't eased for a long time, almost the entire interview. But at some point, there'd been a transformation. Maybe it was simple mental exhaustion that had allowed the other woman's feelings to seep into her awareness. But finally, Mary Frances had begun to have a glimpse of what her counterpart was experiencing and it had transfixed her.

Who was that woman on the screen?

Mary Frances's thoughts began to race as she realized that it might have been her. Not then, but now. Right here in this moment, right now in this place. She knew almost nothing about virtual reality, but it seemed as if the interview could have given her a flash-forward glimpse of the future. A vision of this moment and what would happen here today.

She did know that if she were to have the interview all over again, she would want to be the woman on the screen. She hadn't understood the power of that strange, trembling passion then, but she understood it now.

Was that why she was here?

Where was he?

She glanced down at the same time that her hand came up. The medal was gone. He'd kept it, but her habit of seeking its comfort was so strong that she might reach for it the rest of her life, even if she never found it there.

"What are you doing out of bed?"

"Oh!" The sight of him against the billowing white curtains startled her. Not a shadow this time. He was there in the flesh, but the aura of darkness remained. Maybe it was his clothing. His silky pants reminded her of pajama bottoms. The color of black currants, they clung on his hips, secured by a drawstring. The shirt hung free, revealing a sinewy chest and lower, the expanse of golden hair that graced his belly.

"Are you all right?" he asked.

There was concern in his voice. It wasn't a polite inquiry. She had the feeling that if her legs were to give way and dump her on the floor, which was a distinct possibility, he would be there in an instant, scooping her into his arms. But until that happened, he was going to keep his distance.

Just as well, she thought. She could feel the impact of his gaze from across the room. An eagle watched a skittering field mouse with less intensity. His dark contempt, so evident in their first meeting, had vanished. Even the curious detachment was gone. He had once looked at her as if he couldn't decide if she were angelic or demonic.

He had made up his mind, she realized.

"Yes . . . I'm fine." She swayed dizzily when she tried to move. "A little wobbly."

"You lost some blood."

She touched the bandage on her forearm, remembering. She had escaped Alejandro Cordes. She dimly recalled piercing herself with the needle when the brawl broke out, and her last conscious thought was that she would bleed to death before they got her to the clinic.

"Where did they take me?" she asked him. "And how did you find me?"

"I was there. I carried you out."

"There? In the clinic?"

"In the villa."

"You carried me out of Cordes's *villa?*" It took a moment to make sense of what he was saying, and as she searched his face she realized he was the guard who'd applied the tourniquet and lifted her off the floor when she blacked out. "How did you get in? There was security everywhere."

"That's how. I was part of it. It's a long story, and even if you were up to hearing the details, I'm not up to telling them right now."

"I'd like to know. I have a right—"

His focus was sharp enough to cut. A warning lurked in the marbleized gray of his irises. "I've had dealings with the man who handled the security for Cordes. Let's just say he owed me a favor and leave it at that for now. You need . . . some rest."

Rest? This wasn't about rest. For some reason, he didn't want to discuss what he'd had to do to get her out of

Cordes's villa. That was what the distance was all about. He didn't want her probing into the details of his rescue mission, and she had to know, all of it. He'd deliberately put her in danger, apparently with the plan of getting her out, but that barely mollified her when she thought about Cordes's murderous rage.

"He was going to kill me," she whispered. "Did you know that? For no other reason than because I made him look foolish."

The bones of his face seem to sharpen. "If I'd known that you'd humiliated him in some way, or that he would retaliate the way he did, I—" He broke off and exhaled heavily. "I thought he would deal with you after the meeting, that I'd have plenty of time to get you out."

His voice harshened, and she sensed pain there, such fresh pain she didn't probe any further. But she didn't know whether he was protecting her or himself.

"This is your shirt, isn't it?" she asked, suddenly aware of the gleaming gold of her naked legs as she glanced down. "Why am I wearing it?"

His gaze had taken the same trajectory as hers, down the length of her body. As it swept back up and hesitated at the shirt's string ties, she was caught between two opposing urges, to crouch and cover herself, or to undo the placket and open the shirt. The woman on the screen would have let the shirt drop in a heap. Was that what Mary Frances was supposed to do? Was that what he wanted?

She reached for the ties at her neckline, and his voice stopped her. It was hot and soft. "The truth?" he said. "I wanted you in something of mine. I wanted your body touched by the shirt I'd worn, caressed all over . . . molested."

She caught her breath and the trembling began. Suddenly she could feel the shirt floating around her. She could feel it touching her everywhere, caressingly. It glided over her breasts as lightly as the gossamer scarves. Silky ribbons kissed her nipples and feathered her thighs.

He'd already done it, she realized. He'd undressed her and put this shirt on her. He was letting her know he'd taken the choice away from her. And he was doing it again now, with his eyes, invading her inner forces like a saboteur, stealing through closed and bolted doors with the stealth of a safecracker. His voice, his eyes, his male energy, they all pushed at her intimate boundaries. She had wanted that before, but now, without the anesthetizing force of his rage to stun her senseless, the prospect of outright seduction by Webb Calderon was a fearful thing.

"What happened while I was unconscious?" she asked.

A silvery glint. "Not *that,* I assure you . . ."

Mary Frances didn't know quite what to do or where to go. He was moving, walking toward her with a look that told her if she didn't find a way to stop him, he would finish what his eyes had already started.

"I believe you," she said swiftly.

"No, you don't understand."

He didn't stop, and she didn't move. There was nowhere to go, and he was suddenly there before her, his fingers glancing her cheek as they sought the dark curls at her nape. A soft sound died in her throat. She couldn't even manage a decent gasp. His palm was hot on her flushed skin, sweetly demanding as it curved itself to the back of her head and urged her close. His mouth feathered her temple with mint-scented breath, and had she looked up at him and met his eyes, his lips would have been mere inches from hers.

He did all this with quiet force and surprising tenderness. It was the last that left her momentarily helpless.

"You are a strange creature, Irish," he said, irony filtering through the maleness that textured his voice. "I've wondered more than once if you're made of skin and bone, mundane things like the rest of us. There are times when I think my hand might go right through you, there's so much light. Thank God, it doesn't. Thank God you are made out of . . . this."

His thumb gently flicked the velvety lobe of her ear. "Very soft stuff."

Her slow smile felt like it *was* made out of light. She avoided his eyes and tried to still her hammering heart, but her smile lit up with questions, and with the knowledge that something different was happening. She could feel it in his touch, the sudden pressure of his palm. Yes, she was made out of the same things he was . . . wild hope and hunger—fierce, aching things.

"You didn't really think I would want you unconscious when we made love, did you?" he asked her. "Not only would I want you awake, but every drop of my attention would be focused on you and your reactions. I would be listening for the sighs that got caught in your throat and the words you couldn't bring yourself to say. I would be obsessed with the idea that you might whisper my name when I moved between your legs, that you might shudder and tighten while I held you captive and plundered that dark, fragrant garden of yours like a thief—"

"Held me captive?"

"Gently, Irish, gently. Just so you wouldn't run away."

"Why are you doing this?" she demanded shakily. Something had fundamentally changed between them. She'd recognized that immediately, but what *was* he doing? He seemed bent on sexual conquest and she didn't understand why. Her inexperience had stopped him before, and nothing had changed in that way.

"Did you get the information you wanted from Alex Cordes? Is that it? Your plan worked and I'm the spoils of war?"

"No, my plan failed. I got nothing . . . except you."

She looked up at him, confused. He seemed reluctant to explain, but she had to know. Had he really given up his chance at Cordes? She couldn't believe that was possible, not knowing his obsession with the slaughter of his family. If he was telling her the truth, then he had sacrificed the only thing in life that seemed to hold meaning for him.

His hand dropped away, and the intensity shifted away from her for a moment, long enough for her to breathe—and become even more aware of his effect on her. Someone was perspiring lightly. She caught the faint tang of it in her nostrils and lifted her head like an animal, testing a scent on the wind.

It was her. Her skin was overheating and flushed with excitement. She was responding to the closeness of the man and the thrumming power of his body, perhaps even to the ribbon of nakedness revealed by the opening of his shirt. Lightning curled and streaked in his dark gold hair, hot enough to burn.

"I heard it all," he said finally, "every word that was said in Cordes's *business* meeting. Do you remember that I told you about the implant in your ankle? It was reactivated when I removed the ankle bracelet."

That had been his plan all along, she realized, to put her in that place and let her be his human conduit. She ought to have been enraged that he'd put her at risk that way. She *was* enraged, but the anger lost some of its fiery pain as she remembered what drove him. It was more than revenge. She understood what it was like to sacrifice someone you loved. She knew how that drove you to any

lengths to justify your actions. Like him, she had taken
the life of a loved one. Webb, himself. Unlike him, she
had barely understood at the time that she loved him.

"Sick bastards," he whispered. "I could hear what they
wanted to do to you, I could *feel* it." The icy fury was
back, flickering in the black wells of his pupils. He
wouldn't let her look away. "If one of them had even
touched you, I'd have torn out his throat when I came
through that door."

Stripped raw. His voice was flat and toneless, yet that
was how it sounded. Stripped raw of anything but animal
instinct.

She was right. He had given his mission up for her. The
near riot in Cordes's villa had forced him to choose, and
he'd chosen her. For some reason, it cut her apart to know
that. "That was your chance for revenge on Cordes, wasn't
it, perhaps your only chance?"

For a moment his chiseled face looked as if it might
shatter. Bones and flesh and beautiful taut angles all
seemed to collide. His hands caught in her hair and he
drew her close as if he didn't want her to see this. *Him,*
out of control. She buried her face in his shoulder with a
bewildered moan.

"Christ, Irish, do you think I had any choice?" His
body moved. "That I could have done anything else but
get you out of there?"

"But your family. What about—"

"Shhh, *don't*—"

He held her tightly, and for a moment she was lost in
the hard thud of his heart. She could feel his struggle and
ached for him, but didn't know what to do except to let
him work it through. He *had* chosen her. After everything
he'd been through, all the horrors perpetrated on him and
his family, even what he'd been forced to do to his sister,

he had still chosen a woman he barely knew, a woman he called Irish. As the silence stretched and he sought the comfort of her hair against his face, she wondered if she would ever have an answer to her question, if he *could* answer.

"My family's gone," he said finally. "They can't be hurt anymore. But Cordes would have destroyed you . . . or let his thug friends do it."

She allowed herself to be held awhile longer, until she couldn't stand it anymore. She had to see what was happening to him. One glance told her why she'd been drawn to him from the beginning. God, the exquisite turmoil. His eyes were iced over with agony, but they were beginning to thaw, to bleed.

He managed to stroke the delicate hollow just below her cheekbone. "I have a vision quest," he said.

"I know, the Cordes family."

"No, not anymore. Something happened on that island, to me as well as to you. Perhaps it's been happening since the day I met you. The past is who I am, and I'll never be able to escape its grip, not entirely . . . but it's not who I want to be." His voice changed, roughened as if it might break. "I want to be the man you love—"

Mary Frances stared at him in mute wonder, not sure she'd heard correctly, or if she had, that she understood. But the time for talk was over. He bent toward her, and some ancient part of her responded instinctively, thrilling at his swiftness as he took control of the moment and at the possessive power of his hands as they captured the weight of her hair. Her stomach pulled deeply as he brushed his lips over hers.

He was right. Something had changed. In her, too. There was a time when she would have feared this kiss, would have believed it could freeze her solid. Webb

Calderon was an ice god, a man of such ferocious control he could pierce his own flesh and feel nothing. She knew better now. Whether the source of his passion was ice or fire, it didn't freeze the things it touched, it melted them. His mouth was barely touching hers, but she could feel the burn, hear the hiss. Primordial ice. Primordial fire.

He bent to scoop her up with the clear intention of putting her on the bed. Somehow she found the strength to hold him off. "Not yet!" she said. "You have to tell me why first."

"Why . . . ?" His brow furrowed.

"Why me?" She felt she was the least likely woman on the planet to inspire a man to such acts of passion, such breathtaking words.

"That's impossible, Irish. There are too many reasons, as many reasons as stars." He sighed heavily and touched her lips. "But if you must know, then this is why."

"My mouth?"

"Yes, this beautiful mouth. It's all I want in the world."

She didn't understand. She would never understand. All kinds of erotic notions assailed her. "My beautiful mouth . . . where?"

The mood broke as he laughed and shook his head re-provingly. "You have a dirty mind, girl. This isn't about a religious experience."

She was mystified. If it hadn't been for the thistledown caress of his fingers, she would have insisted he tell her what he meant. As it was she didn't want to breathe for fear he'd stop. The sensations were gorgeous. The light-ness on her lips had exactly the opposite effect deep in her belly. It tugged hard.

"You know the medal you left with me?" he said. "The one I still have?"

"Of course." Did he think she wouldn't remember the

family heirloom that seemed to hold her fate in its golden
depths.

"I watched you bring it to your lips once, in a moment
of need, and it was the most exquisite thing I've ever
seen. The way you held it, the way you trembled. Your
eyelids fluttered and I swear I could feel what was happening inside you. There was passion and longing and
that small naked sound you made."

He knew. He knew how intimate that was for her. The
gesture was infused with vulnerability, so much so that
over the years it had taken on many different meanings.
In a strange way, it had almost begun to feel erotic.
Surely even sex couldn't be as intimate. He knew that.

"I want to taste the longing on your lips. I want to feel
them tremble against mine. If I could draw a fraction of
that passion from you, it would be—" He broke off, bemused and clearly unable to express himself. Finally, in a
moment of helplessness that struck her as completely un-
characteristic, he laughed and said, "It would be like
touching God, Irish. Like a glimpse of perfection. I don't
know how else to describe it."

Mary Frances wasn't aware that the moments of silence were piling up like snowfall. She wasn't even
aware that she'd twined her fingers in the string tie of her
shirt and drawn it to her mouth. She didn't know she'd
done all that until she felt the warmth of her knuckles
against her lips. An odd sound caught in her throat, perhaps even the one he mentioned. She wanted to believe
she hadn't dreamed it, that he really had said she was all
he would ever know of innocence. He must have.

He seemed about to turn away, and she could hardly
think what to do. Her heart wrenched as she realized he
was waiting for a response. He might even be embar-

rassed by what he'd said. She couldn't imagine him affected by that kind of vulnerability.

"Wait." She caught the dark silk of his sleeve. "I need to do something."

He glanced at her, and she felt fear grip her. His marbled gaze held her at a distance, and it took all her courage to continue. "I need to do *this*," she whispered.

She didn't wait for him to tilt his head or touch her face or in any way signal that it was safe to proceed. Just as she'd brought the medal to her lips in an act of faith, she had to do this, too. *By believing in roses one brings them to bloom.* It wasn't from the Bible, it was an old Irish proverb, a favorite of her aunt's. But Mary Frances had never thought much about it until now.

Rising on her tiptoes, she touched her mouth to his eyes and his cheeks and his clenched jawline. Everywhere on his face, she dusted him with trembling kisses, and when finally her mouth brushed his lips, she let out a sob that was laughter and wonder and anguish in equal measure. What opened inside her was a starburst of passion. She had to brace herself against his chest with her fingertips to keep her balance.

He cupped her face with his hands, and whatever sound she'd made, whatever nakedness it held, she heard it now in his throat, in his breathing. Everything he'd asked for in her kiss she found now in his. She could taste the longing in his lips and it made her own throat tighten with need. She could feel her own trembling passion searching through him, reaching deep and drawing up a response that made him shake.

The impulse that came over her made her open her eyes and draw back. She was almost sorry she had. Looking at him *was* like touching God. She could hardly manage it without feeling pierced through and through. Sweet light enveloped her, the radiance that came from cracking the casings of simple human need and letting it flood the darkness. She saw her own need reflected in his eyes. His need, quivering in the muscles of his rigid jaw. Their need, magnified to the heavens.

The lightning in his eyes wasn't ice. Ice was transient. It melted and was gone. This was eternal, the white stab of innocence. Not a reflection of hers. His own. Whoever had executed his family and tortured him hadn't destroyed it all, not every last quiver. There was one indestructible breath of life left alive, and her kiss had found it. That must be the strongest thing of all, she thought, certain she knew the answer to the riddle now. It was innocence.

24

You could die from kissing. Mary Frances knew that for a medical fact. One of her nursing instructors had described a case where an impassioned woman kissed her asthmatic lover at such ardent length he couldn't get enough oxygen. His raspy moans and helpless thrashing made her think he was as thrilled with what they were doing as she was.

Mary Frances could easily imagine expiring from a lover's kiss. As Webb lifted her to him and took control of the situation away from her, she could imagine forgetting to breathe entirely. And if suffocation wasn't the cause, then it would be heart failure.

"Help," she moaned against his lips. She hadn't expected that a man's mouth could be so soft, or so paralyzingly sweet. His hands were hard and forceful. They slid down her back and demanded that her hips come to him, yield to him. His throat was alive with rich, hungry, male sounds. Devouring sounds. And his body was a hotbed of burgeoning muscle and need.

But his lips were milk and honey.

She could have lived and died from them alone. And that was before he slipped his tongue inside her upper lip and caressed the porcelain smoothness of her teeth with slow, delicious strokes.

She moaned again, her own rich sound. She had never had a man do this to her before, any of this. It was exquisite. She was helpless, yet she loved the sensations. They were wild. They made her wild. She wanted to be picked up, tossed on the bed and taken. Stunned with the force that was in his hands. Ravished with the nectar that flowed from his kisses. Yes, please, taken.

She was even being polite about it.

His hands kneaded her hips and moved upward, abandoning them in favor of higher ground. He knew where her flesh was aching to be touched. He climbed her midriff with the heels of his palms and came up against the fullness of her breasts, crowding them until she gasped and wished his hands could be everywhere. Rough and tender, pleasuring her everywhere.

The heat of his groin was a firebrand. She rubbed herself against it and drew a moan from him. She was well acquainted with how hard he could get. She'd felt it burning a hole in her belly before, throbbing inside her. She'd nearly had the beauty she craved then, and the thought that she might have it now left her sweetly drained.

"Help?" He'd just registered the word. "Was that what you said?"

She clutched at his arms as he pulled back to look at her.

"Are you all right?" he asked, steadying her.

She wanted to laugh, but another sound came out, anguished. "Depends on what you mean by all right."

After a probing look at her flushed features and wild,

dilated eyes, he began to shape her lower lip with his thumbs. "You can relax," he told her, applying long, soothing strokes that ended at the sensitive corner creases of her mouth. "I already have what I asked for."

His husky tone told her he meant it. So did the way he was touching her, caressing her as if that really was all he intended. One kiss. The possibility sent her into a "tizzy," as Sister Fulgentia used to call it.

He bent as if to brush her forehead with his lips, and her body screamed no. It was going to be one of those dismissive kisses, the kind that made you long for more. She lifted her face to him instead, and their mouths touched.

Desire. Hunger. The awful anguish of wanting a man beyond anything else. It rose so swiftly in Mary Frances she couldn't breathe, flared into exactly the kind of passion she'd always dreamed of, a blaze out of control.

They were both overtaken by it, unable to stop.

She reached for him, and the rest was a glorious blur. The next thing she knew their clothes were on the floor and their naked bodies were entwined on the bed. White veils floated around them, serene despite the maddened fury for completion in their midst. Webb was pressing into her, entering her, and the rapture of opening herself to the mystery, of letting someone in—*him*—was so great she was afraid she might split apart like an overripe bud.

His voice broke through her thoughts. Low and savaged with desire, it galvanized her. "Hold me now," he whispered, "tightly. I don't want to hurt you."

His body bore down on hers with a dark, sweet force that she wanted desperately to yield to. She would have bargained with the heavens for her deliverance, but a stabbing sensation made her cry out. The tears that

welled in her eyes were frustration more than pain. Her
body wouldn't cooperate. It wouldn't give way to him.

"I've hurt you," he said. "Ah, sweet Christ—"

"No, please! It's all right. I'll be all right." She put up
a valiant argument, tried every way she could think of to
convince him, but he refused to go on.

His voice was a searing sigh. "Irish, there doesn't have
to be pain. I can make this easier for you."

"But I want the pain, I do." She moaned and gasped
and breathed the words all at once, knowing how crazy
she must sound. "I don't want to be denied anything, not
even that. Please—"

Afraid he would withdraw and leave her as he had before, she clutched at his face and searched his white-and-
gold waves for purchase.

"Shhhh . . ." He touched her lips with his to hush the
jumble of words and emotion. "Slow down, sweetness.
You're moving too fast. Your body can't catch up."

With a ragged sigh, he curved himself over her, his
elbow resting next to her head and his fingers laced in her
hair. His low reassurances were meant to calm her, but his
still-hard body was not doing that. It nearly drove her
mad with joy and need to have him envelope her that
way, his heat drenching her senses, his burgeoning hardness pressed solidly against the barrier her body had designed to keep it out. She felt so full of him, crammed full
of him . . . and yet so empty.

It shocked and thrilled her how much she wanted him,
all of him, every love-thickened inch. The fleeting pain
he would give her couldn't be anything compared with
the deep, aching need she felt now. And the mere sight of
him arched above her, his muscles straining to contain the
energy they'd amassed, only made the yearning worse.
She was beginning to think she would never know what

complete love was, not if he was determined to be noble.
Did he know that by sparing her, he was punishing her?
She would take a little twinge if it meant he could finish
what he'd started. She could take a big twinge.

"Your body isn't ready for this," he told her. His hand
curved her throat with a gentleness that made it constrict.
"The gate to the garden is sealed shut and it's not going
to give way to the first intruder."

"How can that be?" The boldness she felt startled her.
"Look at me, look at how flushed and feverish I am. My
throat is splotchy, my breasts are swollen with excitement, my nipples are aroused and er"—she stumbled,
then swiftly reclaimed the word—"erect. I trained to be a
nurse, you know. I recognize the signs of sexual arousal."

His eyes glimmered like icicles, as hot as they were
cold. "I'll bet you got straight A's." He let his gaze brush
over the erogenous zones in question. "You're right about
the erect nipples. God, how could we have let those go
wanting?"

"Well, if it's about things going wanting, my vulva is
aching, too. I think it might be a good idea to give that
some attention as well."

The sparkle that had suffused his eyes became a wry
smile. "You could always write me a prescription for
physical therapy. Nipples first, followed by the vulva. We
could even work on the G-spot if you wanted."

"The Grafenberg spot?" She was intrigued. "They
didn't cover that in nursing school, but Jenny Jones de-
voted an entire show to it. One woman fainted when she
found hers."

"Fainted on the show?"

"No, I believe it was in the funhouse at Coney Island."

He gazed at her, but shook his head, apparently deciding not to go there. "Let's skip the G-spot. We've got plenty to deal with without you fainting."

"It might have been the ride that made her fain—"

A hand clamped her mouth, silencing her gently, but firmly. Undaunted, she moved her hips a little, hoping to encourage him with some body language. It worked. His jaw clenched and then so did everything else. The muscles of his belly rippled in a motion so graceful it felt like water lapping over rocks.

"Mary Frances—" He continued to muzzle her, all the while absently caressing the sensitive spot where her hair swept back from her temple. "I don't need to be convinced that you want me. The problem is you don't trust me, and your body is reacting instinctively to protect you."

"Itrusyu." It was probably just as well that her denial got garbled in his palm. It would have been one of the biggest fibs she'd ever told. She pulled his hand off her mouth. "I *don't* trust you?"

"It's not because you don't want to. You've been thoroughly indoctrinated in the virtues of obedience and submission, probably your entire life, and your way of dealing with things is to yield rather than to fight. But you always hold back some part of yourself. You never yield everything—and that's what you're doing now."

"How do you know all this?" Everything would have been so simple if she could just lie.

His smile faded as he studied her. "I know it because you tell me, just the way you're telling me now. Your eyes invite me and your mouth yields to me instantly, but the garden is off-limits. I'm not allowed in your secret place because if you let me in there, you might reveal too much of yourself in the heat of passion. I might discover who you really are, and why you still need to hide. Once you let me in, there won't be anywhere you're safe from me."

She looked away. He knew what no one else had ever cared enough to find out about her, that she was embryonically fragile, that she could be cracked like eggshells when she was vulnerable to someone. Her father had shown her from infancy that he could only love her in a limited way that depended entirely on her being chaste and untouched. If he'd even suspected her secret dreams, much less her deep envy of Brianna's boldness, he would have loathed her. He wanted a saint for a daughter, so she'd locked every other part of herself off to keep his meager love and to avoid being crushed by his hatred. She had kept her true self so well hidden no one had ever seen it or even suspected it existed . . . until now.

She nodded and felt his hand soothe her cheek caressingly.

"It's only natural, Irish. You have no reason in the world to trust me, and every reason not to. I deceived you and dangled you like bait. I kidnapped you and forced you into marriage. I haven't treated you well, to say the least. There's no way to justify what I've done. I was wrong. But we were pitted against each other as enemies, if you remember. And you got in a couple of shots, too."

It was true. She'd nearly killed him.

"It doesn't have to be this way. We can change all that now," he told her. "We can change everything. But it must be your choice. If you want this to happen between us, you're going to have to give yourself over to it—and to me."

She opened her eyes to his melting gaze, to icicles that were thawing, bleeding. "How do I do that?" she asked.

"I can take you past the pain so quickly you'll never feel it. I can give you pleasure unlike anything you've

ever known. It will rival rapture, but in order to let yourself have this experience, you're going to have to do
everything I tell you to. Everything, without question."

"And if I do," she asked, reminded of the story Africa
had told her, "if I let myself have this rapture you describe, how will I ever be able to settle for anything less?
Won't I just want more and more and more?"

He smiled. "You might. Would that be a problem?"

"Only if you decided to lock me in a room and make
me a prisoner of delight the way Bluebeard did with his
young, virginal wives." She shivered at the thought, actually quite taken by it.

"I'd like nothing better, but you'd never be a prisoner,
Mary Frances. Nothing would be done to you against
your will."

Somehow she knew that he could make her want anything he wanted, that when it came to things of *that* nature, she would have no will of her own with him. That
thrilled her, too. Everything he did thrilled her, although
it made this odyssey he talked about a very dangerous
thing. Would she lose her way, lose herself?

"Webb Calderon's alive and hiding out in Cap Ferrat.
He's rented the Villa del Mare, your family's old summer
place in the south of France, where your father used to
take you when you were a child. He's the one who
snatched that Murphy woman out from under your nose.
Calderon did it. She's there, with him. . . ."

Alex Cordes slid his thumb over the tiny remote-control
device, searching out the power button by feel. His eyes
were protected against the tropical sun by tiny black satin
goggles, and his nude body, still wet from a dip in the
saltwater pool, was slathered with pungent coconut oil.

The phone-message machine sat on the tile counter of

the nearby wet bar. One touch of his thumbnail turned it off. Unfortunately, there was no power button to erase the anonymous male voice from the tape deck playing in his mind.

His plan had been to laze by the pool all day, drinking goombay smashes and nibbling on conch fritters, a local seafood delicacy. He had a great deal to celebrate. Despite the awkwardness with the "Murphy woman," his associates had been so anxious to finish the negotiations, they'd agreed to every concession he asked. It had been a stunning success, and he wanted to savor it privately before he faxed his support base in San Carlos. Now that he had the economic wherewithal to put his country on the map, the next step would be to remove his father from power, swiftly and decisively. And since Ruben would never acquiesce gracefully, there was only one alternative.

The remote control plunked noisily as Alex dropped it on the wrought-iron table next to his lounge chair. He groped for his drink, found the icy glass nestled in a woven bamboo coaster, and brought it to his lips, congratulating himself on his dexterity.

Rich laughter swelled as the rum and coconut liqueur slid down his throat. He didn't need alcohol. He was already drunk. Nothing would be the same from this moment on, he knew that, and it made him giddy with joy. He needed time to adjust to it all, to revel privately and savor a future in which every word he said would be freighted with importance and even his casual gestures would be analyzed for their meaning.

Another deep drink of the smash made him sigh. He set the glass down and let his head loll back against the thick white terry bath sheet. Perhaps the greatest pleasure would come in avenging himself on those who had misused him. There were so many who'd patronized and dismissed him. But the phone call had changed his plans.

Sweat traversed his scalp and trickled down his temple. He wiped it away with the back of his hand, aware of moisture forming in various crevices—the back of his neck and knees. Reaching down absently to rub his thigh, he let the heel of his hand sink into the hot muscles and was pleasantly surprised at the sensations as he massaged.

Calderon wasn't his first concern. Men like him rarely stayed dead for very long, although Mary Frances Murphy's story had been remarkably convincing. The art dealer was also a wanted man, and not just by the law, which handicapped him greatly. The Mafia types who'd supplied the microchip couldn't have received their payment since Alex still had it. No, Alex was reasonably sure a bargain could be struck. He had something Calderon needed, including the authentic Maya figurine. But Alex was curious who might want to pit him and Calderon against each other. And why they were using the woman as bait.

The tingling in his groin encouraged him to continue stroking. Odd that he couldn't remember the last time he'd aroused himself. Sex held little interest for him in and of itself. It was the power games he enjoyed, and he'd been taught by the best, his father's mistress, a manipulative, voracious she-wolf of a woman, who had loved nothing better than to taunt and humiliate and reduce a budding adolescent boy to a bumbling idiot.

The thickening that had begun in his loins fell off as his hand stilled. *"Puta,"* he mumbled hoarsely. Even the memory of that castrating whore could make him impotent.

He'd often wondered if his father knew of Shaheen's

taste for nubile young males. Alex vaguely remembered a blond houseboy who'd spent a summer with them at Villa del Mare. He'd been at Shaheen's beck and call until a nasty fight erupted between her and his father. That night the kid had been shipped off somewhere, never to be heard from again.

A dark, pouty beauty of French and Caribbean extraction, Shaheen hadn't bothered to wait for Alex to mature sexually before she began her instruction. He was eleven the first time she aroused him to the point of pain with her deft hands and lips and then dismissed him as pathetic. "That chicken bone couldn't choke a teething puppy," she'd crowed.

When finally, after years of this torture she had allowed him to mount her, she'd slapped him viciously for coming too fast. He endured her taunting for nearly four years, until one day quite by accident he discovered he was the stronger. That time he'd hit her back. He'd knocked her nearly senseless with the blow and taken her in a violent rage of lust. The satisfaction had been so intense he'd found it difficult to climax after that unless there was force involved. A taste for rough sex was born that day and it had haunted his relationships ever since.

Now he could read a woman's hidden desires for such things. He knew when she wanted to be taken forcibly and when she wanted to be reduced to sexual rubble by degrees. Because eventually those with a taste for it all wanted the same thing, to be sacrificed on the altar of erotic pleasure. And he was happy to be their high priest. Very few had the strength of mind to resist his delicious and deadly subjugation. He could only think of one who might have been able to, had he had some time with her.

He's the one who snatched the woman out from under your nose. Calderon did it. She's there, with him. . . .

Mary Frances Murphy. Her luminous green eyes pierced the darkness behind his black satin mask. Alex wasn't given to reflection on the character of others, but she interested him in a way no other woman had, including her sister. Celeste, or Brianna, as her sister had called her, had defied him and earned his grudging respect, but she had not escaped him. Mary Frances had, twice now. But that wasn't what had absorbed and fascinated him the most. It was her power. Alex was obsessed with power, and she was strong in a way he'd never encountered before.

Her strength came through what most people would have considered weakness. Surrender. Or perhaps a more appropriate word was submission. You couldn't fight someone who simply gave in to you without a struggle. The battle was over and they had won by taking away your ability to defeat them, especially when you knew and *they* knew that they hadn't been defeated, not in spirit.

With her fern-grotto eyes and her delicate freckles and soaring spirit, Mary Frances Murphy's curse was that every man she encountered would be compelled to try to defeat her and own her totally. Own her soul. That was what he wanted, too, the strange woman's soul.

A hot throb in the sea depths of his belly brought his mind and his hand back to that place. "Mmmm, yes . . ." A groan rippled low and lush in his throat as he rediscovered his own body. He was hardening again, already thick with the pleasurable sensations flooding his groin.

The microchip deal had fulfilled his dreams beyond measure. He didn't need Mary Frances Murphy for anything. Or Webb Calderon, for that matter. He'd pried open the Queen Conch and it had yielded a priceless pink pearl. Still, the opportunity to capture what had eluded him held a certain allure. And he was feeling lucky this morning.

Mary Frances watched in confusion and wonder as Webb began to pull veils from the canopy bed. One by one he tweaked the filmy things and they fell into his hands like cirrus clouds being snatched from the heavens. He'd left her curled up in satin sheets and slipped on his coffee-black pajama bottoms to perform the feat, a sight that evoked fanciful thoughts of half-naked Roman deities with lightning for hair and diamonds for eyes, demigods at play in the cosmos.

"What are those for?" she asked. By now her pulse was erratic, skipping beats and stumbling on the pauses.

With a few twists of the veils, he made several white silken ropes. "Your protection," he said. "If you decide to let me take you on this journey, there will be times when you'll think you want me to stop."

"I'll *think* I want that?"

She hadn't yet agreed to anything, but he'd already started the preparations and was being purposely oblique about his intent. "Why can't you tell me what you're going to do? Then I'll know whether or not I want you to stop. Perhaps I won't even want you to start."

He glanced up from his efforts, one eyebrow having risen ironically, the other having stayed put. "Because this is as much a matter of trust as anything else. If you're going into this adventure, you'll have to do it blindly, nothing held back, a leap of faith. The power of a ritual is in its rules, and the more ancient the ceremony, the more important it is that the rules be followed to the letter. If they're not, the power can be lost or subverted."

"Subverted? What does that mean?"

He didn't answer, which she could only assume meant

bad news. She was intimately familiar with rules and rituals and their power. They were an essential part of the religion she'd been brought up in, or any religion, for that matter. "How do you know so much about ancient ceremonies?"

He laid the ropes across the foot of the bed, six of them, in a parallel fashion. "I deal in antiquities," he told her, his gaze flickering over her as if he were measuring her for restraints and a collar. "My work is steeped in the ancient past, in arcane art and its secret uses. Much of it was used in early worship of one kind or another."

A white wicker credenza stood next to the bed. He'd taken a tray from one of its cupboards and some items from a drawer and he was continuing his preparations as he spoke. Mary Frances saw votive candles and a small bronze pot that looked like an incense burner. There was another object, too, but it was obscured from her view by his body.

"Every icon has its own mythology," he explained, "every fertility statue its legend. It's my business to know its oral history as well as its sales history."

"So . . . you do this often?" She couldn't help herself. "Perform rituals?"

He was still turned away from her, emptying a vial into the brass pot and setting it over the flame of a burner, but his hesitation made her think he might be smiling. "Not often," he said. "Only when there's a virgin available."

She tucked the sheets around her drawn-up legs. The potency that swelled from the brass pot had already saturated the air so thoroughly it was making her woozy. Rich, heady smells like burning brandy were ghosted by hints of sandalwood. "You said I might want you to stop, and I'm assuming that's because of the pain. What if I do?"

"There won't be pain in the way you're thinking, I promise you that. The sensations will be new to you, and at their most intense, they can bring a pleasure that's indescribable. It's the sweetest bliss you'll ever know, but torturous nonetheless. If that happens, you'll beg and fight, and that could be dangerous."

"Dangerous?"

"Do you remember the Zin Quai? The drug you used on me? Mixed with other herbs, it has uses that make it essential for the 'pleasure' trade. I'll only need a little, an infinitesimal amount actually, just enough to coat the tip of this."

The object obscured from her view was a ceremonial sheath and dagger. He held it up for her to see, and her breath hitched in painfully. It was the one she'd coated with the Oriental herb and left on the floor for him to find, the scimitar he'd called the Serpent's Eye.

"Dear God," she uttered softly. The breath that had caught in her throat vibrated there as she stared at him, probably the most beautiful, dangerous, and yes, evil man she'd ever known. He admitted to it, the evil. She still didn't know what his involvement was in Brianna's death, or why he'd sacrificed his chance at Cordes to rescue her. He'd said he had no choice, and she'd believed it when she felt him shake and press his mouth to her hair. But there was something dark in him still, something that made her shiver and kept her from feeling totally safe. It was like exploring a subterranean cave with a torch. The beauty was stunning, but you never knew what was around that next corner.

Webb Calderon was the last man she should be entrusting with her virginity, perhaps even her life. And yet it had to be him. There was no one else, no other man who could take her through this experience. They were entwined, he and she, for good and evil, forever, even if forever came with the next breath she took. She knew that, too.

The bright sunlight brushed his bones and contoured his face with shadows. "There's one more thing before we start," he said. "Something I have to know about you."

"What's that?"

"Your sin of impurity. I need to know what you've done."

Mary Frances wondered how to tell him. She'd known he would ask eventually, but that didn't make it any easier to explain. She'd never told anyone for the simple reason that they would have jumped to the wrong conclusion. People were least tolerant of the qualities they rejected in themselves, even emotions. "A kiss. It was an innocent thing, really—"

"Your kisses aren't innocent, Irish, despite what I might have thought once."

The rough edges in his voice told her he'd already made some assumptions about the situation that weren't true. He sounded faintly savage, and she wisely decided not to look at him. This was going to be difficult enough without being riddled by his eyes.

"It's not what you think," she went on. "It happened in the infirmary at St. Gertrude's."

"The convent?"

She nodded and continued, knowing it would be more difficult if she stopped. "Those of us who were studying nursing did shifts in the infirmary. It was mostly uneventful work and left me lots of time to study, but one of the newer postulants tried to run away one night. She only got as far as the grounds, but she hid somewhere, and it was bitterly cold. By the time they found her, she was blue. They left her in the infirmary with me, but I wasn't sure how to care for her. She was so thin, I thought she was going to die, so I . . ."

He anticipated her hesitation. "You held her?"

"Yes, I took her in my arms, poor frail thing, and tried to stop her shaking. She began to whimper and cling to me, I think more from gratefulness than anything else. It probably would have been all right, only we fell asleep that way, and one of the professed nuns found us."

"And she got the wrong idea?"

"She told the reverend mother that we were engaged in unnatural acts and were an abomination in the sight of God. I was called in, and even though I denied there had been anything unnatural, I couldn't deny what I'd felt."

Silence. A rustle of silk as the veils on the bed moved. "What did you feel?"

"Passion, that's the only word for it—unbelievable passion for human contact, for the warmth of another body, for love. I felt so starved for that, all of it, that I never wanted to let go of the poor sick child. We'd all been cautioned against physical contact or developing a 'particular affection' for any of the other postulants. We were also discouraged from private conversations or singling anyone out for friendship, and I never questioned that, because I knew friendship wasn't what we were there for. We had a much higher purpose. But I hadn't realized how much I missed holding and caring for someone until I held a sick girl in my arms. It wouldn't have mattered who it was, I drew more comfort from it than from my spiritual studies . . . and that, I knew, was unforgivable."

"You said there was a kiss?"

This was the part she'd never told anyone, because she knew they couldn't possibly understand. Even she didn't really understand why she'd reacted the way she had. "My mother died when I was child, and my father raised Brianna and me. Thank God for my aunt Celeste, who always seemed to be there when we needed her. Whenever I was ill, she would check me for a fever by pressing her lips to my brow, so when the postulant began to shiver, I did the same without thinking much about it. Her face was turned away, but I must have startled her, because before I could draw back, she came around, and our mouths touched. Our noses hit, too, and our chins, but none of that seemed to make any difference."

"It sounds like an accident."

"It was, I'm sure of that now, but I wasn't then. My poor heart nearly kicked its way out of my chest. I felt such horror, I knew unequivocally that I had to leave the convent. Not because I'd accidentally kissed another postulant, but because of who I'd wanted it to be."

His questioning gaze drew up an answer. "Someone dark," she admitted, "someone forbidden, the phantom who stole my fantasy and turned it into reality."

"Are you going to tell me this fantasy?"

"You *are* the fantasy."

Now his eyes did pierce her, impaled her through and through. They were as sharp as the dagger, as deadly, but they were also as sweet as the bliss he'd described. They promised everything she'd ever wanted. They promised the ultimate . . . but was that ecstasy or agony? Some intuition told her what he had not, that to know ecstasy, you had to know agony first, and that before he was done, she would know both.

She looked to him for reassurance. She needed him to tell her that she wouldn't be hurt in any way, that he would bring her through it safely, but he was oddly remote, as if he had to detach himself in some way in order to follow through with what they'd started. When she confessed her rising fears, he gave her something to drink to relax her, a sweet, tinted concoction that tasted faintly like Angel Water. And when she asked him to tell her more about what he was going to do, he reminded her that all ceremonies had their rules and this one had only two. The first was trust and the second was commitment. If she was unsure in her heart about either, they couldn't proceed without taking precautions.

"You do understand that once we've started, there's no stopping," he told her. "If you fight, I'll have to use the ropes."

He laid the dagger on the bed next to the veils and turned to her. His eyes asked the question that only she could answer.

A tremor shook through her body. She held out her hands, wrists together. "Do it now," she said. "It's not you I don't trust. It's myself."

As he reached for the ropes she remembered another time she'd surrendered herself in this way and realized that gesture had only been a form of preparation. Her entire life had been preparation for this moment. She had never done either of the things he was asking of her. She had never trusted anyone implicitly or committed herself to anything with her whole heart. To do so would be a terrible risk for some reason that completely eluded her at this moment. But it didn't matter why. It only mattered that she take the risk, here, now, with him.

25

The things I do for love. Mary Frances wasn't sure whether the catch in her throat was tears or laughter. She felt like a flower caught in a hurricane. The tremors wouldn't stop. They buffeted her body with one gust after another, tugging and tossing her about. She couldn't imagine how it could get any worse, and he hadn't even touched her yet, except to put the smock shirt back on. All he'd done was arrange her body on the satin sheets, loop a silk rope around her wrists and tie them to the headboard above her, and then, because she'd insisted on it, he'd looped each of her ankles with veils and secured them to the balustrades at the corners of the footboard.

She'd warned him to tie her tightly, because she was weak in the trust and commitment departments, and he'd promised he would. But she hadn't been able to distinguish the gliding motion of his hands from the silken caresses of the veils. The sense impressions had left her breathless, and even now that he'd nearly finished, she couldn't tell if she'd actually been restrained. Perhaps it was because she was trying so hard to lie still, but all she could feel was a warm, floaty pressure against her inner wrists and ankles, where her skin was extra-sensitive.

"Did you tie them tight?" she asked when he was done. "So tight I can't break free?"

"The fighting Irish?" He sat next to her on the bed and caressed her unsteady lips with a tenderness that brought tears to her eyes. "Why don't you just lay down your arms right now and surrender to me, sweetness?"

"I want to," she whispered.

"I know you do." He continued to soothe the shake from her lower lip. "But there's a part of you trying to hold the fort, no matter what. That's the part we have to sneak past, okay? A little military science?"

His strategy included coating the tip of the scimitar with the Zin Quai mixture. Mary Frances watched him do it, and when he turned to her moments later, the dagger in hand, she began to realize what was at stake. She knew how little it had taken to affect him. This went beyond trusting him with her sexuality, this could be her life at risk.

"Be still now," he said, sitting next to her and smoothing flyaway tendrils of raven from her temples. "You need to be very still. No matter what happens, don't move, not even to tremble. If you do, my hand could slip . . . and I don't want that."

"Wait." She felt the restraints tighten and didn't even realize she'd drawn against them. The veils had been tied with slipknots, all four of them. Not only was she was bound, she couldn't move. "You're going to apply the Zin Quai with the dagger?"

"I don't have any choice, love. Anything larger than the tip of this dagger would introduce too much of the mixture into your system. You're not in danger, I promise, not unless you move suddenly."

He set the knife aside as if to reassure her that he wasn't going to use it just yet, and continued to shape her brow with his thumb, gentling her. His touch hadn't lost any of its tenderness. Even his eyes flared with the emotion. They were beautiful. Melting pools of silvery blue.

"Now close your eyes and let me bring a sigh to your lips," he told her. "We're not going to do anything until you're ready. Someone once said that oil poured drop by drop onto the fire revives the flames, but poured in large gushes, it smothers them. That's how we're going to do this, drop by drop."

Her lids fluttered and closed, partly her own volition, partly because they were so deliciously heavy. Was it the Angel Water? she wondered. The incense?

He smoothed away the remaining strands of her hair. She made a little sound of contentment and turned her face up to the warm rain of his fingertips. It sprinkled her skin and lips and hair. And when the shower was over, he began to quiet her body with gentle touches.

"That's it, love, relax. Give yourself to it. Give yourself to me. I want those lips to sigh. I want those eyelids to quiver with pleasure."

The smock shirt caressed her breasts like a shy lover. Now she knew why he hadn't removed it. Rustling under the lightness of his fingertips, the diaphanous material stippled her skin, making it seem iridescent. If the silver that stretched tautly across a moonlit lake had a feeling, it would be this. If the silver of his eyes had a feeling, it would be this.

Every touch sent a shiver along her nerves and brought the sighs he wanted to hear. Only it wasn't enough. It felt as if he'd barely iced her breasts before he was gone.

He'd barely trailed his silver fingertips up the inside of her thighs.

Not enough, she wanted to cry. *Not enough.*

But it was just enough to make her lift toward his hands.

"Don't move, love . . . moving is dangerous. You can sigh, you can cry, you can even die a little, but don't move."

"I'm floating," she said thickly. "I don't think my body's touching the bed."

"Shhh, quiet, Irish," he said, hushing her with a thumb to her lips. "I have plans for this mouth, too."

He left her no time for anything *but* sighs as he continued. She did her best to hold still, but her ankles and wrists strained against the silk ropes anyway, a reflex reaction. Her nerves were dancing, spinning. Yet despite the pleasurable tension, she found herself relaxing, too, flowing like a river under his skillful caresses. A dam had been broken.

Languidly aroused, she felt a tingling sensation along the rim of her bottom lip, where ruby fullness met pale skin. Any sharper and it would have stung. Her pulse began to flutter and rise. As the sensation spread to encircle her entire mouth, she realized he was tracing her lips with the point of the dagger.

The fiery pleasure must be the Zin Quai mixture. It reminded her of the reed switches that Africa had used on her—peppery, yet delightful. Her entire body had thrilled to the vibrant chaos. It was like being tickled and teased with a pincushion, so lightly caressed with the prickly points that you wanted more, yet knew you might not be able to stand it.

"Don't move," he said, tracing the knifepoint along the inner crease of her lips. Her lids shivered spontaneously.

That feels lovely and hot, she told him silently, opening her eyes. *Can't I have more of it, please? Touch me hotter, deeper. Burn me like a candleflame.*

But his gaze penetrated hers like daggers, the tenderness gone. She could see by his warning stare that she had better not voice her request, and even if she obeyed and didn't move a muscle, there was little chance she would get what she wanted. No one knew better than he what too much Zin Quai could do. He was doling it out sparingly.

Her body shuddered of its own accord, testing the silk bonds. He'd said the mixture excited the erogenous zones, and it was doing just that. Every part of her was alive with anticipation. The softness between her legs was tingling as if he'd already stroked her there. What would she do when it was as hot and fiery-sweet as her lips?

She was desolate when he left her that way, tingling and aching, bereft and abandoned, and began to untie the strings of her shirt. A tidal swell of sighs filled her throat. Her lips throbbed for his, but he would do nothing to relieve them.

A sound caught in her throat. Need.

"You were warned," he said in low, reverberant tones. "Every tender pink part of you will be singing like that before I'm through. I ringed your lips with just a tiny bit of it, enough to make them swell and tighten."

"Mmmmm." She moaned faintly in response.

"Shhhh . . . that's only a taste. Your body is next, your breasts. When I encircle your nipples, they'll quiver and reach as if they'd been sucked."

She wanted to nod, to dart her tongue over her feverish lips, but his warning not to move flashed in her mind. All of her fears and doubts seemed to have evaporated. She'd never been so ready for anything. She was hungering for it, and yet her heart was pounding with something that felt as much like terror as excitement.

She breathed deeper, inhaling the hot perfume of her own arousal. He had opened the shirt to her belly, grazing bare skin with his movements. Now the luminous material shivered against her skin, raising gooseflesh so sensitive it started a new round of quaking. The sounds that spun through her were sighs and moans.

He gazed down at her, devouring her. The ice of his eyes burned her. But when he touched her with the blade of the knife, the pressure was so slight she wouldn't have known she'd been touched at all, except for the delicate pink line he left on her flesh.

Another sliding caress made her gasp inwardly. Her flesh rose and reached, covered with glowing streaks. Still as a whisper, the cool, sharp knife edge was testing the fullness of her creamy-white breast. She moaned deep in her throat, and as he began to encircle her nipple she moved against the restraints, unable to help herself.

He hissed a soft "Hold *still*!" But she couldn't.

Sometime later, probably only moments, she realized the sensations had eased, that he'd hesitated and was waiting for her to behave herself. She let out a ragged breath and sank into the bed, whimpering as he began again. Torture. It was torture.

When he'd finished with one breast, he dipped the tip of the blade into the tiny pot where the liquid mixture was being heated. The scent of brandy and sandlewood rose like a fever dream as he began to paint the other side, stroking the aureole to terra rosa and the bud to quaking tautness.

She was weak by the time he was done with her, unable even to quiver as he used the dagger to lay open the rest of her shirt. He exposed her fully, the pale legs, the raven-black pubis that crowned them, and the sliver of a crimson scar he'd left on her belly the last time he'd used a dagger to undress her. Still, she was too limp to protest his methods.

"Lovely Irish, you must be as soft as mink."

She could feel the tip of the dagger sifting through her dark curls and it made her think about drawing her legs together, but she couldn't. Even if she'd had the strength, the ropes held her ankles fast. The feathery sensations along her inner thighs told her he had begun his assault on her lower extremities. Surely he couldn't be using the scimitar, not down there? She was afraid to look, but as the coated tip lightly encircled her sex, sending up flares, she knew that nothing was to be sacred and no part of her body would be spared.

Light pinwheeled beneath her eyelids. It was as sparkling bright as the brilliance in her loins. He needn't have warned her not to move. She couldn't have. She was completely caught up in the wonder of her body to create such a spectacle. She had seen fireworks shows that were less dazzling.

"More loveliness," he said, stroking the fragile pink ruffles that peeked from the bed of dark curls. "The thatch of bramble roses that guards the gate."

Each touch of the blade brought its own little burst of starlight. Each prick and caress intoxicated her and made her anticipate the next one and the next, until she began to feel as if she might expire if the stimulation didn't stop. And yet she would certainly die if it did. It was the sweetest provocation she'd ever known. Delicate feminine muscles reached and tugged, searching for something to embrace in their tight, butterfly heat.

Through lowered lids she was aware of his skill and

precision, of his mastery over the ebb and flow of her flesh. He was attuned to every quake and quiver. He could manipulate even the tiniest response. And when her arousal was complete, he stepped back and studied her, watching her slightly delirious attempts to escape the restraints.

"Please," she whispered, "please."

The black-coffee silk dropped to the floor as he began to undress, and when he was naked, he dipped the dagger in the Zin Quai once more. His muscles were fluid, yet prodigiously hard. His erection glowed in the candle-flame. This time he ringed his own erogenous zones with the herb, burning the perimeter of his nipples first. They hardened like burgundy agates.

He flinched slightly as he painted the head of his shaft next, though undoubtedly with pleasure, if he was experiencing the same fire she had. Male flesh jerked and shuddered, growing even more rigid under the light strokings of the blade. It was a thing alive, as erotically powerful as anything she'd ever seen.

Deep within Mary Frances, something shifted and dropped as she imagined the rapture of having him inside her. Her muscles unfurled and reached. They tightened again. Pining. Her flesh was pining. Every part of her sang out to be penetrated.

She couldn't wait any longer. He had grievously over-estimated her ability to obey. Convent or not, she was only human. She'd been exhorted to mortify physical desires in favor of spiritual ones. But this was more than flesh, more than desire. It felt uncannily spiritual, as if the longing had awakened the sleeping woman in her soul. Love was holy. Fear was reverential, and she felt both for this man. She'd never understood the workings of the

heart, especially her own. She just knew they were powerful.

He had set the knife aside and cupped himself, cradling
the inflamed hardness as well as the taut sacs. She had the
feeling he was preparing his body in some way, but she
had no idea what it might be. Perhaps he was spreading
the Zin Quai mixture. Her experience with naked males
was limited to hospital work and she had certainly never
seen a man handle himself this way. It made her ache all
the way to her bones.

"Now?" she asked weakly. "Whatever it is that's supposed to free me of pain and give me rapture beyond
measure, couldn't you do it *now*?"

He glanced up, his eyes darkening with laughter, and
searingly male. He certainly looked ready, but apparently
he wasn't, because he picked up the dagger and dipped it
again. This time he traced the gleaming blade edge over
his lips and even coated the tip of his tongue. That's when
she realized what he was going to do.

"Lord," she whispered, "oh, dear Lord."

A sudden stab of pleasure nearly lifted her off the bed.
It was anticipation. He hadn't touched her, much less
done what she was thinking. But her imagination had
rocketed out of control, and she couldn't turn it off. Her
response was so sharp and sweet and wild that when he
did move between her legs and lift her to his mouth, she
cried his name and her eyes brimmed with stinging tears.

His tongue caressed her like the fingers of a satin
glove. It pricked her as vibrantly as the dagger. Sliding
along her inflamed layers and petals, all shivering sensation, it delved into her garden of secrets and found her
heart. And by the time he touched his lips to that tiny
swollen bud, and began to draw on it with the sweetest
suction she'd ever known, she was already convulsing

with wonder and shame. Surely this much pleasure was forbidden?

Another stab made her gasp with surprise. And then another and another in a beautiful, endless chain. And though she'd never had one before, she realized she must be having some kind of orgasm. It was a rippling, thundering thing, only the tension didn't let up as the pleasure subsided. It continued to build, making her muscles ache terribly with their need to squeeze something firm and hot. Was that what Zin Quai did? Bring the body to spontaneous orgasm?

She strained against the ropes. "You're done with the dagger! Can't you untie me?"

"I'm not done with it, Irish," he told her gently. Suddenly he was arched over her, bracing himself with his hands as he feathered her mouth with a kiss, a kiss that tasted intimately of her. "We're come to the most important part. Now you must give yourself over totally. Trust me completely. Can you do that?"

"Yes!" She'd agreed even before he had the questions out. Her body gave her no choice. None. She'd never believed in demon possession in the literal sense, but she was starting to now. She felt as if something supernatural had taken possession of her and was making her promise anything to get what she needed. *Him. The man and that beautiful, hard thing between his legs.*

He sheathed the knife, and she realized that everything he'd done so far had been in preparation for this. In truth, something about the sleek, gleaming, evil object he held fascinated her. She *must* be drugged. She was actually looking forward to being deflowered by a vile instrument of death called the Serpent's Eye.

"Couldn't we try again? You and I?" she asked pleadingly. "It's you I need. Not that awful thing."

At least he had the decency to look regretful as he patted her knee and turned her down flat. "Sorry, sweetness,
but we've been there and done that. Twice, remember?
This way there won't be any pain, I promise you. Only
pleasure so intense it makes bliss pale by comparison.
The slight torque of the sheath allows it to probe where
the membrane is most easily breached. And before I use
it, I will have prepared you"—he smiled faintly—"all of
you, including your *aching vulva,* to accept and accom-
modate whatever I put inside you. Once I use the sheath,
it will be over in seconds, and I'll take you the rest of the
way."

"Yes, okay, fine," she agreed breathlessly. It was her
aching vulva that was talking for her now. Otherwise she
would have told him what he could do with his serpent
and his bliss.

"No pain," he repeated as if he didn't quite believe her
miraculous conversion, "nothing to inhibit the pleasure.
The pressure you'll feel will intensify everything, and the
orgasms will continue, but on a different level. They'll be
much deeper and more satisfying. Your muscles will
tighten around me like tiny fists, and your pleasure will
be complete, possibly before I've penetrated fully."

"Yes, I'll have orgasms and make fists," she promised.
"I'll do anything you say, just untie me!"

"I can't untie you, Irish. You're too wild to be trusted
now, and I can't take the risk of hurting you."

He was playing dirty! Either that or he knew she was
demon-possessed. She wanted to struggle, but what was
the point? Instead, she closed her eyes in utter frustration
and felt him move between her thighs. She felt herself
being cupped and lifted, locked in the position he wanted,
and by the time he was done, he'd given himself unfet-
tered access to her throbbing center.

She'd stopped writhing by then in anticipation of finally getting what she needed. Despite what he'd said, she knew there wouldn't be total satisfaction, couldn't be total satisfaction, until he was buried to the wall of her womb. She had to have him as deeply inside her as he could penetrate. Nothing else would release the wildness.

He moved over her as if he were going to thrust into her himself, but she saw the sheath in his hand. Arched above her, he curved his other hand to her throat and pressed her into the bed. His lips touched hers searingly.

"Let it free you," he demanded softly. "You won't be whole until you're broken."

A cry left her lips as suddenly she was full. Everything he told her was true. There was no pain, only a sense of volume and a moment of surging pressure as the barrier that kept him from her gave way. A slight tearing sensation made the lights behind her closed eyes burst brightly. She arched and fell back, everything releasing at once— that tender part of her body, the silken ropes that held her and the wild breath that had caught in her throat. All of the restraints were gone.

"Irish?"

Silver thunder, his voice. Low and iridescent. She opened her eyes to it swirling in her head. To him above her. He hadn't entered her yet, and her need to have him inside was so great she reached for him with sudden force. She hadn't consciously meant to collide with him, but that was what happened. Caught off guard, he lost his balance, and she fell with him. The half roll of their bodies left him on his back and her straddling him.

The ache for sex rocked through her. The ache for him was indescribable. He felt like a wedge of heat and solid muscle between her legs as she pushed herself up and gazed down at him. Her thighs hugged his hips and the dark curls of her pubis were flush up against his hardness.

"I need you," she breathed. "I need you *now*."

"That was going to be my line." His smile was ragged as he caught hold of her wrists. Tenderness flared in his eyes. And rage. Such beautiful rage. But if he had any thought of dominating her now, that was not to be. She was a free woman, and she would have her way. With him.

Her hands were flung above her head, locked in his hold. She used them to brace herself as she sought her one true objective. Her only objective. Ravishment. It ached through and through her to ravish his beautiful, hard body, to love him within an inch of his life, as she knew he would have her.

Wild for release, she rose up and impaled herself on him in one shuddering stroke. A cry swelled in her throat as she slid down the length of him and sank to his belly. She was full of him up to her eyes, it seemed. He felt massive inside her, so gloriously hot and thick and alive.

She ceased to move. She couldn't move. She could only sway there above him, a naked woman, virginal no more, anchored by soaring pleasure and the great throbbing axis that held her in place. He'd said her muscles would grip him like tiny fists and they did, hot little replicas of her hands. He'd said her pleasure would surpass bliss, and it did. This was rapture.

She could have swayed there forever, blissfully engorged, but he wouldn't let her. He had his own objective. He caught her beneath her arms, and the impact of his body as he lifted her and brought her down again made her gasp with wonder. A bright new crisis built, the first with him high and hard inside her, and it drove her into a frenzied quest for completion.

She rode him with wild abandon, shuddering with orgasm after orgasm. She rode him until she felt his body buck and convulse and jackknife into hers. The last thing she remembered was falling forward and gently touching his face. His eyes were crystal shards, but it wasn't their jagged beauty that pierced her. It was his voice, his silver thunder voice.

"Irish," he said. "God, Irish, I love you."

When she came to sometime later, Mary Frances was vaguely aware of a burning sensation on the inside of her elbow. A sharp scent pierced her nostrils, and she recognized it as alcohol. Her focus was pale and blurry, but she could see him sitting beside her. He was intent on the arm that rested on his thigh. Her arm. At first she thought he was caressing her, but then she felt the dampness and saw the cotton ball he was using to swab her skin.

Suddenly a syringe glinted in his hand.

She could see the silver needle and realized he was about to inject her with something. Not Zin Quai? *That would kill her.* Too weak to lift her head, she tried to make him to stop. She struggled with the words, but they were slurred and indistinct. He couldn't possibly have understood her.

She felt a quick stinging sensation, and then he looked up at her, sadness in his eyes. "I'm sorry, Irish," he said softly. "There's no other way."

Horrified, she struggled with a realization that her mind could not accept. She couldn't let herself believe that this was why he'd rescued her and brought her here. He could not have done it all just to get rid of her. It was unthinkable, beyond imagining, especially given his emotional declaration.

But the fuzziness that invaded her thoughts as the drug

took hold wouldn't allow her to fight the brutal reality. It wouldn't let her deny what was happening to her. There was no other explanation. He had given her enough Zin Quai to knock her out before, and now he was injecting the lethal dose.

Her mind went off on tangents as consciousness began to slip from her. Perhaps this was why everything about him had felt inevitable from the first. She had never wanted to believe in premonitions and curses, but something nightmarish had been set into motion from the moment she met him, and perhaps even before she met him. It felt as if the family legacy of tragedy was being realized, and this was her destiny. She was going to die after all, and it would be at the hands of the man who had just told her he loved her.

26

The sun's brilliance struck at Webb's eyes and made him blink away the fire. He turned from the terrace doors to the woman lying on the bed, aware of the lacerating irony of his own thoughts. He hadn't told her where he'd brought her because it would have terrified her. This place was the former summer home of the Cordes family. Webb himself had spent part of a summer here, the year his family was executed.

Villa del Mare. The perfect setting for a family reunion. This was where it would all happen, the culmination of Webb's master plan for the man who had turned him into the mercy killer of his own sister. Even the fates could not have predicted what lay in store, though they might have predicted the twist. Webb Calderon would have his emotional justice, but he could take no pleasure in it. None.

He'd done things most men couldn't live with. He'd played God with human lives and altered the course of events to achieve his ends. Some thought him a monster, and perhaps he was one. That was what you became when you were treated monstrously. He and Alex Cordes had that much in common. Ruben Cordes had created them both. Monsters.

But all crimes weren't evil, Webb had long ago realized. Men like Cordes operated outside the law. Nothing could touch them, and that was the real crime. Personal justice became the only recourse. It was the age-old moral dilemma. If it was the middle of the night, and you had to break into a pharmacy to steal insulin for a diabetic, was that a crime or a heroic act? Was the sacrifice of one hostage justified if the act would save millions? For Webb, there had never been a choice. Nothing had been sacred in the quest for Ruben Cordes.

But now there was her. This time the hostage was an amazing spirit named Mary Frances Murphy. His hand closed over her medal as he walked to the bed. He could feel it burning softly in his palm. He could feel her burning softly in his heart, a flame that would never go out.

The pendant's images were engraved in gold, but in his mind he saw a single bloodred rose, the only relief against an arctic landscape of bitter ice and snow. Those were the symbols of St. Rita of Cascia, the rose who bloomed in winter.

He'd done some research on the spiritual trials of her protector, the patron saint of impossible causes. Rita had earned her canonization. But he could hardly imagine a cause Mary Frances Murphy herself couldn't defend and win. She had the strength and the spirit of ten, and yet indomitable as she was, there were things even she couldn't save. Lost causes.

Her face was pale, a cameo framed by sooty hair and a matte-white pillow. The golden freckles could have

charmed the black heart of an ogre, but it was the tender
pout of her mouth against the tomboy cut of her jaw that
had enchanted him the first time he'd seen her. That and
the way her gaze struck out at you and defied you to
look away.

He could easily imagine her doing what his fierce little sister had done—singing a hymn in her clear, trembling voice, singing in the face of hatred and death, and
shaming them all with her luminous courage. Yes, he
could imagine it.

He sat down beside her and brushed the dark silk
from her brow, aware of the cooling flush of her skin.
Several smoky tendrils were caught in her lashes, and as
he freed them he thought about how beautiful and vulnerable and exposed she'd been when they'd made love,
how all her passion had been spent in one last rapturous
burst.

Her hair fanned out as he lifted her to him so that he
could put the necklace on her. When he was done, when
he'd fastened the chain around her neck and arranged
the medal in the hollow of her throat, where it would
have hung naturally, he pressed his fingers to her lips
and felt his heart break.

She was the rose. He was the winter.

Her patron saint's patient love could bring a bud to
bloom, even in the bitterest cold. But not this sweet
rose. Nothing survived the ravages of an ice storm. Its
grip was too deep, too deadly.

He'd once asked himself what twisted urge made men
hurt what they loved, why they defiled innocence instead of protecting it. She was his answer. He couldn't
have lived if he hadn't been with her, yet he couldn't
live with himself now because he had. Someone had
once said that innocence was the price to be paid for all

things worth having. It wasn't true. There were some things beyond price.

He should not have made love to her. He should not have taken her virginity. He would pay for that. He had started paying already. As for the rest of it— A grimace contorted his mouth as the blades began to turn, flashing and slashing. The pain was unbearable, and yet he couldn't have done anything else. He knew that, too.

He'd always believed he'd been left alive for a reason—one and one only—to bring meaning out of the senseless slaughter of his family. That was his moral imperative. Others might not have been able to reconcile what he'd done, but he couldn't have reconciled anything else.

There was no sun to burn his eyes now, but something was blinding him. Something stung with the acid fire of tears. "Rest well, Irish," he said, his voice harshening as he gazed at her serene face through the blur of this new, fresh agony. "It won't be long now."

Mary Frances was awake in her cradle of night. Awake and aware. She knew everything Webb had done, but she couldn't move. She couldn't even open her eyes. He'd tried to kill her with the drug, just as she had once nearly killed him. Except he had injected it because he didn't want there to be any chance that she might survive.

Pain seared her. He might as well have plunged the knife into her heart. He'd said he loved her, and she'd felt his hands on her as he'd arranged the necklace. She'd heard his mumbled farewell and choked voice. Why had he so elaborately and tenderly taken her virginity if his ultimate goal had been to take her life? The poison must be circulating in her bloodstream by now.

She was· dying, slowly, a breath at a time. *Was* he that evil? Was anyone that evil?

He *was* Bluebeard, she thought. He'd used her to lure Cordes and then brought her here to kill her. The diary was proof that he'd seduced her sister and undoubtedly murdered her, too, and perhaps the other escorts who were said to have disappeared. She could hardly comprehend anything so cold-bloodedly calculated. It would have been too heinous to believe if Africa hadn't warned her.

She would never know the answer to Africa's riddle, or whether it could have saved her, but she had to know the truth about Webb Calderon. She couldn't die, not with all these questions tearing at her.

It took every fiber of her concentration to get a response, but when she channeled all her energy into moving the hand that lay at her side, she felt a nerve in her forefinger twitch. Her next effort sent a painful ripple of energy down her lifeless arm. Her goal was simply to lift her hand off the bed, but the mental struggle was excruciating. Her brow was drenched in sweat before she managed the shaky feat.

Her arm responded next, and then her leg. Each was a ferocious effort of will, and the motion was limited, but at least she could lift them. The lids of her eyes felt leaden as she got her first glimpse of the world outside her corporeal prison. It wasn't night. The room now had a pinkish glow that signaled twilight, though she'd lost all sense of the normal passage of time. It was possible she'd been in this suspended state for days, but she didn't think so.

She sought the medal at her breast with quaking hands. The effort to grasp it exhausted her as completely as if she'd scaled a cliff. Her patron saint had been mar-

ried to a brutish man who terrorized her and her children
for eighteen years. There'd been no hot lines or halfway
houses then, no way to escape emotional abuse. A wife
was chattel, real property, but Rita's faith, even in the
face of her husband's tyranny, had finally toppled him.
She had killed with kindness, defeating his every attempt to break and subjugate her. Mary Frances needed
that kind of courage now.

Moments later she was clinging to the headboard and
dragging herself up to a sitting position. Dying or not,
she had gotten herself this far. Now all she had to do
was find a way to summon help. There must be a telephone nearby. She would fall to the floor and crawl if
necessary.

The jarring clash of men's voices rang out from across
the hallway. Mary Frances heard them as she approached the door of the bedroom. Her heart was an engine, flooding her body with poison. She'd supported
herself against the wall to get this far, but more than
anything else, it was fear and raw nerves keeping her on
her feet. The bitter mix tasted like rusting metal in her
mouth.

The voices were coming from a room just up the hallway on the other side. Great windows and towering
bookcases, filled to capacity with leather-bound vol-
umes, told her it was a library, and the one man visible
through the doorway was instantly recognizable to her.
He was one of Cordes's security guards at the villa.

Mary Frances sank to the floor, not sure what to do. If
her movements caught his eye, it was all over. But if she
waited, she took a chance that the meeting would break
up and the men would appear before she could navigate

the hallway. She barely had the strength to move, but she had to go now.

"Where is she, Calderon? You claimed you were holding her. If you're lying—"

Mary Frances recognized Alejandro Cordes's voice as she inched down the cold marble slabs. There was an alcove at the end of the hallway that looked as if it housed a writing desk and telephone. She was almost out of range of the library doorway. If she could make it that far—

"Put the gun *down*," came the soft, deadly reply. "I make it a rule not to talk business at gunpoint."

Gunpoint? Mary Frances swayed dizzily. That was Webb's voice. She jerked around, dreading what she might see, and felt the cold shock of Webb Calderon's eyes on her. He was looking right at her. Cordes had a gun on him, but the South American's back was to Mary Frances, and the security guard was out of view. Webb was the only one who could see her.

Cordes brandished the gun tauntingly, ignoring the condition Webb had set. "Why would she turn to you for help?" he asked. "She tried to kill you. She hated you."

Webb's gaze flicked to Cordes, but only for an instant. There was rage in his icy glare as it slid back to Mary Frances—or was it horror? She couldn't tell. Stricken, she realized it must be shock that she wasn't dead and once again his plan had failed. He seemed to be warning her not to interfere or reveal her presence in any way, and he looked savage enough to kill her on the spot. Yet her wild heart wasn't responding to that. It was something else in his expression. Despair.

She drew back, cornered and confused. Her breathing was shallow, her lungs aflame.

"I offered her my services," Webb told Cordes, "and she took me up on it, probably because she thought I was the only one who could help her."

Cordes seemed to be weighing that statement. Finally: "What do you want in exchange for her?"

"A piece of the microchip pie. I know about the deal. It's going to be worth billions, and I want to be cut in. In fact, I want half—"

Money. Billions. It had never occurred to her that his motive could be anything so venal. He was going to sell her to Cordes.

"Nunca!" Cordes snarled. He cocked his gun, and the guards sprang to action, drawing their weapons. *"Te mato, primero!"*

Webb was being threatened with death. Mary Frances had picked up enough Spanish at Our Lady to know that. Now was the time to make her escape. Now, she told herself, before they forced him to admit that she was right outside the door.

The guards rushed Webb unexpectedly. One of them wrestled him into a hammerlock and pressed the barrel of his automatic rifle to his temple. The other shoved his pistol-grip machine gun into Webb's gut. Webb made no attempt to fend them off, perhaps wisely. But Mary Frances had the strongest sense that everything he was doing was intentional, including his decision not to fight.

Cordes moved in, still snarling, only now in English. "You get nothing, you son-of-a-bitch," he avowed. "Where is she? Tell me or I'll blow your fucking head—"

"You'll try," Webb cut in softly. "You'll fucking *try,* you imbecile."

Cordes exploded. "You'll *die* for that. My father

made the mistake of calling me an imbecile." He signaled the guard, who wrenched back his massive arm as if to break Webb's neck. Horrified, Mary Frances saw Webb's head snap backward and heard a sickening crack. As Webb grasped for the guard's arm Cordes flew at him and kneed him viciously in the groin.

Webb buckled and Cordes rammed the gun barrel into his mouth. "Tell me where she is!" He shrieked like a madman. "I'll splatter your brains all over the room!"

The safety cracked like a gunshot.

Cordes was going to pull the trigger.

"No!" The word ripped from Mary Frances's throat. She sank to the floor in a heap, screaming it over and over again. She was still sobbing it when they picked her up and half carried, half dragged her into the room. She ended up on the floor next to Webb, who was leaning heavily against the bookshelves.

He pulled her into his arms, obviously enraged at something, at her. "Christ, Mary Frances."

"You wan—" She choked on the word. "You wanted me dead."

"No, shhhh." He smoothed her hair, her face. "You were only supposed to sleep like the dead so he would think you were. I didn't know any other way to keep you safe. He would have found you, killed you, no matter where you went."

"But you knew the Zin Quai would kill me."

"That wasn't Zin Quai. There are other drugs that mimic death, medically approved. I used the exact dosage, but it was still a risk, too big a risk—"

Cordes punched a fist in the air triumphantly. "Now I have it all, don't I, Calderon?" He spun around, waving the gun and laughing helplessly, as if he himself couldn't believe it. "The whole fucking pie. I have the woman, the Maya figurine, the deal with the consortium, and this—"

He made quite a flourish of reaching into an inner pocket of his coat jacket, a collarless pale linen affair. His eyes darkened, sparkling with lights that could have been sexual as he drew out a primitive bluish-green amulet. "The blue jade pendant that Brianna stole from you the night she died. Exquisite, isn't it? Like Brianna? Did she enjoy it when you tied her up and used the cane on her?"

"I don't use canes on women, Cordes."

"Which must be why she preferred me, hmm? I often wonder what the coroner's office thought of the marks on her body. She liked it everywhere, even her breasts. She liked a lot of things that left marks—"

Mary Frances let out a shaking breath. It was him, Cordes. He was the one who tortured her sister, the man Brianna wrote about in her diary. "Did she ask you to call her Celeste?"

Cordes's wary expression answered her question.

"Your sister was a freak," he said contemptuously, as if that could justify how things must have escalated beyond sex.

"And that's why you killed her?"

"I didn't kill her, I loved her—"

Webb moved as if to silence Mary Frances, but it was too late for that. She was on the brink of discovering the truth about her sister. It was right here in this house. She could feel it, just as she could feel Brianna's presence in some form. She'd been here with him. He'd even tortured her here.

"Then who did?" Mary Frances demanded. "Who killed her?"

Webb stopped her before she could say anything

more. Turning her head into his chest, he muffled her long enough to challenge Cordes. "You don't have the whole pie," he said. "Your father has San Carlos. He runs the country, and he'll never turn the reins over to you—to a fucking *imbecile*."

Webb was clearly attempting to bait Cordes. But the other man didn't respond immediately. He was studying a huge framed map of the world, his smile odd, distant.

"My father was a brilliant man," he said, traces of regret in his voice, and perhaps even reverence, as with the gun barrel he touched a place on the map that might have been his country. "His fatal flaw was that he was shortsighted. He failed to see how much like him I really was. Ruben Cordes will be dead within twenty-four hours. He may be dead already. They've sent someone to assassinate him. That was part of the deal."

"You are my *son*!"

The tortured hiss came from the library doorway. A gaunt silver-haired man stood on the threshold, draped in an overlarge black Armani blazer and slacks, one hand braced against the frame. He was clearly shaken by what he'd heard, yet every inch the aristocrat. His accent reflected an Oxford education more than his Latin homeland.

"I gave you everything," Ruben said.

"Father?" Alex was frozen with fear, but only for an instant. One swift, incendiary word burned it away. "Take him out," he ordered his bodyguards. "Kill him! Do it now."

The two thugs had the older man lined up in their sights, but neither pulled the trigger. They were clearly torn. They were the security detail, not assassins.

"Idiots!" Alex reached inside his coat, apparently for a weapon, but that was as far as he got. A whistling stiletto pinned his hand to his chest. The deadly knife had curved brass talons and what looked like a family crest carved into its ivory handle. His father had thrown it.

The younger man dropped to his knees in shock and fell forward, driving the stiletto in deeper.

Mary Frances averted her eyes, but she had seen the blood. It was an invasive wound. The blade may well have entered his heart. Alex Cordes had almost surely killed her sister, but she couldn't quell the instinct to help him. She couldn't let him lie there, his life seeping away in a dark stain on the carpet, when there might be some way to stop the bleeding.

Webb's head lolled back as if he were about to lose consciousness. Given the blow he'd received, Mary Frances wasn't surprised. But as he slid down the wall away from her, she saw the quarter ladder and extension pole that were propped against the bookcase nearby. The pole had calipers and was probably meant for retrieving books from the top shelves. But it would also make a nasty weapon, and Webb would soon be close enough to reach it.

She couldn't be certain that was his intention, and if she waited to find out, Alex Cordes would be dead. Panic flooded into her throat. It forced her to move, and as she did she realized she could draw attention away from Webb.

Ruben Cordes's stricken expression transformed to one of naked hatred as he saw Mary Frances spring up to help his son.

"Let him die," he said, his voice shaking with rage. "This is a matter of family honor. No one interferes!"

The report of a gun brought Webb up and to his feet. He saw immediately that Mary Frances had made a run

for Alex's fallen body, and Cordes had taken a shot at
her. He was getting ready to fire again. Webb whipped
the extension pole up and launched it like a javelin at
the older man, hitting him square in the chest and
knocking him into the wall.

The two security guards swung on Webb, ready to
open fire. If they weren't exactly clear who the enemy
was, at least they knew he wasn't a friend.

Fortunately neither was prepared to be charged head-
on. Webb plowed through the startled thugs like they
were stick figures. They'd made the mistake of posi-
tioning themselves together, which allowed him to im-
mobilize the first one with a karate chop and ram him
into the other.

He finished off the second with a knee to the groin
and an uppercut and left the two of them in a heap.
There wasn't time for anything more lasting. His only
thought was to get Mary Frances out of the line of fire.
She was bent over Alex Cordes's prone body, struggling
to roll him to his back, and as Webb scooped her up he
heard her scream something. It sounded like her sister's
name.

"Brianna!"

Mary Frances only knew she was being assaulted
from behind. She had no idea who had caught her under
the arms and jerked her back. She hadn't even realized
she was being shot at. But as she was whirled around
and lifted into someone's arms, she saw the face of a
ghost. She saw her sister.

"Brianna?" she whispered, gaping at the woman
who'd entered the room. She couldn't tell if she was
having an hallucination or if what she was seeing was
real. But Brianna looked as much there, as much flesh
and blood, as Mary Frances did. Her sister's hair wasn't

blond anymore. It was flame red, but one glimpse of her eyes told Mary Frances this wasn't a vision. Brianna's eyes were a shade of china blue that lived up to the romantic cliché. Her soul seemed to reside in their depths.

More significantly, Brianna had a gun and she was holding it to Ruben Cordes's head. The older man was on his feet now, his only apparent injury a scalp wound that had soaked his linen handkerchief, but probably wasn't serious. Most scalp wounds bled profusely.

Brianna winked as Webb settled Mary Frances on the floor. "Don't say I never saved your life, sis."

Mary Frances was still in a state of utter confusion and shock. "You're alive? You weren't killed in the accident?"

The smile that shimmered revealed her pride in her plan. "That was no accident. It was staged, all of it. I faked my own death and vanished without a trace, thanks to one of my best customers at Cherries."

She ordered Ruben's hands in the air and went on. "He's the head administrator at County General, and when I suggested that his wife and teenage daughter might be interested in a photo of him in his 'Thumbelina' costume, he seemed more than happy to help. He had the clout and the connections to take care of everything—the hospital records, the death records. I walked away from it without a scratch and assumed a new identity."

"Why did you do it?" Mary Frances bumped up against Webb and wondered if any of this was known to him. One glance told her it wasn't. He was studying Brianna through narrowed eyes, clearly suspicious.

"I had no choice," Brianna said with sudden vehemence. "He would have killed me if I hadn't." She pushed Ruben deeper into the room. He complied, but stumbled as she dug the gun barrel into the base of his skull.

Mary Frances thought she meant the elder Cordes at first, but it was Alex Brianna indicated when she was close enough to probe his slumped body with the needle-sharp tip of her high heel. He showed no signs of life as she gingerly lifted his arm and let it drop, and Mary Frances realized with a certain numbness that he must be gone.

The situation was too incongruous for her to feel anything but disbelief. Her sister was obviously a battered woman from the evidence of her diary, yet she showed none of the fear and loathing of one. Instead, she exuded an icy control that Mary Frances found unnerving. Brianna seemed perfectly comfortable with the gun and more than capable of using it. Even more macabre, the white patent-leather slingbacks she'd used to assure herself that Alex was no longer a threat matched her chic vanilla-white pants suit, and the outfit, coupled with the ivory combs tucked into her fiery curls, made her look like an angel of mercy on a death mission. It was surreal.

"Who would have killed you?" Mary Frances asked. "Alex?"

A faint smile surfaced as Brianna's gaze brushed over both Mary Frances and Webb. Apparently she was satisfying her curiosity about the possibility of her little sister's transformation from saint to sinner—and the man responsible. Naked except for the flowing white shirt, totally disheveled, and huddled in the protective circle of Webb's arms, Mary Frances couldn't have looked anywhere near as pristine as her sister. Except for the gun, Brianna could have been the former postulant and Mary Frances the call girl.

"Alex, yes," Brianna admitted. "I wouldn't be standing here today if I hadn't escaped him. I tried several times, and he finally caged me like an animal. He enjoyed seeing women beg and cower. Fear was like a drug to him—"

"My son," Ruben Cordes broke in, revulsion quavering in his voice, "he was a pig."

Mary Frances felt the rigidity in Webb's arms and knew he must be remembering the inhumane things this silver-haired wraith had ordered done to his family. Was it enough, she wondered, that Ruben had killed his own son? Was that the act Webb needed to put this behind him? Ruben's brutality had forced Webb to destroy his own sister, and now Webb had turned the tables on the dictator. She wanted to believe it was over, that there might even be some biblical retribution to the tragedy— an eye for an eye—but intuition told her it wasn't.

Ruben was standing close enough to his son's body to spit on it, and the older man looked as if he might want to do that.

"This deal of Alex's, the money, it will all come to me now," he said. He was speaking to Brianna, appealing to her. "Millions? Billions? Whatever the amount, it's an embarrassment of riches, and given what my son put you through, the least I can do is compensate you for your pain and suffering. How much would it take to heal the wounds? Name your price, Brianna. Anything."

Brianna laughed as if he'd made a polite joke. "Turn around," she said, drawing back with the gun.

For a moment Mary Frances thought her sister was going to kill him in cold blood. She watched with bated breath as Ruben turned warily, a study in physical grace as the meticulous tailoring of his black blazer and white slacks rustled against his lean frame. He seemed to be

waiting for the coup de grâce as well, a bullet in answer
to his proposition.

Brianna touched the gun barrel to her lips and smiled.
"Fifty million now," she said, "and a percentage of the
gross yearly take from the manufacture of the chips."

Webb's arms released so abruptly Mary Frances fell
against him. "Wait," she whispered, afraid of what he
would do. She couldn't believe what was happening either, but something told her to hold off. "Don't do anything yet," she implored, sotto voce. "Brianna has a gun.
I don't want either of you hurt."

"Fifty?" The dictator didn't seem ruffled in the least.
He looked Brianna over admiringly. "It seems a fair
price for what you went through. There might be other
ways I could make it up to you as well. I've been gov-
erning alone for years now, without the support and
companionship of a strong helpmate. I need someone to
succeed me, my own Eva Perón—an heir to the presi-
dency as well as the wealth. . . ."

He hesitated, letting the last word hang as he gazed at
her.

Brianna flushed and beamed him a smile. "Is that a
sincere proposal, Ruben? El Presidente?"

"I never make any other kind."

"Well, then—" She seemed a little shaken, almost
flustered. "I think a toast would be appropriate, don't
you? To celebrate our happiness?"

"Are you saying yes?"

Brianna dipped her head coyly. As if to prove her own
sincerity, she left the gun on an occasional table within
easy reach of the dictator, and walked to the nearby
liquor cabinet. She seemed to know exactly where the
cabinet was, which indicated she might have been there
before. Mary Frances also had the feeling that, coyness

aside, Brianna knew exactly what she was doing, and that every action and reaction, even the faintest smile, were carefully calculated to distract and disarm.

But Cordes was a master player, too. There was no way to know how much of his proposal was sincere and how much ploy, which was why Mary Frances didn't dare take her eyes off either one of them.

Within moments Brianna had removed a chilled bottle of champagne from the small refrigerator and filled two crystal flutes to the brim. She swung around with great ceremony and held one of the bubbling glasses out to Ruben. The sip she took was dainty by anyone's standards, but the mirth shimmering in her blue eyes was tantalizingly sensual. Ruben responded with a macho swallow. Laughing, he drained the entire flute.

Mary Frances could feel Webb's barely contained fury. He wanted to kill someone, and she didn't know whom to protect anymore. She pressed back against him, her arm covering his. If he decided to act, there was no way to stop him, but at least she could try to delay things as long as possible.

Brianna picked up the champagne bottle. "More?" she asked. Ruben declined, but she filled his glass anyway, letting the champagne flow over the rim. Even before the droplets had hit the marble tiles, the flute joined them, exploding in a shower of crystal.

"Something's wrong." Ruben's voice was raspy and his eyelids fluttered uncontrollably. "What have you done?" he whispered.

Brianna's smile wasn't quite so polite this time. "Let me introduce myself, El Presidente. I'm the hit woman hired by the consortium."

There was no time to recover from the shock. The older man staggered to the occasional table and dropped to his knees. As he toppled over he grabbed for the gun and caught the handle in his grasping fingers. Brianna dropped to the floor as he wheeled around and fired. The bullet went high, missing her.

Enraged, Cordes began to fire wildly, spraying the room with bullets. He was going to kill someone, anyone. *He was going to kill them all.*

Webb pulled Mary Frances to safety, shoving her behind a high-backed chair. Still crouched, he searched the room for something to heave at Cordes.

"Cobarde!" Cordes ground out. "Coward! Show yourself!"

Coward. Mary Frances flinched at the word, remembering Webb's reaction when she'd used it.

A snarl of pure animal rage rattled in Webb's throat.

"No!" she pleaded, but there was no way to stop him. He couldn't even hear her.

Staring down the barrel of a cocked gun, Webb rose up and sprang at Cordes like a jungle cat. Mary Frances had never seen such savage grace. Even Cordes seemed mesmerized in the seconds before he pulled the trigger. The weapon fired an instant before the two men collided, but the strange metallic click told Mary Frances that the gun was empty.

She touched her saint's medal, dry-eyed with wonder. Had Webb known the gun was spent? Or was heaven playing favorites?

Webb's brutal backhand slammed the dictator against the occasional table and sent the man and the furniture sprawling. The rifle dropped by one of the guards lay nearby. Webb scooped it up and targeted his lifelong nemesis. But Cordes was already down, either dead or so far gone a bullet would have been pointless. Webb dropped the gun and turned away, shuddering.

Mary Frances wanted to go to him, but it was all she could do to stay on her feet. The Cordes men were dead, both of them. Her sister was alive and Webb was safe. Why was she suddenly sobbing?

27

Wrapped in a plush white terry robe and fresh from the shower, Mary Frances struggled to brush the tangles from the jungle wilds of her damp hair. One particularly nasty knot brought a pained wince. It seemed a hopeless task, but when had that ever stopped her? Some people thrived on hopeless. Well—two people. She and Ingrid Bergman in *Inn of the Sixth Happiness*.

"Give me that brush," Brianna said, feigning impatience as she caught Mary Frances's reflection in the vanity mirror. She turned from her own efforts at damage repair and scrutinized her baby sister. "The world's sexiest hair, I swear, and you still can't do a thing with it?"

She rose and patted the elegantly scrolled antique chair. "Come sit down. Let me."

Mary Frances reacted with a shy, startled smile, aware that they had never shared this sort of thing as girls. We should have, she realized. A bittersweet sense of irony welled as she settled herself in the chair and offered up her thick raven mop to her sister's surprisingly gentle touch.

They might have been at home in Sweetwater, squabbling affectionately in the cramped bedroom they shared as teenagers, except that they had never squabbled affectionately. They'd fought tooth and nail. And this wasn't their boxy stucco rambler in Sweetwater. It was a quaint Normandy-style beach cottage in the south of France.

They'd vacated Villa del Mare with swiftness and stealth that afternoon after Webb made a single phone call. A car with darkened windows had arrived and whisked the three of them to this lovely hideaway down the coast, and they'd been here ever since. It had all been very clandestine and frightening, and Mary Frances's nerves had been as tangled a rat's nest as her hair. Both were just beginning to relax now. The shower helped. And, surprisingly, so did her sister.

Still, Mary Frances had so many unanswered questions they probably numbered in the millions. She wouldn't have put much past the Brianna she remembered, but the stunning redhead combing her hair had claimed to be a hit woman. Mary Frances simply couldn't comprehend that. And then there was Webb. Apparently she was married to some kind of double agent.

Webb had refused to say anything about his mysterious phone call other than to assure her and Brianna that his support came from the highest levels of the U.S. government and the "official" version of the two men's deaths wouldn't involve the three of them in any way. That hadn't satisfied Mary Frances, but she'd lacked the stamina to question him any further. She'd told herself there were things one was better off not knowing, to relax and be grateful they were all safe.

But now that she had Brianna alone . . .

"What's that look, Mary Frances?" Brianna glanced at her sister in the mirror. "Do I have an extra eye? A hairy mole growing on my chin?"

"Sorry, but when I think of contract killers, I think of a guy named Vinnie."

Brianna's laughter was quick, soft. "What about Kathleen Turner in *Pritzi's Honor*?"

"I saw that movie, Brianna. She *died*."

The brush slowed its strokes and stopped. Brianna's smile lost its sparkle as she met her sister's gaze in the mirror. "Men like Alex Cordes should not be given power—and not just because of what he did to me. He would have been even more corrupt than his father. Ruben was a tyrant by nature and a butcher when it came to preserving his own power, but he wasn't in it for the glory. Alex was. He wanted nothing more than to feed his own ravenous ego. He had to be stopped and what more fitting way than by his own father—who made him what he was."

"Then it was you who arranged for Ruben Cordes to be at Villa del Mare?"

"No, that must have been part of Webb's plan to pit Ruben and Alex against each other. Each man thought Webb was on his side when he was actually luring them there for a confrontation. I wish I had thought of it. It was a brilliant move."

There were moral arguments Mary Frances could have made, and she would have once, strongly. But not today. Not after having lived through what she had. "Then you really are a hit woman?"

The sparkle returned. "You witnessed my one and only hit, sis. But the concept has some merit, all things considered. There are depraved people out there, men who operate so far above the law ...no one can touch them. If

women like me can get to them, and we're the only ones
who can—"

She shrugged and resumed grooming her sibling.
"Don't worry, I'm not going to make it my new job description, not just yet."

An *aspiring* avenging angel, Mary Frances thought,
still having difficulty with the idea. "How did you happen
to get so involved with Cordes? I know he was gorgeous,
but ugh, that shriveled soul."

"In a strange way I owe a debt to him," Brianna declared. "It took a brush with death before I realized there
was a reason I always ended up with the service's violent
clients. I sought them out, apparently because I harbored
some notion that I deserved abuse. After all, I was never
a virginal nun like you, Mary Frances. Our father never
held me up as an example to you, did he?"

Her voice was tinged with hurt, even bitterness. She
tried to disguise it with a knowing smile, but Mary
Frances knew this was something else they would need to
deal with someday, another step to be taken. They had
both been hurt so much, even by their father, a man who
meant well.

"Alex finally made me see the error of my ways,"
Brianna continued, "but not through love, through hatred. He cured me *by* beating me. At some point I knew
I didn't deserve what he was doing to me. Even I wasn't
that vile a human being."

"You were never vile, Brianna, just—" Mary Frances
smiled, bemused and saddened, yet very aware of how
grateful she was to see her sister alive and to have this
second chance with her. "Just gutsy in a way I wish I
could have been. And Alex Cordes did love you," she insisted, remembering how he'd sobbed out apology after

apology when he thought she was Brianna. "Obsessively, I think."

Mary Frances found herself staring into the mirror, studying her sister's reflection and wondering where the strength had come from to do what Brianna had done, wondering if she herself could have summoned that kind of mettle.

Brianna glanced up, seeming both puzzled and pleased by the near-reverence in Mary Frances's expression. "I'm not the Amazon you think I am, Mary Frances. I had help—and not just from my doctor/client friend. There was someone else who came to my aid, someone you know very well."

She'd been feathering delicate bangs across Mary Frances's forehead. Now she set the brush down. "I suppose I should tell you everything, shouldn't I, especially since he's more your friend than mine, and he can't tell you himself."

It must have been Mary Frances's expectant silence that prompted Brianna to go on. "There was only one person I stayed in touch with after I went to work for Cherries," she said. "And when I finally got free of Alex, I went straight to him, straight to Our Lady. I confessed everything, including my plan to disappear—"

"Father Rick?" Mary Frances broke in, stunned. "Rick Caruso knew? He let me think you were dead? He let us all think that?"

"No, Mary Frances, not dead. He allowed you to think I'd *disappeared*. He didn't have any choice. He was a priest, taking my confession, and he knew what kind of danger I was in . . ."

Brianna went on talking, explaining the situation with Rick in more detail, but Mary Frances was only half-listening. As the shock of her sister's news wore off, she began to nod. She was remembering that afternoon in the bar when she'd collapsed in Rick's arms and blurted out her narrow escape from Cordes. He'd been terrified for her. Now she knew why.

"It's all right, Brianna," she said after a moment, aware that she'd alarmed her sister with her reaction. "I understand why you had to do it, at least I think I do. Alex Cordes would have killed me, too, if he could have."

She considered her sister's reflection again—the fiery beauty, the soulful blue eyes—and realized how drastically things had changed since their childhood. Mary Frances wasn't envious anymore. She was concerned about her sister's welfare. She wanted to know if Brianna was going to keep working for the service, if she was happy. But Brianna had picked up the brush again, and a tug on her head made Mary Frances look at her own reflection. Her jaw dropped in surprise. "One more question? What are you doing to my *hair*?"

Brianna had gathered a mass of crown hair into a ponytail, and dark tresses were cascading all over the place. All Mary Frances would need to complete the Barbie doll look was Spandex pants, a tube top and backless heels.

Brianna pretended surprise. "You don't want to look like a young Bardot, only dark-haired? You know there are women who would scalp you for this hair, don't you? They get perms and crimps. They buy hair extensions from José Eber."

They both laughed, but Mary Frances realized with a sinking heart that Brianna was going to leave her this way. The Flying Nun meets Cosmo Girl! Webb had told her he would be waiting for them on the terrace with a light meal, something he'd ordered in.

With a quick shake of her head, Mary Frances watched

her hair take wild flight. This was crazy. It wasn't her. It
made her look sort of sultry and sex kittenish. But even
before the raven mane had come in for a landing, a secret
smile was taking shape. Who knew, she thought, maybe
he would love it. She was already beginning to see the
possibilities.

"The story will be that Ruben and Alex killed each other
in a power struggle that turned deadly," Webb said,
moonlight flickering on the dripping wine bottle as he
took it from the bucket and refilled their glasses with pale
pinot grigio, first Brianna's and Mary Frances's, then his
own.

"Everyone knew there was no love lost between Ruben
and Alex," Webb explained, settling back in his chair.
"Alex publicly disassociated himself with his father
every chance he got, so it will come as no surprise that
there was a war for control between them."

"You said it will be made to look like they killed each
other?" Brianna toyed with the pâté on her plate, making
little designs in its jellied surface with a toast point. She
had barely touched her food.

Understandably, none of them had much appetite.
They'd just had a light supper of the pâté, cheese, and
fruit on the open-air porch of the cottage and were sitting around at an umbrella'd patio table. Mary Frances
was curled up in her chair, wearing a silk blouse, jeans,
and a pair of sandals that Brianna had loaned her. If
Webb had noticed her sex kitten hair, he hadn't mentioned it. He'd drawn her into his arms and asked if she
was all right when he'd first seen her, then led her to a
chair at the table. She understood why, of course. Life
and death issues took precedence, but still . . .

"They'll say Ruben summoned Alex to the family's

summer house to confront him," Webb continued, "and things escalated to violence. Father stabs son with a knife from the family collection, and then celebrates by drinking champagne that was poisoned by the son with the intention of killing him."

"And the French government will cooperate?" Brianna asked.

What she didn't ask was whether or not Webb had been the mastermind behind the confrontation between father and son, but Mary Frances was virtually certain that he must have been. Their meeting could not have been coincidence. Webb had undoubtedly orchestrated both the opportunity for Alex to betray Ruben and for Ruben to discover the betray.

Webb took a drink of his wine and held it in his mouth a moment before swallowing. It wasn't clear whether his smile had to do with the pinot grigio or the question. "The government will get the same story everyone else does. Only those with a need to know will learn what actually happened today, and yes, they'll cooperate."

"What about the microchip?" Mary Frances asked him. "Will the consortium make a manufacturing deal with some other third-world country?"

"There was no microchip."

"What?"

Webb's glance held such startling megawattage, she forgot the question for a moment. The low gleam in his eyes stirred her loins as sweetly as it did her heart. She ached for him, absolutely ached for him. The urge to touch him, to be in his arms again, temporarily overwhelmed every other thought. Did he like her hair this way? It was so childish a concern, she could hardly believe she was thinking about it. But he had a thing about innocence, and she wondered if an experienced woman would appeal to him, much less a sex kitten. Did he want a woman? Did he want her? Talk about a need to know.

But he'd just said something so shocking.

"There is no microchip," he repeated. "The consortium bought a dud. The chip they got was designed to fail after initiation. Cordes gave them a brilliant demonstration of its powers, not aware himself that it was a one-trick pony."

"What about the Mafia types," she wanted to know, "the ones who were going to kill you if they didn't get the original figurine?"

"That was a little story to motivate Alex Cordes. Clever?"

His sexy smile did its best to distract her again, but she resisted him with a cast-iron will. She wouldn't quickly forget the gruesome fate he'd said would be in store for him if she didn't get the figurine back. "And to motivate *me* as well?" She shot him her best glare, which clearly needed some work.

"Mistress? It's time to go."

Mary Frances recognized that deep, musical voice. They had another visitor, she realized with a start—an ebony-skinned giant, who was so tall he must have had to stoop to get through the terrace doors. She rose from the chair. "What are you doing here?"

Garbed in madras plaid instead of white robes, Africa laughed uproariously and lifted his arms, as if to say that life, after all, was theater. "I told you it would be a grand adventure, didn't I?"

Grand adventure was a relative term, Mary Frances thought. So was confusion. "What's going on?"

"Africa works for me," Brianna explained.

"Do most hit women have their own cosmetician?" Mary Frances was slightly rattled and glad when she

heard Webb come up behind her. The touch of his hands
on her arms told her he was there if she needed him. But
it also made her long to know that he would *always* be
there if she needed him. He had been in her life such a
brief, tumultuous time, and yet she couldn't imagine what
she would do without him.

Clearly delighted to see Africa, Brianna joined him and
linked her arm in his. "Can you keep a secret?" she asked
Mary Frances. "You know me by another name, and it's
not Celeste."

To Mary Frances's astonishment, her sister grinned and
winked.

"No!" Mary Frances couldn't believe it. She was so
certain it couldn't be true, she repeated the word over and
over again. "You're Wink? My Wink? The anonymous
Wink? That means you're still an escort, then. You work
for Cherries."

"I run Cherries."

Mary Frances tried to step back, but Webb was there,
holding her. She could feel his arms tense, and realized
this must have come as a shock to him, too. "You run the
escort service?" she said. "How is that possible?"

"Maybe you'd like to sit down?" Brianna suggested.
"Maybe we should all sit down?"

But no one took her suggestion, and it would have been
impossible anyway. What Brianna had in store was not a
cozy yarn suitable for a spring evening at the seashore. It
was a shocking, riveting confession, and as the four of
them stood in a circle on the terrace, sheened by moonlight, she recounted a labyrinthine tale of evil, greed, and
dishonor among underworld thieves.

She explained that she never intended anything so
elaborate as faking her own death. She was going to
evade Alex by disappearing, but the perfect opportunity

presented itself when the retired judge who ran Cherries died of a chronic illness. Brianna had started as an escort, but she'd always been good with computers, and her suggestion that Cherries utilize the Internet resulted in her becoming the architect of the current streamlined operation. The judge had been impressed and made Brianna his assistant, but as his illness progressed he became bedridden and began to operate exclusively through the Net. At the time of his death, Brianna was the only one who had access to him.

"If someone were to exhume Brianna Murphy's body tomorrow," she told them, "they would find a seventy-two-year-old man, who died of congestive heart failure."

The difficult part, she went on to explain, was coming up with plenty of murder suspects. Alex Cordes was obvious, since she'd been dating him, and Webb became implicated when she discovered the secret compartment of the Hermès suitcase. By removing the smuggled blue jade pendant and ostensibly stealing it from Webb, she gave him a motive and made him another suspect.

"What about Blue?" Mary Frances asked. "She's the one who got me involved. Did she know all along that you were alive?"

Brianna shook her head. "No, and she very nearly blew the whole thing with her investigation. She assumed it was Webb because of what I told her the night I 'died.' I finally managed to scare her off and make it look like Webb had done it. That's the point at which she came to you and complicated things even further. Once Webb had insisted on having you at his party for Cordes, there was little I could do but go along with it—and try to keep you safe. Traci did her best to protect you while you were in the hacienda. She works for me, too."

Perhaps it occurred to all of them at that moment that

Wink's instructions to Mary Frances in Webb's hacienda had nearly resulted in his death.

An awkward silence fell. It was Brianna who broke it, addressing herself to Webb. "I was trying to protect both my sister and myself. I thought you were going to kill her, and to be honest, it would have been far safer for me, too, with you out of the way. I do regret dragging you into it—"

He stopped her. "You couldn't have kept me out of it. I was after Alex Cordes, and that alone would have brought me into the investigation of your death, if only in the attempt to prove it was him. Besides, all's fair."

Mary Frances sensed that some understanding had been reached between them, but she doubted they would ever be fast friends. They were probably too much alike. "What will you do now?" she asked Brianna.

Her sister's hair shimmered brilliant reds and golds, rebounding to cascade about her face in waves as she tried to comb it back. "Who knows?" she admitted with a shrug. "I may become one of most powerful women alive by playing dead."

She studied Mary Frances and Webb for a moment, then smiled with genuine affection and blew them both a kiss. "You two deserve a real honeymoon. And you deserve happiness, too. Every happiness." Fighting emotion, she tugged at Africa's arm as if they should go.

But Mary Frances didn't want to lose contact now, not after they'd just found one another again. "Will I see you again?" she asked.

"Try getting rid of me," Brianna said, laughing. "I'll be the sister of a thousand faces—the caterer at your first wedding anniversary and the new fashion consultant at the spa and maybe even the gypsy fortune-teller at the local carnival."

"Africa!" Mary Frances called out, an afterthought as he and Brianna turned to go. "Remember that riddle you asked me? What is the strongest of all things?"

The gentle giant cocked an eyebrow and acted shocked that she would ask. "I can't tell you that, Irish. The riddle only brings luck if you guess the answer."

"Hey—have mercy! I've done nothing but guess."

Mirth rolled from him in rich, irresistible waves. "Let me ask you a question, then. Do you consider iron strong?"

"Yes, but—"

"Shhh." He hushed her and waited until she was a properly appreciative audience, until they all were. "You're quite right, iron is strong. But the blacksmith is stronger, wouldn't you agree? And what, if anything, can subdue the blacksmith?"

Both Webb and Brianna said it at once. *"Love."*

"Love?" Mary Frances protested vociferously over Africa's whoops of delight. "No fair! I guessed that the day you asked the riddle."

"You guessed it and negated it," Africa reminded her. "You said it couldn't be love, that love was too simple, remember?"

Perhaps for the first time in her life Mary Frances wasn't giving in gracefully. "But how could love have helped Bluebeard's wives?"

"You assume that his wives didn't love him enough. Perhaps if he'd loved himself more, he wouldn't have felt the need to make them prove their devotion." Africa's eyes were smiling now, aglow with lights. "Whoever said love was simple, hmm?"

This time the two of them did turn and disappear through the doorway, and the moment they were gone, Webb drew her closer. As her back came into contact with his front, Mary Frances felt a sensation rush up her legs like static electricity. Instantly her silly heart began to thud and her thighs to quiver. She'd been about to concede that Africa might have a point before that happened. If love was so strong, why did she feel so weak?

But there was no time to ask, and ultimately, no need.

He'd already turned her around and bent to kiss her before she could speak. The prickly sensations flared to her throat, needling like a heat rash. Maybe it was the way he'd tilted her head, but Mary Frances felt as if she were brushing her lips over an electric grid. His mouth was wired with the hottest charge imaginable. It was painfully exciting, *painfully* sweet. If this was weakness, she conceded, it was a powerful thing.

It seemed to startle him when she drew back.

And suddenly she was curious about something, very curious.

"What is it?" He seemed faintly uncomfortable at being put under the microscope. "I guess there must be a couple things you want to know about me?"

A couple hundred! Starting with the fact that she didn't have a clue who he was. She knew absolutely nothing about Webb Calderon's past and next to nothing about his present. He could have been a government agent, or an undercover operative.

But in all honesty there were just two questions she felt compelled to ask, and the first one barely mattered. It was more a matter of mental bookkeeping than anything else. "Are you a spy?"

His frown eased into the faintest of smiles. "If you call working for the Italian Foreign Office spying, I guess the answer is yes." Her mute surprise prompted him to explain. "The Italians have the best Art Squad in the business. I've worked for them and several other governments over the years. The U.S. Treasury Department was in on this assignment—and it was my last."

Startled as she was, she could deal with his having been a spy, but what she couldn't deal with were the personal unknowns. She was down to the last question and she had to have it answered at that very moment. This was the concern that would burst its seams if she couldn't voice it. She took a moment to clear her throat of its huskiness.

"Are we really married?"

28

THREE MONTHS LATER . . .

"Bless me, Father, for I have sinned."

The muffled female voice came to Father Rick Caruso through the mesh of the darkened confessional booth. Few Catholic churches had booths anymore, but Our Lady was a venerable old structure and Rick had wanted to preserve the history and the tradition.

"I'm ready to hear your confession," he said, leaning closer to the screen. Her voice sounded familiar, but he was probably imagining things. It couldn't be Blue Brandenburg. He hadn't seen her since Webb and Mary Frances's wedding over two months ago. They'd held the ceremony here at Our Lady, but Blue had seemed mysterious that day. She'd told Rick she was involved in some kind of volunteer work, but wouldn't elaborate. That was the last time he'd seen or heard from her.

"What have you done?" he asked the woman.

"I did a bad thing for a good reason."

His mouth was dry as ashes. It did sound uncannily like Blue. But what could have brought her back here? What had she done? "That might absolve you," he said, "but I would still need to hear the bad thing."

"I'm so ashamed."

"What did you do?"

"I made up with my mother."

"What?"

The shock in his voice must have told her what he was imagining. "What did you think I'd done," she asked defensively, "gone back to selling my body?"

"Blue—" He fell forward, his head bumping the mesh, his voice low and despairing. "What are you doing here?"

"Confessing. I told you, I did a terrible thing."

"By making up with your mother?"

"Yes, I lied. I told her I liked her, but I don't. I can't stand my mother."

He wanted to laugh, but she sounded halfway serious. "Maybe you were trying to make amends with her?" he suggested.

"No, I was after money."

"Oh, that *is* bad. Why?"

"So I could give it to you."

Muffled laughter erupted from her side of the booth, and Rick was immediately suspicious. "Blue, what the hell are you doing over there?"

"Watch your language, padre," she warned him. "You're speaking to a real-live angel of mercy. I just raised a half-million bucks for my favorite charity, Father Rick Caruso and his church. I've got letters of commitment from banks, computer companies, grocery chains, fast-food franchises, you name it. They all want to sponsor you in an outreach program, teaching barrio kids the wonders of cyberspace."

Her voice bubbled with excitement. "How's that sound?"

Rick could barely talk over the lump in his throat. "It sounds like a miracle. How did you do it?"

"I ran a major guilt trip on my mother, and she hit up all her old-biddy friends with Fortune 500 husbands, most of whom, it turns out, are scared shitless of gang violence and the growing juvenile crime rate. Hey, they're thrilled to be getting these kids off the streets. You're a going concern, Father."

"I don't know how to thank you, Blue." His voice harshened, threatening to break. He didn't know what else to say. He really didn't. He wasn't good at this, at thank-yous and good-byes and sentimental stuff, especially with her.

"What's to thank? I loved every minute of it. Felt like Robin Hood, only with breasts."

She heaved a satisfied sigh and went quiet for a moment, just long enough for him to realize that she *was* an angel, and that she probably had been sent to him by the heavens. All he had to do was look at what she'd done, the difference she'd made in his life.

"You okay over there?" she asked.

"A-Ok." His throat ached, but he said it again. *"A-Ok."*

"So . . . what was it between us?" she asked after a long, palpable moment. "Lust or love?"

"Love," he managed huskily, "without a doubt.

Quick and hot and pure, like the flare of a struck match."

"But it's gone now? Flared out?"

He drew on the air around him, on the strength and stability of the very structure he was in. "It has to be gone, Blue. You've given me the way to change lives, to save lives. These kids need me just as I am, their priest, their spiritual father, and in some cases, their only father."

"You're right, of course." Her voice was tight and full, resonatingly sad, but not without hope. "And you are going to change things. I've never doubted that."

"What about you? What will you do"—his smile warmed the words—"now that your *charity* work is done?"

"I'm off to find the wizard, of course, accompanied by my traveling companion, the Cardinal. You remember Cardinal Fang?"

A throaty meow told Rick she had the cat right there in the confessional with her. He imagined there were rules about that, but he wasn't the right one to enforce them, and when had rules ever applied to Blue Brandenberg anyway?

"Do good things and know that you've already changed someone," she told him forcefully. "Me. I'm a better person because of you, Father Rick Caruso. This crazy lady who robs from the rich and gives to the church, I couldn't have become her without you."

She laughed and then her voice caught hard, struggling with something bittersweet, like tears. Godspeed," she whispered, "to both of us."

The confessional door opened and closed. The click of her heels faded down the aisle and was gone in the quick roar of traffic and a flash of sunshine bright enough to penetrate the cracks of the antique booth.

The wooden bench groaned under Rick's weight, and he sank back with the inner knowledge that he would have a burden weighing on his own conscience at his next confession. He had lied, too. The match he and Blue struck had lit a candle that would burn inside him for all of his days. He would always love her, always hold her passion in his heart, and that was why he would do good work. Why he *had* to do good work. He owed it to both of them, to her and to him . . . and maybe even to God.

SEVEN YEARS LATER . . .

A voice rang out, piercingly clear in the bright summer morning, a child's voice, as sweet as the breezes that carried it to him. Webb dropped the photographs he was holding and rose from his desk, struck to the core by the haunting song. As he wheeled toward the door his pant cuff caught on something and he kicked the chair out of the way, his heart as noisy as the cart-wheeling furniture.

Who was singing in that haunting voice?

His office was in the south wing of the English country estate he and Mary Frances had bought shortly after their marriage. The art seasons in London required him to be here both summer and fall, and they'd wanted a place where the children they hoped to have could run and play freely. The stately old Tudor, with its rolling grounds and terraced gardens had seemed the perfect choice. Mary Frances had named it Winter Rose.

Webb's siren song seemed to be coming from the

east end of the house, where the rose gardens were in
full bloom. Every window on the second floor had
been thrown open, drenching him in fragrance as he
made his way down the narrow halls that would take
him to the bedroom he shared with his wife.

He found her on the balcony, standing at the rail, and
his heart wrenched pleasurably as he saw how the
breezes lifted the collar of her blouse and played with
the dark tendrils of her hair. The mere sight of her
could still do that him, tighten the cords of his belly
and flood him with a lust so pure it felt holy. In the
nearly seven years they'd been together, she had
aroused his heart as well as his loins to a state of sweet
and almost constant anguish.

She was looking out at the garden now, and when he
joined her, he saw what the attraction was. Their small
raven-haired daughter, April, was serenading her bemused golden retriever as if he were the prince come
to rescue her from the tower. It was a song from her favorite Disney movie, *Snow White,* and her voice
cracked and quavered with all the longing a five-year-
old heart could render.

The sound of it set Webb's own heart on edge.

"Shall I stop her?" Mary Frances asked. She gazed
at him searchingly.

"No," he vowed softly, "nothing will ever stop her
from singing, not while I'm alive."

He felt a yank on his shirtsleeve and realized his
wife was pointing out a small dark form creeping
through the cover of the rose garden toward April. The
interloper, lurking in ambush, was their six-year-old
son, Tyler, whom Webb referred to affectionately as

the little fiend because of his affinity for stealth and
surprise.

"Why does he stalk her like that?" Webb wanted to
know.

"Because he's her brother, because he's a boy, and
because he's your son." Mary Frances laughed and
nuzzled Webb's shoulder. "You won't always be able
to protect her, Webb. You have to let her grow up."

The little drama on the lawn unfolded to no one's
surprise, except April's, who shrieked and toppled
over when Tyler sprang at her. The dog leaped to his
feet, barking furiously, and a flock of sparrows took
flight from the sycamores.

Tyler frowned mightily at his sister's sissy behavior.

"Stop crying," he demanded as she began to sniffle.
When his command didn't work, he threw an elaborate
shrug of indifference and dropped to his knees, watching her. His grudging concern grew obvious as he
inched toward her until he was finally close enough to
knock her over again. Instead, in a move that seemed
to startle even Tyler, he tilted toward her and brushed
her damp cheek with a kiss.

Webb watched them in bittersweet agony, wondering if he'd been brave enough at six to be that tender.
God, he hoped so.

Mary Frances drew Webb's arms around her, and he
embraced her tightly. If his children were caring souls,
he had her sweet nature to thank for it. Mostly he had
protected them like a lion, perhaps too fiercely.

"Tyler's birthday party is this weekend," Mary
Frances mused, as if she were thinking aloud. "I wonder if his godmother will be here. I haven't heard from

her since she RSVP'd the invitation and that was three weeks ago."

"Blue?" Webb buried his face in his wife's rich dark hair and felt the familiar weight in his loins, the familiar heat. "She'll be here. She's never missed before. Doesn't she usually combine the visit with a buying trip in London?"

Their friend had turned her talents to interior decorating some years ago and then launched her own design firm, to great success. Every time she visited, she stormed through their place, threatening to throw out all Mary Frances's needlepoint.

"She's taken a side trip to Ireland this time," his wife confirmed, "for some Irish lace, I think."

"You don't suppose she's met someone?"

"Blue?" Mary Frances sounded genuinely shocked. "Lord, I hope so, Webb. She's been alone so long."

Webb regretted at times like this that it was beyond his ability to help everyone in the world who was lonely, their friend included. No one knew that pain more intimately than he. But his isolation had been self-imposed, a protection, and Blue's was about independence. She had never seemed that unhappy.

At least he could be grateful that there were things he could do, here, in his world. He had made a promise to himself when he became a husband and once again when he became a father—vows he'd kept locked in the confines of his heart and had shared with no one, not even the soulmate afloat in his arms. They were his covenant with the heavens, the fates.

As long as he was alive, his wife would have roses in winter and his children and his children's children would play in the sunshine. It had to be that way, and not simply because he loved them more than his own life. He owed it to a little girl who would always be eight years old, and who would forever sing in the far reaches of his memories.

"Stop!" Blue cried to the taxi driver. The black-capped older man had taken the rutted country roads of County Kerry like they were an Indie 500 track and nearly shaken Blue's artificially whitened teeth from her head. But that wasn't what made her scream.

The car had just whizzed past an old church, and Blue had caught a glimpse of the quarry-stone edifice with its tiny courtyard and statue. "Stop!" she insisted, nearly sliding off the seat as the taxi careened to a halt.

The driver shouldered around and glowered at her.

"Sorry—" She apologized profusely and sheepishly, knowing she must have given him a near heart attack, but thinking it was only fair. "Will you wait while I walk back to the church?"

She made him promise and then called back as she swung out the door, "It'll only take a minute."

A gust of wind whipped long golden strands from her French braid and made her wish she'd worn something a little warmer than a lavender blue silk jumpsuit. It was the height of summer, and she'd only been in Ireland a few days, but she'd already learned that when the sky turned overcast and the clouds rolled in, it could get as chilly as a California winter.

The thatched-roof church lived up to her fleeting glimpse. Small and quaint, but with none of Our Lady's Spanish influences, it was a charmer nonetheless. Blue couldn't decide whether to go inside or visit the courtyard, but finally it was the garden that drew her. Its arbors and trestles were loaded down with climbing vines and hanging flowers.

The statue was a Madonna and Child from what Blue could see as she approached, much smaller than Our Lady's St. Catherine, but a lovely thing. Limestone white and mossy with age, it graced the courtyard with a tranquillity that seemed to glow.

Someone had left flowers on the path, she realized, hesitating. A bouquet of forget-me-nots was lying on the stones at her feet. Curious, she knelt and touched them, wondering why they were scattered about as if they'd been dropped.

"Miss, those flowers, they're—"

Blue glanced up into eyes so green they rivaled the verdant meadows that Ireland was known for. Eyes so green they were all she could see for a moment. Gradually she realized she was staring at a full-grown man with disheveled dark hair, a smile that hinted at intrigue, and a white turtleneck sweater that snuggled up to his powerful jaw.

When she stood up, she had his flowers in her hand. "They're lovely," she said, feeling unaccountably awkward. "I guess they were meant for the Madonna?"

"Not exactly," he was quick to explain. "I set them down so I could climb that tree."

He was pointing to a huge gnarly oak, a soaring work of nature that was probably as old as the church. Blue's heart did a strange flip. "Was there a cat caught up there?"

"Yes, how'd you know?"

"He wasn't orange, was he?" No, it couldn't be Fang. Her traveling companion was back in the hotel, snoozing.

"Sorry, black and white with long white whiskers—
and not much more than a kitten."

Blue stared at him helplessly for a moment, entranced
by the lilt in his whiskey brogue. The view was a little
different from eye level. His hair was wild and
windswept, and his face as ruddied by the elements as the
hills around them. But he was also as handsome as a
young girl's dream, and Irish to his soul, Blue imagined.
Black Irish, with her luck.

"Your flowers," she said, handing them to him
abruptly.

"No, you keep them," he insisted. "I think you were
supposed to have them anyway. They match."

"Match?"

"Your eyes, miss. They're blue like your eyes."

"Oh, I—well, thank you."

He was staring at her now, perhaps wondering why
she was plucking the petals from his handpicked bouquet. But more than that, he seemed to be studying her
in a way that made her think he wanted to know her—
or already did know her, even the vulnerability she
was trying so hard to hide from a green-eyed stranger
who rescued kittens from trees.

"Maybe I'm out of place," he said, "but you looked
a little sad before . . . when you saw the flowers."

"Sad, me?" Her fingers began to tremble as she
arranged and rearranged the bouquet in her hand. "The
forget-me-nots are lovely, or did I already say that? I
guess they were intended for someone, right? They
must have been—"

He hunched his great shoulders and shoved his
hands in the pockets of heavy tweed trousers that

seemed incongruous in the middle of summer, yet perfect for the blustery day, perfect for him.

"No one who's going to miss them until I can get back with some more tomorrow morning," he told her. "My grandmother's buried in the yard out back. She loves forget-me-nots, but she's in no hurry these days, and I come here often."

Blue made a mental list. There was a graveyard out back. He had a grandmother who loved forget-me-nots, and he came here often. The sun might be hiding under a bushel, but the saints were smiling on Blue Brandenburg today. Once again she was in the presence of a good and honorable man.

"You remind me of someone I know," she said finally. When she looked up, he was gazing at her a little more boldly than before.

"A lover?" he ventured.

The question played havoc with her heart. But it was the answer that resonated in Blue's mind as she remembered the last time she'd picked up a bouquet of flowers and someone had insisted she keep them. Humbled by the generosity of a child, she'd offered the flowers to St. Catherine and asked for a blessing.

"No, a friend," she said, stirred by the sweetness that touched her heart, the sadness that touched her smile. "A good friend. His name was Jesse."

She brought the flowers close to feel their softness against her face and drink in their scent, but it was a green-eyed stranger she saw in her mind. Jesse would be pleased, she thought, if he knew what blessing she was going to ask for today.